HE SAW A BILLION WORLDS...

...a billion billion worlds, all dead and deserted. He saw the interstices between the worlds, alive as they had never been before...waiting.

But waiting for what?

Waiting for the End...and for you.

For me? he thought.

For you, if you will serve.

D1373977

Worlds of Science Fiction from Avon Books

ALL THE TRAPS OF EARTH
by Clifford D. Simak

THE ARCHITECTS OF HYPERSPACE
by Thomas R. McDonough

BRIGHTSUIT MACBEAR
by L. Neil Smith

A DOOR INTO OCEAN
by Joan Slonczewski

THE LEGACY OF LEHR
by Katherine Kurtz

TOOL OF THE TRADE
by Joe Haldeman

WETWARE
by Rudy Rucker

XORANDOR
by Christine Brooke-Rose

DESTINY'S END

TIM SULLIVAN

AVON BOOKS ◆ NEW YORK

Grateful acknowledgment is given for permission to reprint the excerpt from the poem "Proteus" by W. S. Merwin; copyright © 1954 by W. S. Merwin. Used by permission of the author.

AVON BOOKS
A division of
The Hearst Corporation
105 Madison Avenue
New York, New York 10016

Copyright © 1988 by Timothy R. Sullivan
Front cover illustration by Ron Walotsky
Published by arrangement with the author
Library of Congress Catalog Card Number: 87-91838
ISBN: 0-380-75352-9

First Avon Books Printing: July 1988

AVON TRADEMARK REG. U.S. PAT. OFF. AND IN OTHER COUNTRIES, MARCA REGISTRADA, HECHO EN U.S.A.

Printed in the U.S.A.

K–R 10 9 8 7 6 5 4 3 2 1

To Lil and Bill: Long may they wave

Acknowledgments

The author would like to thank the Dirda family of Silver Spring, Maryland, as well as Val Smith, Bob Collins, Joe Mayhew, Gardner Dozois and Greg Frost, for their invaluable help. Special thanks go to John Douglas for editing this book, and to Joanne Burke for the chicken.

No voice came but a voice we shared, saying,
"You prevail always, but deathly, I am with you
Always." I am he, by grace of no wisdom,
Who to no end battles the foolish shapes
Of his own death by the insatiate sea.

—W. S. Merwin, "Proteus"

Prologue

On the barren fourth world of a dying sun, I wait. Bathed in the hot blue rays of that merciless star, I sift the songs and laments of all the worlds through my analytic gyri, so that the Seers may read and interpret them to Man. Here, at the tip of a spiral arm stretching forth from the blazing core of the galaxy into the infinite, I have functioned for a thousand centuries.

I have heard the voices of the stars, and there can be no doubt of what they say: the universe is doomed.

Man knew of the universal fate long before I was constructed. In fact, that is the very reason *why* I was built. The matter of this universe has expanded as far as it ever can or will, settling once and for all that most ancient dispute on the probability of eternity. For eons, all has hung in relative suspension— a brief, decadent moment in the long history of the cosmos—before its increasingly rapid decline . . . before the start of its inexorable fall.

Before the End of All Things.

Man is one of the last intelligent races to accept the imminent End of All Things. From time to time he discovers the remains of civilizations that once flourished and then vanished in mere millennia. There was the garden world of Doazwa, its full, lush tiers grown wild until there was no surface trace of its once great cities; the planetary network of the Trikshulairt, whose lightships now speed the sacred Seers across vast distances in a twinkling; the Rewyjhoy, whose metaphysical arts were once the envy and mystery of the galaxy. These great races left us, one by one. Where have they gone? Investigations lead only to the eventual disappearance of the curious. The Kra'alnsen, a vibrant race, turned inward rapidly and, incredibly, were soon gone, leaving only their machines humming behind them. Their neighbors, the Dllotaw, missed them and tried to find out where they had gone. Only a few centuries passed before the last Dllotawan was seen. This intrigued the Sknah of Tinus, who were soon no more themselves, and then the burrowing, indus-

1

trious Rocinthans. Indeed, the Rocinthans were the first to detect the pattern of disappearance, so far flung was the galaxy even in those later days of easy star travel. They too looked at the evidence and soon began to dream of Otherness, as had so many races before them. In their obsession to learn the answer, they had lost their hopeful dreams.

Not so Man. The dream of forever, so characteristic of his race, remained an irresistible lure, a quest he could no more abandon than life itself. And he came to live for a very long time, a span of centuries, millennia, tens of millennia, hundreds... until he lost count. Just as he at last grasped immortality, he found that he somehow had been cheated by time itself. Wherever Man existed, eternal life had been bestowed on a single gifted person on each planet by its worldmind, but now even these privileged ones would die. And yet Man fought oblivion, as he had never fought before.

Once, in the exploration of collapsars, he believed that he had actually discovered a gateway to eternity, but all routes sent him home—though sometimes by peculiarly indirect ways—to the universe of his birth. And that universe, infinite in his youth, still spacious enough in his maturity, grew ominously mean and cramped with at first the possibility, then the probability... and at last the certainty of final return to the infinitesimal.

Nothing could contain his despair, neither science nor art nor philosophy—not even pleasure. Had he come all this distance only to learn that he knew nothing? It was as if the End of All had supplanted all; Man's origins were forgotten, the worlds he had remade in his own image hung like playthings in the waning light. For it had become late afternoon, twilight for a race that would have become gods, had they but time.

There is no escape, it seems. Man must at last bow to the inevitable, as have other thinking beings long since. And yet ... and yet he still gazes outward, even knowing what must ultimately come. Still he clings to a vestige of hope, though many believe this is senseless. These optimistic ones are, of course, a minority, for Man is essentially a logical race ... or so he believes.

There is always a chance, the last hopeful humans say, that there might be some way out. It is sensible to keep trying to find an answer to this final question. Logic tells us that there is no eternal life, but logic has not always proven correct. Not always.

And so, on this tenuous framework a new and desperate dream is born. Engineers have designed and built me, filling the crust of an entire world with my bulk. My purpose: to monitor the whispers that find us from beyond the stars, for nothing is ever truly lost, even in the vastness of space. My outer shell listens and absorbs; the rest of me, secure beneath the planet's surface, clears away nonessential data and analyzes what is left. The Seers examine the results. What their specially designed brains cannot comprehend, they submit to those who possess a special Gift, a Gift used and misused throughout Man's long history. These gifted ones are scattered throughout the galaxy, lonely aristocrats on myriad worlds. They are known as the Receptors, and they are the only true immortals.

Together, the Seers, the Receptors, and I search for the answer to Man's ultimate question, while the rest of the human race loses itself in decadent games. It is a question that cannot even be phrased without paradox:

After the End, what? . . .

Part One

Chapter One

Bilyf's Prophecy

Angry, drunken shouts reached Danna in the crystal garden, where she tended the gleaming, prismatic flowers her mother had seeded before forever leaving the world of Rocinth. Danna set her nutrient sprinkler on a jewellike outcropping, and hurried up the garden path towards the villa, inhaling the salt smell of the sea. Her father had been drinking all day, and she was afraid of what he might do if he didn't pass out soon. Under her sandaled feet, tiny nafs scurried for safety on their many nimble legs, momentarily abandoning their foraging for insects.

It was getting dark, and firelight shone brilliantly through the villa's central archway; against the orange flames of the dining hall's braziers, Danna saw two moving silhouettes—her father's shadowy figure lashing his Mennon servant.

"What did you see?" her father shouted at the Mennon. "I won't ask again."

The Mennon, called by the human name Bilyf, barely flinched as his master savaged him with a riding crop. Even so, Danna knew that he was in terrible pain, and that he would be forced to submit sooner or later. If only Bilyf were given a moment to articulate, he might be able to reply; Mennons were incapable of lying when asked a direct question. Had her father been sober, he would have realized this and wouldn't have acted so brutally.

Wincing, Danna saw Bilyf's multi-jointed fingers writhe like snakes, bands of muscle tensing under his nacreous flesh with each crack of the riding crop. Still, the crest of his elongated head remained erect.

Sickened, Danna wanted to run away. She turned, seeing the darkening sky begin to obscure the villa's perfectly landscaped grounds. But she could not leave Bilyf in her father's cruel hands tonight. She had to help her tutor and playmate. Resolved, she turned back toward the dining hall. But when she looked again at her father, she dared not draw his attention to her.

Her father, Acrios, Receptor of Rocinth, reeled drunkenly, running his long fingers through his dark, graying hair. "Out with it!" he screamed.

Bilyf's oral cavity quivered with the effort of duplicating human speech, difficult for him at the best of times. No sound came forth.

"Out with it, I said." Acrios's sharp features twisted into a snarl.

His ferocity was a terrible sight. Each time he drank, he grew worse. Of late he had frequently awakened in his chair early in the morning, his memory of the night before blank. He had tormented Bilyf on many occasions. Danna had tried to deal with it like an adult, but she had begun to despair of ever changing his habits. If only her mother were here... but even her mother had not been able to control him. Danna suspected that she had gone over to the strange blue mystery of Otherness at least in part because of him.

There was a terrible crack as Acrios brought the riding crop down on his servant's back with terrific force. Pale gray ichor bubbled from the wound and streamed down Bilyf's side, landing in spattering drops on the tiled floor. The alien began to tremble, and a burbling rose from his oral folds.

Still Bilyf did not speak. Eyes reddened with the wine and the firelight, Acrios raised the riding crop and struck again, and then again, and yet again.

Bilyf was on his knees, his arms splayed, tentacular digits writhing on the floor like dying worms.

"You *will* tell me what you know!" Acrios screamed.

"One cannot—cannot be certain—" the Mennon began gibbering.

"I've never known you to be wrong before," Acrios said, his voice softening. "Now tell me what you saw."

Bilyf's smooth flanks bunched, and his dark, oval eyes retracted into their deep cavities. Danna recognized involuntary resignation in his posture, but she was not prepared for what he said next.

"One has seen—the death of Acrios."

The Receptor's thin face was pale, even in the lurid firelight. He stared at Bilyf. Then he sighed, a deep bellows sound of unexpected relaxation.

"An end to... eternity...?" he murmured. "When?"

"One—cannot see."

"How, then? By starvation, thirst, accident...?" The Receptor again lurched toward Bilyf, threatening him with the upraised riding crop. "How?"

Acrios had named all the ways an anthroform could die . . . all but one.

"By the hand—of another—killed."

Danna stifled a sob. This was too horrible. It was bad enough for Acrios to be deprived of his immortality—but killed! No wonder Bilyf had been so reluctant to share his vision.

"Ah," said Acrios. "Murdered?"

"One cannot—see enough—to be certain."

"Does one see who commits the act?" Acrios demanded, stumbling and striking his thigh on the edge of the dining table. A decanter of wine toppled to the floor and smashed, showering crystal fragments from which emerged a sinuous ruby serpent, swiftly arcing and splattering on the tiles and on Acrios's white tunic. The Receptor ignored the spilled wine, asking, "Does one see who kills me?"

Bilyf remained silent. Never before had Danna seen him hesitate to tell the truth.

"Answer me," Acrios said, "or so help me . . ." He stopped and picked up a jagged sliver of crystal. This he thrust toward Bilyf's eyes, which drew back still farther.

Danna was terrified, but she couldn't make herself look away. The flickering shadows cast by the fire threatened to overcome her with darkness. She felt dizzy and nauseated, but she had to know what was going to happen next.

"Answer me!" Acrios roared like a force of nature.

"One sees—one sees—" the Mennon stammered. If he could lie, Danna sensed, he would have done so now. "One sees—that it is—the child of Danna—who kills Acrios!"

The crystal shard dropped from Acrios's hand, clinking on the colored tiles. Slowly he turned from Bilyf, and for the first time saw Danna under the archway, framed in the dying amber light of the sun.

"Danna . . . ?" he murmured.

She shook her head in disbelief. What was happening here?

"Little Danna," Bilyf said, "the truth must—always be told —by the eggsharer."

Danna hardly heard him. She was unable to break her father's icy gaze as he came nearer, the brazier's flames behind him forming a corona around his slender form.

"This . . . this . . ."—Acrios's voice was hoarse—". . . is my reward for conceiving a child by woman as my ancestors did . . . for choosing flesh and blood instead of a . . . a . . ." He wept, and fell into a terrible, dark place he hadn't known since childhood.

He had been punished for playing in the ruined well. His father had pushed him into a place with no light, locking him in.

He hardly ever thought of it anymore, but the memory was always lurking just below the surface, like some aquatic predator. What had happened there had ultimately made him the greatest man on Rocinth. Punishment and reward. . . .

He looked now into the worried face of his pretty daughter, her blonde ringlets tickling his rough skin as she embraced him. How could she be here in the dark place with him? And these flames were orange and red, not blue. . . . No, this was not the black prison. He remembered now. This was the dining hall . . . where Bilyf had been seized with a vision . . . a vision prophesying his death. . . .

"Your child," he said to Danna.

"Bilyf must be mistaken." Danna took his hand.

"No, no. Mennon chronopaths are never wrong."

"They can't be infallible," Danna persisted.

"Yes they can, and they *are* in such matters. Their prescience is the equal of any species in the galaxy, if not the most controlled."

"Well, even if you don't live forever," Danna said, "we can get you restored, can't we?"

"Restored," he snorted. "Death and Otherness are not conquered by siphoning one's memories into a clone, Danna."

"Father, when I was a little girl, you told me that the pleasures of the physical world are worth the suffering we have to endure in the anthroform."

"But it can all be taken away!" Acrios cried. "I didn't think it could happen to me, Danna. I believed that I would go on forever. Now I wish . . . I wish that I had never taken the anthroform." He stared through the archway at the lambent dusk and beyond, the acrid smoke of the brazier stinging his nostrils. Brooding, he slumped into the chair at the head of the table. He knew the future, and it was filled with dread. But the future might be changed, as his ordeal in the dark had proven. There might be a way out of the prophecy.

"Father," Danna said, "I don't even have a child yet, and you talk as if you're already dead."

"Yes, yes, that's true." In her innocence, she was suggesting her own punishment, even her own death as a way out of fulfilling the prophecy.

"Come, Danna," he said, smiling at her, "let's go for a walk. The evening air will do us good."

"Be careful not to step in the broken crystal," Danna said. He remembered that she had designed this decanter, shaping it in the garden as it grew. She helped him out of his chair and through the dining hall toward the archway, steadying him as he staggered.

Bilyf reflected mournfully that one could not see what was about to happen. One could only be certain that it would come to no good, and yet that it was inevitable. He watched the two humans pass through the archway.

Acrios and Danna walked through the crystal garden and past it. Stopping for a moment by the stables, in a field of disc-shaped flowers that swayed in the soft breeze, Acrios said, "I am sorry, Danna . . . for so many things."

"Shush, Father."

Acrios did not look at her, but stared ahead toward the foot of the path, at the ancient well that lay there.

"You might have hurt Bilyf, you know," Danna said.

"I only wanted to frighten him," Acrios said, holding up the riding crop for her inspection. It was still looped about his wrist. Laughing bitterly, he tore it from his arm and tossed it in the direction of the stable. At the hum of its impact against the stable's restraining field, the sleek racing garoms stirred in their sleep. Originally bred by the extinct inhabitants of Doazwa, the huge, hexaped creatures were used for sport on many worlds. Their pungent, but not unpleasant odor cut through the mild evening air, reminding Acrios of those halcyon days when he raced the beasts. That was long ago, before Bilyf had been taken from the eggsac. "Bilyf has been with me since before your birth," he said absently. "I could never really harm him."

Danna didn't say anything, and he felt a flush of resentment at her discreet skepticism. So the little ingrate didn't believe him. He led her to the brink of the well.

The crumbling well was riddled with tunnels and passage-ways, some leading deep into the planet's crust, others seeming to go nowhere. The Rocinthans had left an enigmatic record of their passing amid a handful of these peculiar architectural ghosts, scattered over the planet. In one or two of them, grotesque artifacts of great sophistication had been unearthed. Apparently biochemical in nature, these had been composed of synthetically constructed nucleic acid helices. It was even argued that they might still be functioning, given the proper conditions. As to their purpose, there was some speculation that they might have been used in the way Man used machines, though there was no conclusive evidence. Most of Rocinth's present anthroform human inhabitants gave it little thought. Archaeological detritus interested few of them. Nevertheless,

Acrios had built his home within sight of a well. He had no interest in the ancient Rocinthans, other than their dwellings. These wells had made him the man that he was. This was where his punishment had begun.

"Cousin Dictys brought me down here when I was little," Danna said. "Bilyf went with us. He never let me out of his sight."

"No, of course he didn't." Acrios was tired, his alcoholic fervor drained by shock and anger. He wanted only to be relieved of this horrendous new burden. A monstrous part of him wished that he could rid himself of this chattering little creature at his elbow. She was nothing but a child. How absurd that he should die by the hand of her as-yet-unborn brat. But she was his daughter, and he could not kill her, not even now. She must be cleansed; from her suffering might come salvation for both of them . . . just as it had come for him long ago.

"Let's go down into the well, Danna," he said.

"Oh, yes!" She was as breathless as a little girl. "Let's go down and explore."

Danna wanted desperately for all to be forgotten, everything from the time that her parents had first quarreled, before her father became so preoccupied with the wine, and with his many lovers—and especially with the Seers' transmissions.

The path swung to the lip of the well, curving below its overgrown rim. Trampling weeds, they worked their way down to the highest level of tunnel mouths. At the first entrance they came to, Danna made as if to go inside, but Acrios stopped her.

"No, not that one," he said. There was something in his voice that troubled Danna, a tone she'd never heard before. "Come."

She looked at her father thoughtfully. Behind him she could see the lip of the well against the faded yellow sky, a pitted, weed-bewigged parabolic sweep just a few meters above. Below, the shadowy well yawned, a hungry naf's mouth patiently awaiting its unwary prey.

"Why?" she asked.

"It is too near the surface." Acrios was smiling, but Danna still felt that something was wrong. He exhaled the foul stench of wine. "There are far more interesting tunnels below."

She wanted to run, but she didn't dare to. She had rarely disobeyed her father, and it was too late now, anyhow. He had taken her hand. His skin was cold and damp. It seemed to Danna that they walked for hours, spiraling ever downward as night filled the well. At last they stopped before a gaping tunnel mouth, barely visible in the gloom.

"Here," Acrios said, his voice echoing. "This one."

There was no time to discuss the matter. Danna was pulled roughly inside. She was afraid.

Deeper and deeper into the tunnel they went, feeling their way, until a faint glow appeared ahead. Startled, Danna recalled the legendary sign of the Others—a ghostly blue glimmer. But this light emanated from tiny phosphorescent creatures, partially replacing any artificial lighting the Rocinthans might have used. As a child, she had once asked her father if the Rocinthans had bequeathed them this microscopic light source so that she and Bilyf and cousin Dictys could find their way in the honeycomb of tunnels. Acrios had told her no, scholars believed otherwise. Still, she had imagined the hoary natives, strange beings scudding through these same tunnels, lit by these same luminescent life-forms. He had chuckled paternally and shaken his head. If he acted that same way now, she wouldn't distrust him, but he was behaving like a stranger.

"Not much farther now," Acrios said.

"Where are we going?"

"To a place I discovered as a child. I want to show it to you."

Now that there was light shining ahead, Danna felt a little better. After all, Acrios had always been good to *her* . . . just as he had been good to her mother until they argued and he struck her.

They entered a spacious chamber. It was empty, but brilliantly festooned with glittering bacteria.

"We're almost there now," Acrios said, his voice echoing. "I remember the way clearly—just down there." He yanked his daughter along a steeply inclined passageway branching off from the main chamber.

"Please, Father." Danna was out of breath, her legs ached, and her feet hurt. A needle of fear pierced her heart as Acrios stormed ahead into the darkness, ignoring her pleas, his fingers as hard and cold as bronze gripping her wrist. What was it he was so determined for her to see? Why did he—

She was hurled forward, her wrist released, and she tumbled out of control. Her knees scraped a hard surface. Rolling to a painful stop, she tried to catch her gasping breath. She was dazed, shaken, and her bladder had let go, soaking her clothing.

From behind her came a shifting sound, something heavy moving.

And then a clank.

After that it was perfectly still.

Chapter Two

The Cloud Master

Acrios stood motionless in the dark passageway, his hand on the smooth metal panel separating him from his daughter. He imagined Danna screaming hysterically in the room beyond, but heard nothing save his own ragged breathing. Trembling, he told himself that it was for the best. Now she would be purged, and now he would have time to circumvent what Bilyf had seen . . . if that was possible.

He shook his head and turned, taking long, purposeful strides back toward the brightly lit chamber. Surely Danna couldn't get out of that room. If anyone should know that, it was Acrios. And surely she would be safe there for a while, at least until he returned from Bethes with a physician. Damn this whole preposterous situation! What good would it do to lock Danna up? True, he had been trapped in there by his own father, his fear consequently triggering the Gift, but what effect might it have on Danna? Was the Gift's seed already planted in her psyche? Or perhaps something even greater . . . ? But there was nothing an anthroform could possess that was greater than the Gift, no higher calling on any world than Receptor of the Seers' transmissions.

Whatever came of this, it was doubtful that Danna could already be pregnant . . . though it could happen so easily to a girl of her age. She might think she was in love, and then, in a single moment of lust. . . . He had to see that it *never* happened.

Acrios picked up his pace. It was here that he had been punished, cleansed, instilled with the Gift. This place was both awesome and sacrosanct. A place of transcendence . . . of blue, glimmering Otherness.

He ran across the bare chamber now, and down the dimly lighted tunnel leading to the outside world. As he forced his wine-heavy legs to move, the memory of his rescue from the dark room came to mind. His mother, Stallea, had been drawn to him by the sheer power of his fear, an almost palpable, magnetic force. She'd rushed to him, for the first time knowing that

14

her son possessed the Gift. And, while the Gift was terrible, she
was thankful that her son possessed it, for it had saved his life.

Soon after that, Acrios's father had become an Other.

Then the Seers came in their lightship. Acrios had awakened
one morning not long after his father's death to find his mother
cowering in the dining hall. An unnatural light shafted through
the archway, and Acrios knew that they had come for him. He
stepped out onto the grass, and a shower of antigravitons carried him up to the blazing triangle hovering over the villa.

Inside the lightship, three Seers spoke to him, their huge
eyes insectile and emotionless.

"Come with us," one of them said with his mind. "We will
take you to the Machine."

"The Blue Star," Acrios whispered in awe. "Parnassus."

"You have the makings of a Receptor, perhaps the greatest
of them all." How many millennia had these strange men and
women been bred for the task of deciphering the Machine's secrets? And yet Acrios could not help believing that they had
made a mistake. Surely *he* could never be a Receptor.

"I feel the doubt that is in your mind," the Seer said. "There
is no doubt in ours."

And Acrios sensed that it was true. His mother had known,
and his poor, mad father. He was going to be a Receptor.

"You must come with us now," another of the Seers said.

"Now?" Acrios suddenly realized that he was speaking to
them with his mind, just as they had spoken to him. If he had
had any doubts about his abilities, they were gone now. Not
everyone could do this . . . only those with the Gift.

"Now."

"I must say goodbye to my mother."

"No, you must decide at this very moment. We leave now
with or without you, Acrios of Rocinth."

And he had gone, never to see Stallea again. There was a
distortion, a physical queasiness, an emotional and psychic un-
focusing, and they were suddenly easing into orbit around the
Blue Star, a gem of cold cobalt brilliance.

The lightship cut through the planet Parnassus's pitted crust
like an invisible dagger. Inside was a mantle of machinery, endlessly humming for a depth of hundreds of miles under the entire surface of the planet.

There he learned the ways of the Seers. A node was surgi-
cally implanted in his cortex to enhance his Gift to the maximum. He would always be in contact with the Machine,
whenever he wished, periodically receiving an allotted quantity
of information for as long as he inhabited the anthroform. Once
he absorbed the quantitative information, his mind intuitively

distilled its essence. What remained was instantaneously re-turned to the Machine. This was the power of the Gift, properly refined and guided by the wisdom of the Seers.

By the time Acrios had left the pristine, subsurface world of the Seers and gone home to Rocinth, he was a man. The Ro-cinthan mundomentus—the planet's great mass mind, the most advanced planetary consciousness developed before the Ma-chine—awarded him a secondary node, opening all the planet's considerable resources to him, for he was now the Receptor.

All anthroforms received cortical implants, the primary nodes, keeping them in constant contact with the mundo-mentus. The secondary node was reserved for the statespersons and thinkers of this world, and Acrios was the greatest of them all. But on the day he had returned to Rocinth, he had not imagined the agony and loneliness that was to define his life as Receptor.

With each step it grew darker now; he must be near the tunnel mouth. Before he could slow his pace his momentum carried him past it, to the very edge of the outside path. He flailed his arms, a sickening heave in his guts as he teetered on the brink, the seemingly bottomless well yawning below. Some-how he managed to collapse back onto the cracked stone, heart pumping.

"Fool," he gasped, "you'll kill yourself in your eagerness to prolong your miserable life."

Perhaps that would be for the best, but he could not let it happen. Determined to see this thing through, he rose and began to walk deliberately up the spiraling path. Despite his weakness, he forced his legs to work.

How had it come to this? There were only a few million like him, one on each of the human worlds. Did such monstrous things happen to them? He suspected not.

He alone among the Receptors, the greatest of humankind, had somehow incurred the wrath of something beyond even what the machine knew. He was certain it could only be the Others. But why? Was he so close to their secret that they had to stop him, even by so unholy a means as using his own daugh-ter as their instrument of murder?

For murder it was, no matter how those blue wraiths might perceive it. He was the only anthroform that they actively plot-ted against, and he had known for some time that they wanted him dead. Hadn't they taken his wife, Lehana, from him?

They didn't have Danna, not yet, though they were clearly trying to capture her soul. Those monstrous things, those hid-eous, monstrous things.

He must be vigilant. Their perfidy was beyond even human

treachery. They studied him from some other plane or dimension, from beyond death itself. He had to fight them. He could not permit himself any sentimentality or weakness.

He forced his body to move. No matter how drunk he was, he had to act *now*. He didn't want to hurt his daughter, but he had to make sure that she could never bear a child. Bilyf's vision was not to be taken lightly.

Danna would be all right. Her captivity would last at most a few hours. And perhaps something wondrous might happen to her while she was below the ground . . .

As he passed through the garden, Acrios saw Danna's nutrient sprinkler resting on a crystal ledge. Her mother had seeded the living crystal, a Kra'alnsenian marvel he had presented to her as a gift. Many of his drinking vessels were grown from this parent block, but if left alone the block would spread all over the grounds like some glittering blight. It had to be dealt with before it got out of hand.

He entered the dining hall. There he found Bilyf staring at the well through a window.

"What has Acrios—done with—little Danna?" Bilyf asked, looking as miserable as the day he had been torn from the egg-sac.

"Don't worry about Danna, Bilyf. She's all right." Annoyed, Acrios glared at his servant. "It was necessary to take her to a place where she will be safe while you and I are gone. She'll be back in this house as soon as we return from Bethes with a physician. Get ready to go." He climbed the stairs to his bedroom.

"One must ask—why?" Bilyf called up to him.

"That is none of your concern!" Acrios shouted.

On the sleeping mats, several of his lovers stirred at the sound of the Receptor's angry voice. One of them, a young man named Crophyam, opened his eyes.

"What is it, Acrios?" Crophyam asked.

"Go back to sleep, damn you!" Acrios roared.

Obediently shutting his eyes, Crophyam nestled his head between the breasts of a woman, feigning sleep. Acrios selected a purple cape from his wardrobe. Then he rejoined Bilyf, the garment swirling around him as he stalked through the dining hall.

"Come along," he said to the Mennon.

Acrios bolted through the archway. Behind him, Bilyf churned his short legs, struggling in vain to keep up. Outside, they crossed a rolling expanse, the ground rising until they stood on a cliff overlooking the sea. Below, where tidal waterspouts did not erupt, some of Rocinth's twelve moons were reflected in the water.

"We shall travel in the clouds," said Acrios.

Laboring up the steep grade to join his master, Bilyf hesitated for a moment. He had never liked cloud travel. "One wonders—if this—is necessary?"

"Prepare yourself," Acrios said, ignoring the question. He stared out over the sea, silently calling on the mundomentus to bring the clouds to him. Stretching out his hands towards the stars, he felt his will drawn through his fingertips to shape the very elements of Rocinth. He was like a god, one of a handful in the entire galaxy who could work such miracles. Gods did not answer to anyone but themselves . . . and gods surely did not die.

The air grew still and warm, the sky very black. Clouds gathered, quickly obscuring the moons' minute crescents. On the underside of the rushing cloud strata, huge, baggy tufts erupted and sank towards the land.

"Ah." This was a moment that Acrios always loved, even tonight. Who could comprehend this but another Receptor? And there was no other Receptor on Rocinth. He alone possessed absolute power here. Nothing would make him lose it. Nothing.

Acrios's cape billowed as a cold wind blew in from the sea. Chilled, he caught the cape and drew it around him. He shivered—not so much like a god there. It was hard to rise above the world when one wanted for something, or was cold . . . or was afraid.

The wind whipped at the roiling clouds. Instead of dissipating, they began to intertwine, forming an intricate design of grays, blacks, and smoky whites. Then they met cold air pushed toward the cliffs by convection currents, displaced by the manipulation of the mundomentus. These had been shunted about in the worldmind's unceasing efforts to afford Rocinth perfectly balanced weather, a climate comfortable enough so that anthroforms could walk naked anywhere, anytime, and so that robots could tend the plants for food and aesthetics easily, the better for their masters to enjoy the luxuries of this most beautiful world.

Now the clouds mingled and began to slowly rotate in a single immense, dark disc. It spun faster and faster, as Acrios played the storm like an artist through the medium of the mundomentus, Bilyf cowering at his side.

At last the disc began to extend downward like a finger, a gigantic vortex blotting out the stars. Winds wailed like a million crying souls, as the artificial cyclone swallowed the waves and undulated towards the cliff.

"See what I have done!" Acrios shouted. But his exultation was lost in the howling cacophony.

Whitecaps lashed at the cliffs, the spray stinging Acrios's face. Bilyf shriveled into himself, cold and wet, dreading the coming journey. Acrios laughed as the funnel drew closer. It curved under the cliff and looped upward, so that they could see down into the black tube of sheer force.

"Come on, Bilyf!" Acrios grasped Bilyf's arm and pushed him roughly towards the edge of the cliff.

Bilyf peered down at the bobbing tornado. Its opening now remained more or less stationary, but he still wished that he did not have to do this.

Laughing, Acrios pushed Bilyf into the storm's maw, and then leaped off the cliff himself. Their fall seemed endless to Bilyf, but it was over in a moment. Jerked into the tornado like bits of paper in the wind, they were buffeted helplessly but harmlessly. It was disorienting, blood rushing to the head, limbs flailing out of control as though they belonged to marionettes instead of living, thinking beings.

The Receptor spun dizzily on the furious air currents, quickly losing sight of Bilyf in the dark. He was flung down into the tornado's curve and then shot upward at a tremendous velocity. He flew into the heart of the storm like a dancer, his body pirouetteing, his arms clinging to his torso or stretched out for an upward dive. No man was as alive as this. Ecstasy!

"Let me gaze upon my world." Acrios couldn't hear his own voice over the roaring gale. With a flick of his hand, he made clouds part below him. Through this crack in the great, churning cylinder, he could see the coastline as they moved along it. Inland were the Phallic mountains, carved for the amusement of the masses out of solid rock; the nearby Vaginal Caverns had been the artist's inspiration. From this height, they truly did resemble sexual organs, forests in the foothills simulating human hair.

The funnel damaged no crops or habitations, for its altitude was too high. And yet Acrios knew what a spectacle it was from the ground, a twisting rope of dark power. It was his to command. Everyone on Rocinth, on all the civilized worlds, knew him. He could not die, not before the universe itself was gone. As the dark streamers whirled about him, he tried to imagine himself dead. Nothing, gone to ashes, or . . . Otherness.

Lightning flashed, illuminating the cavernous interior of the funnel. A blue afterimage remained on his retina, a vision of Otherness, as if nature itself were conspiring to remind him of his hitherto unsuspected mortality.

The crack in the clouds sealed itself, and he cast out his hand again, revealing the stars and the Rocinthan moons. As the storm rotated, he was slowly treated to a vista of perfectly manicured valleys and rounded hills softly lit by moonlight. But the vast landscape was soon darkened by the storm's enormous shadow.

No longer exulting in the raw power of his elemental mount, Acrios laughed bitterly and soundlessly in the deafening maelstrom. An extension of his will it might have been, but there were difficulties. He could not rid himself of the storm's shadow. Indeed, it might be that blotting out the light was his greatest gift.

But he would not permit his melancholy to rob him of his pleasure. He was at the very core of the storm, of this world, of the galaxy itself. He could do what not even the Seers could do. There was no man or woman greater than he.

And was anyone so alive as he at this moment?

Alive . . . but Bilyf had seen the end. How could he take pleasure in this mechanistic toy when his very immortality had been threatened?

Grim laughter seemed to override the winds, and the lightning created ghostly glimpses of Otherness. Acrios saw sparking blue figures where it arced and played, knifing into the concave black cloud banks and vanishing before he could be sure that they were really there.

He could not watch this. It was madness. He opened the clouds once again, and fastened his gaze on the rolling land beneath the storm so that he would not be obsessed with such morbid thoughts. Instead, he concentrated on the interwoven clouds—nimbus, cumulus, and cirrocumulus spiraling around him. He marveled that he could be held here at the eye of the storm without being torn apart, idly watching the scenery pass beneath it all.

He could see the mighty serpent vines of Somtovia coiling around that marble and gilt city, semi-sentient tubes attracted by the warmth and movement of human habitation. But he wished to avoid the crowds of that rollicking place. He would obtain a physician where no one would take notice. Only the mundomentus would know.

Mighty forests passed beneath them, their billowing sail trees shrunken in the dark, tropisms relaxed now that the sun was gone. The darkness deepened even as Acrios watched, making the lightning flashes all the more irritating . . . all the more disturbing.

He thought that he heard laughter again, over the tempest's din. It was in his mind, of course. This thing he had embarked upon troubled him, as it would any man. But he was not just a man, was he? He tucked his knees up to his chest and dived backwards into the whorling funnel.

No acrobat had ever spun so gracefully and with such speed, the force of the storm buoyed him, drew him back to the height whence he had dived. It was as though he could never descend below this level, that even his human frailty had become elevated, gigantic . . . almost beyond his control.

Nothing was beyond his control. He was the Receptor of Rocinth. No one was greater than he—no one. On the ground, rain fell from the storm, giving sustenance to the world. He absorbed the pain of space/time in a great swirling tempest of emotion whenever he lay in the reception pool, suffering for all humankind. His tears gave Man hope, just as the rain he brought gave life to the plants of Rocinth.

But already the storm had moved past the forests and now spattered its raindrops on the broad, placid lakes where meteors had gouged the planet's crust before Man had come to Rocinth.

With outstretched hand, Acrios sealed the clouds. He would ride the rest of the way in darkness. As he spun, he tried not to think of what he was doing to his daughter. His life depended on it . . . and so many lives depended upon his survival.

Or did he, in his megalomania, attribute more to himself than he really possessed? Another Receptor could be trained, if a youth with the Gift could be discovered in time. But that could very well take centuries. No, his survival was in the interest of every single anthroform in the galaxy. This was no mere personal matter.

And yet here in this perfect darkness, where no sound came but the sound of the storm, he knew that he was lying to himself. He could rationalize his decisions, no matter how monstrous, no matter how terrible the consequences, but he could not live with them. He could not stand the pain, but he could not bear to see it end. It had come down to such a simple equation.

"Life or death," he said, but his words were lost in the tumult.

A flicker of whiteness came out of the surrounding dark. Bilyf's flailing figure tumbled upward toward the Receptor; the alien's fear was palpable. Bilyf had courage, though. Acrios had known that ever since the day he had taken the Mennon from the eggsac. Acrios loved Bilyf, and had not enjoyed tormenting him. It had been a necessity.

There was no time for pangs of conscience now. Below them the entire world of Rocinth turned. Acrios was a god, looking down at it, willing its very elements to do his bidding.

And yet he could be slain by his own grandchild. How was

such a thing possible? It couldn't happen, not in a sane universe.

The universe is dying—there is your sanity. All is fading from existence, entropy ensuring that there would one day be no trace of it, not so much as a single dead asteroid to mark its passing.

Grim laughter seemed to override the winds once again, as the powerful funnel slowed its dizzying speed almost imperceptibly. It tilted and swayed, its direction altering in response to Acrios's desire to be taken to Bethes. He closed his eyes in the darkness, not needing to consciously direct the storm's movements.

What of Danna? Even if he had her fixed so that she could not bear children, she could have a clone made. Wouldn't that be her child as surely as one that came out of her belly? And if he had that one put to death, might she not have another? And, hating him, another and another and yet another, until one was finally produced that would do the job?

He would have to risk it. The prophecy was clear; Bilyf could not be mistaken. Acrios must change the future so that he would not have to die. He could do that. He was the Receptor; it was his task to find a way to change the inevitable. For the good of humankind. In the end, that was his justification. He was about to commit a crime, but he might very well get away with it because of who and what he was.

The storm's ferocity abated a little more. They were nearing Bethes now, the funnel slowly and deliberately angling toward the ground. A crack opened in the swirling clouds like an eye, so Acrios could take one last look before they landed. The domelike, blue hills north of Bethes were below. Birds craned their necks to gaze up at the storm as their shadows passed over the sapphire vegetation.

Acrios closed the gap and spun in the darkness, protean gusts tossing him this way and that as the storm settled toward the hills. He was wafted downward, buoyed up for a few moments, then dropped down again. Bilyf bounced above him as though on a string. Soon they were dangling in the winds more or less alongside one another.

Incrementally, they drifted towards the soft hills of Bethes. Each drop was shorter than the last, the buoyancy at the end a little less pronounced so that their descent was as steady and gentle as the fall of snowflakes. Floating, floating down as if they were all but weightless.

Acrios's heel touched solid ground. He saw the pale form of his servant light beside him. The clouds, which had coalesced into the tempest miles away, scattered and dispersed, seeming to dissolve, revealing a hilltop overlooking a small village.

The air was calm and warming as the storm blew out to sea. Below, Acrios saw the clean, white curve of the Bethes amphitheatre. Here, he and his wife, Lehana, had attended many plays. Here, too, he had brought the infant Danna to have her first look outside her home, her first encounter with art.

He called to Bilyf, and together they walked down the hill. "We must find a suitable physician here, Bilyf," he said, pointing to a row of orderly, low structures beyond the amphitheatre.

The scent of flowers was carried on the mild night breeze as they approached a gleaming building where robots were stored. As they entered, the walls glowed in response to their body heat. Large metal cubes became visible, stacked neatly from the floor almost to the ceiling. Bilyf examined the markings on them.

"No—physicians," he said.

Nodding unhappily, Acrios led the way back outside. In the clear night air, he thought he heard the distant sound of laughter.

"Do you mock me?" Acrios shouted at the voice. "Do you dare mock me?"

"Acrios—" Bilyf grasped his arm.

The Receptor made as if to pull away, then thought better of it and relented. "Bilyf," he said, "I . . . I hear . . ."

The laughter sounded again, faint and damning. Acrios couldn't quite find the courage to ask if Bilyf had heard it too.

They renewed the search, until they found a building containing physicians. After checking a few for corrosion, they narrowed the machines down to a pair that appeared serviceable. In order to select the better of the two, Acrios deferred to Bilyf. The Mennon had an uncanny knack with machinery—one of the main reasons why the Receptor had wanted a Mennon to begin with—as well as his species' prescient ability and commitment to servitude.

One at a time, Bilyf opened the folded robots, his multi-jointed digits flowing like serpents through their filligreed intricacies. When he was finished, he indicated the more tarnished machine with a flick of a foredigit.

"Come," Acrios commanded.

It took only a moment for the mundomentus to energize the robot. Its response was to nimbly unravel itself and spring to attention, a faint hum of electrical current audible in the stillness.

"Display—please," Bilyf said.

The robot projected three-dimensional images of itself, indicating its medical and lifesaving functions by means of subvocalization and color-coded diagrams. Bilyf was fairly certain that this machine was adequate for the task at hand, in spite of its shabby appearance.

"This one looks a bit old to me, Bilyf," Acrios said, his voice slurring with wine and fatigue. "Are you sure it will be safe to use it?"

"Its medical facilities—are concealed inside—its casing—for protection."

"Very well." The Receptor turned to the physician. "You will follow us."

The robot stepped softly behind him in metronomic cadence as he left the storeroom. Bilyf lumbered silently behind it, watching for any odd movements that might suggest a structural flaw.

"If this goes badly, Bilyf, I'll hold you responsible," the master was saying. "I don't like the looks of this one, not one bit. I admit that you've never been mistaken about this sort of thing before, but if you're wrong this time . . ."

But Bilyf saw that he was not mistaken, and even if he had been, it would not matter in the final analysis. It was best not to tell Acrios now, though . . . best to let him learn in his own time.

As the three of them reached the crest of the hill, Acrios gazed up at the moons.

"Such is my power, Bilyf," he said, "that I can summon forth anything on this world, even the clouds themselves. Do you know how many others on this planet can do the same?"

"Very few—Acrios is a great man."

"Acrios is a great fool." His strength was fast leaving him, and he felt his sense of mission slipping way. Even his wine-soaked mind knew that it was futile to try to change the future. "I can ride the clouds, yet I fear an unborn child."

This time he did not gesture. He silently called on the mundomentus to bring the clouds. Soon the smoky column pointed at Bethes like the finger of a colossus. Just before all sound was smothered by the storm's shrieking cacophony, Acrios thought he heard the hint of laughter a third time.

Sucked up into the cyclone again, Acrios felt the chaotic winds draining the warmth from him. It was as if the life were being pulled out through his limbs. He was no longer the master of the tempest, but its impotent plaything.

The journey back seemed to take forever, but at last they were set down on the grounds of Acrios's estate, on the cliff overlooking the sea. Acrios led Bilyf and the robot. On the downwardly spiraling path he ran ahead, down into the weed-infested depths of the well.

Beginning to feel that he had made a terrible mistake, Acrios ignored the danger of moving so swiftly in the dark. Poor Danna. Why had he felt compelled to incarcerate her? Drunkenness was no excuse. It was the act of a madman—an act that could cripple his daughter.

He was sprinting down the tunnel now, Bilyf and the robot physician somewhere behind him. Nearly out of breath, he barely found the strength to dash across the big, brightly lit chamber. He had reacted much too harshly to Bilyf's prophecy. But that was his way—action first, reflection only when the deed was accomplished, if then—and it was a way that made things work . . . until now.

Danna was all he had now that Lehana was gone. Why did he punish her when he knew she was innocent? She had no influence over future events.

The metal panel loomed before him in the tunnel's dim light. He stopped, catching his breath, while Bilyf caught up with him. The robot whirred to a halt behind them.

"Help me move the panel back!" Acrios's head pounded with hangover and guilt. The three strained until the panel rumbled and slowly rolled on its ancient runner. They slid it open.

"Danna!" Acrios cried into the gloom.

Silence.

"She must be asleep," Acrios said, desperate. "Danna!"

The room was as still as a grave.

"Danna! Answer me!"

There was no answer.

Chapter Three

The God Factory

"Father!" Danna screamed. "Father, help me! Don't leave me in here!"

She had been crying out for a very long time, knowing all the while that no one would answer. There was nobody in these caverns, unless her father was still down here. But he certainly wasn't going to help her. She couldn't understand why he had done this. He had never been cruel to her before, not like this.

There could only be one possible reason for it: so that no one would ever find her. Here she would die ... so that her baby would never be born.

"Father, no!" she cried. "Please, Father!"

When the echoes faded, only silence remained. Acrios wasn't down here anymore.

Danna screamed as she had never screamed before, a long wail of loss and hurt and frustration that left her lungs heaving for air. And then she screamed again. But when her cries had shrunk to nothing more than pitiful sobs, she decided not to carry on like that anymore. It wasn't doing her any good.

She had to open that panel. That was the only way out, and she had to do it. It was as simple as that. Of course she had tried to move it when she had first been trapped in here. She had tried again and again, until her muscles ached, but she couldn't budge it. That was when she had panicked for the second time.

She would never get out by screaming and crying. She had to sit down and think, rest until she got back some of her strength, and then try something that might help her. If she didn't, she would just be stuck in here until she died. Would she become an Other, or just a skeleton lying here in the dark?

And to think that her father had been the one who had talked her into rejecting Otherness in the first place. He had so prejudiced her against it that she had selected the flesh without question. Her cousin Dictys, a great intellect, agreed with Acrios, and Bilyf had offered no opinion—that was so like him. Only the scholar Verra, visiting the estate just before she had

26

become Prime Mystagogue of Rocinth—a position second only to Receptor in importance—had halfheartedly explained to Danna the virtues of Otherness. Verra had been so vague, though, that Danna had not been moved.

Her father, on the other hand, had argued so strenuously for what he termed "life," that Danna had felt that she would have dealt him a mortal blow had she even considered Otherness. Acrios quite logically refuted Verra's feeble defense of the Other world. He had not always been so logical, Danna thought as she sat cross-legged on the cool, slick floor.

"You can run forever, Danna, playing on this garden planet until the end of time"—that was how Acrios had put it. Remain forever a child or turn yourself into something as vague and insubstantial as the wind... something she could not even understand, much less desire.

No one understood; that was the trouble. But now she wished that she *had* chosen to be one of the Others when she had had the chance. They said it didn't hurt if you did it when you were little, but the older you got, the harder it was. No wonder Father was afraid of Otherness, old as he was.

She moved her feet, her sandals scraping hollowly against the hard floor. Her legs were stiff and her toes were asleep, and she stretched them, massaging until the feeling came back. She was a little tired, and ached here and there, but she was all right. She was a long way from dying. It was silly to sit here sobbing. If she was overcome with exhaustion and hunger in the end, so be it. But now she was still alive and healthy. Now was the time to act.

There had to be a way out of here. There just *had* to be.

Standing up, Danna took a step forward, arms outstretched so that she wouldn't run into the wall head first. She fumbled about for a few minutes until her fingers met a glassy surface. It squeaked as she rubbed her fingertips over it, echoing softly in the darkness. Slowly, she ran her hands over the wall in a circular motion. She groped for a long time, hoping to touch something—anything—besides the icy hardness defining the dimensions of her prison. She had no way of knowing how much time had passed before she reached a corner. She made her way deliberately along the contiguous wall.

She had not yet reached the next corner when she felt a cool breeze blowing against her bare legs. Turning, she expected to see the panel slide back, her father reaching out to her, somber and repentant. She would forgive him, she would...

The panel was not open, but there was light coming from somewhere. A shimmering, blue glow caught the corner of her eye. She turned towards it, but where the light source should have been, there was nothing. Her eyes were playing tricks on her.

As the hours dragged on, Danna kept searching for some way out. It was probably futile, but she refused to be overcome by despair. She had come to think of her father in a new way, as a man she hardly knew. How could the man she had thought she knew do such a thing to her?

Maybe Bilyf would come after her. He hadn't been with Father when she was brought down here, but he might be able to see where she was. Surely he would help her if he could.

But she was forgetting that Bilyf was Acrios's servant, and he would not disobey his master even if it hurt him to do so. That was the way Mennons were. And even if he could defy Acrios, Bilyf's prescience might fail him. It was not something he could turn on and off like a tap.

She was getting very tired now, edging endlessly around the little cell, constantly moving her hands around and around. But she would not give up. A small stirring of resentment had taken hold and was growing steadily into defiant anger.

She had always been quiet and submissive, as Bilyf had taught her... and as her mother had shown her by example. What good had it done either of them? And what good had it done her, who ended up here below the world's surface, in danger of wasting away without food or water?

But she wouldn't die, not unless she wanted to. She was the daughter of a Receptor, her cells able to repair themselves and maintain her body for a very long time. But the suffering might prove to be too much... starvation while the body kept on living....

Suddenly she touched something. Her hand passed over it, and it took a few moments to find it again. But there it was, a protrusion, raised not more than the width of a finger from the otherwise featureless wall. She stopped her groping and felt it: a small, oblong piece of metal pinioned to the wall by a thin rod. It was so small she doubted that she would have noticed it even if the room were well lit. How many times had she been around the room without touching it? Five, six? It must serve some purpose, she thought, and that thought gave her hope.

But what was it? And what could she do with it, even if she had known what it was? Her heart was thumping wildly in spite of her misgivings. If this didn't lead to something, she would die.

No, she must not think that way. She wouldn't die. But she had to *do* something with this thing.

But what?

She squeezed it.

Something stirred, a groaning from the bowels of ancient Rocinth not heard for a million years. Rainbow images leaped out at her, lapped end over end like a caricature of a running human figure's legs. The images were all inside the running figure, shifting so rapidly she couldn't make them out very well. At times they seemed mysteriously familiar, and then they were like nothing she'd ever seen.

The legs stopped running, their mass displacing until a human form faced her, rings of light encircling its torso and moving up and down as it waved its harlequin arms. A noise burst inside her head, a thousand chattering voices buzzed at her in some staccato language never spoken by a human tongue. It really didn't sound like a language at all in the usual sense, but she knew it was one, somehow. It was as if the figure were running around inside her head, instead of just being a projection she was watching.

It was trying to tell her something: she was sure of it. But what? Why couldn't it calmly show her what it wanted?

Now the flickering rainbow apparition cast out its hands, and dazzling light spiraled into her brain. Only it wasn't light, but pictures. Information. Talking and moving and light and feeling and smell and . . . and even taste!

She suddenly knew things in a blaze of light. She knew that the builders of this communication device—and all the technology that lay beneath her in the endless warrens that had been still for a thousand millennia—were active again, and that she was the reason for it. These wonders had been built by the Rocinthans, but they were now controlled by the Others. She knew this as she had never known anything in her life. They wanted her for some purpose. Destiny, her father would have called it.

Something was about to happen to her . . . something she had been created for.

The sensations changed. Now the light probed at her mind. It hurt her head. She couldn't take it all in, and her brain hurt, as if it were swelling up and getting ready to explode.

"No!" She twisted the piece of metal savagely, trying to make the pain stop.

The images swirled, eddied, shifting and melting. They didn't go away exactly. Instead, they transformed into a single scene, a vista of coruscating colors and bizarre shapes, angles and curves dipping and rolling in impossible ways. Was this how the Rocinthans had seen things? This must be—what was the word Bilyf used?—synesthesia. It was teaching her things, but at the same time it was examining her, right down to the cellular level. Analyzing her, testing her perceptions, the patterns of her logic, her mind itself.

But it was hard to think now, with all this going on. It was as though she were crawling on her belly through these tunnels. No, not crawling, sliding—swiftly and gracefully gliding along in an environment designed for her body. The vista ahead of her was strange and beautiful, a way of *seeing* that was entirely new to her. The trembling light, changing colors, mutable realities, revealing new and different things constantly, symmetrically. And the smells seemed to come right through her pores and tingle every bit of her body. Sounds rolled over and turned themselves inside out, while her body responded sensitively to everything she touched.

There was another sensation too. Just a suggestion, but she was aware of it. Perhaps it was something the Rocinthans alone had possessed, some sixth sense an anthroform could never know.

Danna found that she was beginning to like it. All these new sensations excited her, made her feel alive again. The terror of her situation shrank into a corner of her mind as she thrilled to the total sensual stimulation.

What would happen if she turned the metal thing again? Perhaps she could make it do something even more exciting.

She twisted it, and was dismayed to feel it receding into the wall. She tried to hold onto it, but it slipped through her fingertips. It was gone in an instant. She tried to find some trace of it, but the wall was as smooth and seamless as glass to her touch.

The last afterimages faded from her head, and she was left alone again in the darkness.

"Come back!" she cried. Her voice reverberated through the chamber. Why had she done such a foolish thing? If she had just left it alone. . . .

She thought she heard something rustling in the dark. Standing perfectly still, she listened.

Her ears must have still been ringing from the sounds of ancient Rocinth. There couldn't be anything down here but bugs or nafs or some other small animals.

Could there be some life-forms, some strange creatures left from the days of the ancients? No, they were all destroyed before the planet was terraformed, long, long ago. And no naf would come down this far beneath the surface.

She must have been imagining things.

Suddenly something brushed against her leg. Before she could react, it coiled itself around her.

"No!" she screamed.

But it had her. She couldn't get loose. She screamed again, but it was no good. Whatever it was, it was starting to move forward, taking her with it.

It held her firmly but gently, as a faint breeze was stirred by its forward motion. Where had the wall gone? It must have opened to let the coil through, or had it actually turned *into* the coil?

It began to move faster now, the breeze becoming a wind, drying the perspiration on her face. The speed increased until she was giddy with fear and motion sickness. She was afraid she would throw up if it didn't stop soon. But there was nothing in her stomach to throw up.

At least she was out of that awful room. She didn't know where this thing was taking her, but at least she could hope to get away, now that she was free of that horrid little cell.

The coil turned corners abruptly, making the ride even wilder. Danna started to get used to it after a while; she began to believe that the ride was going to last forever. She was tired, but how could she sleep while flying through the darkness in the grip of this strange creature?

Perhaps creature wasn't quite the correct word. This was a biologically created machine designed by Rocinthans ages ago. Their method was similar to the ancient human art of bioengineering, with one major difference: the cells of the coil replaced themselves in precise proportion to the cells that died. This was a living device that never wore out. Unfortunately, the Rocinthans had been unable to introduce the same property to their infinitely complex form, so they had not achieved immortality . . . though they had been on the verge of it when they gave themselves up to Otherness en masse.

In the dim light, Danna saw a golden river flowing out from between two banks of writhing, flexing, lashing shapes.

The coil came to an abrupt halt, trembling for an instant before releasing Danna. She cried out as she fell. The drop was cushioned by a soft mound, luminescent bacteria inside it lending it an eerie glow. Blinking, she watched the tensile coil flick into the darkness like a frightened snake.

Her eyes soon adjusted to the faint light. She laughed, amazed to see where she had ended up. She was sitting in the midst of the last scene she'd looked at before she twisted the metal rod and shut off the images. The Rocinthan sensibility was so alien that nothing really looked the same here, or smelled the same, or even felt the same. But there was a pattern underlying her sensual awareness of her surroundings that she equated with what she'd seen earlier.

She was a long way away from where she started. How far did these tunnels extend? As far as Bethes? Or even throughout the planet's entire crust, each well's arteries branching off into tributaries and ultimately connecting with all the others? She knew that this golden river, and the living machines that labored over it, was at one time the central manufacturing focus for all the technology on Rocinth. It was a vast chamber, the end of which was far beyond her vision . . . and yet, because of the knowledge she'd been given, she had some idea of its protean dimensions.

It seemed as if she had discovered something very important. If—when—she got out of here, the mundomentus would have a new store of knowledge about Rocinth's original inhabitants.

Her thought was cut short as the mound swelled beneath her and bubbled. She was pitched backwards, and the mound rose up and sucked her inside itself. She felt herself go under, spinning in a sluggish yet powerful whirlpool. Slowly and steadily, she went down. She was afraid she would smother, but then she suddenly emerged into the air once again.

She was encased in a clear, warm bubble from head to toe. Near her face globules formed, bursting around her bubble on contact.

Curled up in the fetal position, Danna was not uncomfortable in the least as her bubble rolled aimlessly among others of its kind. She saw that the globules grew into bubbles, but these were empty. She seemed to be inside the only one that held any contents.

She was on a collision course with one of the other bubbles. Would they burst? Just before they struck one another they both darted off reflexively at right angles. Danna tumbled end over end, laughing as she rolled through a gregarious crowd of transparent spheres. She didn't know if she were pointed up or down, and she didn't care. This was fun.

A sense of well-being permeated her body. Warmth and happiness flowed through her just as her bubble flowed through this murky stuff—an orange, oily liquid.

She and the bubble were popped into the air, landing in a trench filled with the orange fluid.

Through half-closed, but still wondering eyes, she saw clusters of tendrils, like plant roots twisted into delicate hands. Her bubble was heading towards them, and she saw them lift other bubbles out of the trench and probe them.

What was it going to do to her? She should have been afraid, but she was too sleepy for that . . . sleepy, and yet wide awake.

The tendril fingers reached for her, carefully picking her bubble out of the orange slime. They meticulously peeled the bubble away from her body and discarded its remains in a deep pit behind them. They carried her, like a mother cradling an infant, to a sloping bank peppered with meter-wide holes. She was placed inside one of these and abandoned.

Inside the niche, her entire body tingled as she was brushed from head to toe with tiny filaments. These seemed to grow out of the solid walls of the niche, which was quite deep, set at a forty-five degree angle in the bank so that she couldn't fall out. In her partially comatose state, she doubted that she could have even climbed out, had she wanted to.

But she didn't want to, not the way she felt. She was relaxed, and at the same time excited. It was as if an electrical current passed through her body, only pleasurable. The hairy fibers stroked her, soothing her and driving away all her fears.

Below, the living machines whickered and bubbled, producing the nucleic acids, proteins and chromosomes needed to duplicate human cells. Danna knew what was going to happen to her, but she had drifted into such a dreamlike state that she didn't care.

Outside the niche, the tendril-fingers labored over the pit where her bubble's remains had been deposited. Suddenly they flipped over and scurried away on their tips, like walking hands. In a moment they were out of sight.

Through heavy-lidded eyes, Danna watched the bubbling, spurting organisms perform their inexplicable tasks. This place was a factory, and these living things were pursuing their labors single-mindedly, relentlessly.

The fingers sprinted back into sight, two digits carrying a wad of pink, gummy stuff. From time to time a tear-shaped run would drool out of the wad, but the digits would snap out of joint and catch it before it eluded their grasp. Assuming their position again, the fingers pulled the pink stuff into thin strands as a long, pulsing column rose from the pit.

Something warm and sticky spurted over Danna's body, leaving only her head and legs untouched. A coil wrapped itself around her waist, lifting her carefully out of the niche.

Still lethargic, she felt giddy as she was borne high over the viscous river on which the bubbles floated. She dripped a runny, scarlet patina from her breasts and belly. Her clothing was gone, dissolved by the pink stuff, even her sandals.

The column rose higher, huge and throbbing, below her.

Seeing that it was coming right for her, she squirmed, trying to free herself from the coil's powerful grip as the column drew nearer and nearer.

Hot threads looped around her ankles, unwrapping themselves from the tendril-fingers. They pulled gently yet firmly until her thighs were parted. She was afraid, but not as much as she should have been. Filaments stroked her body as she waited in an almost hypnotic state.

The filaments touched her between the legs, making her

tremble and moan. She didn't want to struggle anymore. The pulsing column pressed against her as the filaments pulled her legs up until her knees nearly touched her chin.

The column thrust up inside her. It hurt, but it felt good too. It moved up and down, and the filaments rocked her rhythmically as it moved in and out, in and out. Each movement thrilled her more and more, until she could hardly bear it.

Her eyes were closed, and her head rolled helplessly from side to side. Her muscles moved now so that the filaments were able to relax their grip.

"Oh," she moaned, "oh." Then louder: "Ohhh!" And louder and louder still, until her screams echoed throughout the cavern. She writhed at the tip of the throbbing column like a dancer.

Then she felt something like warm rain on her skin. In her ecstasy, she opened her eyes. It *was* rain, but it was shining, brilliant yellow. Liquid gold. At that moment a momentous spasm racked her. She felt as if she were dying of pleasure.

It didn't take long for Acrios, Bilyf and the robot to search the room where Danna had been imprisoned. They found no trace of her, and Acrios was growing frantic. Had he actually left her here, or, in his drunkenness, done something else? Something he couldn't remember now. No, it was impossible. He had brought her here, to this very room just a few hours ago. There could be no doubt of it.

"Could this be—some other room?" Bilyf asked.

"No, no," Acrios said, annoyed that Bilyf's thoughts were so much like his own. "I know this place very well, Bilyf. I was trapped here once, in this very room. That was when I . . ." But there was no time for a story that Bilyf knew only too well. "I assure you that there is no exit from this chamber except for the way we came in."

"Little Danna—has perhaps not—gone back—but forward?"

Acrios turned and stared at the pale, lumpy figure of his servant. Did Bilyf know something that he didn't? "What are you talking about?"

"The organic machinery—of the Rocinthans—could conceivably still—"

"Bilyf," Acrios replied, trying to remain calm, "these tunnels have not been occupied for millions of years. Surely you don't believe that any of the Rocinthan artifacts can still be working?"

"Little Danna—is not here—there is no way out—therefore one deduces—that she has found—another way."

"And which way is *that*?" Acrios demanded angrily.

"One—does not know."

"You think some mouldy Rocinthan device popped out of nowhere and whisked her away, do you?"

"It has been said—that the tools of the Rocinthans—might last as long—as this world itself—that they are self-renewing."

"Have you ever heard of such artifacts still working today?"

"One has not—but one sees that—"

"I thought not," Acrios said. "Now kindly stop spouting these absurdities and help me look for my daughter before I lose my temper." He bowed in thought, his shadow a black stripe on the floor, thrown by a light on the robot's head. It was so easy to shut out the world here, to be perfectly alone. Solitude had revealed the Gift in him; perhaps Danna had evinced it too, and someone had heard her mind calling and come for her? No, *he* would have heard, not some stranger.

"We shall search the room again, Bilyf," he said. "There must be some hidden panel, or seam, or..."

Outside, the robot physician stood like a sentinel, its beam shining on Acrios and Bilyf as they searched for a girl who wasn't there.

Danna floated on a thick substance with a life of its own, a crawling river that welled up through a shaft into a pool, depositing her on the edge of a circular platform. Her pink covering slowly desiccated and crumbled to nothing, leaving her torso as bare as her legs. She lay naked, sleeping peacefully. The liquid retreated down the shaft, gurgling into the labyrinthine depths.

As she slept, she shifted her position from time to time. At last she stirred, stretching and trembling luxuriously with the pleasure of awakening. She opened her eyes.

Gradually, memory returned. She didn't know where she was, didn't recognize the platform she was lying on, or the cavern enclosing it, but she knew that it was far away from her father. That was something to be thankful for. Cautiously testing her hands and feet, then her legs and arms, she decided everything was in working order, although she felt a little weak.

She got slowly to her feet and walked unsteadily to the edge of the platform, peering down into the shaft's gloomy depths.

She couldn't go that way. Languidly, she looked around, seeing a number of tunnel mouths where the edge of the platform joined a concave wall. The only thing to do was select a tunnel and see where it led. Stepping off the platform, she entered the nearest, still not fully awake.

As she walked, she began to feel more alert. What had happened to her hadn't been as frightening as she had thought it would be. In a way she had enjoyed it, but she wouldn't want to

go through it again. Right now she only wanted to find her way
back to the surface. The tunnel darkened as she went deeper
into it, but she soon detected a faint light in the distance; not
the luminescence of troglodytic bacteria, but the lovely amber
glow of the sun.

She ran to the light, eventually emerging from the tunnel on
one of the upper levels of a well. The fresh smell of growing
things deliciously filled her nostrils. Above, rank vegetation
crept over the rim; in practically every respect, the well was
identical to the one she had known since she was a baby. She
climbed to the surface, careful not to injure her bare feet on the
rock fragments.

She couldn't see what was over the rim, since thick creepers
and vines overran it, and weeds reached a jumbled height of
two meters in some places. In spite of her nakedness, she fought
her way to open ground.

Beyond, she saw land rising and falling in gentle hummocks.
There were many trees, and colorful bursts of wildflowers.
Birds circled overhead. Insects chirruped.

In the distance was a city, its white columns stark against the
flaxen hills. It was much, much larger than Bethes. She had
been carried a great deal farther than she had guessed. In this
city, she would hide from Acrios. He had always had trouble
hearing her thoughts, and now he thought that she was gone.
She would seal up her mind like a tomb, and the mundomentus
would not reveal her whereabouts; it would do so only if she
committed a crime.

She pushed both the mundomentus and her father from her
mind as she walked on soft humus towards the city. Its spires
seemed to beckon, twinkling in the bright sunlight. She stepped
on a root, nearly twisting her ankle, nafs scurrying out from
under it in fear. Steadying herself against a tree trunk, she
called softly to the tiny creatures: "I won't hurt you."

The nafs disappeared into the tall grass.

She felt as though she had died and been reborn. Her father
had tried to kill her, but the Rocinthan organisms had brought
her back to life. They had even brought her back to the sun and
the clouds. What else they had done to her was fading into a
hazy memory. Analyzed her, prepared something—a serum of
some kind—with which to impregnate her. But why?

Perhaps this was her destiny, then. She would have a baby.
Her body and mind both told her it was so.

By trying to prevent her from having a child, Acrios had
ensured it. If he had simply asked her not to have children, to
spare his life, she could not have refused him.

Instead, he had tried to kill her.

One day, when this child growing inside her was big enough, her father would hear from her again. Oh, how he would hear from her. The mighty Receptor, a man so evil he would sacrifice his own daughter to save himself. She was filled with such loathing for him that she forgot her surroundings for the moment and stubbed her toe on a stone. She cried out in rage, but after the first flush of pain she forced herself to remain silent. There was time now, at least. Time to live and bear a child, time to enjoy her precious life and its pleasures. It was wonderful to be alive, just to feel the grass tickling her feet, to smell the sweet odor of flowers, to hear the cheerful birdsong. There was so much to live for.

She did not hope to live forever, unlike her father. She only hoped to live long enough to see that he was not granted his most profound wish.

One way or another, she would see Acrios dead before she was gone. *This* was her destiny.

Far away, in a tiny room deep underground, her father remembered what it was like to be trapped in the dark, alone. He felt that he was imprisoned in a cell of his own making.

"What have I done?" he cried.

Bilyf bent in silent pity, his crest drooping; the robot remained stationary outside the chamber as Acrios, Receptor of Rocinth, wept bitter tears, not for his daughter . . . but for himself.

Chapter Four

One Loves

Bilyf could not rest, though his body was curled in the sleep mode. His mind ranged aimlessly through the events of his life, past and future. He saw the hive of his infancy burst, its fragments flying outward to cling to the eggsac of his siblings, helping to nurture it as it was absorbed into the thin, veined skin that sheltered them.

The humans said that the hives were like cancers, and were intrigued that they brought forth life instead of death. But to a Mennon, it was all the same.

He remembered his teacher, the old, wise one who came and spoke to the eggsharers, squatting just outside the eggsac in the mud. And he remembered the warmth of the Mother...

If only his knowledge of what was to come was as complete as his memory of the past. The human concept of *time* had muddied his thinking, had made him less than Mennon. It was not like a Mennon to make so much of the passage of events. But the humans! They thought of little else.

It was not enough for them to live till the End of All Things; they hoped to outlast the universe itself. Acrios's reaction to the prophecy of his coming death was not at all unusual for a human. Acrios might just as well resign himself to death by his grandson's hand. But he would not, of course. He would try to cheat death, and there would be dire consequences... especially for poor Danna.

As he lay curled on the webbing here in his little cubicle in Acrios's villa, the bare details of his surroundings dimmed into the flow of time, perceived in the Mennon fashion. He thought of the futility of his master's desires: immortality, or at least as near as anyone would ever come to immortality, and (dare he even think it?) reconciliation with his daughter, even if she had become an Other.

But she was not an Other, and Bilyf knew that he would see her again. He also knew that she would never forgive Acrios for what he had done, and that because of this, Acrios's flesh was doomed. These things Bilyf saw as clearly as he saw. . .

   . . . the

       eggsac

          of

             infancy. . .

   . . . where the membranous covering was drenched in sudden, chill shadow. A fogbeast roaming the swamp in search of food? The eggsharers huddled together, fighting the urge to cry out in terror, for fogbeasts were known to rend the veined dermis of the eggsac, seeking the warm blood of those inside. But fog-beasts should not have been here in the swamp during their mating season. Now they were rutting in highland caves, far away.

What, then, lurked outside the eggsac?

A vision. Not now. Not now. Bilyf struggled to clear his mind. He must not drift to the future now, not when danger was near. Why could he not see what he wished? his frustrated mind cried out in anguish. Why did he not see what this creature was?

He only knew that it had not come for the siblings, but for him alone. He could almost see it now, a long, long way into the future. . .

Nutrient fluids spurted as the dermis was torn open, wrench-ing the brothers and sisters to their very souls. Bilyf was jarred from the vagaries of the future back to the terrible reality of the present. He stared into a grotesque, alien—yet somehow strangely familiar—face. Yes, it was the same towering creature he had seen in his vision only a moment ago. Its clawed limb reached into the home of the eggsharers.

Fighting the monster, Bilyf coiled his tiny digits around its hairy limb, but it overpowered him with ease. Its stiff digits shot toward him and clutched him by the throat. Bilyf struggled, but the tight grip choked him. The wails of the other eggsharers grew faint. Bilyf knew now who this monster was. His destiny was inextricably linked with the destiny of—

"A—cri—os!" Bilyf cried.

The death grip relaxed. Bilyf had called the creature's name, frightening it. He sensed now that it had never meant to harm him. He had struck out at it reflexively while locked in his vi-sion, and it had reacted violently. It did not want Bilyf to escape, but it was not his killer. It was his abductor.

Mist poured through the eggsac's rent. Through it, the mon-ster's pale eyes shone. Bilyf trembled, and it bared its fangs, a whooping shriek escaping its maw. Bilyf saw that he would come to know that terrible sound intimately—the sound of the crea-ture's pleasure.

"So you already know me," it said.

Bilyf understood its words from a time yet to come. Of course he knew this Acrios. Most of his life would be spent with this monster, an alien already old beyond reckoning. It knew how to find the eggsharers, so it was shrewd. And it would take him from his home without compunction, so it was ruthless. It had chosen him alone from the eggsharers because he had known it and cried its name. He and he alone had seen through the veil of time.

This was to be the beginning of servitude for him, the function of an adult Mennon. The teacher had told the eggsharers that aliens sometimes came to steal young Mennons for servants. They had been told to submit, to willingly go with any such aggressive creature who might come after them. Remembering this, Bilyf did not struggle as the violator of the eggsac cradled him in its powerful limbs.

Again the creature shrieked in pleasure, a horrid echo reverberating through the swamp. Then it moved on through the fog, its pedal extremities slogging through muddy water, bearing Bilyf forever away from the eggsac . . . the home.

Already the monster Acrios became less terrifying as Bilyf remembered it from the future more clearly. It would use him for that very purpose, to look into the future. This was a talent Acrios's people did not possess.

Bilyf felt something tugging at his middle. It was the umbilical cord, stretching to the heart of the eggsac itself. Its length determined the limits of the eggsharers' territory. Bilyf was too young to venture outside alone, and now the transition period from infancy to adulthood was lost to him forever.

He feared that his guts would be pulled out along with the umbilical cord. But the monster Acrios reached out and snapped it as easily as one might snap the twig of a splintertree.

It was done. Bilyf grieved that he would never again embrace the Mother, who had borne him in growth on her breast. When the growth had become too large, the Mother and the teacher had removed it painfully from her body and placed it in the hive inside the eggsac, there to be nurtured with the siblings, the other eggsharers whose thoughts Bilyf had shared. He would never see them again; not the mother, nor the eggsharers, nor the teachers, the knowledge sharers. Never again, except in his mind, as he had been taught. There, his loved ones would always be with him.

They would lament his passing while they repaired the gaping wound the monster had made in the eggsac, using tissue from their own bodies. But they would rejoice in the knowledge that Bilyf would always be with them, even so.

Acrios broke through tendrils of mist, making his way to-

ward a glowing sphere larger than the eggsac—larger than any
fabricated object that Bilyf had ever seen. It opened like the
jaws of a fogbeast, and they went inside it. A whine, a jarring
sensation, and...

   ...they
       were
           gone...
           ...they
       were
     soon...
   ...on Rocinth...

Bilyf had never seen the world of his birth since, except in his
visions of the past. He would never see Mennon again. He had
remained with his master, Acrios, his fitful prescience aiding the
Receptor, helping him to retain his vast power. This was one of
the reasons Acrios had wanted a Mennon, of course, but the
master had grown fond of Bilyf, genuinely fond. The scars of
the beating were healing quickly, and Bilyf had already forgiven
Acrios.

Bilyf had not envisioned his adeptness with machines, but he
had nevertheless come to enjoy working with them. He tinkered
endlessly with the estate's robots, maintaining them superbly.
Odd that Mennons should work so well with beings made of
metal and silicone, unheard of on Bilyf's homeworld. Perhaps it
was because the robots *were* beings, something more than machines.

Plugged into the great mundomentus, the worldmind of Rocinth, the robots shared a vast intelligence. But they were limited by the mundomentus to use only what they needed for
assigned tasks. In this way they were not like humans or Mennons. And yet they thought like men and Mennons. Did that
not mean that they were beings with souls, if souls could be said
to exist at all?

As Bilyf wrestled with the concept, his consciousness gradually returned to Acrios's villa and his own tiny cubicle. He
slowly came to realize that an ethical problem had brought him
back from the past. The past...a human word, a concept of
reality wherein events were locked into patterns which could
never be changed. This was, of course, foreign to the way Mennons perceived the passing of events. Nothing was immutable,
though one accepted what was. It was a paradox.

But the humans and their concept of time were something
quite different. Indeed, the humans spoke of the past, present
and future as if they were discrete entities, warring island na-
tions separated by a vast sea...or worlds, distant from one another through the gulf of space.

Perhaps it was actually so. Perhaps such sharp distinctions did exist; perhaps the Mennon perception, in its fatalism, though different from the human idea, was no less false. Perhaps.

It was certainly true that events *developed* in time—no doubt about that, no question at all. There was, for example, the odor of tragedy reeking from Acrios when he took Bilyf from the eggsac. The infant Mennon had sensed something unhealthy about the shrieking, whooping creature who had taken him away from all that he knew and loved. This, humans would say, was merely a distorted memory, what they called hindsight. Bilyf had come to learn that Acrios was sick, and attributed his first impression of the master with this astute observation. But Bilyf knew better. He recalled the stench of fear, and the diseased odor that overpowered even that. The odor had remained, and pervaded the entire villa and its grounds, now that Acrios had by his own hand lost his daughter.

But Danna was not dead, nor was she an Other, as Acrios believed. Her existence would ensure that things would go differently than the master had planned.

And Bilyf could see now, through a shimmering, golden rain, that his vision of Acrios's death was to become real—as humans knew reality—unchangeable, like the past. The future and the past, both the same . . .

The rain became a gleaming downpour, and something thrust powerfully up from the dark. There was pain and pleasure. It went on until his body quaked, and then there was release as it slowed and stopped.

Bilyf lay in his webbing until a vision came through the darkness . . .

        . . . there
                was
                    a
                    street . . .

 . . . alive with merchants and vendors, shoppers and thieves. In it were the scents of fruit and sweat, dust and perfume; the sounds of barter, conversation, anger, and laughter (still a sound that frightened Bilyf), and the whine of human misery. More: brilliant lights, rainbow colors; robots, all shapes and sizes; clones for every conceivable purpose, male, female, and neuter, grotesque and beautiful.

One such, a clone-mother, was central to his vision. He was in her mind, but they would never meet physically . . . their lives would never touch in time and space. Yet there was a bond, for

Mennons never saw those who were totally dissociated from them.

Siula was excited, elated. This was a special night for her, the first time in ages that she had been called out to assist in a natural childbirth. As she careered down a broad avenue toward the House of Life, her enormous udders tingled with anticipation. This was, after all, what a clone-mother was grown for—the first had been bioengineered to provide milk in maximum quantities—and Siula possessed a built-in maternal instinct to match her matronly, ample physique. It was an instinct satisfied all too seldom these days, she thought, as colossal projected figures appeared in the night sky. Athletes were leaping over the dark spires of the city, hurling dikoits and riding six-legged Doazwanian garoms. Siula slowed her pace without realizing it, enjoying the spectacle of light and movement even in silence. She had no desire to listen to the audio presentation that went with it. Besides, she saw no lightbox nearby. Without a talker she couldn't listen in, and there was no time to stop and look for one.

When she was younger, there were many spectacles for children. Not anymore. Perhaps children might enjoy the giant athletes towering over the city, but it was really for adults. In a world of near-immortals, fewer children were born each year. The thought saddened her.

She passed the burnished dome of the mundomentus and walked through the shadow of the city's amphitheatre. The graceful towers of the anthroforms' homes rose like needles threatening to pierce the starry firmament.

Turning a corner, Siula was greeted by a projection of the Prime Mystagogue herself. Verra's enormously magnified figure, stately and handsome, stood astride the great city of Nathe where the athletes had been. A living marble statue, Verra motioned toward a configuration of the Rocinthan moons like a teacher pointing at a palimpsest. But the moons were real, all of them full in the Rocinthan night sky.

The Mystagogue smiled and opened her cavernous phantom mouth to lecture those who might be interested. Siula thought to avail herself of the Prime Mystagogue's wisdom on the way to the House of Life. She looked around for a lightbox, and still seeing none, waddled as fast as her bulk could carry her until she saw a glow ahead on the deserted street. Hurrying to it, she poked her hand into the lightbox and felt a talker pop into her open palm. She stuck the talker under her right ear, and it clung there to the porous skin.

"Night sky," she said, and the mundomentus patched her into the presentation.

". . . precisely the same configuration as a constellation seen from the homeworld in the distant past," Verra was saying. "The dominant star in that constellation was the binary Algol."

Magically, Verra materialized a chart of the constellation, superimposing it over the pattern of Rocinth's twelve moons.

"As can plainly be seen," she went on, "the constellation has been coincidentally reproduced by our satellites. Such an incredible occurrence cannot easily be accounted for. However, their relative positions might . . ."

"Enough." Siula caught sight of the pillars of the House of Life. She didn't want any distractions now, for she relished the task before her. Besides, the twelve moons, whose names she had never memorized, might fleetingly form any shape in their relative positions. There were so many of them that they might even trace her rounded outline if she lived long enough to see such a thing. As she heaved her weight up one polished step at a time towards the House of Life, she chuckled at the notion of awestricken millions staring up at a celestial clone-mother.

Reaching the landing at the top of the stairs, she leaned against a balustrade to catch her breath. Suddenly a burly man, a sentry-clone, stepped out of the shadows to confront her.

"Whom do you seek in the House of Life?" he demanded.

Siula was amused by the somberness of his expression and his stilted speech, but she managed to stifle her laughter. Sentry-clones could no more help their brusque nature than she could disguise her joy at the prospect of once again nursing a baby.

"I'm looking for a young woman who's gone into labor tonight," she said.

The sentry took one look at her enormous breasts and knew that she wasn't lying. Not that there would have been any reason to stop her even if he had suspected her of lying. His was a job that no longer mattered, but he lived on, designed to last for a millennium or more. Rocinth was full of useless clones. Siula herself was almost useless. Almost.

"Go up the first flight of stairs," the sentry said, scowling, "past the organ bank. Then take the third corridor to the maternity ward. There you'll find her waiting for you, mother."

He backed out of the light, powerful musculature held in abeyance until his acute senses told him that another intruder was approaching. The only one likely to come tonight was Tovia, Nathe's other clone-mother, and she would be too late. Siula was delighted, for the rivalry with her sister was an old one, dating back centuries. The paucity of newborn children had made the archrivals even more antagonistic. Siula supposed that they were too much alike, and that was why they didn't get along. They had never learned to share; it had always been a contest to see who would reach the expectant mother first.

But this expectant mother had been very secretive. A clone-mother had been sent for, but only at the last moment, and Siula had been lucky enough to hear about it first. Tovia would never forgive her.

She went inside and laboriously dragged her bulk up one step after another, until she reached the organ bank. There she passed crystalline vaults stocked with the guts and limbs of her fellow clones. She was not subject to such horrid treatment, since there was still an occasional call for her services, but her protected status might not last forever. An anthroform couldn't kill a clone in cold blood, but the mundomentus could select useless clones for dissection in the House of Life. Siula shuddered to think of being cut up by robot surgeons.

The smell of chemicals permeated the place, nearly gagging her. Chilled, she quickly made her way to the third corridor and entered it, relieved to be away from the organ bank. She staggered to the nearest room, wheezing from her exertions. Peering inside, she saw that it was empty. It was spotless, not a speck of dust on any of the arcane surgical devices within, but Siula was left with the impression of a place that no human, clone or anthroform, had entered in a very long time.

There was a series of rooms along the corridor, stretching into the darkness. Gingerly Siula stepped from one entrance to the next until she heard a girl moaning. She found an alcove, a little room set off by itself. Through its doorway she spied a robot going about its duties. This was doubtless the room she was looking for. Sighing, she entered, heart pounding. She felt as if she had climbed a mountain. Why had they ever built the House of Life on such a vast scale?

Come to think of it, she'd once heard that many children had been born every day when the House of Life was built, making it necessary for all medical facilities to be enclosed in one structure. It was a far better arrangement than many human worlds had managed. Of course, that was before the womb-borns could call on the mundomentus to send them a physician whenever they wanted one, rather than depending on these archaic robots. And that was long, long ago.

But why did this woman choose to come to the House of Life, instead of having her baby at home?

Another robot had entered through a sliding panel in the wall, where it had been stored until the first robot needed its assistance. Now the two machines fussed over the prostrate

woman. Their gleaming, economical movements were dwarfed
by a projection seen through the transparent wall. Abstract geometric patterns turned, striking in their brilliant three-dimensional shapes and colors. Such nonrepresentational figures were
all very well, but Siula preferred something a little more lively.
Even the athletes she had seen on her way to the House of Life
had been more interesting in their way. The geometry lesson
over Nathe would soon be over, and something else would take
its place. She'd soon have no time to watch, no matter what was
shown.

The girl was already pulling her knees up high, and one of
the robots was probing with a delicate finger. It wore a glove
made of a soft, warm synthetic coated in a polymer that consumed bacteria.

"Come here, mother," the girl said weakly, seeing Siula
standing in the doorway. "I have need of you."

Siula did as she was told, taking the expectant mother's
hand. It was hot and damp.

"I'll be with you through it all," Siula said.

The girl smiled, but her expression turned to a wince. A
spasm. The girl moaned, and Siula squeezed her fingers. She
was *so* young.

When the pain temporarily subsided, the girl relaxed a little.
Siula pulled back her long, dark tresses, swabbing the sweat
from her brow. No robot could ever replace this comforting
function, Siula thought proudly.

In the night sky, the giant figure of Verra appeared again
through the transparency. The girl's hand twitched, but
strangely, there was no sign of pain on her face now—she appeared to be staring directly at the Mystagogue's image. But
why should that disturb her?

Siula took another look at the night sky. As far as she could
see, the presentation was identical to the one she'd looked at
out on the street: the twelve moons covered by a star chart to
show their similarity to some constellation or other, just the
same as before. Perhaps the poor thing was delirious? After all,
anthroforms weren't used to physical pain. But she seemed to
be frightened, or at least apprehensive, of Verra's hologram.

Now the girl licked sweat from her lips. She strained, trying
to push the struggling life within her down towards her pelvis.

"Push harder," one of the robots said in a commanding, yet
soothing voice.

Another spasm. Her entire body trembled.

"The child is large," said the other physician as it bent over
her, "but it will come easily." The robot's smooth, featureless

head disappeared from Siula's sight behind the girl's swollen belly.

Gasping, the girl stared at the flickering projection in the night sky as the robots skillfully brought the baby into the world. A cold steel appendage induced the child's first cries.

Her burden lifted by the sweet music of the baby's squalling, the mother sighed and closed her eyes. Fading now, an afterimage over the childbed, the ancient star map cradled Rocinth's moons.

In her dream, Danna saw the baby in Verra's arms. No, not the baby, surely not the baby . . . Verra held the moons of Rocinth in her mountainous limbs, trying to shelter them from a golden rain . . . until she came to realize that the rain was not harmful, but nourishing in some way beyond human ken. The Prime Mystagogue was humbled by this knowledge, abandoning the pedant's somber expression for a look of wide-eyed wonder. She lifted the moons slowly, exposing them to the rain. Once again, the moons became an infant, the lines connecting them on the star map gaining plump, pink flesh. The child slept peacefully . . . floating in the night sky over Nathe.

The warm orange rays of the morning sun woke Danna. Opening her eyes, she saw an unfamiliar place, bare with the exception of a vase of silver disc-flowers. There was a fat woman—a clone-mother—asleep in a chair next to her. Oh yes, this was the House of Life. She had come here to have her baby, afraid to permit the mundomentus's robots to come to her home: Acrios's gift was far too powerful for her to take such a risk.

The clone-mother's girth hid an enclosed crib from her, almost entirely. She tugged at one fat arm until the woman opened her eyes.

"Is it a boy, mother?" Danna asked.

The response was an eager smile, showing the gap between the front teeth characteristic of clone-mothers.

"Yes," she said, "a fine boy. But I'm afraid he doesn't look much like you. He's very fair."

"But I'm—" Danna was about to say that she herself was blonde, when she remembered the cosmetic surgery that had darkened her hair and complexion, making her look several years older. "Is he all right?"

"He's a healthy, beautiful baby," the clone-mother said, rising and sliding back the transparent cover of the crib. "He'll be the prototype of a million clones who'll be grown just to be admired." She carefully lifted the baby out of the crib and gave him to his mother.

"Yes, let me see him." Danna stretched out her arms, feeling the weakness in them. She gathered the child to her breast. As the clone-mother gently withdrew her hands, Danna saw her son's face for the first time.

"He's not beautiful at all," she said. "He's as wrinkled as the skin of a dried bhel-melon."

"All neonates are like this," the clone-mother said, "but this one is special."

"In what way?" Danna demanded. Did the child's alien conception somehow show?

"He's just . . . special, mistress."

The baby stared at Danna through wise, clear eyes.

"You didn't tell me your name," Danna said to the clone-mother.

"Siula, mistress."

"Well, Siula, I think you're right. My son *is* special."

"Do you have a name for him?" Siula asked.

"Yes. I remember a name from a dream play, the first one I ever saw. The name of a character was taken from one of old Earth's oldest tongues."

"What was the name?"

"Deles." She lifted the baby to her face and kissed the tangled hair on his little round head.

"Deles? It *must* be an ancient name. I've never heard it before. What does it mean?"

"It means 'You destroy.'"

Chapter Five

The Receptor's Agony

Bilyf awoke, undergoing great emotional stress. He felt the creaking of his cartilaginous frame, and this reminded him of his shortcomings. He still did not know precisely when Acrios's death would occur, and he now suspected that he never would. But he did perceive that the instrument of the master's death was already in existence. Acrios's grandson had been born.

Bilyf heard steps outside the cubicle. He rose from the webbing, willing his tired body to awaken fully. Quietly he followed the footfalls. They led him down the stairs and through the dimly lit dining hall. There the brazier's dying flames revealed the stooped figure of the Receptor.

Acrios stared into the fire. The presence of this elemental force in his home was an anachronistic touch, but was somehow appropriate. It burned brightly, always under control, the household robots tending it. But now it appeared to be in danger of guttering out. Acrios left its comforting glow, passing under the archway and out into the garden. Bilyf followed him silently, through the crystal garden and beyond.

At the well's rim, Acrios halted in the light of the twelve moons. Motionless, he stared into its black depths.

Bilyf stood quietly behind him. How odd, he thought, that humans continue to grieve after such a long time. Perhaps he should tell the master that Danna was still living? No, not unless he was asked. Acrios's guilt was disheartening, but his temper was swift and violent, as well. Bilyf's vision must be kept a secret this night, and for many nights to come.

Strange that the master had never asked if Danna were still alive. No, not so strange, for he must have feared the answer. Still, if Acrios should ever suspect the truth about his daughter. . . .

"Acrios," Bilyf said, "one is—concerned."

For a moment, the Receptor showed no sign that he had heard. Then he slowly turned. His face was as thin and pale as a Mennon's.

"Bilyf, do you . . . regret that I brought you here when you were small? That I gave you a human name and forced you to live among us as a servant?"

"Regret is not—a Mennon emotion. If—Bilyf should feel—regret—he would only be—more human."

"Yes, always the one for abstruse philosophical musings, aren't you?" Acrios said, but there was no malice in his tone. "Come, Bilyf, I have need of you tonight."

"In—what capacity?"

"As a friend, I hope," Acrios replied. "In spite of all." Acrios put his hand on Bilyf's gnarled shoulder.

Bilyf had hoped that the master would ask him to stay close by, so that the night would not end in a drunken stupor. Such a condition might adversely affect reception. An unpredictable thing, Acrios's Gift. He had been trained by the Seers on Parnassus, a desolate world of the Blue Star, his psychic talents channeled, supposedly for the good of humankind. Clairvoyance, precognition, even a hint of telepathy were all at least inchoately alive in all anthroform humans. At one time these talents had been considered mysterious, even dangerous, but of course they were only a part of a larger phenomenon, which came to be called simply the Gift. Those who possessed it in great abundance were special cases, whose fitful cosmic visions might someday combine like the pieces of an infinite puzzle. The Machine would join the projected visions of the Receptors into one unified answer . . . the answer that might save humankind from the heat death of the universe, from the End of All Things itself.

Since Danna's disappearance, Acrios had neglected his duties as Receptor. And, even if he hadn't been cursed with such a great burden, the master's solitude was clearly weighing heavily on him. During his long period of mourning he had sent all his lovers and household clones away.

Earlier, before Bilyf had taken his rest, Acrios had spoken of receiving the whispers of space/time tonight. If he could in fact successfully receive, it might help to distract him from his sorrows. But Bilyf feared that Acrios would use the Gift to try and find out if Danna still lived. He might not be able to help himself. It was inevitable that he would sooner or later make the attempt.

And if that failed, he would almost certainly demand a chronopathic effort on Bilyf's part. If Bilyf saw nothing, he might be beaten. And if the master asked him what he knew of Danna's existence, Bilyf would have no choice but to tell him the truth.

Even if Danna's survival were somehow not revealed, there

could be trouble, for prescience was a Gift that often revealed facts one did not want to know. If that were to happen tonight, things might become very unpleasant indeed.

Sadly, Bilyf followed Acrios back up the garden path. His duty, according to Mennon ethics, was to comfort his master. He had been Acrios's constant companion since being snatched from the eggsac, and had never really known any other life. He had been present at Danna's birth. He had loved Danna and her mother, the lady Lehana, deeply in his way ... just as he loved Acrios.

Before they reached the crystal garden, Acrios said, "I must look after the garoms."

They stopped at the stable to feed the racing animals, six-legged creatures brought from Doazwa before the demise of that world's jovial people. The sleek beasts, with their rodent-like incisors had provided sport for the Doazwanians in the old days. Acrios tossed them some plants. As the garoms gnashed their huge front teeth on the tough stalks, he watched them thoughtfully.

"Bilyf," he said at last, "I am going to pose a question to the Seers tonight. Do you know what it will be?"

"One—cannot presume—to know."

"Very tactful of you, Bilyf. Very tactful." Acrios picked a root from the feed pile and lobbed it towards the animals. The restraining field buzzed, and a gargantuan head jerked, snatching the tidbit out of the air. "But don't you think I would want to know what those wise beings have to say about killing one's own child?"

"Acrios does not know—that she is dead."

"You are not only tactful, Bilyf, but charitable as well. One would think that Verra raised you, not Acrios." He tossed another root to the garoms. "But I forget the Mennon knowledge sharers. If Man had possessed such rigorous ethics, he could never have traveled to the stars."

"One sees that—things could not—have been otherwise."

"Such things as my treatment of Danna?" Acrios replied. "You know, Bilyf, at times I am convinced that she is alive. But I can't be sure if the Gift tells me this, or my guilt. It is such an unreliable thing, this Gift ... I cannot trust it in this matter."

Bilyf said nothing.

"She cannot be alive, of course." Acrios turned towards the sea.

"One must—remind Acrios—that his intention—was not to—"

"Yes, yes," Acrios said. "But wouldn't you think that such a tragedy would move the very cosmos? Strike a responsive chord in the Great Intelligence itself, if there is such a thing? A parent responsible for the death of his own child, and not through accident but through malice... In all the centuries I've been alive, Bilyf, Danna is the only child I ever had." His voice broke, and tears came to his blue eyes.

"There is more, Bilyf, much, much more... You see, when Lehana left me, I was very close to a breakthrough. Yes, I could feel it coming together... some knowledge that might help us escape the End of All Things. I could almost see it, but it was unfocused. A bit of fine adjustment was all that I needed, but without that essential clarity it was meaningless. It nearly broke me, this unending frustration. I began to brood, and desire solitude. My drinking grew more and more frequent....

"For those times that I was cruel to you, Bilyf, please forgive me, for I am not the man that I once was. Yet my external power is still great, for the mundomentus provides me with a semblance of..."

"Acrios is—a great man."

"No, Bilyf, it's all a sham. Wherever I go, robots spring to attention at my command. I can do what I wish, when I wish, enjoy every sensual and sensuous pleasure there is..."

Listlessly he tossed in the last of the feed. "If the mundomentus should decide that I am no longer useful, even the semblance of power will be stripped from me."

"But Acrios is—Rocinth's Receptor."

"Yes, Bilyf, but to what end? I've gained wealth and power, quantities as fleeting as Man's life once was."

"What would—the master desire instead?"

Acrios bowed his gray head. "Some spiritual quality, I suppose. A quality I have forsaken in my pursuit of power, something I did not know I needed until it was too late."

"Yet—is it—too late?"

Managing a weak smile, Acrios said, "It seems too late for many things, my friend. In spite of this, the foolish mass mind that runs our world would have me continue." He extended his arms and whirled suddenly, like a dancer.

"Hear me, mundomentus," he shouted. "Foolish, I said. Do I hear the distant sound of thunder as you mull that over in the once-great city of Nathe? Well, examine the evidence for yourself. You would have me remain in contact with the Seers, who so carefully edit useless information distilled by a Machine even more ponderous than yourself. And to what end? To ask of the void a question that has no answer."

Bilyf trembled as Acrios threw back his head and laughed, the hideous sound echoing into the night.

"Is it any wonder that I have become bitter?" the Receptor said. "Or that I have lost my mind?"

Bilyf remained silent.

"Come along," said Acrios. Bilyf followed him back to the villa. Just before passing under the archway, he was alarmed to see the master slump to his knees on the path.

"Danna!" Acrios cried. "Danna, my baby!"

Bilyf wrapped his digits gently around Acrios's heaving shoulders, waiting for the fit of grief to subside. When the master was calm at last, Bilyf raised him to his feet and took him inside. Leading Acrios to his quarters, Bilyf helped him to a chair.

From there, Bilyf climbed the stairs to the villa's third and highest level. Here was the reception pool. No robots were allowed in this room, and so Bilyf prepared the pool by himself. He opened the main valve, and the spigots poured a crimson desensitizing fluid into the pool. As soon as it was full, Bilyf shut off the valve and went back downstairs to the master's room.

"One has prepared—the fluid," he said.

Slowly Acrios rose, and without assistance climbed the stairs to the pool. Crimson wavelets reflected on his emaciated body as he removed his tunic. Before stepping into the blood-warm bath, he said, "Sometimes . . . sometimes I think I am beginning to understand what the universe has to say to us. Then I remember that I am nothing but a man, and I become frightened. It is all too much for a man, far too much." He stared at the crimson fluid. "But then, sometimes I feel that I am on the verge. . . ."

"One sees—that it is so."

"Yes." Absently, the Receptor eased his body into the sparkling red desensitizing fluid.

The ceiling drew back to reveal the moons and the neighboring planets—including two inhabited worlds, Sripha and brilliant, demonic Tartarus—as well as the myriad stars. Bilyf would remain by the master until the sun rose, its amber light extinguishing the night's bejeweled elegance.

Several times during the night Acrios cried out. Once he laughed; often he wept. And while he listened to the cries of infinity, the lamentations of forever, Bilyf remained alert. For him, time did not drag on, hour after hour, as it would for a man. He was often away, but just as he had once fought against Acrios while in the throes of a vision, a part of him remained by the reception pool this night . . .

... while
    a
       part
          of
             him
             is
        here
    another
night ...

... he sees Acrios emerging from the receptive mode; the master's fingers grip the edge of the pool, twitching; Acrios gapes, his eyes roll. Bilyf reaches for a robe, terribly concerned. Never have the master's contortions revealed such anguish. His writhing creates a miniature red tempest.

Rising to his knees, the fluid running down his gaunt limbs like blood, Acrios grimaces. His head swings from side to side, and his breathing is heavy and uneven. He opens his mouth as if to speak, but no sound comes forth. Slowly he stands, joints cracking; a trembling leg is thrown over the pool's edge. The Receptor pauses, seeming to stare right through Bilyf at something far away. At last he steps shakily onto the tiled floor, raising his arms.

Alarmed, Bilyf drops the robe and starts towards him. But before he can be assisted, Acrios collapses in a dead faint. Bilyf wants to rush to the master's aid, but he is transfixed, not by a vision, but by the familiar sight of the moons. He recalls a star map, and a human infant. But as soon as he foresees these images

    from the future ...
        the
          moons
             are
                fading ...

Chapter Six

Verra's Guest

Verra tried to immerse herself in her work until the time came to prepare herself for a disagreeable but, unfortunately, necessary task. She didn't look forward to addressing the mundomentus formally, even on behalf of an old friend. But Acrios was much more than an old friend. He had been both lover and mentor to her in the past. Nevertheless, she found the entire affair deplorably wasteful. She busied herself with the study of a three-dimensional model of the rectilinear universe of the ancients. Eternal expansion, what an appealing idea. How comforting to believe that things would go on forever.

It seemed incredible that Man had ever been able to convince himself that such a thing was possible, but there it was, a historical fact. He had always dreamt of immortality, his myths and religions preoccupied with the concept, until science finally made the dream appear to be within his grasp. Not only was eternal life possible—and this conclusion had been reached through ostensibly empirical research!—but inevitable. Man's life span grew longer and longer, until most people could not remember the earlier centuries of their lives. As memory faded and time became meaningless, the universe itself began to close in. But even then there were those who claimed that it was not really so, that it was all a matter of interpretation, that humankind would indeed live forever. Such optimistic forecasts had somehow won the day, and no one, not even the most hardened cynic, ever imagined that the End could come so quickly.

"What a reassuring notion," Verra said, waving the model away. So reassuring that it had never fully died, she thought as she watched the archaic image dissolve. It had merely become reality—after a fashion. But was this, as the conventional wisdom had it, the only myth that survived Man's journey to the stars? There were times when she thought she saw traces of the old stories everywhere. . . .

Acrios, for example, seemed to have become a puppet, acting out a story at once so ancient and familiar. He would be here in a little while, come to see her after all these years. Would she become a part of his myth, too? No one had ever believed more strongly in eternal life than Acrios. He had almost become a god himself, but his human failings had overpowered him. Perhaps it was his destiny.

One of the reasons she was developing a reputation for eccentricity, she supposed, was because of her interest in such unfashionable concepts as destiny. But she couldn't help wondering. Humankind was supposed to have transcended all the primitive urges developed during the race's long evolution. How could humans be so foolish as to deny the savage, superstitious beast lurking below the anthroform's placid surface?

Once when she had prepared a night sky presentation on the subject, the mundomentus had refused to project it. She had given only token resistance, not willing to jeopardize her comfortable existence, for hers was a good life, if a bit static these days.

And now there was this troublesome business to attend to, concerning Acrios. Verra felt a little ashamed of her attitude, but there was really very little she could do for him. It was true that Acrios had helped her when she was a poor student, but he had also taken his price out of her flesh . . . and out of her soul. Acrios was by no means an easy man to get along with. Charming when he wanted to be, he was mercurial, willful, and frequently duplicitous. Of course, that was to be expected. He had gained power and fame, not through any innate integrity or greatness of spirit, but simply because of the intensity of his Gift. He had used his position to advance Verra until she was eligible for initiation as a Mystagogue. The rest, she could say without flinching, she had managed by herself.

But could she have made that first essential step without the aid of the Receptor? She couldn't deny that there was a debt; a large debt, at that. Now that Acrios had fallen upon difficult times, it must be repaid. The best thing she could do for him was to make a formal plea to the mundomentus.

She didn't have to, of course, and a negative decision on her part could easily be rationalized. After all, Acrios had taken from her at least as much as he had given. But in those days she hadn't minded. The Receptor was magnificent once . . . and perhaps he could be again.

How clearly she recalled that pristine morning when she had walked with him to the very base of the mundomentus's dome. He had kissed her and walked away, leaving her to enter the worldmind's endlessly complex machinery by herself. Her training had begun that very day, and she had not seen Acrios for many decades thereafter.

Each meeting had been marked by a deterioration in his physical and mental state. Of course, his body repaired itself and was looked after by physicians, but there was no doubt that his excesses had hurt him. And then, not so long ago—was it more than two or three years?—he had done that terrible thing to Danna.

At that moment, the curtain covering the room's entrance was swept aside, and Acrios entered. He was very pale, nervous and unsteady.

"Good morning," he said.

"Good morning." Verra kissed him on the cheek. Touching him, she noticed that he was too warm and his skin sticky. How long *had* it been since he lost Lehana and Danna? Three years? Four years?

"Acrios, I've been thinking about the case I'm going to present to the planetary intelligence," she said cheerfully. "A defense might be built upon the claim that you have already suffered inordinately for something over which you have had no control."

"There is truth in such a claim." Acrios was distracted by figures on a frieze capering near the ceiling.

"Even if you are relieved of your duties," Verra said, "we might persuade the mundomentus not to remove the secondary node."

"I . . . I don't want to have either node removed," Acrios replied, toying with a puzzle on the Mystagogue's desk.

"Frankly, you might not be permitted to retain even the secondary node."

"Tell it that I must have them, Verra. Both of them. Tell it that there is something in my mind I have suppressed . . . but I have come very close to . . . to understanding Man's place at the End of All Things. These past few years have been . . . difficult ones. One night, not long after . . . after I lost Danna, I had a vision. I saw something so clearly while I lay in the reception pool . . . and yet I cannot recall anything about it."

"That is precisely why the worldmind is concerned, Acrios. If you have locked in some hidden place in your mind what the Machine needs . . ."

"After a rest I shall be capable of unraveling all the thoughts in my brain."

"Acrios, do you think the worldmind can wait forever?"

"I need only a little more time."

"Shall I say that to the mundomentus?" Verra asked skeptically.

Taking his hand from the puzzle, Acrios stared pensively at his old friend, tears starting in his eyes. "No," he said after a moment. "I cannot be sure if I will ever be able to retrieve it."

"I didn't think so," Verra replied, not unkindly. "If you promised such a thing, you'd be expected to follow it through. The attempt could destroy you."

"Verra," Acrios cried, his voice breaking, "I am already destroyed."

"Oh, Acrios." Verra embraced him and led him to a chair. "Sit down."

Acrios allowed her to seat him at her desk. "Forgive me," he said.

"There's nothing to forgive." She stroked his gray temples. "We have been lovers, and now we are friends. Friends need not be told they are forgiven, especially when they have only revealed honest feelings."

"Thank you." Acrios wiped his tears with the back of a shaking hand. "I must tell you something, Verra, something no other human being knows but me."

Verra waited.

"I will die by the hand of Danna's child."

"What?" But Verra knew that she had heard him correctly. "But how *could* you know such a thing?"

"Bilyf."

"Bilyf prophesied that Danna's child will kill you? But that's madness."

"Yes."

"Acrios, even if it were true, you must take comfort in knowing that we will all be gone by the End of All Things."

"True, but I have the distinction of knowing of my own death beforehand."

"You believe in this prophecy even though—even though Danna is gone?"

"I do." Acrios's eyes were frightened.

"Then you must believe she's still alive?"

"I don't know. I only know that what I did to her has led to my present sorry state." He stared at her as though from a nightmare, saying, "I should not have come here."

"My dear Acrios," Verra said, stroking the back of his neck. "Stifle your pride."

Acrios attempted a halfhearted smile. He would stay.

"Once we have eaten and I've had a chance to think the matter through, I'll plan our defense and go to the mundomentus. But not a moment before I am ready."

"Then you'll go today?"

"Most likely. Is that too soon?"

He smiled again. "I don't suppose your arguments will be

enhanced by the further passage of time, like a good wine," he said.

"I should think not." Verra was pleased to see him amused. "Now if you'll excuse me, I'll see what the stasis field has in it that looks good to eat." She disappeared behind the curtain.

Acrios watched the curtain swish back and forth in ever-diminishing arcs. Rising, he went to the window. As he peered down at the sparsely traveled street below, he wondered what had brought him to Nathe today. His difficulties with the mundomentus were nothing new. It had been years since the worldmind had begun its rumblings about taking away his privileges. He'd spent so much time drinking since then that he'd hardly thought of it. But then he had awakened this morning still dreaming of Nathe.

Was the Gift telling him something?

Absently, he scanned the rooftops while he waited for Verra. It was as if he were looking for something. But what? He only knew that he would know it when he saw it.

Insects buzzed in the dingy room Siula shared with two others—the city's other clone-mother Tovia, and a drone. The latter, sexless Bothos, rarely spoke. When he did, he usually complained about the filthy jobs he undertook. Most of them were unnecessary, since machines took care of the drudge work around Nathe. Bothos chose to work so that he would not feel useless; besides, he had been designed for such labor. What choice did he have? It was either find some labor to justify his existence or risk ending up in pieces in the House of Life.

"I found a walkway that hadn't been cleaned in an age," Bothos said. "The robots assigned to it had malfunctioned long ago, and it had become a positive hazard to pedestrians."

Siula was impatient with his babbling, and so did not reply.

"All right, mother, don't say anything," Bothos said. "I've work to do anyway. Goodbye." And with that he was out the door, gone to slave over some meaningless, menial task.

Siula sighed, glad to be left alone. Tovia was at the marketplace, so she wouldn't be tempted to argue with her sister. Perhaps they should turn their energies to commiserating with Bothos instead of fighting, but that wouldn't be natural. Their rivalry was centered on the function for which they had been created. Siula and Tovia were the only two clone-mothers in Nathe these days, and that was one too many as far as Siula was concerned.

Well, since everybody else was out, she would go out too, after cleaning. She removed her robe and threw it on the webbing, walking downstairs to the baths.

The smell of sweat permeated the steamy rooms just outside the baths. Those coming out wore color-coded wraps signifying their labor functions. Those entering, after working through the night, often wore soiled wraps. Peeling their clothing off, the tired clones discarded them in bins before entering the baths. As they returned to the clonarium, which housed them at the heart of Nathe, they were almost oblivious to their surroundings. Siula consequently found that clammy flesh slapped against hers all too frequently. At such moments she wished that she were a biotech, working in the subterranean levels where bodies were grown. There was hardly anyone down there anymore. The city no longer needed clones, and it had been like this for centuries now.

"Hurry up!" a voice shouted from behind her. "I want to get cleaned up so that I can get some sleep."

"That's right!" bawled another. "We don't have all day, mother."

They really did have all day, of course. They could have just stayed in the clonarium instead of going out to search for jobs. But they couldn't help it; that was the way they were made.

The clonarium was too crowded, since virtually all the clones left in Nathe lived here now. Once it had been fashionable for anthroforms to keep domestic clones, but the fashion had swung back to robots. Robots were easier to store, easier to control, and they didn't gossip about their masters. Even so, Siula dreamed of leaving the clonarium and living in the little house with Danna and Deles. She had suggested this to Danna to no avail, even after pointing out that there would always be someone at home to care for Deles. It was probably true that Danna couldn't afford to keep her; even so, Siula could tell by Danna's manner that she was used to giving orders. More than likely Danna had grown up with robots in the house, perhaps even a clone or two.

"Come on, mother!"

Startled, Siula saw that it was indeed her turn under the cleansing spray, and moved forward. She had been daydreaming again.

The warm chemical shower caressed her. It was over much too soon, and she reluctantly waddled to the garment room. There she selected a pink wrap from a shelf and dressed herself. Cool, clean, and freshly attired, she stepped into the winding corridor and made her way to the irising east gate. Emerging from the clonarium, she blinked in the bright morning light.

The mundomentus dome was burnished gold as she caught a glimpse of it between the struts of a building. And there was the dark cube of the Prime Mystagogue's house near it.

Siula walked to a rack of graviton platforms. Mounting one, she was lifted over a high terrace to a point from which she could see most of the tiered city. The breeze caught her long, black hair, pulling it behind her as she rose. Now the mundomentus took over, her neural analogue somewhere inside that vast dome informing the planetary intelligence where she wished to go. She looked down, always an enervating experience on a graviton platform. In the midst of the dawn-tinted spires of the city, the clonarium resembled an ugly, gray plug that had been pounded into the ground by an enormous sledgehammer.

Siula paid her surroundings little attention, however, as she was carried over the graceful buildings and the bustling marketplace, too high up to see if she could spot Tovia. The other clone-mother would be one of the few shopping at such an early hour. Early as it was, however, Siula's dear little Deles would already be up and making a nuisance of himself. She could hardly wait to see him.

Chapter Seven

The Crime of Acrios

The sweet smells of morning were everywhere as Danna stepped through the open doorway into her crystal garden. The block was not as large as the one she had worked on when she was younger, but it would grow. Its gleaming, rainbow brilliance hurt her eyes as it caught the morning light. Both hands full, she set a glass of bhel-melon juice on a small outdoor table and adjusted the nutrient sprinkler's nozzle.

Before her were several goblets, a bowl and a sculpture of layered prisms. These had been commissioned, and Danna would spend the money on Deles. She had nearly completed two of the goblets, though the sculpture would take longer. Soon she would begin cutting them carefully away from the parent block.

Through the outcroppings of transparent stone, she could see the buildings of Nathe in all their multi-leveled complexity and beauty. Even the house in which the Prime Mystagogue lived was visible, an ocher cube, sedately earthy in color, perfectly geometric in shape. There were times when Danna was tempted to visit the lovely woman on whose lap she'd sat as a baby. If Verra only knew that Danna lived right under her nose! But Danna had long since decided that the risk was too great.

"Mistress."

Without turning, Danna knew it was Siula. Each morning the clone-mother made her ponderous way from the clonarium to the tiny three-room house where Danna and Deles lived. Siula hated to let a day pass without seeing Deles. Her great affection for him was at least partly because his was the last birth at which she had been present. As for any other reasons— well, there was little else for Siula to do. But she genuinely loved Deles, and Danna had come to depend on her a great deal. Siula was often a great help, and had practically become a member of the family.

With Siula's aid, Danna had made a reasonably happy and comfortable life for her son in Nathe. Danna was happy too, for she was never lonely, not with Deles and Siula both to keep her company—and to drive her to distraction. In the dusky body the cosmetician had created for her, Danna had remained anonymous, quietly raising her son and growing her sculptures.

At first she hadn't thought of Siula as a true human being, but she had gradually come to feel differently. The clone-mother possessed every human trait—love, compassion, curiosity.

"Good morning, Siula," Danna said, continuing to sprinkle the crystals. "Did you sleep well?"

"I never sleep well in that madhouse."

Poor Siula, hinting once again that she'd love to get out of the clonarium and come to live with Danna and Deles. But it would attract too much attention for people of such modest means to have a clone—a clone-mother, at that.

High-pitched laughter came from inside the house, and a moment later Deles dashed out into the garden, barefoot, chasing a naf. He sprang, capturing the slippery creature under his cupped hands with astonishing speed and agility for a child of his age. The creature blinked its frightened eyes from between his fingers.

"Don't hurt it, Deles," Siula said. "Nafs are good. They bring gifts to those who are kind to them."

"Siula, stop filling his head with nonsense," Danna scolded. "These animals were brought to Rocinth to keep down the insect population. There's nothing magical about them. Deles, let it go."

Deles reluctantly opened his fingers. Free, the naf blinked again, scurried away on its eight legs, and was gone.

"That's a good boy."

Deles watched his mother in his strange, thoughtful way, as she sprinkled the parent block. She faced away from him, and yet she knew that he was still watching her. Sometimes she suspected that he knew things, that he had the Gift. At times like these, she tried not to show apprehension, for there was no real evidence that there was anything...unusual about Deles. He was bright and physically precocious, but that was all. She was the only one on this or any other world who knew the circumstances of his conception. He had been created for some purpose, but Danna couldn't even begin to guess what it might be—unless it was to kill Acrios.

But no, she would not bring her child up to be a killer, as much as she would have enjoyed seeing her father die. It had taken her some time to recover from the shock of what Acrios had done, and at first she had thought of little else but killing

him, but there was too much to live for. Still, she hoped to
never see him again.

Verra's proximity was a problem. Deles and Siula had both
been after her for weeks to let the clone-mother take the boy to
see the Prime Mystagogue. Danna could cite no good reason
why Deles shouldn't go, not without revealing her identity to
Siula. She knew that Siula would never intentionally expose her,
but a slip of the tongue might lead Acrios to her ... and Siula's
tongue had slipped on more than one occasion.

One solution was to explain the truth to Deles and conspire
with him not to tell Siula what they were up to. Siula had to
take Deles to Verra's, after all. Danna could not take him, for
she feared that Verra would recognize her even though her face
and voice had been changed. She might be able to persuade
Verra not to reveal their whereabouts to Acrios, but she
couldn't be sure of it.

"Mother," Deles said, "when do I get to see Beara?"

"Verra, dear," Danna sighed. Here was the question being
raised again.

"Ver-ra!" Deles stood corrected.

"That's right, dear. Verra."

"Why won't you let me go see her?"

"Because . . ." she temporized, trying to think of a new excuse. None of the others had been convincing enough. "Because
all the children in Nathe go to visit her, and you are not like all
the other children—you are special."

"Now who's filling his head with nonsense?" Siula demanded, forgetting her subservient social position, as she so
often did. "You'll make him think he's odd."

"Not odd. Different."

Deles listened attentively, frowning in concentration.

"Run along and play now, dear," Danna said to him.

Deles, relieved to be excused from all this serious business,
ran whooping and screeching out of the garden.

"You're right, Siula," Danna admitted, "it's not good to tell
Deles such things."

"Then why do it?"

"I . . . have a good reason for not wanting Verra to know
about us."

"Yes," Siula prompted.

"It has to do with my former life, Siula. That's all I can say."

"Oh." Danna knew that Siula had gleaned a little about her
"former life" from isolated comments, and yet she was certain
that the clone-mother didn't suspect she was Acrios's daughter.

"Well, mistress, *I* would be taking Deles to see Verra, not
you. So where's the danger?"

"You don't know the person I fear," Danna replied. "He has ways to get to people. He is in a . . . high societal position."

Danna could see from Siula's frowning expression that the clone-mother didn't understand. In Siula's view, all anthroforms occupied lofty social positions. Only such godlike beings as the Prime Mystagogue were above them . . . and the Receptor.

"Perhaps we can show Deles the importance of keeping my existence a secret," Danna said.

"I think he can do it. He's very intelligent, and he *is* different from other children."

Danna was chilled by Siula's words. If a simple clone could see Deles's uniqueness, how much more could someone like Verra see? "What do you mean, different?"

"Why, you said it yourself!" Siula was clearly surprised by Danna's sharp tone. "I only meant that he is special—intelligent, handsome, charming."

Danna stared deep into Siula's eyes, trying to fathom the dullness there. Did Siula see something more than she now admitted? It didn't seem so, for all Danna detected were confusion and a little hurt. She relented, knowing how sensitive Siula was about Deles.

"Have I done something to make you angry, mistress?"

"No, Siula. I am suspicious by nature, but I have no doubt that you are our friend. I must do everything in my power to protect my son. Surely you understand that."

"Of course, and I will protect him, too. But there is no danger if we keep your identity a secret, is there? Surely Deles and I can be trusted to do that to our dying breaths."

"Dying . . . Siula, perhaps if you tell Verra that Deles's mother is dead. . . ."

"*If* she asks about you at all. Yes, that's a very good idea, mistress. But . . ."

Did Siula see a flaw in this plan? "But what, Siula?"

"But how did you die, mistress?" A mischievous look came over Siula's face. "After all, death's not an everyday occurrence among anthroforms."

"An accident . . . crushed to death . . . no physician there to repair me."

"How dreadful!"

They both laughed at the sincerity of Siula's shocked cry.

"We can create more details until we have a full-blown account of my sad demise. No matter what she asks about the accident, there'll be so much to the story she'll have to believe it."

"So we must teach him to lie, so that he can meet the great Verra, and perhaps become a great man himself someday."

"I'm afraid so, Siula. We don't want to deprive Deles, do we?"

Siula's face brightened as she realized that she would finally get her wish. "No, of course we don't, mistress."

But Danna wasn't so certain.

Alone in Verra's small dining room, Acrios still sat, dour with the weight of memory. He had brooded for hours, and at first the wait had seemed interminable, but he found now that he didn't mind being alone as much as he had thought he would.

He considered looking for something with which to pass the time, but decided against it. There was much of interest in this house—toys, puzzles, scholarly tracts—but these things were not for him, not today.

Instead, he meditated, finding the ambience of the Prime Mystagogue's home as conducive to deep thought as a pool of desensitizing fluid. Everything about the place seemed to stimulate his intellect. It struck him as odd that the simple decor and total silence should achieve such an effect, but Verra had doubtless designed it to be that way. She had always possessed a special insight, a genius expressed in the simplest (though never simplistic) terms. This had been clear to him from the first time he had spoken with her . . . as though she were a point in the continuum where the diffuse lines of his life met.

Of course, he'd always convinced himself that it was her statuesque body and handsome features that he found most attractive, but it was really something far less tangible. A rare intelligence coupled with an animal sensuousness, compassion, wit, tolerance . . . and a forgiving nature.

Lately he had found it strangely moving to contemplate his past; not just the halcyon days of his youth, but his whole life. Since the terrible night of Bilyf's prophecy, he'd been able to face the memory of what his father had done to him as a child. He had done the same thing to Danna, and only lately had he begun to wonder if it were some kind of bizarre family ritual. Shock had released the suppressed emotions of childhood, but now there was something else to gnaw at him.

Was it the Gift, or merely a delusion? He couldn't be sure. Madness passed from father to son to daughter to . . . grandson? Madness ending in his own destruction? No wonder the Gift could not function properly in his tormented mind.

The cream-colored wall flushed, brightening momentarily to scarlet, a signal that someone wished to enter. It began to acquire the semblance of depth, showing the street in front of Verra's house. The sentinel eye had discerned a person or persons unknown to it. As if imprisoned in a box, the image of a large woman and a boy appeared within the wall.

Acrios assumed that they sought admittance to the Prime Mystagogue's home. Those who still had children often brought them, in the belief that Verra would take special notice of their brats' precocity. Well, why not? That was precisely how Verra's parents had revealed *her* talents to the world—by taking her to Acrios himself. She had been a fine pupil, but hundreds of others had been brought to him, and these had not fared so well.

Verra customarily admitted them, since only a few hundred were born in Nathe these days. Besides, she enjoyed them.

Rising, Acrios stretched his cramped muscles and left the room, moving toward the entrance facing the street. The door, transparent from the inside, revealed the visitors more clearly. Acrios was puzzled to see that the woman was a corpulent clone-mother. The child, too, made him uneasy.

The door slid silently up into the ceiling.

"Hello," Acrios said.

"Hello, master," the clone-mother replied.

"That's not Verra." The little boy frowned.

"Are you sure?" Acrios said, studying the tyke. This little one had a solid, graceful figure, a handsome face, and curly blond hair, like Danna. Perhaps the resemblance was what he found troubling about the boy. "One may change sex if one so desires, young man."

"Not Verra."

The Receptor nodded. Indeed, he thought, not Verra.

"Deles," said the clone-mother, "mind your manners."

"Deles," Acrios repeated. "What an interesting name. It seems to me I've heard it somewhere before, but I can't seem to remember when or where. Deles . . ."

"We've come to see the Prime Mystagogue, sir," the clone-mother said. "If we may."

"I'm afraid she's not in just now."

"Oh." They both looked very disappointed.

"How old are you, Deles?" Acrios asked.

"Three years old, almost four," said Deles. "How old are you?"

"Very old." What strange, beautiful eyes the child had. How odd, yet assured was his manner. "I sometimes feel I'm as old as the world itself."

"Will you live forever? Siula says that anthroforms can live forever."

"It is possible, Deles, but it never seems to happen."

"Why?"

"Perhaps we could come back later when the Prime Mystagogue is in," Siula said before Acrios could answer.

"No, no, mother, I wouldn't dream of turning you away. You must come in and wait for Verra with me."

"Well, if you think it's all right."

"Yes, she'll be back soon," Acrios said, "bringing me news about something very important."

"Since you're waiting, I guess we can keep you company."

"Exactly," Acrios said, smiling. "I'm alone here, and will enjoy talking to you." He couldn't resist the opportunity; he had meditated long enough, and now felt the contagion of Verra's pedagogical zeal in the presence of this bright young mind. There was something about this boy. . . . He led the way back to the dining room and sat them at the table, reaching into the stasis field to draw forth cool fruits for them to eat.

"Perhaps I can answer some of the questions you intend to ask the Prime Mystagogue?" he said, still smiling.

In transit, neural analogues flashed around Verra as she made her way through the core of the mundomentus on a suspensor bridge. Each spark was a message, a bit of information to be codified, compiled and syndeticized into Rocinth's central nervous system. From here the entire planet was run.

Verra almost wished that she'd had a node implanted, to save her this long walk. She had addressed the mundomentus in the usual way, using a restricted talker, but that wasn't good enough. Her body would temporarily function as a kind of node—her nervous system a synapse—in the vast planetary brain, yet without a node in her own cortex she couldn't physically command the forces in play here.

As she walked, she pondered the irony of a technology that duplicated the sapience of every man and woman on Rocinth, controlled the climate, provided every imaginable service to those it represented, and yet still could not provide perfect justice. Even so, the people did govern their world without the bother of active participation, fulfilling an ancient dream of Man, flawed as the reality was.

Pausing for a moment on the suspensor bridge, Verra stared at the endless twinkling motes.

"Is this the best we can do?" she said aloud.

The mundomentus did not answer, understanding that this was rhetoric. Indeed, Verra was not certain herself of what she meant. She only knew that somehow the attainment of Man's ancient dreams had not created happiness, had in some respects killed his spirit. But these thoughts should not preoccupy her now, not while she was on a mission to save a man's soul.

She threaded a path through the intricacies of the worldmind without touching, or being touched by, the millions whose thoughts blended here. A node would have made this impossible, here at the core of the mundomentus, which was as vulnerable to her as she to it—and as it was to no one else.

Such was the power of the Prime Mystagogue. She alone could communicate with the mundomentus. She could even direct it, shape its actions to what she believed to be the best course for Rocinth's people. Perhaps Acrios could enjoy its privileges and communicate with the distant Machine itself, but he could not influence the Machine as she did the mundomentus. No one could. It was better to rule here than to serve the Machine.

Of course, she did not enjoy as much power as did Acrios. But then, power did not intrigue her as it once had. She had loved it for a time, but ultimately had found it lacking. She had come to think of it as nothing more than a tool. It could be used for good or ill, whether its source was the thermal energy of a planet or the will of that planet's people. The long quest for power had left her unsatisfied; she needed something more.

Call it truth, an intangible yet understandable entity that Acrios had never faced. But who was she to say that? How could she know truth any more objectively than he . . . or more than any other sapient being? In a very real sense, it was imperfection that defined what it was to be human.

Consumed by these thoughts, she continued along the bridge. Her shadow shifted length and direction, jumping as the reproduced light of human thought exploded silently everywhere. The suspensor bridge snaked around the great shaft of the core tap. The reactor globe, the furnace stoking this awesome construction, loomed as a perfect sphere above her.

She was almost at her destination. The central disc was just ahead, where she would communicate with the worldmind as no other could. The bridge spiraled up to the disc's swollen belly, which irised open at the bottom to admit her.

Inside, she reclined in a shell contoured to her body, and fit the skullcap over her head. It took her a moment to relax. Strange, she had never felt so anxious, even when matters concerning the entire world had been at stake. The fate of this one man unnerved her much, much more.

She concentrated, counting her breaths to clear her mind. Soon she felt ghostly filaments enter her consciousness, seeking her motivations for defending Acrios. They picked through the minutiae filling her mind, searching, probing. A myriad invisible tendrils pride gently at the convolutions of her cortex, midbrain, amygdala, thalamus, hypothalamus; pulses from the reticulate formation were monitored.

No matter how thoroughly the mundomentus explored, she was confident that it would recognize that she was armed with the truth. She had searched her conscious mind carefully and was prepared to counter any doubt the planetary intelligence might harbor. Any doubt but one. To obviate that one, she stated it immediately.

"I have come to plead for Acrios, to stake my reputation as Prime Mystagogue of Rocinth that he is innocent of willfully withholding from Man the answer to the question concerning the End of All Things."

Chapter Eight

Family Reunion

Deles didn't know if he liked this tall gray man. There was something wrong with him. It wasn't a smell, but it was something like that.

One thing that bothered him was the man's smile. He didn't smile because he was happy, but to make them *think* that he liked them. It was a kind of game, the way he used that smile. But Deles and Siula weren't really allowed to play. Only the gray man knew the rules.

"Perhaps the child would care for a sweet?" he'd asked Siula. Half the time he called Deles "the child" or "the boy," as if Deles weren't there—or as if he didn't think Deles understood what he was saying.

Deles now chewed the candy the gray man had given him, listening to an exchange between the two adults.

"It seems that there are few womb births to draw you from the clonarium these days, mother."

"That is true," Siula replied.

"Perhaps that's why you're so attached to this little one?"

"Deles is special."

"In what way?" The gray man leaned forward in his chair.

"Intelligence, beauty, strength, agility—in every way. I've never known a child like him."

"I see . . ." He appraised Deles with new appreciation.

Deles gulped down the soft lump of candy.

"Where is your mother, Deles?"

"My mother is dead," Deles recited from rote. "Her name was Jila, and I never knew her."

The gray man stared into Deles's eyes for a moment, before returning to Siula. He sank back into the cushioned depths of his chair, silently gazing at the blue curtain draped across the entry. It seemed to Deles that he had completely forgotten their presence.

Siula forced a cough, asking, "Is the master feeling well?"

"Yes, mother," he said without looking at her, "I'm fine."

"I hope we haven't offended you, sir." She shot a warning glance at Deles.

"No, no," the gray man said. He had looked up unexpectedly and caught Siula's admonitory glance. He smiled his strange, empty smile. "You see, this is a very important day for me. I am . . . in danger of losing something vital to me, and my friend Verra is trying to help me keep it."

"I see," Siula said, but Deles could tell that she didn't see at all, and neither did he.

"I have something," the gray man went on. "Something that has made life easy for me . . . but now I seem to have misplaced it somewhere. . . . It is no longer dependable."

"I'm sorry to hear that, master," Siula said, clearing her throat. Things were becoming more confusing all the time.

"I hope that, with Verra's help, I can restore it to its former fine state."

Siula did not answer, having finally realized that this was not really a dialogue. She chewed her lip and fidgeted on the divan next to Deles.

"Will Verra be here soon?" Deles asked, tiring of the gray man's enigmatic manner.

"Yes." A penetrating stare was directed at Deles. "I'm sure she won't be much longer, Deles."

"Can we play a game when she gets here?"

This time the gray man's smile was more genuine. He said, "We'll play a game right now, Deles."

As he rose, the curtain parted, and a woman wearing the white robe of the Mystagogue entered. She was tall and stately, very beautiful. Deles recognized her immediately; he'd seen her image in the night sky dozens of times.

"Ah," said Verra, her voice low and friendly, "we have guests."

"Yes," the gray man said. "This young man's name is Deles, and he's escorting the clone-mother Siula."

"I am pleased to have you visit my home," Verra said, "but now I must have a few minutes alone with my friend. I am sorry, but perhaps you could come another time?"

"Of course," the clone-mother said, taking Deles's hand.

"No, please stay," said the gray man. "There is no need for you to go." He turned to Verra. "All Rocinth will know the outcome soon enough. What does it matter if they hear?"

"Very well," Verra said. "I won't keep you waiting any longer."

The gray man nodded somberly.

"The mundomentus has decreed that you will be permitted to retain both nodes."

Frozen by the news, the gray man could only stare at Verra in apparent disbelief.

"But there is a condition," Verra said. "Each day, you must make a genuine effort to recall the thing that has been blocked out of your mind. Otherwise . . ."

"Yes, go on."

"Otherwise a searcher will be sent into your brain to extract it."

"A searcher!"

"I'm afraid so."

"I—I hadn't thought of that." He sank into the cushions of the chair, overcome. "Couldn't the mundomentus examine my mind instead?"

"It wouldn't work."

After several disconcerting seconds of silence, the gray man asked, "How much time do I have?"

"While you show progress, as long as it takes."

The room became so quiet that Deles thought he could hear the faint sounds of people out on the street.

"Can we play now?" he asked.

Before Siula could silence him, Verra said, "Yes, we can, Deles." She smiled. "Now we can play all you want."

"That is what I told him," the gray man said. "I must resign myself to this. . . . So let us play a game to help me start."

Verra took his hand, helping him out of the chair. He looked right at Deles, seeing the first sign of a tentative smile on the boy's handsome face.

"Thank you, dear Verra," he said. "Now, young man, just what sort of game did you have in mind?"

Anxiety plagued Danna as she made her way through the crowd of pedestrians, who languidly strolled in the midday warmth. She had decided that the best way to pass the nerve-wracking wait for Deles and Siula was to get out of the house. She had walked all the way to market, ostensibly to look over the day's fresh fruits and vegetables. As she neared the busy marketplace, the gold bubble of the mundomentus's housing glinted in the distance.

The worldmind's knowledge of her existence dictated her every waking moment; even while she slept, her mind guarded against Acrios's prying Gift. She made no special requests of the mundomentus. It terrified her to think that an extension of the planetary intelligence—a node—was implanted in her father's brain. And yet Acrios still didn't know she had survived the ordeal in the well, apparently. Whether this blessed anonymity could go on forever, she couldn't say, but perhaps it would be

wise to feel Verra out. It must be done slowly, though, and
Deles's visit was a good start. Verra was a woman of great integrity; surely she wouldn't arbitrarily inform Acrios of their
whereabouts? Danna would simply have to wait and see. And,
she reminded herself, there was no need to worry about today
—Deles had memorized a good story.

She passed lovers who dallied in the cool shade of sculptured
fountains, and walked through the rainbow hues of a color wall,
on into the sunny market square.

There were offworld traders and entrepreneurs numbering in
the hundreds, hocking wares from all the worlds the human
tongue could evoke.

"... and from Ca'anaz, the sofizshiz, so brilliant the eye cannot look upon it unaided ... the flowering fungus of Doazwa,
still growing, though the race who cultivated it has been gone
for millennia ... elegant Quifiton feathered pikes ... pottery
from the tribal natives of Bulog ... tattooed skin from Lemohlat—have no fear, they part with their skins quite willingly on
Lemohlat. In fact they shed them twice a year, and their economy depends on selling them. At tremendous cost and great
personal risk, these peerless art objects have been brought to
Rocinth, this most earthlike jewel of a planet. Indeed,
these ..."

Indeed, indeed. It was true that Rocinth was reputed to be
much like ancient Earth, but who really knew what Earth had
been like? Who even knew where it *was* anymore? In spite of its
distance from the more settled parts of the galaxy (or perhaps
because of it), Rocinth had long been a popular spot for trade.
Trade was just a game now, of course. Rocinth was an entirely
autonomous, self-sufficient planet, unlike many other worlds,
and trade here was a luxury, nothing more than an ancient
human habit that some still enjoyed.

Danna fingered precious stones, tasted exotic foods, sipped
wines, gazed in wonder at projected sights from faraway worlds
—not to mention sounds, smells, and even textures.

But she soon abandoned it all, turning instead to the more
mundane food staples on the far side of the square. By this
time, holographic images were playing in the darkening amber
sky. She examined comestibles through the wavy optical effect
of a stasis field. Mounds of fish reminded her of her childhood
home by the sea. She turned away, toward the fruit.

As she squeezed a ripe bhel-melon, with its characteristic
inverted side puckered invitingly at the edges, she noticed that
everyone seemed to be looking up. She didn't want to watch
any projections, for she was likely to see Verra, which would
only unnerve her. Still, everyone was so rapt on the early night

sky image—many going to the nearest lightbox for talkers—
that she couldn't resist a peek.

To her horror, she saw her father's face, immense over the
city, fierce eyes seeming to bore into hers. She dropped the
fruit.

What could this mean? Was Acrios dead? Her heart
pounded, and she wished that it were so, for the alternative was
too dreadful. Running to a lightbox, she grabbed a talker and
slipped it behind her ear.

"... amid speculation that Acrios will remain Receptor. The
true will of the people—through the good offices of the mundomentus—reveals that the intercession of the Prime Mystagogue
was instrumental in the decision, which involves the eventual
use of a searcher, if all else fails. The Receptor, arriving at the
home of Verra yeste—"

"Deles!" Danna screamed, tearing the talker from her ear
and dashing it to the ground. Several startled onlookers stared
at her. Pushing them out of her way, she prayed that her father
had not yet discovered who Verra's young visitor was. She
fought her way to the color wall, her gown trailing awkwardly
behind her as she began to run. Her father was much too clever.
A child's lie might work with Verra, but if Acrios suspected...

She had to stop him.

Deles rode on the shoulders of the gray man. Siula laughed,
showing the gap between her front teeth. Verra looked on in
amused tolerance.

"I despair of teaching Deles anything," the Prime Mystagogue said, "especially with you here, Acrios."

"*Acrios!*" Siula cried. "I had no idea!"

Before anyone else could speak, the back wall flushed and
brightened to scarlet. It gained depth, showing a raven-haired
woman trailing a diaphanous gown. Halting, the woman looked
nervously toward the front door of the house, seeming to stare
right at the small group gathered in Verra's study, though of
course she could not see them at all.

"Now, who's this?" Verra asked of the clone-mother. "Do
you know her?"

"I—I don't think so." Siula's sharp intake of breath was
clearly audible in the quiet room.

Deles held his hands over his mouth, stifling a giggle.

Acrios nodded. In his eyes was dim recognition. He did not
know the young woman's face, but something in her carriage,
the shape of her neck, her movements...

"I think Deles knows this dark lady," he said as the little boy
giggled again. "Don't you, Deles?"

"Yes!" Deles burst out with pent-up laughter.

"Then why don't you tell us who she is?" Acrios swung the boy around and held him up so that they were face-to-face.

"She's my mother!" Deles cried, delighted at this new wrinkle.

"Indeed." Acrios threw Deles into the air and caught him. The child's fat legs kicked as he squealed mirthfully. Acrios said softly: "I thought she was dead."

"Not anymore!"

Acrios squatted, setting down the laughing child, but still holding him by the waist with one hand. "Perhaps we should invite her in." He glanced at the Prime Mystagogue. "Verra?"

"Yes, I suppose we should, although I must admit that this all strikes me as a bit odd."

"Very odd," Acrios said. "But I think I understand what is happening. It seems that my Gift has not failed me after all."

Verra looked puzzled as she pulled back the curtain and went to welcome the young woman to her home.

"You, mother," Acrios said to Siula, his face darkening, "your game is more complex than Deles's . . . and a good deal more dangerous."

"Master, no—I didn't—" Deles sensed that she was very frightened.

Danna's muffled voice came from the vestibule behind the curtain, her words indistinguishable. But Verra's reply was clear.

"Don't worry," she said. "You're among friends here."

The curtain was flung aside, and Danna stared in horror at the sight of Acrios holding Deles. She told herself to remain calm, that her father could not recognize her. She had a different face and hair color than when he had last seen her, even her vocal chords had been changed . . . and he thought she was dead. Why, knowing all of this, was she so frightened? He could not look into her mind if she didn't let him. If she controlled her fear, they would escape.

She looked directly into her father's cold blue eyes.

"So this is your mother," Acrios said, loosening his grip on Deles, but not yet releasing him.

"I thought you were supposed to be dead, Mother," Deles said.

"So you told us, my boy," said Acrios, "and yet she is standing here before us."

Danna did not turn away from Acrios's burning gaze.

"She seems far too substantial to be an Other, don't you agree?" Acrios turned to Siula, who did not reply.

"What is all this about, Acrios?" Verra demanded.

The game had turned serious, and Deles was disturbed. When his mother had first arrived, he thought she was joining them, but now the puckering of his mouth showed her that he was frightened. She wanted to get him out of this house more than she had ever wanted anything in her life.

Acrios released Deles, who ran to his mother and flung his arms about her neck as she stooped to pick him up.

"How rare and touching," Acrios said. "A child and his mother. Deles and ... what did you say your mother's name is, Deles?"

Desperately, Danna tried to think of a way to stop Deles from speaking. If she silenced him, shushed him, clapped a hand over his mouth, Acrios would know that what he suspected was true. She waited an eternity for her son to speak, her heart beating wildly.

Deles buried his head in her breast. "Danna," he said softly, "my mother's name is Danna."

"Danna." Acrios's tone was triumphant.

"Danna?" Verra murmured. "Alive? Here?"

"The Gift has brought you to me," Acrios said, the wonder in his voice revealing that he could hardly believe it himself. "You could not escape me forever, my daughter. But I hasten to add that you needn't worry, I have no intention of harming Deles."

"Just as you never harmed me, I suppose."

"Danna," Acrios said, a world of sadness in his eyes, "I meant to leave you only long enough for Bilyf to select a good physician."

"Liar!"

"When we opened that panel, I ..." Here he broke off, choking with emotion.

"You're a fine actor." Danna's voice was as cold as death.

"I admit to emotionalism," he said, "but what I say is no less true for that." His words seemed lame, conveying none of the turbulent passion surging through him.

"The mighty Acrios," Danna said contemptuously, "Receptor of Rocinth, tormentor of women and children."

Rage and compassion warred like two armies within Acrios's still-powerful frame. He wanted to kill them, but he could not. It was not for fear of the mundomentus, or even of the Machine. He was past all that now. They were mere toys next to the murderous hatred swelling up inside him, threatening to rip out his soul and cast it into the infinite reaches of time and space.

He had to exorcise the demon that threatened him, but he

could not harm his loved ones. He turned toward Verra and took a step, seeing fear in her eyes.

He could not strike out at Verra.

He turned on the babbling clone-mother.

"Who would believe it?" she was saying to Danna. "You, you are the daughter of Acrios. *Acrios!*"

"Yes, she is my daughter," he said in a soft tone. "And you tried to keep her from me, didn't you?"

"No, mighty Receptor, I never—"

"Silence!" he screamed. "You played your part in this charade, didn't you? You made a fool of the mighty Receptor." His face reddened, the veins on his temples and neck swelling. He had to do something, or the demon inside him would burst out of his skull. A fine spray of spittle erupted from his curled lips as he shouted, "Did you really believe that a clone could get away with mocking the *Receptor of Rocinth?*"

She gaped, cringing before the wrathful figure towering over her. He had to strike out at her—or die of rage himself.

He lunged, kicking at the soft flesh of her belly. He felt the hard bone of his foot sink in. Siula was driven back, colliding with the wall in a sickening thud. Moaning, her face livid, she slid like liquid to the floor.

"Siula!" Danna screamed.

"Acrios!" Verra cried. "No!"

But it was too late. Acrios smashed his sandaled heel repeatedly into the body of the clone-mother, hearing the cries of horror only as distant, muted sounds through the ringing in his ears. He kicked her head viciously, and it knocked against the wall like a single beat on a timpani. The clone-mother's eyes rolled up to show the whites, blood dribbling from her open mouth.

His rage spent, Acrios gazed upon the fallen woman. What had he done? In a moment of uncontrollable anger, what had he done? Did it matter? He was Acrios, Receptor of Rocinth, was he not? Why then this ringing in his ears?

Deles screamed. Danna put him down and ran to Siula, cradling the clone-mother's broken skull in her arms. Blood seeped into her gown like an angry red flower.

"Siula." Tears were in Danna's eyes. "Oh, my dear Siula."

Verra knelt beside her, taking the clone-mother's pulse as if she somehow believed there might still be a chance.

Outside, the wind began to howl. The room darkened, and Acrios thought he saw a flash of blue phosphorescence in the gathering gloom. So the Others had come to bear witness to this spectacle. Well, he would give them a show. Not even they could stop him from gaining immortality. He had become a god,

taking a life. It had been necessary, and if he had taken a life
. . . perhaps he would also spare one. He could not kill his own
flesh and blood.

Danna heard her little boy crying, but all she could think of
was Siula. If she had only argued more forcefully against the
foolish idea of visiting Verra. . . .

This couldn't have happened, not to poor innocent Siula. It
hadn't really happened, had it? But here was the corpse growing
cold in her arms, and nothing could be done about it. Clones
weren't repaired when they died. They just died.

"I want to go home," Deles bawled. But a strong hand
gripped his shoulder.

"You'll come home," the gray man said, breathing heavily.
"You'll come with me, to your real home."

Events had conspired against him, but Acrios had emerged
victorious. Whatever doubts he had entertained were erased
now. His immortality was that of a god, not a man. He picked
up the screaming child and started out of the room.

"No!" Danna cried, leaving Siula's body and running after
them. "Father, no!"

But she knew that her father would have his way at last.
Nothing could stop him now.

Chapter Nine

Adrift in a Sea of Stars

The sun vanished, blacked out by a whorled mass of clouds rushing in from the sea. A drizzly shadow hung from it like a shroud as it moved steadily towards Nathe. Pedestrians frowned in puzzlement, stopping to watch the approaching storm, for this was unheard of. Storms simply didn't appear unannounced.

The storm was here because Acrios had called it. He dragged his daughter out onto the street with one hand while holding the boy against his chest with the other. He was a giant, a force as irresistible as the interactions that bind together quarks. Danna did not resist him, as did the squirming Deles. He looked down at her and spoke.

"Do you see now that there is no limit to my power?"

Danna fell to her knees as if she were a sack of flour. She was incredulous that the mundomentus would permit this to happen. Surely her father would be struck down in his madness and arrogance before his tempest destroyed Nathe.

But the storm slithered ever nearer, exuding the odor of ozone, a black serpent in the sky. It pointed directly at them, spinning on an unerring trajectory. A man on a graviton platform could not descend quickly enough to evade the onrushing winds. Overturned, he fell screaming to his death. The peaks of the city's taller buildings crumbled and flew apart. Roaring winds accompanied the thunder of debris crashing into the streets.

Just before she was sucked into the storm by its enormous vacuum, Danna saw, through a miasma of churning dust, enormous chunks of masonry glancing harmlessly off the mundomentus's protective force field.

Then all was howling darkness. Danna was not thrust toward the calm eye of the storm, as she had expected. Rather, the winds seemed to pummel her aimlessly, for the storm was no longer controlled by the mundomentus, but by the unhinged mind of her father. She thought her limbs would be torn off and the life sucked out of her. But somehow she remained at points

80

of equilibrium through the storm's cold, merciless fury.

Why did the mundomentus send the storm to Acrios, after what he'd done to Siula? His privileges should have been terminated immediately. He was a murderer, and yet he still maintained the power of a god.

Danna pulled her knees up to her chest and clutched her legs, tumbling end over end in the whorling black womb.

If she and her child survived this, she would see to it that Acrios's future was as black as this storm. She had almost forgiven him, forgotten her vow to see him dead. It had seemed too terrible a burden for her child, and as time passed, she had softened. But she must be relentless now. It must be done for the good of all thinking, feeling creatures. If there was evil in the dying universe, Acrios was its black heart.

Deles would be his destroyer, after all.

Acrios took pleasure in manipulating the storm. It would carry them to the estate, and he would allow no light inside on the way, no glimpse of the world below or the stars above. He was free to do anything he chose; it was his right as a god. He had always suspected that he possessed a divine nature, flawless even beyond the physical perfection of the anthroform. Now he was certain of it. He was no longer frightened of the Machine, the mundomentus, the searcher . . . he did not even fear the Others anymore. Sealed in the swirling darkness of the storm, he exulted in his magnificence. He rode the winds in triumph, a man like no other who had ever lived . . . and he, Acrios, would live forever.

To him, the journey back to his estate ended soon enough, but to Danna it was an eternity before the churning winds slackened. She began to drop towards the ground with sickening speed. Then she was buoyed up by a powerful gust, and dropped again. Her erratic descent stopped at last, light began to cut through the clouds, and she found herself rolling awkwardly onto her stomach on a carpet of close-cropped vegetation.

Rising to her knees, she saw on one side trees lashed by the abating winds, and on the other the agitated whitecaps of the sea. The storm clouds retreated until the air was still and clear, a matter of only a few seconds.

Acrios stood over her, a deranged god, still holding Deles, who was now crying silently.

"What kind of father would I be," Acrios asked, "if I permitted my daughter and grandson to languish like pariahs in the company of clones?"

"Murderer."

"The clone-mother may not be dead," Acrios replied. "But

even if she is, another can be grown for you. She can even be given the same name."

"Siula was a human being," Danna said softly.

"I hear Verra's pedantry in your words, my daughter. But no matter what idealistic nonsense you may believe, a clone is only a clone, and has been since time immemorial."

"She was my friend."

He shook his head.

"Siula loved Deles so much." Now Danna was not speaking to her father. A terrible sense of loss overcame her, and she was drained of anger.

As the last formless wisps of the storm vanished over the sea, the Receptor said, "It seems that the mundomentus did not think so highly of her."

"Give me my son," Danna demanded.

"Danna, Danna, I have no wish to harm him . . . or you."

"Liar!"

"Daughter, I am in the grip of things too vast and awful to suffer your hatred also. Have a care."

"You dare speak of caring, you monster?"

He shrugged. "It's time for us to go." This argument was getting them nowhere, and he did not feel compelled to explain himself to Danna, or to anyone. "Come."

"I am not going anywhere, Father," Danna said. "You'd better kill me right now, because if you don't I'll find a way to repay you, no matter if it takes me an eternity."

"You will not have an eternity, Danna, not in this universe. Only *I* am destined to live forever. The rest of humankind is doomed." But even as he spoke them, his words rang false in his own ears. He could not ignore the sheer hatred in her glare. There was something in her manner, her expression, her voice . . . something new. It was something he recognized, nevertheless. It chilled him.

Had *he* done this to her?

"Danna, if you seek revenge you will only destroy yourself. Try to understand."

"When have you tried to understand?" Danna demanded. "I saw you beat my mother. Were you so understanding then?"

"I tried to be, Danna, but I could not." How was this possible? How was this child, still in her teens, cutting him as if she wielded a dagger? He did not have to explain himself, but he felt a need to make her see how it had been. "Your mother was moribund, despairing. She thought of nothing but death and Otherness, for these two really are one and the same. I tried to reason with her, but nothing worked. I wanted to make her *feel* again, even if all she felt was pain."

"Liar."

"No, I am not lying." But even as he spoke, he was uncertain of the truth. Had he driven his wife to suicide, then? He could not think about it now, not when he had so much to do.

A pale figure waddled across the lawn, coming from the villa —Bilyf. As the Mennon joined them, he saw the child in the Receptor's arms.

"This is my grandson," Acrios said to him.

Bilyf's crest bowed in understanding. He saw that a terrible thing was happening, and that the repercussions would vibrate into the future, poisoning and destroying . . . but also that ultimately some good might come from it. The good, however, was so nebulous that he could not see it clearly at all. He turned to Danna, whom he recognized easily for all the superficial changes that had been wrought upon her by cosmetic surgery. "Little Danna."

"Oh, Bilyf." Danna embraced him, weeping. But beneath her sorrow, Bilyf sensed an unfamiliar hardness, a sick resolve . . . a madness.

Bilyf's flowing digits gently touched her face.

Acrios pulled her away. "What do you see, Bilyf?" he asked.

"One sees only that—nothing has changed."

Acrios's eyes narrowed. This was not what he had expected.

"Don't you see, Father," Danna said, "you have only en-sured that the prophecy will come true."

But Acrios wasn't listening to her. He had turned to gaze out over the sea, where a deathly stillness held dominion. The sky was tinted an unwholesome green.

"Something is wrong," he murmured.

Danna felt it too. Something that made the fine hairs on the nape of her neck stand up. Something . . .

Acrios's cape rippled with a sudden breeze. In moments the breeze had become a hot wind, enveloping them and whipping them pitilessly. Bending under its fury, they ran towards the villa. The rapidly building storm pushed them forward, through the archway and into the dining hall. A transparent shield slid down from the arch, as well as all doors and windows that led outside, sealing off the house.

"If the mundomentus cannot stop this," Acrios said, "it must not be functioning properly."

This was unprecedented in the history of Rocinth. It terrified Acrios, deadened his spirit to think that the mighty worldmind could fail. Would it be repaired? Or would the forces of nature run amok, demolishing the planet's delicate artificial balance?

Danna did not care. She only knew that the failure of the

mundomentus could mean that her father might get away with murder.

"This is the reason the mundomentus didn't stop you, Father," she said. "Not because you are the Receptor, but because it is breaking down. You are not a god, but a common murderer, and justice will be served sooner or later . . . one way or the other."

"She was only a clone," Acrios said, his eyes wild. "What has this storm to do with the death of a clone?"

"Can't you see? Whatever prevents the mundomentus from controlling this storm has also prevented it from dealing with you."

"But what power on Rocinth can override the mundomentus?" he cried desperately.

The house began to shake and rumble. No one answered him.

Danna had never seen a storm like this. She had always taken the domesticated climate of Rocinth as a given. This storm was savage, pounding at the walls of the villa like the fists of an enraged giant. It was a wild beast, ravenous and bloodthirsty, threatening to raze their home and consume them, as if it had sought them out in their anguish. At least it would all be over quickly, for she was certain that the villa could not withstand such elemental force. She was not frightened anymore, strangely enough. She only wished that Deles could be spared.

But the howling winds grew no worse. Instead, the storm subsided as quickly as it had come. In moments, their breathing and the beating of their hearts were the only sounds they heard.

A magnetic crackling disturbed the stillness of the unnatural green sky. The huddling group stared through the archway at the motionless trees. Beyond the trees, the sea was glass, as if there had been no wind at all.

Deles began to whimper.

"Give him to me," Danna said.

"Soon."

"Father, what do you intend to do?"

"What choice do I have?" Acrios said, sliding the shield up and tasting the clean, still air. He cradled the sniffling child.

"You can send us away," she said, pleading. "You can send us where we can't possibly harm you."

Renewed gusts of wind blew Acrios's hair back from his high forehead, framing his gaunt face with strands of gray.

"How do I know that the mundomentus will give me a ship?"

"It just worked that screen over the archway for you, didn't it? When it's functioning normally again, it will take away your privileges for killing someone who didn't want to die. Now is the time to call for a ship. If you don't, you will never be rid of us."

"What will stop you from coming back to Rocinth?"

"I'll see to it that Deles stays on whatever world you send us to, Father. I'll make a home for him there, I swear it to you."

The wind gained strength, howling so that they were forced to shout to be heard. The storm returned, but diminished almost instantly. All was placid again in seconds, as if the hot winds had never blown.

Acrios knew he was incapable of killing Deles. He cursed himself as a weakling, but he could not do it.

"Who is Deles's father?" he demanded.

"There *is* no father," Danna said. He saw no fear in her, only hatred, as if the passion of all her charged emotions had melded into this one evil thing that glared balefully out at him through her lovely eyes.

"No matter. Deles exists, and that is all that is truly significant." He wouldn't yet tell her that he would allow the boy to live, for the plan he had conceived was not yet fully formed. But it would be a simple thing. He could not kill the boy, but he might be able to bring himself to kill Danna—for he could see that she was already dead.

He had always wanted to pass on his bloodline. The idea had become of paramount importance as the centuries, then the millennia had accumulated. It was not merely sensual pleasure that made him cling so tenaciously to life, that made him deny Otherness as an alternative. As the likelihood of accident or even murder preyed more and more on his mind, he suspected that the Others had selected him for their target. He was the very symbol of life, of vibrancy, and they were death incarnate.

Never mind the Others now. He was faced with a terrible dilemma. Danna was the only child he had ever had, in all the thousands of years he had lived. He still loved her, but she no longer loved him . . . and she never would love him again. All of this rationalization was irrelevant, however, in view of one overriding fact. He could not kill Deles. That was the one thing he could never do. Deles had broken down all his defenses in the few short hours Acrios had known him. The Receptor had to be merciful . . . but he would not be a martyr.

"Very well, Danna," he said. "You shall have your wish. I will send you away."

"To where?" Her relief was palpable.

"To the farthest civilized world that is still inhabited. A place where your needs may be provided for."

"A world that does not send ships to this part of the galaxy?"

"Yes." Acrios looked straight into her eyes. "I cannot kill

this little one, but I must protect myself as much as I can."

"One would ask—" Bilyf said, the peculiar tint of the sky coloring his pale skin a sickly green.

"What?" Acrios demanded.

"One would ask—for the privilege of—accompanying little Danna—and her child."

"Would you leave me now, Bilyf?" Acrios said, realizing just how alone he would be without the Mennon.

"Little Danna—will need Bilyf—more than will—the master."

"Yes, yes, I suppose she will." It was better this way. Bilyf's presence would only remind him of the past, of the prophecy that had initiated this tragic chain of events.

"Then Bilyf may come with us?" Danna asked.

"Yes."

"Give Deles to me, then. We'll leave as soon as you have a ship ready."

The wind rose again, tearing at them within seconds, and Acrios felt great trepidation, even terror at the power of the uncontrolled elements. The storm rose and fell suddenly, like his own capricious moods . . . waxing and waning as though it possessed a will of its own—one moment cruel and dangerous, the next calm and peaceful. It was like him, but it was not his creation. This storm had not sprung from his will, nor was it controlled by the mundomentus. Could it be caused by the Others?

Turning toward the villa, he handed Deles to Danna. What did it matter, any of it? He would soon be rid of them. Never seeing them again, he would live beyond the End of All Things . . .

"I will send for a ship," he said. He let the mundomentus know what he wanted—a sphereship capacious enough for comfort. He would set them adrift in space. If they should be fortunate enough to put down on some uncharted world where they could eke out an existence, so be it. He wished them well. And if they could not survive . . . at least he had not been their executioner.

"One will serve—little Danna—as one has served—Acrios."

"Ah, Bilyf," Acrios said, "you've been a good and faithful servant. More than that, a friend. I don't know if I have ever told you so before, but I find you wise in your way. I will miss you."

"One carries the master—with one—always."

Acrios wept, for Bilyf, for Danna, and for Deles . . . but most of all for himself.

Danna watched him with contempt. She would see to it that Deles wasted no pity on the old monster when he was big enough to avenge her. Burning to articulate that thought, she remained silent, fearing that her father might still change his mind.

A low thrumming sound permeated the cyan atmosphere.

"Come," Acrios said as the humid wind blasted them again. They leaned into the gale, Acrios leading the way to the descending ship. Danna followed him, carrying Deles, Bilyf behind them.

The storm was an endless babble of angry voices as the ship settled onto the seaside cliff. To Danna, it hardly looked like a ship at all. It was a bristling, radiant globe, its systems housed inside ten columnar extrusions. Floating a few centimeters off the ground, it rested on a field of antigravitons.

"It's going to be all right now, Deles," she shouted over the wind. Despite her reassuring words, however, she actually feared that the ship's cramped space would force them to go into adiabatic suspension—a long sleep from which they might never awaken.

The ship opened at the bottom like a hinged jaw, and Danna carried Deles inside without hesitation. The inner airlock swung in on the cavelike interior, and she laid Deles down in webbing that cushioned him comfortably. Easing in behind them, Bilyf ran his multi-jointed digits over the gleaming surfaces. Danna looked into his opaque eyes, seeing strength and assurance there.

The portal closed on Acrios's drawn, staring face, as the wind was silenced inside the ship once and for all.

"Well," Danna said, lying down next to Deles on the webbing, "at least we're alive."

Just as Bilyf crawled in beside her, there was a mild sense of emotion. The visuals winked on in a three-hundred-and-sixty-degree arc, fish-eyed and three-dimensional. Acrios's distorted figure stood alone before them, braced against the wind. He slowly looked up; they were over his head now. His figure shrank, disappearing into the enlarging land mass. The edge of the sea appeared.

Hardly feeling the effects of propulsion, they were in space within seconds, the great green and white-streaked disc of Rocinth seeming to fill the inside of the sphereship. In the blackness behind the globe was an auroral display so bright and colorful that some of the smaller moons were obscured completely. The stars were awash with pale blue, green, yellow, orange, red, violet. Not confined to Rocinth, the freakish storm extended far into space.

"The solar wind—flares into—an ion storm," Bilyf said.

"What is causing it?" said Danna.

"One does not—pretend to know—but the eruption may be—to our advantage."

Bilyf had removed the cover of the directional systems column, and had crawled up inside it. He had not explained what he intended to do, but Danna suspected that it involved the effects of the ion storm, which now swept through the entire solar system. She stroked Deles's curls as they peered into the niche where the Mennon worked. Bilyf's haunches slid out of the compartment, his milky body dropping onto the webbing beside them.

"One sees—that the electromagnetic disturbance—affects the sphereship—mnemonically."

"What does that mean?" Danna asked.

"Its memory—is gone."

"But its program is locked, isn't it? I can't believe my father would be fool enough to leave a flexible course unlocked."

"One sees that—it is so."

"Then we are lost." There was little chance of the ship's monitors finding an earthlike planet close enough to land on.

"One sees—that when—the program is lost—the lock opens—" Bilyf said, "enabling one—to plot a new course—in place of the old."

"Then . . . ?"

"We may go—where little Danna—chooses." His crest bobbed in satisfaction.

"Can we go to Sripha?"

"One—believes so."

"Oh, Bilyf." She threw her arms around him.

Deles was confused by their apparent joy. He could think of nothing but the terrible thing the old man had done to Siula.

"What about my father?" Danna said. "Will he know?"

"Acrios's power weakens—allowing Deles—to live."

"Did you hear that, darling?" She hugged Deles to her breast. "We're going to be all right."

Tears of joy ran down her cheeks. She could ask for asylum at her cousin Dictys's home on Sripha. On that primitive world, Dictys's half-brother was the master of an estate far larger than Acrios's. Surely they would be welcome there. She could raise Deles properly, and when Deles grew to manhood, he would be very near Rocinth . . . very near to Acrios.

"Mother, I'm afraid," Deles said, worry etched into his little face.

"Don't be afraid, Deles," she said. "It's going to be all right now. Your grandfather can't hurt you."

But the terrible expression on his mother's face frightened him almost as much as his grandfather did. A change had come over her, and Deles didn't like it. Still, he didn't cry. He was too exhausted for that.

As the endless black sea drifted past on the sphereship's panoramic visual scan, Danna thought: For what you have done, Father, you'll pay. Your transgressions will one day take from you the very thing you love best—life.

But could she use Deles as her instrument? One look at the terror in his blue eyes convinced her that his childhood was gone forever, that he would always be haunted by the nightmare of Siula's murder. The child must kill Acrios, as she had originally planned.

It was her son's destiny.

"Go to sleep now, darling," she said, thinking of how difficult their task would be. "Much lies ahead of you."

The scintillating colors of the solar winds began to fade, and soon the stars shone with a clarity possible only in space. The storm had subsided . . . at least for a while.

Part Two

Chapter Ten

Danna's Advice

Deles spun, releasing the dikoit at the precise instant that would ensure its maximum ascent, for the higher it flew the more its skimmers would play on air currents. Up it soared, pirouetting like a living thing. Exhilarated, Deles sprinted to keep pace with the shining, diminishing circle before it was lost forever in the clouds.

The grass whipped his bare ankles as he pounded through a furrow between two hills. This was where he had spent his life, and now that he was a young man he knew every nearby stone, tree and flower. In these hills he had competed in childish contests that helped him grow into a tall, strong young man ... and, in the nearby woods, he had learned the secrets of love from some of Ploydekt's favorite concubines.

Less pleasantly, he had first joined the hunt in the meadow beyond the woods, and had killed his first and only chakta there the summer puberty came upon him. He had not enjoyed it: often, in his dreams, he still saw terrified rolling eyes; heard pitiful squeals break the cool air; recalled the urging of the men to finish off the wounded animal, blood and passion in their excited voices; felt the hunting garom's flanks, sleek and hot against his thighs, as he dismounted.

And the thrust. The red spurt. The convulsive twitching of furry limbs. The lingering death wail.

Somehow he had forced himself to partake of the chakta's flesh at the solstitial feast. It had been no different than any other meat, and yet the memory of its death—by his own hand —made it difficult for him to chew and swallow. The following year, when he had declined to join the hunt, the men had not commented, but the master had been increasingly cool to him ever since.

Deles ran up the hill, chasing the dikoit as it veered unexpectedly to the right. At the top of the hill he stopped and stretched out his hand, the dikoit drifting back toward him. He caught it easily and stood looking down at the land of his boyhood. Below was the labyrinthine stone maze of Ploydekt's estate, a complex pattern of walls and tunnel openings. Although its bulk was underground, its surface features sprawled over a vast expanse. But Ploydektum, as the master so humbly called it, was not truly Deles's home. His home was Rocinth, a bright, unwinking star in the evening sky, as his mother so frequently reminded him.

Squinting into the autumnal sun, he watched a bird circle overhead. He had a vague memory that the sun had been a different color on Rocinth, brighter and larger; there had been no snow; there had been hordes of people and bleached white buildings; there had been the giant golden dome of the mundomentus. Cousin Dictys once told him that Deles had regaled his playmates with tales of Rocinth for months after he'd come to Ploydektum.

Ploydekt was not a blood relation to Danna and Deles, being the half-brother of Dictys. He had inherited the estate at an early age. In those days he had been feuding with Dictys over some matter long since forgotten by both of them. Even so, the master had at one time been sufficiently provoked to banish his half-brother. Dictys had then traveled to Rocinth, living for a few centuries in the house of Acrios, whose wife Lehana he claimed as a cousin. At last Ploydekt had forgiven him and Dictys had returned to Sripha, when Danna was thirteen. Ploydekt had been married in the interim, and his wife Mella had exercised a benign influence over him. But then, a few months before Deles's seventeenth birthday, she had gone over to Otherness, and things hadn't been the same since. The master now possessed an insatiable lust for lovers of both sexes. He increasingly turned his attention toward Deles's mother, and commensurately Danna resented it.

Cousin Dictys seemed oddly unconcerned about the brewing conflict. It was up to Deles alone to defend his mother from Ploydekt's advances. The master of Ploydektum saw Danna as merely being coy, Deles as an ungrateful pup. As far as he was concerned, it was only a matter of time until he won Danna over. Like Deles's grandfather Acrios, Ploydekt was an imperious, self-serving man. Still, he had been good to them until recently. At one time in Deles's early puberty, he had even taken a special interest in the boy. His doting had ended after Deles's first hunt.

In the distance, Deles saw two figures coming from Ploydektum. One was diminutive, his movements economical. The other was a lumpy biped with a crest on his head, shuffling along as if he wished that he were on some other planet.

"Bilyf!" Deles shouted. "Cousin Dictys!" He effortlessly

bounded the thousand feet separating them and embraced Bilyf, his strong arms nearly disappearing in the bunched muscles of the Mennon's back. He laughed as the dikoit fell to the ground, and turned to give his graying cousin a hug too.

"My brother will be pleased to have you represent Ploydektum in the solstitial games," Dictys said, pointing at the fallen dikoit.

Deles nodded. He knew that his cousin didn't believe what he was saying, but the pretense would do no harm. But why had they come looking for him?

"One has learned—" Bilyf began.

"Yes?"

"One has learned—that Verra—is lost on Tartarus."

"Verra?" A faint memory of a tall woman dressed in white. This news would do his mother no good. Verra was a link to the happier days of Danna's girlhood, before Acrios went mad. But there was nothing happy about being lost on Tartarus. That demonic world was the abortive result of a primitive attempt to acclimatize it to Rocinthan tastes. As it turned out, it was a hostile environment to humans, a reducing atmosphere that reacted badly to oxygen. Verra's chances of survival were slim.

"I'd better go to Mother," Deles said.

"One—believes so."

Deles nodded. His mother often had need of him now. She'd never taken a lover, and her antipathy toward Ploydekt made her all the more insecure. Verra's disappearance would surely be a shock to her.

"How did Verra come to be on Tartarus?" Deles asked as the three of them started down the hill toward the enormous estate.

"She was searching for something believed to be crucial to the Seers' inquiries," Dictys said. "Since Acrios was relieved of his nodal privileges, Rocinth has been without a Receptor. The Prime Mystagogue was trying to attend to his duties as well as her own."

Surprised, Deles kept silent. No one ever spoke of Acrios, except in the most circumspect terms—no one but Danna, who had always implied that Acrios was the most powerful of men. Deles had never heard about the Receptor's privileges being revoked. His memory of his grandfather consisted entirely of a gray man using awesome power for the most selfish ends conceivable, a memory his mother had done everything she could to reinforce.

"One—leaves Deles—here," said Bilyf at the south entrance to Ploydektum, a gaping wound in an enormous stone wall. "Little Danna—wishes to share her sorrow—with Deles alone."

Deles nodded at Dictys. He watched them walk away, and then entered a tunnel slanting beneath the surface until it leveled off amid a warren of cubicles and passageways. Past these, he hurried down a stairwell, around a curving corridor, and along a gradually descending ramp, finding himself deep underground. The entire estate was a renovated Sriphan ruin, much like a Rocinthan well. Indeed, the Sriphans were of the same genetic stock as the Rocinthans. These extinct beings had even attempted to settle Tartarus, forging a new biological construct designed to survive on the immense fifth world. A few descendants of Tartaran colonists were all that remained of that once-enterprising race.

He softly drew back the curtain to his mother's salon. Her back to him, Danna sat working on her tapestry. The needle hummed softly as she set the figures in a variety of postures—moving them, freezing them, moving them again—until she found a grouping that satisfied her. Silently, Deles watched her work.

"Thank you for coming so quickly," she said, wielding the needle efficiently as she spoke.

"How did you know it was me?" he asked.

"Everyone has a little of the Gift," Danna replied, leaving her work as she stood and walked to her full-length mirror. "The difference between the Receptors and the rest of us is merely a matter of degree and control, not of kind. But even a Receptor does not always know why he does something. It took Acrios years to find us . . . and yet he did find us."

"If he comes here, I'll kill him," Deles said. There was no emotion in his tone. It was simply a statement of fact.

"He will not come here, Deles. You will have to go to him." She tapped the needle against her palm.

"Perhaps." Deles watched her as she looked away from her reflection and studied the nafs frolicking in her tapestry. Clearing his throat, he said, "You have heard about Verra?"

"Yes." Danna set her needle down on a chest.

"Mother, why did she go to Tartarus?"

"An ancient monograph, recently unearthed, mentioned some Rocinthan artifacts there. With her boundless curiosity, Verra had to seek them out." Danna did not seem to be speaking to Deles. She stared into the middle distance as if she saw something there besides wall and tapestry. She did this often these days, and Deles found it unsettling. At last he spoke to break the silence.

"Do you need anything?" he asked.

She shook her head slowly, not so much as a reply but as if she were waking from a dream.

"Last night Ploydekt came here," she said, turning again to the mirror. The master's cosmeticians had long since restored her original appearance. Though her blonde hair was now threaded with gray, she was still very beautiful. She looked directly into her son's eyes, through his reflection in the mirror. "He was very insistent," she said.

Deles clenched his jaw.

"I don't want you to say anything to him," Danna said. "You must remember that it has been difficult for him since Mella became an Other."

"That gives him no right to victimize you."

"His rights are unlimited on this estate. You must give him no excuse to harm you, my son."

"If he is angry with you, why should he want to harm me?"

Danna sighed. "You know so little of human vanity, Deles. Perhaps it's because Bilyf is your tutor. In any case, you ought to know by now that a man like Ploydekt cannot face rejection. He must have someone to blame, and he has taken a dislike to you."

Deles remembered the concubines he had trysted with. Did Ploydekt know? It didn't matter. He didn't want to upset his mother by saying so, but he would take only so much of Ploydekt's badgering . . . no matter what the consequences.

"We will go to the solstitial feast as we do every year, Deles," said Danna. "If the master speaks to you, answer him with civility. Remember that he has treated us as if we were part of his own family."

"We *are* members of his half-brother's family."

"Nevertheless, we were nothing to Ploydekt when we came here. You must promise me that you'll try to forget the rancor of recent days, and remember the master's generosity."

"I'll try." How well she knew that he wanted to defy Ploydekt. Perhaps she had inherited more than a little of the Gift.

"What of Verra?" he asked.

"She must be an Other by now. There is nothing we can do."

"She could still be alive."

"As yet, Bilyf has had no vision concerning her destiny."

"That doesn't prove she's dead." Deles went to the curtain, bunching the cloth in his brown hand.

"Does your Gift tell you that she's still alive?" Danna asked.

Deles grew uneasy when she spoke of such things. "I have no Gift, mother," he said. "I see nothing beyond what is happening on this estate. I can't ignore Ploydekt's intrusions into your life any longer." He turned and left the room.

Danna watched the swishing curtain, fearing that her son's dramatic exit was not the end of this. Why couldn't she make him understand that he should overlook temporary difficulties and prepare himself for his confrontation with Acrios? The time for the old monster was almost at hand.

She picked up the needle and fingered it. The tapestry had become her avocation, much as the crystal sculptures had been back home. But the crystals did not flourish on Sripha, just as Danna did not get on well on this barbarous world. Better Sripha than Tartarus, though. Poor Verra, dead on that hellish planet... while Acrios went on living. It was *his* fault she had gone there... the life of everyone he touched turned ultimately tragic... poor Verra.

Danna would soon see to it that the Prime Mystagogue too was avenged... very soon.

Before he emerged from the west portal, Deles heard shouts and raucous laughter coming from the surface. Running the last few meters underground, he blinked as he came up into the harsh daylight. As his eyes adjusted to the glare, he caught sight of the object of all the merriment.

A force field held a huge volume of water in a blue-green, amorphous blob. Within swam an amphibious trun, a phenotype bred by its Nauriian ancestors to survive in the dark waters of Sripha. When humankind had first come to this world, millennia of interspecies warfare had resulted. The struggle had retarded the growth of human civilization here, while virtually destroying the trun society. And yet the amphibious creatures still populated hidden waters. The murky Sriphan lakes were theirs.

"He's a big one," a man shouted. In blue, glimmering shadow, the hooting spectators gathered around the slowly drifting, aqueous cage.

Hating them, Deles thought of Bilyf.

The contained liquid's parameters were stretched and narrowed by pressor beams, in order to maneuver it between the trees. The crowd stepped back, surrounding Deles. Unable to evade them, he was jostled until he found himself very close to the floating water. Its proximity was disconcerting, and he looked up at the captive trun. The plated lids of its strangely beautiful green eyes were opened wide, and the creature stared plaintively at him, as if it understood that he alone was an unwilling participant in its humiliation. Startled, he turned away.

When he had broken free of the jeering crowd, he looked back. The trun had swum to the far side of its watery prison, waving webbed claws at its tormentors. He watched it until the entire quavering mass drifted behind a stone wall. He did not move until the noises of the crowd had faded and were gone.

Chapter Eleven

Ploydektum's Secrets

In his cavernous but well-appointed rooms, Dictys sat at a desk compiling a list of all those who would attend the solstitial feast. That annual hedonistic revelry would mark the most important day of the year, as always, and as always Ploydekt would entertain as lavishly as possible, and the estate would ring with laughter and song for days. None too soon, the way his brother was moping about. The feast would take Ploydekt's mind off whatever was troubling him, if the prefatory hunt did not.

Dictys had let it be known that the master's preferred gift would be a hunting garom from each of his guests. It was time to infuse the stock with new blood.

He checked off names with a stylus, intending to invite only the most powerful people on Sripha. They would suffer Ploydekt's boorishness for the sake of the feast. As an extra touch this year, he would dispatch robots to invite the guests ... not that Dictys himself approved of such ostentation, of course, but Ploydekt would like the idea.

He carefully set the stylus in its cradle. Ordinarily, he was able to lose himself in such tasks, but today something was troubling him. The boy Deles, like a son to him, was at loggerheads with his half-brother. No good could come of it, especially for Deles. Instead of trying to mend the rift between himself and the master, the boy exacerbated it. Deles was still a boy, but Ploydekt wouldn't permit that to dissuade him from exercising his vile temper. If only Deles were not so headstrong. If only he would listen to those who knew more than he. But of late only the opinions of Bilyf seemed to matter to him. Admittedly, the Mennon was not without wisdom, but there were some things he couldn't teach a human youth. Quite a few things ...

It was up to Dictys to make sure that any problems would be minimal by the night of the feast. Surely, as the time grew near, the master's annoyance with Deles would lessen.

The boy would hardly be noticed.

Ploydekt lay on the cushioned webbing, an imagemaker draped over his face. His retinas perceived exotic visions, hypnotically powerful light patterns that were the result of shrewd analysis by its manufacturers, designed to provide maximum cortical effect. It was a plaything from some distant world, but made for humans. Unfortunately, not even the narcotic delights the imagemaker provided could assuage his foul temper now. He tore the flexible mask from his face, blinking in the subdued light of the master bedroom. Here he was, at the very core of the great estate's subsurface level, just under the banquet hall—Ploydektum radiating about him like the spokes of a gigantic wheel, a wheel that turned at his command, for he was at the hub, its heart—and that great heart was in pain.

The cause of his pain must be removed.

Slapping a buttock with his pudgy hand, Ploydekt roused the sleeping boy to his right. Simultaneously, he forced his short fingers into the yielding flesh of the lissome girl on his left.

A moan was followed by a sleepy grunt of acquiescence. As he fondled the girl's soft breast, the boy's blond head rose up in his face, reminding him of Danna's snot-nosed brat. First the little puke had rejected his every advance, pretending to be unaware of Ploydekt's intent, and then he had turned Danna away from him. Deles refused to join the hunt, and he was always in the company of that revolting alien. And now this. The little bastard—and both mother and son so proud that there was no father! The high and mighty Rocinthan exiles. Ploydekt laughed, the flesh quaking on his small frame. He would have his way yet.

He continued laughing as he rolled the boy over and parted his slender thighs, preparing to force his tumescent penis into the tender young anus.

. . . falling

      drifting

            swimming

                  in time . . .

              . . . the eggsharer

          is

    consumed

by the . . .

...love of the oviparous mother...a love tempered with wisdom and pragmatism (though education was the primary function of the males, not the mother, never could Bilyf say that he had not learned more from her than from anyone). She had been, was, is, good, of the swamp...a Mennon. Aided by the knowledge sharers she made the eggsac with the flesh of her body...she builds it even now, just as even now the function of the males is carried on as they dream of this strange world of the alien, *human* now...the now that only seems to be...the now whose shadow lasts forever....

Bilyf was the male, and he educated the young master Deles as best he could. But there was much that stood in his way. What was it that led Deles through the continuum like a needle pulling threads through the twisted patterns of a tapestry?

The truth unravels slowly. Slowly. Just as Bilyf left the eggsac to lead a life of servitude on Rocinth, just as he abruptly abandoned a lifetime of servitude to Acrios to go with Danna and Deles, so Deles begins his unwilling journey...a journey that will ultimately carry him beyond Bilyf's sight....

...there   is
a   blue
fire
....

...and the baked surface of a dream world...far, far away ...the throb of energy...and here is purpose.... But it is all so very distant...so maddeningly elusive....

He must come much closer to it before he grasps its terrible essence...for he cannot travel beyond it and look back to see what it is....

...*being*...

...*always*...

life/death
death/life
life—
—death
...is...
...am...
...one is...
I am...
one will be...
I am...

...serving a greater purpose than even the knowledge sharers can know on this cracked and blistered world of
the
blue
sun

—the blue sun—

the

blue

sun . . .

. . . Parnassus . . .

. . . place of birth

death . . .

. . . Home.

Chapter Twelve

The Hunter's Prey

From the top of the hill the hunters were bright swatches of color on the backs of their swiftly moving garoms. The hum of discipline rods murmured through the still morning air as they were applied to the animals' flanks, punctuated by the shouts of the men, the click of clawed feet on the hard ground, and the flicking of the reins. Rising from the trail were clouds of dust, lending the scene a hazy overlay.

When the hunting party was out of sight and the dust had settled, Deles stood staring after them. Incrementally, the sounds of nature returned: the chirping of birds, the twittering of insects. And yet behind these tiny animal noises the stillness was ominous.

He turned toward Ploydektum. As he began to walk, he remembered that the garoms were all gifts from those attending the feast. Ploydekt had led the hunters, mounted on a magnificent white beast. Dictys had suggested that Deles present the master with a garom too, to appease him. Like the others, he could have reined in his mount, deferentially permitting Ploydekt to take the lead. Deles would rather have died.

Down the side of the hill he abruptly ran, hoping to diminish his confusion through the exertion of his body.

As the hunters returned to Ploydektum, there were a host of revelers out to meet them. A dozen drone-clones labored under the weight of a thick pole bearing the slain chakta. Its eyes stared sightlessly back at the crowd. Ploydekt could have used pressor beams to bring the animals in, but he preferred this triumphantly atavistic entrance.

Deles watched the hunters with Dictys, from the balcony of his cousin's spacious quarters. Depressed, Deles turned away from the window and looked at a whirling display of colored light particles, an art object created by Dictys.

"It is astonishing how swiftly Man can regress, given the opportunity," Dictys said. "By remaking his environment—or should I say environments?—he has succeeded only in turning back his intellectual and spiritual state to the point of barbarism."

Deles looked up from the dancing color motes. "When you speak like that," he said, "I am reminded of Verra . . . or at least what my mother has told me about her."

"You flatter me, Deles," said Dictys. "Verra's mind was perhaps the most stimulating I've ever had the pleasure of knowing. Though much of what she said was beyond my capacity, she was very patient with me. In fact, she was always kind to everyone . . . especially to your mother, though, when Danna was a little girl. She was an astonishing woman."

"Then you believe she's dead too."

Dictys didn't answer, but his uneasy expression was eloquent as he turned back to the window. Over his shoulder, Deles saw the hunters as they dismounted. Clones attended to the animals and the noisy crowds dispersed, until at last only a few drunken stragglers remained in the courtyard below, basking in the orange sunset or lying with their lovers beneath the columnar trees.

The silence soothed Deles now. He didn't want to argue with Dictys, only to enjoy his cousin's company in the time left to him before Ploydekt struck out at him.

"What were you saying about Man's development?" he asked.

"I was saying that, like the universe, Man has gone as far as he ever can. Eons ago, he gained complete control over his environment . . . and has changed but little since then."

"What about the Others? Did they exist before Man took control of his environment?"

"If they did, they existed only in some other dimension."

"Then Otherness is not the natural order?"

"No, because it is an anthroform's duty to go on living, no matter what."

"Even if life is nothing but pain?"

"Sometimes it seems that way, but life is cyclical. Would you trade the joys you have known, Deles? Without suffering for contrast, you would not recognize them as joys."

Deles thought this over, watching the kinetic light sculpture. He tired of it, passing his hand over it to make the color motes fade into nothingness.

"Deles, you must go away," Dictys said in a low tone. "No one can help you if you stay here."

"Not even *you*, cousin?" said Deles. "Is that what you're saying?"

"I've never had much influence with my brother . . . and in a case like this . . ."

Deles wondered if Dictys would even try to help. Hypotheses were all very well, but Dictys had felt Ploydekt's wrath in the past, and feared it more than he feared impugning his own integrity. Even so, Deles knew that his cousin loved him, and that he was pained by this turn of events.

"You will still enter the games tomorrow, won't you, Deles?"

"Only the games, I hope, and not the hunt."

"The hunt?" Dictys gestured toward the window. "The hunt is over."

"Is it?"

Dictys bowed his head in shame and sorrow.

Color and motion. Carnival sounds. The distant sun's light faded into evening through the dusty thunder of the garom races, the quicksilver grace of the acrobats, and finally the ritualistic contests from Terra's distant past: foot races, long and short; the decathlon, grueling test of endurance; the archery match; the javelin throw—and the dikoit.

Deles waited his turn. Just before he stepped up to the circle, he looked around to see Ploydekt watching from atop his huge, white hunting garom. In the master's hand was a goblet, spilling over with red wine.

Ignoring him, Deles took his place inside the circle. He concentrated, as Bilyf had taught him to do in any endeavor, until he felt himself sufficiently poised and relaxed. He spun and released. As the dikoit left his hand, he felt that it was a good throw... but not his best. Robots recorded the intricate series of figures his dikoit's flight described, but he knew that his throw would not win. There was too much on his mind today.

The prize for the dikoit throw went to Zetik, a powerfully built young man from Baregtum. His master, Baregt, slapped his beefy shoulder with drunken pride. It was not often that Ploydekt was beaten on his own turf.

Only a few games remained before dark, which marked the time for the feast to begin. Ploydekt watched, a brooding figure mounted on his garom. When he became too drunk to sit up in his elaborate saddle, a palanquin was summoned. Six clones carried him about for the duration of the games.

When the stars came out, all the guests assembled in the great hall as music filled the crisp air. The roof had been drawn back so that all was bathed in moonlight.

Ploydekt sat at the head of the largest table, an absurd, hiccoughing figure, a blemish on the alien splendor of the estate. To his right sat Dictys, smug yet clearly uncomfortable among the throng of revelers. To his left were two of his current lovers, a boy and a girl. Frequently the master turned and spoke to one

of them, propping his flabby body against the table as he offered comments intended to amuse his guests. His voice alone
was amplified, and the diners laughed dutifully at his vulgar
jokes.

Deles sat next to his mother at a separate table on the far
side of the banquet hall. Seated with them were participants of
the dikoit throw, including Zetik. Bilyf, as always, had declined
the invitation to join them. Had he come, the special foods that
sustained him would have been served to him, of course, but the
menu wasn't the reason he didn't attend. Drunken feasts were
foreign to Mennon sensibilities. Danna explained this to the dikoit throwers.

"You see, it's impossible for a Mennon to—"

Her explanation was cut short by Ploydekt's strident voice.
"There is one last item of entertainment to be savored while we
eat and drink," he said. "I'm sure you'll all enjoy it."

He clapped his hands.

For a moment nothing happened, and the crowd began to
murmur. Then a dark, rippling edge appeared high above Ploydekt, at the summit of the wall behind him, some five meters
over his head. The amorphous shape rose higher. Many in the
crowd gasped as a moon shone through it in a wavering, luminous oblong.

They applauded as they saw the clawed figure swimming in
it: the trun. Slowly the watery cage floated up until it was suspended over the banqueters. They craned their necks to look at
it, laughing and shouting uproariously.

Ploydekt silenced them with a wave of his right hand.

In the ensuing hush could be heard a low hum; then another
hum, higher in pitch, harmonizing; then another, and another.
Soon the air was filled with the sound. A figure riding a graviton
platform rose up beside the mass of water, like a floating statue,
pedestal and all. He was a sentry-clone armed with a burner—a
powerful, lightweight weapon. Another clone rose up on the
opposite side. A few seconds later there were dozens of them,
weaving back and forth in front of the irritated trun. It angrily
waved its claws at them. Deles pitied it, even though he knew
there were still places on Sripha where human sacrifices were
made to its kin. This was no less barbaric.

"A protective field over the banquet hall is now energized,"
Ploydekt said, "and the field containing the trun is . . . no
more!"

A huge volume of water rushed down at them, and the spectators involuntarily cried out. But the deluge was arrested by a
force shield, a transparent canopy protecting them as violet
sparks poured down the walls of the banquet hall.

The trun was pitched onto the foaming field, writhing as its hide was burned by raw energy. Its gills expanded and contracted desperately, for its metabolism hadn't enough time to adjust aerobically during its swift fall. It opened its powerful jaws to suck in oxygen. Through an awkward combination of crawling and rolling, it attempted to make its way to the nearest wall.

As soon as it made progress, one of the clones fired his burner to head it off. The trun then made its trembling way in another direction, meeting more fiery resistance from another clone. Now its scaly head glanced furtively about, searching for some avenue of escape. But as soon as it neared the limits of the protective field on any side, a volley sent it back to the center. Its tormentors swooped and soared, buzzing the trun to the delight of their audience.

One of them came too close. The trun leaped at him, upending his graviton platform. Before the others could get off another shot at the trun, it throttled him and threw him headlong off the force field. His body fell behind a wall, a lifeless husk.

Angered, the clones renewed their attack. Practicing their marksmanship, they burned off the trun's appendages a little at a time. Soon the suffering amphibian began to gasp, not only from pain, but from being out of the water too long.

Sickened by the clone's death, the wheezing trun, the sadistic crowd, Deles rose. Danna tried to stop him, clutching his arm, still clinging to the notion that he should do nothing to offend the master. Forcing himself to sit back down for her sake, Deles saw that the trun's movements were becoming feeble. It was dying. He didn't want to watch, feeling like an intruder at life's final and most intimate scene, but he did. The trun's flailings were reduced to shudders. Then even its spasms ceased.

The crowd applauded heartily as the clones floated out of sight, four of them carrying the armored corpse with them. But it was some time before conversation resumed at Deles's table, and even then it was extremely subdued.

"I'm glad Bilyf didn't see that," Danna said at last.

Though he was shaken, Deles did his best to entertain the dikoit throwers. Since none of them felt like eating, they fell into a halfhearted discussion about the dikoit.

"Our dikoit throwers are amusing only one another," Ploydekt's voice boomed. "Perhaps they will share their secrets with us."

There was a short silence, followed by a rustling as the crowd turned to stare at Deles's table. Embarrassed, Zetik and the others stared into the cold food on their plates.

"We have no secrets, unlike some of Ploydektum's inhabi-

tants. And, as for amusement, isn't that the purpose of the solstitial feast?" Deles said, annoyed. "I have heard a great deal of
laughter."

"We have been amused by the trun." Ploydekt sat forward
until his thick waist overlapped the table. "And I was very
amused by the outcome of the dikoit throw."

Snickers came from the crowd.

"It was also quite amusing," Deles said, not to be outdone,
"to see the master attempt to remain on his mount."

A startled murmur arose from the guests.

Reddening, Ploydekt glared across the banquet hall. His
bloodshot eyes spoke his hatred more eloquently than his thick
tongue ever could. When he finally did speak, his voice was
surprisingly calm. "Our young Rocinthan shows great courage
by his answer," he said. "Don't you agree, my friends?"

Approbation was muttered here and there, but only by those
who did not really know the master.

"Excellent!" Ploydekt clapped his hands. "Then you will also
approve of the task I have selected for him . . . a very special
task."

"State your purpose, Ploydekt!" Deles started out of his
chair, but was again restrained by his mother's hand.

"Deles . . ." She was pleading with him. He sat down.

The banquet hall was still.

Ploydekt leaned forward, smiling, his manner oily.

"Our dear friend, Verra, has not returned from Tartarus, as
you all know. Our hearts are heavy as we think of her marooned
there, vainly awaiting succor." He paused dramatically, swaying
a little with the wine.

"No," Danna whispered.

"Deles, you are a brave fellow," Ploydekt said as if he had
just thought of it. "You and the Mennon Bilyf will mount an
expedition in search of her. I am confident that *you* can find
her."

"No!" This time Danna cried out.

"What's wrong, Danna, aren't you feeling well?" Ploydekt
turned to two immobile clones. "Please assist the lady to her
rooms."

They sprang into action, crossing the floor and taking
Danna's arms in their big hands. Others surrounded the table,
armed with burners. Deles could do nothing.

Danna rose. Casting one last disdainful glance at Ploydekt,
she allowed herself to be ushered out of the banquet hall.

"We cannot afford to waste another moment if we wish to
see Verra alive again," Ploydekt said with mock earnestness.
"Your ship will leave for Tartarus tonight."

A murmur of comprehension came from the crowd.

"If you harm my mother . . ." Deles said, nearly choking with rage.

"*Harm* her?" Ploydekt lifted his eyebrows. "I'm only interested in her well-being, Deles, and you should know that. I'll see that she's taken care of . . . while you're away."

Deles tried to speak, but he couldn't work any moisture into his throat to form words. He'd never dreamt that Ploydekt would go this far. This was tantamount to murder.

"You will be taken to the ship now," Ploydekt said. "The Mennon is already there waiting for you."

Deles pushed back his chair and stood. "I'll be back," he said.

Ploydekt smiled. Next to him, Dictys sat, livid and shriveling under Deles's gaze. He had anticipated exile, even lifelong banishment, but nothing like this.

"Did you hear me?" Deles shouted. "I said *I'll be back!*"

One of the sentries grabbed his elbow roughly. Without further protest, Deles walked with the guards out of the banquet hall. They left Ploydektum's dark walls behind them as they climbed the nearest hill, a silver curve in the moonlight.

But why Bilyf? Did Ploydekt believe that Danna's loved ones were all that kept her from him? Had he so little knowledge of the human heart that he didn't know he could never possess her? How could he be such a fool, Deles wondered as he heard the first low hum of the approaching graviton ship.

A glowing horizontal hourglass, the graviton ship droned softly at the hillcrest. It was one of the finest of the few reliable Sriphan spacecraft—a Rocinthan import, one of Ploydekt's most valuable possessions. No expense had been spared to kill Deles in an acceptable fashion; Deles had underrated his own importance.

The airlock hatch swung open, and Deles clambered inside. With armed guards behind him, he hadn't much choice. He could not fight back, but at least he could take a certain grim satisfaction in knowing that his mother would never give in to Ploydekt's demands. Any debt she owed that foul martinet was cancelled once and for all. All Ploydekt had coming to him now was death.

With a hollow clank the hatch closed behind him. The inner airlock hatch opened, revealing Bilyf and two sentry-clones standing on either side of him, as if placed there by an artist to complement his ungainly form. They got out of the ship, jostling him in the airlock, and waited for Deles to board.

"Bilyf," Deles said as the airlock closed behind him, "I'm sorry."

"One must consider—not sorrow—but survival."

"Yes." Deles crawled up into the body of the ship and put his arm around Bilyf. "We'll find a way to get back."

"One—shall see."

"Then you don't know what's going to happen to us."

"One sees—only—" A vibration interrupted Bilyf, and there followed the unmistakable sensation of lift-off. They were bound for Tartarus.

"One sees—that the ship is sturdy—and its memory intact," Bilyf said as they escaped Sripha's gravity well.

"Then we really are being sent to Tartarus? It won't explode in space."

"One sees that—both surmises—are correct."

"Very sporting of Ploydekt," Deles said. "I suppose that he didn't want to be seen as a murderer by his aristocratic friends."

"One—believes so."

"So he sent us on a mercy mission, looking for Verra," Deles concluded bitterly, watching the visual display. Sripha was a shrinking green ball floating in the cabin, a pall of darkness surrounding it. Deles half expected some bright auroral torrent to appear from nowhere—the solar wind, carrying them miraculously to safety once Bilyf tampered with the ship's memory.

But there was nothing, only the black depths of space studded with gleaming stars, a million suns winking so far away.

Dictys sat in the roof garden, overlooking the mud-colored, superficial walls erected over the remains of the original Rocinthan burrowings. The sun was setting, its slanted rays piercing the forest peaks, dappling the softly rounded hillsides with orange. It would be dark soon, and the perfume of the flowers seemed overpowering. Guilt consumed him for not helping Deles. He had been brooding about his cowardice—intellectual and moral cowardice, nothing less. He had been exiled once, and he had feared another such punishment if he took Deles's side. But exile would have been preferable to what he was going through now. He could have withstood another extended stay on Rocinth, and he might have saved the lives of Deles and Bilyf. How like Ploydekt to choose the same method by which Acrios had rid himself of the young boy Deles . . . except that Acrios's error would not be duplicated, for Ploydekt had no compunctions about killing those who stood in his way.

Dictys wept for the boy, the Mennon, and himself—particularly himself.

"Why did you leave my grandfather's service to come with me and Mother that night on Rocinth, Bilyf?" Deles asked.

"The needs of—little Danna and Deles—were greater than —Acrios's—and so one was—compelled."

"But then, why were you so content to be my grandfather's servant for all those years?"

"There is—virtue in servitude," Bilyf replied. "One learns from it—the refinement of humility."

Deles mulled this over, drifting through the bottleneck opening to the opposing compartment. "What good is humility," he called over his shoulder, "in a universe filled with creatures like Ploydekt and Acrios? They devour those who are not strong."

Without turning away from the cannibalized mnemonic cylinder he was examining, Bilyf asked, "Is there no strength—in humility?"

"Maybe." Deles had heard all about the virtues of humility many times before. "But it's hard for me to accept the Mennon way at this time."

"Time—the Now That Seems to Be."

"It just doesn't seem to be, Bilyf, it *is*." Deles thrust out his hand. "We're really here, at this moment. If we weren't, we'd have nothing to worry about."

Bilyf's digits were white rivulets running over the cylinder's components. He said nothing.

"Well?"

"What does—Deles wish to know?"

"Explain what you mean by 'the Now That Seems to Be,'" Deles said. "I've never really understood it."

"One sees the truth—as one sees the truth," Bilyf said, still working on the dead husk of machinery.

"Do you mean that there's as much truth in human philosophy as in your own?"

"One—believes so."

"Then why do you prefer the Mennon philosophy?"

"One functions best—in the discipline—that shapes one."

"I see." Deles relished this opportunity to lose himself in abstract thinking. Dreamdiscs, with their ephemeral images, were the only entertainment they had, and he had quickly grown tired of having them fastened to his scalp. He found Bilyf's alien thought patterns infinitely more stimulating. "Then you recommend whatever system of thought works best."

"One believes—it is pragmatic."

"Pragmatic? What about the spiritual side of all this?"

"The pragmatic—and the spiritual," Bilyf said as he lifted the cylinder, "—are not exclusive."

Deles floated back to help him slide the cylinder into its compartment. "I still don't understand."

"One admits that—it is complex."

Deles shrugged. The albedo of Tartarus was a gleaming circle in the lightless cosmos. He wondered how these philosophic ruminations of Bilyf's might help them when they set down there.

As he lay in the reception pool, Acrios was taken with a spasm that shook him to his marrow. At first he thought it was only the searcher, crawling through a pain center in his brain. He deserved this suffering for coming here to play at being Receptor again, something he had found no comfort in. Another spasm came, and he knew that it didn't originate inside him. He flailed his limbs, his eyes rolling wildly as he spattered crimson fluid on the floor and mosaics. He had come to bathe in the desensitizing fluid to free himself from pain, but he struggled now to free himself from an agony more unbearable than any he had suffered in all the millennia he had lived. Pulling himself out of the pool, he collapsed, his angular form lying supine on the tiles.

"He lives..." Acrios whispered between racking breaths. "He lives..."

Slowly his respiration resumed a more regular rhythm, and the too rapid beating of his heart stabilized. Fluid ran down his back and gathered in sanguinary puddles on the floor. At last he collected enough strength to prop himself up on one elbow.

Deles was alive—he was certain of it. He looked up at the stars, only to see them obscured by rushing clouds. The wind began to blow, chilling his wet, naked body.

Chapter Thirteen

Tartarus

They came down from space into the swirling clouds of Tartarus, the landscape dun through the vapors as the ship lit on the surface. Immense slabs of wet rock jutted out on one side, the result of recent geological activity, and a steaming, brackish sea was almost lost in the churning gases on the other. Lightning sporadically illuminated the swift movements of the only immediately apparent animal life—crawling, multi-legged creatures the length of a human arm. Plant life was limited to a few clumps of pale violet stalks and dripping, spotted fungi.

The atmosphere was generally reducing, but there were many pockets of oxidation, held by inversion in the valleys where steam spewed forth from fumaroles. The free-floating oxygen, derived from plants and water vapor, often ignited explosively when it met with methane, the least bit of friction creating an inferno.

The conventional view of Tartarus held that the autochthonous Rocinthan-Sriphan species had bred colonists who planted vegetation with the intention of converting Tartarus's atmosphere from reducing to oxidizing. The attempt had been only partly successful, and air breathers couldn't live here without oxygen recycling generators. Because of the planet's huge mass, a graviton shield was also needed. These tiny devices Deles fastened behind his ear and under Bilyf's oral folds. Then he removed a box of provisions from an overhead panel.

As he rummaged through the box, Deles wasn't surprised to find that there were no burners in it. Of course, they might be better off without them. If there was any oxygen floating in the path of a burner's beam, it would immolate the one who fired the weapon, flames leaping into the generated field enveloping his body.

"Are you ready, Bilyf?" he said.

"One—believes so." Bilyf had taken no rest during the journey to Tartarus. Nor had he used a dreamdisc, though it probably would not have helped him anyway. Dreamdiscs were for

114

humans, not Mennons. When he had to go without rest, Bilyf somehow drained the toxins from his cerebrum through an act of will.

"Well, then . . ." The inner hatch opened. Deles entered the airlock first, pressing the generator behind his ear with his index finger and feeling a static tingle on the fine hairs of his arms, the cool breath of oxygen. He stood still in the dark chamber as Bilyf joined him. The inner hatch closed behind them as Bilyf activated his generator. He pushed the provisions box, which floated on a cushion of antigravitons in front of him.

The outside hatch swung open with a hiss.

Misty gases swirled in, breaking on the graviton shield just a few centimeters from Deles's flesh. Bathed in his cocoon of oxygen, he was separated from asphyxiation by less than the width of his hand. He stepped out into the world of Tartarus.

As Bilyf joined him in front of the ship, all was still but the steady drip of foamy fungus falling from a finger of glistening rock. Deles caught a glimpse of crawling things scuttling off as the airlock hatch closed. Some of these timorous creatures might have been the descendants of Rocinthans.

They began to walk, their feet forced down cruelly by the planet's huge mass, even with their graviton shields fighting it. Their heavy heels sometimes met the resistance of air pockets.

"It's impossible to walk with these generators," Deles complained.

"One would not—care to walk—on Tartarus—without them," said Bilyf.

Mollified, Deles shut up and made his way through the vapors as best he could. Where to look for one woman and her companions on a world so large and inhospitable? For he fully intended to find Verra, if possible. With her help, there was a better chance of getting off Tartarus . . . and if her ship's memory was intact, Bilyf could replace their ship's locked memory with it, and their return to Sripha would be assured. The chances were not good, however.

Cliffs of porous stone rose on either side of them as they gradually gained some poise and economy of movement. A chasm—a great gash in the skin of the planet—confronted them. Down they went, coming to a series of slabs laid one on top of another by some great upheaval millions of years in the past. These they laboriously climbed, heading straight up toward the erratically breaking clouds.

When they reached the summit, they saw through the haze enormous cracks where monolithic shards had fallen after being pushed up through the crust. These fissures could serve as rough trails; they would be relatively easy to walk through.

They found the downhill march a relief, almost a pleasure, after the agonizing climb up the other side. Soon they were in the nearest fissure, making reasonable progress. Deles found it irritating that he could see no more than a few meters ahead, even under the best conditions. Furthermore, the almost total silence added to the sense of isolation as they sweated in their protective oxygen wombs. It was maddening to know that death literally enveloped them, that this entire world was hostile, waiting like a stalking fogbeast for just one minor malfunction . . . just one mistake.

Deeper and deeper into the fissure they went, their oxygen shimmering around them in ghostly outlines against the murky gases. The effect gradually vanished as they became lost in shadows, the walls of the fissure now rising thirty feet on either side. Stalks grew from fungoid puddles, some as tall as trees, creepers, and vines connecting them.

Deles wasn't certain just when it occurred to him that they were being followed. He noticed a peripheral movement, so slight he couldn't be sure he really saw it. At first he didn't want to worry Bilyf needlessly, and didn't mention it. It was probably nothing, he thought, and yet the ghostly presence became ever more obvious. Blue apparitions intruded on the fringes of darkness, blending with wisps of vapor. They shimmered, glowing like cerulean methane, intent on some unknown and unknowable purpose. When he tried to look directly at them, however, there was nothing.

The stalks grew ever more densely, becoming a kind of forest, groaning as they sawed back and forth, moved by the wind. Lightning flickered, casting quicksilver rays through the thick, misty vegetation. Deles tried to convince himself that it was this that had created the illusion of ghostly moving figures. The blue tint could have been a result of the gases. It didn't seem likely, but at least it was an explanation. But where did this wind come from? The forest surrounded them for several miles all around now. How could the wind penetrate these thousands of massive stalks? Was this normal meteorological activity here?

"Bilyf," he said, "do you see . . . ?"

There. There it was again. But when he turned to face it, there was nothing.

"What can it be?" he whispered.

"Others." This time Bilyf replied without hesitation.

"Others. But I thought they never show themselves. What are they doing here?"

"One sees—only that—they are here."

Lightning flashed, as if to punctuate Bilyf's comment. Simultaneously, the heavy plants snapped like whips in the powerful wind, glowing blue patches appearing among them.

"What do they want?"

"One cannot as yet—be certain of—their purpose."

From between the boles of huge plants, blue stripes spiraled through the churning gases. These flitted about Deles and Bilyf, stroboscopic ghosts in the alien forest. Abruptly, one halted a meter in front of them, assuming a vaguely humanoid shape. Then it began to float backwards, beckoning for them to follow. Deles noticed that its companions were all gone now, as it stretched a glowing appendage toward him. He stumbled after it until it stopped. Deles hesitated. He was close enough to touch it, but before he gathered the courage to do so, the Other fragmented, pieces of it vanishing and reappearing, smaller and smaller. Soon there was nothing left of it but a few disconnected blue motes. Then even these were gone.

The wind ceased its howling.

Trembling hand outstretched, Deles stood rooted to the spot as the lightning continued to flicker.

"Did you see?" he murmured. "Bilyf, did you see . . . ?"

"One has—seen," replied Bilyf. "The Others—have indicated—that this direction—is desirable." He nodded toward the dark passage where the Other had last stood, between two towering stalks. They started out, moving with some difficulty through clustered, pale blue giants fringed with frilly growths. It seemed as if this strange forest had just sprung up around them as they walked. The going became more and more difficult, the stalks growing in ever denser clumps as the path became steadily steeper. Progress was made only by the most strenuous effort. Then a lightning bolt revealed a mist-enshrouded path descending through the giant stalks like a corridor.

"This way," Deles said. Bilyf protested that it was not the way the Other had indicated, but Deles insisted that they take the new route. They moved swiftly, for the path was virtually without impediment. But the mists became unusually thick as they made their way down the side of what surely must have been a mountain. So gradual had been their ascent that they hadn't noticed the elevation until now. The new path cut across the sloping land, so that they were nearly running downhill.

"One sees—that we must—slow our descent," Bilyf said.

"How?" Deles panted. The grade now seemed almost vertical, making it virtually impossible for them to stop moving, and the visibility was steadily worsening.

Above, lightning pierced the clouds, revealing that they were hurtling toward a deep chasm. They threw themselves onto the steep ground just as a bolt ignited the accumulated oxygen rising from the chasm. Flames shot miles into the air, furiously burning the atmospheric gases. At the edge of the sheer drop, stalks were starkly outlined against the awesome blaze.

Deles spoke, but his words were inaudible against the roar of the flames. He helped Bilyf up, and they started the painful climb back up the mountain, before the grumbling inferno behind them could catch them and invade their oxygen bubbles.

When they finally reached level ground, hours later, they found a small clearing. There they stopped to rest, nurse the bruises they had suffered at the chasm's brink, and eat. At least Deles ate. There were nutritional beads for Bilyf, but he consumed none of them. Deles knew that he should have followed Bilyf's example, stretching his food, but he buried his face in his hands and ate greedily. Two suspensor beds were furled inside the provisions box, as well as food, containers of water, and eating utensils. Ploydekt had given them as little help as possible.

"I don't know how long we can survive here," Deles said as he lay down, the distant roar of the fire in his ears. From Bilyf's silence, he knew that his friend must have had his own doubts, though Bilyf obviously preferred not to say so. He had, after all, not been asked a direct question.

When Deles awakened, the fire still raged. They were soon off again, traveling until the forest began to thin at last. Before long they came to its end—the lip of a mile-wide pit. There was a small pool of bubbling liquid at the pit's bottom, and its sloping sides were riddled with holes, which were apparently tunnels bored by the pit's inhabitants. In the dancing shadows cast by the fire, it was difficult to make out details.

"This must be what the Others wanted us to see," Deles said. "But what sort of things live down there?"

"Tartarans—descended from—Rocinthans."

A few meters below them, a creature as big around as Deles's leg crawled out of a tunnel mouth. It was long and wormlike, some twelve feet, a complex network of nerves and seemingly little else. As they watched, it unraveled parts of itself to serve as temporary limbs or palps.

Several others slid out of their holes, one of them coiling an appendage carefully around something round and white, approximately the size of a human hand.

"What is it holding?" Deles asked.

"One believes—that it is—a biological machine."

"Made by the ancient Rocinthans?"

"One—believes so."

The creatures were making their way toward the pool, following the one carrying the milky sphere. More of them squeezed out of the tunnels on the pit's sides and joined them.

As they gathered by the bubbling pool, the leader picked up the white orb, using two ersatz appendages, and held it high. It resembled a ball of yarn that had started to come unraveled.

All of the creatures touched, forming a single entity that wound around the pool several times. The leader extricated itself, passing the orb to the one behind it. Then it felt its way to the end of the spiral of living ganglia and attached itself there.

"They share it," Deles whispered, excited and yet fearful that he would disturb them. Dictys had told him about these creatures once, though he had said their existence might be more myth than fact. They combined into one living brain. But what was the white orb? He asked Bilyf.

"One sees—that it is a kind of—artificial sensorium."

Bearing the sensorium, the new leader eased into the bubbling liquid. It was now an extended tendril, projecting from the giant communal brain. As it submerged with the sensorium, the writhing mass of ganglia shuddered pleasurably en masse, though remaining untouched by the liquid. But when the leader partially emerged, the sensorium faced the edge of the pit, and the tribe disported itself no longer. The pit was completely still.

"It sees us," Deles said, noting that the tribe's squirming had ceased. "I'd better acknowledge them."

He started down the side of the pit, half walking and half stumbling, having miscalculated its steepness. The rest of the creature bathing the sensorium in the pool backed swiftly out of the bubbling liquid, as if it had been sucked back into the living mound.

The tribe suddenly heaved about and crawled swiftly toward Deles, clearly on the attack.

Chapter Fourteen

The Eye of Time

Horrified, Deles turned and scurried back up toward Bilyf on all fours. Clammy feelers clutched at his ankle. He had trouble making it until he felt Bilyf's digits wrap around his bicep. Pulled up to level ground, he turned to see that the tribe had halted.

"They tried to kill me!"

The creatures separated, crawling back and forth below Deles and Bilyf, as though challenging them to come near again.

"Bilyf, that sensorium," Deles said after catching his breath, "did you learn anything about it from your vision?"

"One sees—that this tribe fear their world—nearly as much —as do we."

"What does their fear have to do with the sensorium?"

"It is their only escape—from terror and misery."

Deles pondered this. No doubt he had reacted too strongly to the advance of the tribe. These creatures had no fangs, talons, prehensile digits, or even beaks to rend and tear. As he looked down upon them now, he saw that they were timid beings who felt threatened by the intrusion of an alien.

"When you say that it is an escape, do you mean that it is something more than a sensorium? That it's not just a dreamdisc or imagemaker for Rocinthans?"

"One sees that it is—like these devices—and much more— but beyond that—one cannot see."

"Can we communicate with them?"

"One believes so—but only outside their—territorial boundaries."

Deles smiled. "That means we have to find a way to draw them out of the pit—or make them welcome us into it."

He had an idea.

Bilyf had been gone for quite some time when he reappeared carrying the thin, hard membrane of a dead plant. On it he

scratched symbols, which stood out in pale contrast to the brin-
dled husk. He held it up before the curious white orb of the
tribe.

The creatures ignored it.

Bilyf then attached the membrane to a ropy vine, dangling it
into the pit. The creatures continued to ignore it. Groping
blindly with their ad hoc limbs, they slithered about their business. Only the possessor of the milky orb was still, transfixed by
the intruders at the rim of the pit. Occasionally its sightless fellows nudged it in their peregrinations. It remained rigid, however, staring at Bilyf and Deles, who retreated to their camp a
few meters back, where they maintained a vantage over the pit.

"I think I understand why they have so much nerve tissue on
the outside of their bodies," said Deles. "Since they have no
other senses, it's the only way they can get around."

"Without—the sensorium—this is so."

They ate, Bilyf engulfing a few tiny black beads in his oral
folds, Deles chewing on half a curd cake in an attempt to control his appetite. They were already running low on food.

"Bilyf," he said, "do you think we can find edible . . ."

The sensorium, grasped in three threadlike appendages, rose
over the edge of the pit. Slowly the tribe began to crawl up over
the rim, one linked to the other, until they formed a pulsing line
stretching into the forest. The entwined, living cable came close
enough to Deles that the crunching of dead vegetation was
clearly audible beneath its flowing weight.

"One sees—that they are foraging."

"And they can all see through that thing when they're
linked?" Deles asked.

"One believes so—" Bilyf replied, "—and more."

"More than just see? The entire sensory apparatus is enclosed in the orb, isn't it?"

"One—believes so."

"They don't seem concerned about us anymore," Deles observed.

"One believes that—the tribe considers us—no danger to
them—since we have not—as yet attempted to harm them."

"Good," Deles said, smiling, "very good."

Determined to make himself useful, Deles walked to the
edge of the forest to gather water in an empty container. Con-
densation ran down the dun stalks to form pools in large cavities
at their bases. By pressing the container to the bottoms of these
natural bowls, he was able to get a few grams of water from
each plant. When the container was nearly full, he carried it
back to camp, encumbered with its weight, and searched for a
portable heater to boil the water, finding it in a compartment

near the bottom of the provisions box. Removing it, he set it on the ground with the sphere resting on it. He sat down and waited for the water to boil, and then removed the container.

"It shouldn't be so difficult to communicate with them," he said as Bilyf joined him, "if we can make use of the sensorium."

"They have no desire—to communicate with us—or to share with us—the sensorium."

"Then we have to find a means to make them come around."

"The tribe is unlikely—to communicate willingly."

"Then they'll communicate unwillingly," Deles said, lying down. The vast fire was a distant rumble as he dozed. As he slipped into unconsciousness, he dreamed that it actually burned inside him, a flame that would lead him ultimately to survival . . . and to vengeance.

Time passed slowly. Even if the days had not been so lengthy, it would have been impossible, without a timepiece, to tell how long they had been on Tartarus, since the stars were never visible. There was faint sunlight, but even that was obscured by the fires reflecting off the clouds. As yet there had been no progress in the communication attempts. The only way they had found to affect the denizens of the pit was to set foot within it, the tribe's territorial perimeter.

"They're afraid," Deles said, stroking his thin growth of beard. "That's why they don't let outsiders near them, because they're afraid. Anyone would have run away from them, the way they turned on me." Deles tossed a stone into the pit. The present possessor of the orb shuddered at the impact, but the rest were oblivious.

Though Bilyf chose to say nothing, Deles went on talking, "It seems to me that they should be going out to forage for food soon."

They watched until the tribe's leader, swaying gracefully, suddenly laid the sensorium in a small depression on the sloping side of the pit. Content that the orb was safe in the niche, since a human arm could never have reached it, the creature groped its way to the nearest of its fellows. With a liquid, sucking sound they entwined, within moments joined by the remainder of the tribe.

"One sees—that they propagate."

"Where is that vine you were using as a rope?" Deles shouted. "Quickly!"

Bilyf fetched the vine. Winding one end around a short, stout stalk, and the other around his waist, Deles lowered himself down into the pit—he kicked his way over towards the niche where the sensorium was hidden. Calling to Bilyf to unwind a loop from around the stalk, he thrust with the strength of his calves. The coiling mass of nerve tissue had partially flopped over toward him, and for one harrowing moment he swung out from the slope directly above the tribe. Then, feet spread wide apart to brace himself, he landed flush over the niche.

"Unwind more rope," he called to Bilyf.

Bilyf slowly let out the line, his striated muscles bunching with the effort.

Deles's feet and shins disappeared into the niche. It would be a tight squeeze, but he had to make it.

"More rope!" he shouted, glancing over his shoulder to be certain that the tribe was busy. He was relieved to see that they were still at it. Even after they were through mating, it would take their leader some time to grope its way back to the niche. Bilyf could pull him up very quickly if need be.

"One more loop." He slid a few more inches inside, a small, ragged circle of smoky orange sky overhead. In the dim light he could just make out the sensorium between his feet. The aperture was too narrow for him to bend, so he squatted to pick it up. He felt the pressure of generating air against his back as his oxygen bubble was squeezed, and stone scraping against his skin.

He had it!

"Bilyf!" he called out. "Pull me up! I've got it!"

The orb was warm and oily in his hands, and it pulsed like the living thing that it was. He felt Bilyf tugging on the vine, and he scrabbled until he had worked his head and shoulders free of the niche. He pulled the rest of his body out and swung over the pit. He was able to make his way up the side with only a little help from Bilyf.

Out of breath, he stood on the edge of the pit with the slimy white orb in his hand, triumphant.

"Now they'll be a little more reasonable," he said, grinning.

"One does not see how—since they cannot communicate—without the sensorium."

"That's just it, Bilyf: they can't get along without it, and it's in our hands. We have them at a disadvantage." Deles could almost tell what his moralistic Mennon friend was thinking. That the sensorium was really of little use to them. That stealing it was cruel. That maturity had not yet taken hold of Deles's consciousness. That, in fact, this was an act of regression. But what difference did any of it make? It was just as Danna and Dictys had always told him—there were some things Mennons simply didn't understand, things their obscurantist philosophy couldn't account for. Action was needed now, not rumination. If

Deles didn't do something, they'd both die...become Others....

"Look." Deles saw that the tribe was pulling apart at last. As the individual creatures disengaged themselves from the massive pile of nerve tissue and organs, it became clear that something had formed at the core that had not been there before the mating. The last of the tribe slithered off to their tunnels, and Deles pointed out what he saw to Bilyf—a greasy, squirming lump near the pool.

"It is the result—of propagation."

"You mean that is a baby?" Deles laughed. As Bilyf had said, the people of the pit *had* propagated, but this was the end result, not the beginning. Here was the reason they had seen fit to go without the orb, in spite of the intruders lurking at the edge of the pit. Perhaps they feared harming it in their sexual frenzy.

"What are they doing now?" Deles asked as several of the creatures emerged, carrying gray-green plants. They crawled back to the quivering newborn and held the colorless fruits over it, squeezing with their whiplike appendages until thick juices dripped down onto the throbbing bundle of neural fibers.

Once the infant was fed, the creatures went about their business as if nothing had happened. One of them—Deles assumed it was the same one who had hidden the orb—returned to the niche after feeling over familiar ground for a few seconds. It unleashed a lengthy feeler, which snaked into the niche with assurance. After it had groped about for a while, it tore another appendage from itself and continued the search. Soon it had shoved half a dozen frenetic limbs into the chimneylike niche without success.

At last it withdrew them, lashing them onto its larger mass. For some time it lay perfectly still; then it slid across the pit, feeling its way, until it collided with one of its fellows. It entwined its appendages in the fibers of the other creature, which joined with another. Soon the entire tribe were a writhing mound, locked in a traumatic communication that informed them of the unthinkable—the sensorium was gone.

"They can't hear us or see us!" Deles cried, laughing uproariously. "They're completely helpless without the orb."

But Bilyf's disapproving eyes took the pleasure out of his victory.

"I'm not hurting them," Deles said defensively.

"One sees that this—is not so."

"But now they're not dangerous." Deles held the glistening, pale orb out dramatically against the scarlet sky, its ganglia dangling like threads. "And even if they were, this thing could help us."

"They cannot survive—without it."

"But you saw them try to attack me!"

"One sees—that they live—as they must."

"Please don't lecture me, Bilyf," Deles said. "I, too, do what I must. The orb will help us to survive." The artificial nerve endings twitched as Deles turned the sensorium to examine it. "Why is it moving like that?" he asked nervously.

"One sees—that it responds—to the impulses—of the nervous system."

"Then it's reacting to me," Deles said. "I had hoped that it would." The sensorium clung to his hand and wrist, ganglia crawling like worms to gain a better hold.

Deles stared at it with new understanding.

The orb faded into the burning sky. The sky split into a thousand blazing variations of red and orange, yellow, violet and blue. A rainbow overlapped into two long strands of pure light, turning end over end like an exaggerated human figure running.

There was the world, a bowl-like basin at its center. From the basin, the self extended out to the loved ones . . . the pit, the tribe . . . the tribe's memory, in all its visual and aural glory . . . singing pleasure color touch . . . oh, the touch . . . the touch . . . but now, the tall running ones . . . living . . . like, and yet not like . . . the Others.

"The Others!" Deles shouted. "They've seen the Others! With this!" He held the sensorium before his eyes, seeing once again *through* his own eyes as it clung to his fist. "They've seen it with this, Bilyf."

Bilyf bowed his crested head.

"Bilyf, we might be able to communicate with the Others themselves using this sensorium." Deles couldn't contain his excitement even in the face of Bilyf's dismay. "It showed me that they are still human in a way, even though they're dead. They exist in more than one dimension. Surely they'll help us if they're capable of it."

"One sees—that the Others—have already helped."

"They've helped by leading us to this!" Deles thrust the orb towards Bilyf. "They wanted us to take it."

"One does not—see."

"Do you think it was just a coincidence that the Others showed us a path that led directly here?" Deles was puzzled by Bilyf's lack of awareness. Perhaps it was because the Mennon had not seen through the orb, as he had. "Don't you see, Bilyf? Don't you?"

"One sees—only suffering." Bilyf pointed a stiff digit down

at the churning mass of neural tissue. "One sees—starvation and misery—without the sensorium."

"Once it's served its purpose, I'll return it to them," Deles said. "I promise you that."

Again, Bilyf bowed his crest.

In the Now That Seems to Be, Bilyf sees nothing, and yet it is clear to him that Deles will soon transcend his teacher in intuitive power, if not in ethics . . . if not in true vision. It concerns him that the boy begins to exhibit such puissance while still so morally undeveloped. Disturbed, Bilyf remains silent . . .

He perceives also that Deles is inspired. Perhaps what he has said about the Others is indeed the truth . . . and yet Bilyf cannot shake himself free of his belief that stealing the sensorium is immoral. These beings have adapted to its constant use in a uniquely dependent way, their senses becoming first vestigial, then vanishing altogether . . . relying always on the orb, for the orb is not confined to any one sequence on the continuum . . . it more clearly *sees* . . . once an object has come under its scrutiny it is forever there . . . for the sensorium has memory . . . a memory more thorough than that of any human device . . . except perhaps for the great Machine itself. . . .

And there is more: the biological constructs of the Rocinthans, it is said, renew themselves at a rate that perfectly balances their decay. Perhaps they might all be working yet if only one knew their secrets . . . here, in Deles's hand, is one such living machine which still functions . . . which responds to the nervous system of a human being, curiously enough. This should not be so, and yet it is . . . and one cannot deny the potential of such a thing . . . only the pathetic, crawling creatures in the pit, lost without the orb, prevent Bilyf from acceptance of Deles's actions. It is against his principles to gain from the misfortune of another, and he tells Deles so.

"When we were on our way to Tartarus," Deles replies, "you spoke of the pragmatic and the spiritual being part of the same thing. It is pragmatic for me to keep the orb, and therefore there is rectitude in what I have done."

"One sees that Deles has reversed—the dictum," Bilyf says, "and yet the truth remains—in spite of his cleverness."

"Bilyf, if you could see through the sensorium as I have, then you'd understand why we must have it."

"But one—does not see." Somehow Deles knows that he alone may use the sensorium, Bilyf sees . . . that no other human or Mennon may derive any benefit from it . . . only Deles, who fails to understand Bilyf's objections . . . nevertheless, Bilyf is saddened to feel himself losing touch with Deles, and to find that he can see less perfectly on Tartarus. . . . The same is true when he first arrives on Sripha, in the Now That Seems to Be . . . the focus is always in the minds of those whom one comes into contact with, directly or indirectly . . . Tartarus and its inhabitants are too unfamiliar . . .

Deles, he sees, is once again entranced by the sensorium . . . Deles visits other times and other minds, not unlike a Mennon chronopath.

"Bilyf," Deles says, his eyes dreaming, "your moral attitudes won't work here. Please don't make things more difficult than they already are."

"One must—for it is—the Mennon way."

Deles could not sleep, long into the fiery night. It was not the lurid glare of the burning hydrogen that kept him awake. Still, the conflagration was something to look at while he tossed on his suspended bed. The blaze was still several kilometers away, but it crept ever closer to the pit. If it kept on consuming the atmosphere at the same rate, they would be forced to leave the region in a few days. They would be driven away from the pit long before that. Deles had to make a decision—he must either send Bilyf back to wait for him at the ship or be constantly tormented by his friend's accusations.

Propping himself up on one elbow, it occurred to him that he might best search for Verra alone. If he found her—and if her ship was still intact—he would bring her back, with the mnemonic cylinder. Bilyf could work on the rest of the ship while he was gone, to make sure that it was in good shape for the flight to Sripha. And if they never made it back to Sripha . . . well, Tartarus was a big planet. They would find some way to get along here. The Rocinthans had done it.

The only movement in the pit now was the reflection of churning flames. Earlier, Deles had watched the helpless denizens grope their way to their tunnels like lost souls. He had felt an undeniable pang of guilt. In the morning, nevertheless, he would select what he needed from the provisions box and send Bilyf back to the ship. It was their only chance.

Rolling over on his side, he faced the wall of fire, knowing that he could do what he must only if he were alone.

Chapter Fifteen

The Other's Warning

Bilyf did not protest the decision. Deles had prepared a kind of speech explaining himself, but had not needed to deliver it.

"One sees—that Deles—is in thrall—to a vast and urgent force," was all that Bilyf said.

Together they made a small satchel out of a container and attached it to Deles's back with a length of vine. They put food in it, along with a pointed metal implement with a cutting edge. There were a few more items included that might be of some use, while others were discarded as too bulky.

"If I haven't returned to the ship within five days, I'll probably be dead," he told Bilyf. "My food is practically gone now."

Bilyf bowed, his crest level with Deles's chest. Then he turned, and pushing the provisions box ahead of him, started toward the forest of giant stalks. Before Bilyf entered a dark passage between the boles of two monstrous growths, nearly invisible in the mist, Deles called to him.

"If I live, I'll return the orb to them," he said. "I promise this to you, Bilyf."

As Bilyf bowed once more, he was a bright ghost in the swirling vapors. A moment later he was gone.

Deles stared into the silent forest long after his friend had left him. The silence was disconcerting, eerie, almost preternatural. It wasn't until the tribe began to poke their appendages out of their tunnels, venturing forth gingerly into the world, that he fully realized he was alone... alone as he had never been before, on a hostile world with no way home.

Through the orb, Deles saw that the tribe considered themselves the same as their ancestors. Their tissues were the same; therefore *they* were the same, only some of their functions having changed. They did not build, as they once had, and they didn't teach, as they once had. They survived and reproduced ... and lived the past.

But their history was real to them. Deles experienced it too.

He crawled down elaborately designed and well-lighted tunnels, made use of biological constructs synthesized for his amusement, consumed viscid foods, wrapped his ganglia around the erogenous ganglia of others. He saw alien sights, smelled alien smells, thought alien thoughts, dreamed alien dreams. Alien and dead, dead yet alive.

He wrenched the orb from his fist with his free hand and stood on wobbly legs overlooking the pit. It took him a moment to temporarily perceive where he was—in the Now That Seems to Be, as Bilyf would have it—and for his eyes to focus on the aimlessly milling creatures below him. They were little more than neural voyeurs, having adapted minimally, wasting themselves on the useless sensory input of the past. Deles pitied them. Now that he saw them as they really were, it hardly seemed possible that only a few hours ago he had feared them.

Reaching into his makeshift sack, he withdrew a single curd cake. He would eat and then relax for a while. After he had digested his food, he would use the orb once more before pushing on. Perhaps he could learn more about the Others through it.

Before he had swallowed his first bite, however, a snaking appendage jerked over the edge of the pit, startling him. Was the tribe forming a train to search for the orb? More likely to forage, for they must have been hungry by this time.

The leader slithered blindly toward him, forcing Deles to move out of its way. Feeling about, the creature slowly worked its way along the plateau between the pit and the forest. By the time the entire tribe had emerged, the tendrils of the last creature were still submerged in the bubbling pool. They foraged for food, and yet, linked together, never left the pit.

It saddened Deles to see them groping about. At first he had believed that he was only blinding them temporarily, but it was much worse than that—he had taken away both their means of survival and their racial memory. He mustn't deprive them any longer than he had to. Now he would look through the orb again to see what he could learn.

Only a short time ago, he saw, the Others had first come to the pit. The people of the pit had no trouble grasping the nature of the Others, because there was always a part of the tribe escaping with their expiring neurons, like methane drifting into the atmosphere—a ghostly essence that Deles recognized as Otherness. They had seen few flesh and blood humans until Deles abruptly appeared in their midst.

In spite of their fear, they had come to accept the presence of the watery bipeds, which was how they perceived Deles and Bilyf. Nevertheless, they associated Deles with the Others in

some indefinable way. They were confused because he had
feared them, as the Others did not. The Others had revealed
themselves to the people of the pit when man had first settled
this solar system.

The magnitude of Deles's discovery was somewhat dizzying.
Surely he was the first anthroform to know of the orb . . . or was
he? How many humans, who had never left Tartarus in the
anthroform, had stumbled on the pit? Perhaps some of them
had seen the orb, but without Bilyf's vision they couldn't have
discerned its significance. And even if they had, no one could
have divined the full extent of its powers without touching the
sensorium itself, and that meant taking it away from the tribe.

Only Deles had done that.

Now he saw the Others, those who had died horribly on the
surface of Tartarus, on Sripha, and on Rocinth; those who had
given themselves over to Otherness without a struggle; and those
who had simply willed themselves into Otherness. Those who had
opted for Otherness to save themselves anguished lives were
incomplete, tormented, often troubling the people of the pit with
their visits. But the tribe had gradually learned to accept them.
They did not harm the tribe, and were therefore ignored.

How did the tribe know that these tortured ones were the
Others who had not finished out their lives as they should have?
This sensorium did not reveal, but there was a hint that they
knew it intuitively, as if the passage of their own flesh into Otherness had made them aware of it. They were always dying a
little bit—and continually giving birth—and so were no
strangers to those who had already surrendered their physical
forms to Otherness.

The people of the pit were joyous over the simplest things.
Their remembrance of such mundane pleasures as food, sex,
and affection overwhelmed the events and migrations of the
past in their long decline. They were aware of the existence of
other tribes believing them to be inferior. This tribe alone possessed the sensorium; therefore they alone had never abandoned the ways of the ancients. They had no notion of their
degeneration, how meager their tunnels were in comparison to
those of Rocinth and Sripha. The orb was a mask, its glory a
veneer disguising the harsh truth.

In its grip, Deles had nearly as much difficulty in discerning
the concrete reality about him as did the tribe. Caught up in
their past, he became vicariously guilty of their vices.

His reverie was at last disturbed by a presence in the forest
behind him. Others. They must have been with him all the time,
he thought, right there among the eddying clouds of gas. They

revealed themselves to him only when they wished, a matter of suggestion. They straddled two or more dimensions, like acrobats. This simultaneous existence was effortless, unconfined by time and space—even though an Other was always somehow rooted to the world where its anthroform had perished.

Now he could see them clearly, twisting around the boles of huge stalks. Others, forming vaguely humanoid shapes, glowing in the dark forest . . . they would speak to him.

One stepped forth from the shadows. Cool, blue walking fire in the figure of a woman, overwhelmingly beautiful. In spite of his awe, Deles felt that he knew her, that he had always known her.

"Who are you?" he whispered.

She responded in a breath like the wind itself, her shimmering arm reaching out toward him, an unmistakable gesture. And yet he hung back, shrinking from the approach of this strange revenant.

Deles, she whispered.

Yellow curls played around his face as the wind rose and blew his hair, passing through his shield.

"Are you . . . Verra?" he asked.

No.

"Who, then?"

I am Lehana.

It took a moment for the name to register. This Other claimed to be his grandmother. He had never known her. She had run away from Acrios by killing herself. But how could she be here?

Again, a limb of blue flame reached out to him. Again he shrank back, fearing that the apparition could see into his mind, that she had picked Lehana's name out of his subconscious.

"What do you want?" Deles cried.

I want to help you. The figure advanced, not swiftly, and yet easily overtaking him. *Deles, my grandson.*

She touched him.

His fears faded; her touch was a warm breeze, caressing him with love and care. He felt the pain of her anthroform existence as if it were a fishhook penetrating his skin. He felt her sadness for the way her daughter's life had turned out. But where he had expected to find hatred for Acrios, he sensed only pity.

This *was* Lehana.

"But how," he asked, struggling to keep the tremor out of his voice, "how did you come to be here?"

I left Rocinth, bound for Sripha, she told him, *but never arrived.*

"Why not?"

While I was in space, I saw that there was no place for me on Sripha . . . or anyplace else.

"So you . . . gave yourself over to Otherness." A single tear traced its way down Deles's cheek, losing itself in his sparse beard.

There is much hatred in you, Lehana said as he wiped his face with the back of his hand.

"Yes," Deles admitted, "I think it's what's keeping me alive."

Lehana said nothing.

"I'm trying to find Verra," Deles said. "Do you know if she . . . is one of you?"

She is not.

"Then she's still alive?"

Yes.

"Where is she? Is she very far from here?"

Very far.

Well, that was all right. He had never expected things to go this well. He threw back his head and laughed. It was as Danna had always told him, there was something special about him. His luck had held.

Verra is not well.

"There are physicians on Sripha," he said, "as soon as we . . ."

She has murdered all those who came to Tartarus with her, so that she could have their food. She is mad.

"Mad?" How odd to have an Other pronounce the Prime Mystagogue mad. "What of it? Who wouldn't go mad after being stranded on Tartarus?"

If you go near her, she will try to kill you.

"No she won't," Deles protested. "She knows me."

Just as she knew those who were with her.

"I'm sure that she didn't have any choice."

Didn't she?

"It must have been a matter of survival." The orb seemed to weigh down his arm terribly.

She will fear you . . . and try to kill you.

It was useless to argue with this specter. Deles really knew nothing about Verra. But he had to bring her back to Sripha with him if he could.

"Tell me where she is," he said.

Chapter Sixteen

A Gift from the Past

Verra was half a world away—a world larger than Rocinth and Sripha put together, with all the difficulties attendant to such huge mass.

"How can I get to her on foot?" Deles asked.

I will show you.

He followed Lehana for half the long Tartaran day, down a sloping grade and across a lava flow's hardened ripples. At last he stood at the rim of an enormous well, peering into its black depths. He had almost come to believe that he was losing his sanity, that Lehana was only his imagination's feverish creation. But there was no doubt in his mind that the well beneath his feet was there. Vapor trails swirled and broke on the eroded stone. Below, gases lay trapped in languid streamers within a cylindrical prison. He felt the itching of his sticky flesh, for the flow of oxygen around his body could not cool him after the arduous march he had just undertaken. Pebbles dislodged by his heel slid over the well's edge, rustling softly against the spiraling ledge. This was no illusion.

"What is down there?" he asked.

There is a device below that will take you to Verra.

Deles nodded. He reached over his shoulder to adjust the sack and started down the winding path, whistling a tune he remembered from childhood. As he descended, he found the going easy in most places, although here and there the ledge had crumbled. Only once was he unable to make his way through the rubble. On the single occasion when he could not, he hesitated over a gap nearly two meters across where a huge, jagged shard of rock had cracked and fallen into the seemingly bottomless well.

"I can't get across," he said.

You must.

"I can't . . . it's too far."

You must go on. Lehana glided before him, her flaming,

133

quasi-human form elongating and re-forming on the ledge across the gap. *You must.*

"Why this way?" he asked pleadingly. "It's too dangerous, don't you see?"

There is no time to find another way. A cobalt arm beckoned him on.

"No time? What do you mean?"

You must hurry.

"I don't understand," he cried, trembling. "I've been here this long—Verra's been here even longer—so why can't it wait until we've found a safer way to go."

There is no time, Lehana repeated.

Surely she wasn't lying. She had no reason to want him to fall to his death. But why was it so urgent that he go on? "Please tell me why I have to do this. It isn't that I don't want to trust you," he said, giddy as he looked down, "but I don't know if I can make it across."

You must. There is so little time.

"All right." He loosened the sack and pulled it off his back. He lobbed it across the gap, but the heavy gravity pulled it down before it had traveled a meter. It tumbled into the well, diminishing and disappearing without a sound. Now he had nothing.

"Why didn't you stop it from falling?" he asked.

Did you not say that you trust me?

"What choice do I have?" Inside his womb of oxygen, antigravitons contrived to prevent him from being crushed by Tartarus's immense mass. They also permitted him freedom of movement. He tensed his thighs, loped to the brink, and hurtled through space. Landing on his feet, he fell forward on the narrow ledge, striking his forehead and shoulder against the stone wall. Dazed, he rolled onto his back, head and arm dangling over the side of the ledge. He had made it.

Head swimming, he rose on wobbly legs and followed the figure of icy flame. He soon began to feel better, though he was angry at himself for throwing the pack away. If he had just kept it on his back, he would still have it. Now he had to depend on Lehana to care for his needs.

Intermittently, she vanished, reappearing a few moments later. Sometimes she was in front of him, sometimes drifting out away from the ledge, sometimes behind him. At last she floated like a streamer of blue vapor into a tunnel mouth. Deles followed. Within a few paces all light was absorbed in the shadows, only the glimmering of Lehana visible. She was always just ahead.

Several hours passed as they traveled through endless tunnels into the bowels of Tartarus. They came to a bisecting passageway and turned to the left. Soon they had taken a number of other turns. If Lehana were to desert him now, he would never find his way out. . . .

After shuffling forward in the dark for several more hours, he called out to Lehana, "I'm tired and hungry." He remembered that his food was gone. "I've got to stop and rest. I'm still an anthroform, not tireless like you." He sat down on the tunnel floor. "I can't go any farther right now."

There is no need for you to go farther, Deles.

How could this be the end of the journey? There was nothing here. What was she talking about?

"I don't underst—" Something in the dark touched him. Before he could react, he was firmly gripped in a thick coil winding around his torso, pinning his arms to his sides.

"Lehana!" he cried as he was lifted off the tunnel floor. He couldn't see her or anything else as he was rushed through the tunnel, blind, and at a sickeningly high speed.

You will be given what you need. Lehana's disembodied words called from somewhere, seeming to the terrified Deles to be nothing more than the wind in his face as he was carried faster and faster. *Don't be afraid.*

As soon as the first dizzying wave of fear and disequilibrium had passed, he tried to compose his thoughts. This thing holding him like a giant hand had to be the device that Lehana had mentioned, the device that would take him to Verra. It was alive, like the orb, he was sure of it. Doubtless, it was one of the biological constructs of the Rocinthans. If this thing possessed a rudimentary nervous system, its function had been narrowed to a particular task or series of tasks.

Calm yourself, he thought, it isn't going to hurt you. As the coil abruptly changed direction, his heart seemed to leap into his mouth, but after the coil had snaked around a few unexpected curves and corners, he became used to it, laughing hysterically at the exciting sensations. From time to time the dark world seemed to drop out from underneath him, the coil clutching him like a benign fist as he was conveyed swiftly down and down. On the lower level, his forward motion resumed a steady, uninterrupted flow. Deles fell into the monotony of it. He was very tired, dozing and at last falling into a deep sleep.

Dreaming of sunlight reflecting off a cool Sriphan lake, Deles awakened to find himself speeding through a dimly lit corridor, a bubble of filmy protection around him and the smooth, fat loops of the coil. Ahead, he saw nothing but the corridor stretching to a vanishing point, its sides wildly rushing by. How much farther was this thing going to take him? It seemed that he'd already gone halfway around Tartarus on this subsurface route, but of course it must have only been a tiny fraction of that in reality, perhaps a few thousand miles. He'd slept, but he was very thirsty and hungry. This mode of travel had its disadvantages.

He was sleeping again when he felt his forward motion arrested. The coil came to a smooth stop, drooped, and unwound. It snaked away, leaving him standing on trembling legs that could barely support his weight. He turned to watch it flip out of sight in the darkness, and turned back to blink at the brightly lighted chamber ahead.

Slowly, he entered the chamber. Everywhere were slimy pools, dormant organic lumps, and sleeping ophidian shapes. They would do what was needed, but would he have any more control over them than he exercised over the coil? It seemed that only the Others knew how to activate them, and once one was in motion, there was no stopping it until its job was done.

"Lehana," he called, his voice soft and shaky. He took a tentative step and nearly collapsed. He hadn't used his limbs in days, the gravitation field notwithstanding. The oppressive weight of his artificial gravity field felt like the equivalent of Tartarus's. Even so, he had no desire to be swept away by another coil. He consciously thought in negative terms on the subject of motion, just in case they responded telepathically.

"Lehana," he called again. Where was she? Had she taken him all this distance only to abandon him now? His own grandmother? But she wasn't really his grandmother anymore. She wasn't even human. . . .

He was very thirsty. It was hard for him to think, he was so parched. And hungry. Well, it wouldn't do him any good to dwell on it. He had to find water and boil it with the heating device he had in his sack. But the sack was gone. It had fallen into the well when he leaped across the broken ledge.

An elongated shape stretched toward him, its tip curving into a bowl. It halted in front of him, and he saw that the bowl was filled with clear liquid.

"Water?" he whispered.

If it wasn't water, it certainly looked enough like it that he could hardly resist splashing it into his mouth. He somehow restrained himself long enough to dip his fingers into it. It had the consistency of water: it was crystalline, the drab gray of the biological construct showing through. He lifted his trembling hand to his face and sniffed. There was no discernible smell. He tasted.

Water—there could be no doubt of it.

He thrust his face into the bowl, drinking greedily. After he had drunk several mouthfuls, he splashed cool water over his head and neck. When he had drunk some more, he stepped back, wiping at his sopping beard.

Flaming azure appeared by his side. Lehana.

"Where have you been?" he demanded. "I thought that thing was going to carry me forever."

You are near your destination now.

Deles felt a mild thrill of fear. Lehana, having brought him this far, flickered expectantly before him. But he was having second thoughts. She had told him that Verra was mad, that the Prime Mystagogue had killed all of her companions.

"Is there nothing among these constructs to protect me?" he asked, acutely aware of his dependence on Lehana.

You shall have what you need. The coruscating blue figure fragmented and vanished, reassembling several meters away, inside the vast chamber next to some slumbering, fleshy mounds. Deles's limbs were now sufficiently limber for him to walk to her without stumbling. Then she pointed out to him a minute object nestled in one of the mounds.

"What is it?" he asked.

Lehana did not answer. Deles lifted his hand and stared at the orb perched on his wrist, feeling its tendrils tighten their grasp. In all this time he had hardly thought of it, because by now it was almost a part of him, responding instantly to his will. There had been many occasions on his long journey when he had delved into its mysteries, and he had been glad to have it with him. Now he opened his mind to it, to see if it had any knowledge of the thing lying half buried in the mound.

It informed him of the purpose of each of the constructs in the chamber, but nothing about the tiny object was forthcoming.

Take it. Lehana gestured at the mounds, and they slowly opened like the petals of an enormous flower.

Deles walked cautiously between two of the ungainly things to get a better look. He saw that they stretched out from a central cushion of fleshy stuff on which the mysterious object rested. And the object was nothing more than a thin, colorless disc, perhaps ten centimeters in diameter at its broadest point. So innocuous was it that at first he hadn't even seen it, had thought that there was nothing there at all. But here it was, once his eyes had become accustomed to it.

He stepped up onto the fleshy cushion. It gave slightly but held his weight, enabling him to touch the disc. The outstretched mounds, columns now, would close around the disc if it was endangered, he had seen through the orb's memory.

"If I should take it," he said, "will these things crush me?"

No. Take it.

Reaching down, he grasped the disc between thumb and forefinger, feeling its smooth coolness. Around him, fleshy columns folded inward on him. He cried out in anger and disappointment as their bulk blotted out the light.

Chapter Seventeen

The Face of Death

Like monstrous fingers, the columns bent to grip Deles. He took a deep breath, readying himself to fight them. Snarling, he struck out, but no sooner had he hit one of them than they all collapsed, falling to lie limp on the floor.

"You said they wouldn't attack me!" he shouted, more embarrassed than angry now.

I said that you would not be crushed by them, Lehana corrected him, *not that they wouldn't frighten you.*

"Well..." Deles couldn't argue with that, but he was nonetheless resentful. He felt as manipulated as a puppet, but there was nothing he could do about it. At least he had the disc. He turned over his hand, and it clung to his palm as if through some mysterious attraction. "What is this?" he asked.

Something to help you.

"Must you always be so cryptic?" he said testily. "In *what* way will it help me?"

It is time, Deles.

"You haven't answered my— Time for what?"

Time for you to meet Verra.

Chilled, Deles wondered what good this tiny disc was against an insane murderess. "You haven't yet told me how the disc can help me," he said.

Are you afraid?

"No, I..." Why not tell her the truth: she obviously sensed his fear. "Yes, yes, I'm afraid."

Don't be. You have what you need.

He sighed. His momentary panic—fear of betrayal—had set his stomach churning, but he wanted to get on with it all the same. If he had to die, then he might as well die now, instead of waiting for a slow, painful death by starvation, or asphyxiation when his recycler finally failed...or being crushed to death by atmospheric pressure when his gravity shield gave out...or being burnt alive in a methane inferno.

"Take me to Verra," he said.

139

Then you are prepared?

"Yes." No sooner was the word out of his mouth than a coil sprang from the shadows and encased his body. Deles swallowed, expecting another long, breakneck journey, but this time it was surprisingly brief and gentle. Soon the coil eased to a stop, releasing him in front of a dark oval opening in a concave wall.

"Is she in there?" Deles asked Lehana as she flickered back into existence next to him.

Yes.

This was it, then. Deles drew a deep breath and started into the darkness beyond the oval. Once he had progressed a few cautious feet, he detected a faint light, although he couldn't tell where its source lay. Wherever it was, it grew brighter as he followed the downward sloping floor. He continued walking, reaching a vast open space, the limits of which he could not discern. But as he made his way deeper into the innermost recesses of this underground chamber, he perceived figures in the distance, silhouetted by the dim light.

There were people down there!

"Hello!" he called to them.

They didn't answer. They didn't even turn their heads. As he came nearer to them, he began to think that they weren't people after all; statues, perhaps. They were so still and strangely formed, there could be no other explanation. But what were statues doing in this place?

As he approached them, he saw what they really were—and it made him thankful that he couldn't smell anything outside his gravity shield. These were corpses, somehow propped up in the attitudes of living people. Their flesh was drawn and desiccated, in some cases actually falling from the bones. One of the bodies had collapsed in an awkward heap, but the other six miraculously stood, their muscles and tendons turning to jelly on their skeletons.

There had been seven people in Verra's ship—excluding the Prime Mystagogue herself.

"Lehana," he said, "how has Verra done this?"

A blue flame flowered into a woman's outline. *She has found a device that generates a vibration capable of constricting cellular material.*

"Constricting cellular material? I don't understand."

The vibration stiffens the organelles, the microtubules, creating a kind of internal latticework within the cell, and the organism dies frozen in its last position.

"Where did she find such a—" Out of the corner of his eye, Deles caught a glimpse of something diamondlike, an angular gleaming. It was gone before he could tell what it was, but as he turned he saw another, and then another. And yet another. Slowly a pattern emerged, a scintillant network, a web of energy. In its dazzling center there reclined a human figure.

"Verra," Deles said.

She raised her head to look at him, her scalp covered with tubes that writhed like a nest of snakes. Her hair and ears were obscured by the coiling tubes, only her face remaining visible. Like her once stately body, that regal visage had become gaunt and scabrous. She lay naked on the web, swinging her splotched legs around so that she faced Deles.

"I am Verra," she rasped. "Who are you?"

"Deles."

"Deles? . . ." For a few moments she seemed lost in thought, and then she said, "I knew a child named Deles once, but he died. You can't be him."

"But I am," he said. "I was set adrift in space with my mother, but we survived. It happened a long time ago."

"Time . . ." The word affected Verra strangely. She seemed troubled, and to have lost the thread of dialogue. "For all of time, I am the Prime Mystagogue."

"Yes, but you seem to be confused, Verra."

"*I* am the Prime Mystagogue," she repeated, her tone as cold as ice. As she stared at him, head cocked, her eyes bottomless wells of madness. "What do you want with me, child-man?"

"I've come to take you home," he said softly.

"Home? *This* is my home," she said, flinging out a scrawny arm, "my palace. Time stops here . . . and there is so little time left."

"That's true. There is little time left, and you can't survive here for much longer. Your graviton shield will fail, or your oxygen recycler will quit, or your food will run out." It was the same ghoulish litany that had run through his mind a thousand times since he'd come to Tartarus.

"Do you think any of this matters to me?" Verra demanded. "I exist like an Other. . . ."

"In what way are you like an Other?"

"I am at the beginning . . . which is also the End . . . when the holes in the continuum bring us all back to the beginning again . . ." She drifted off, muttering to herself.

Deles let her go on babbling while he tried to think of a plan. He was counting on Lehana to help him, but where was she?

Here. And yet he did not see her. In the darkness, she should have been highly visible. But all he could see were the crumbling bodies, intermittently lit by the flashing of the energy web.

"I killed them, you know," Verra said, nodding toward the corpses. "All of them. It was better that way."

"Better for them to die? How could that be?"

"Because now they can make it through..."

"Through what?"

Verra's head sank to her bony chest, and she did not reply. She seemed to be staring past him, as if his question had induced catatonia in her. She did not move, much less speak.

"Through what?" Deles repeated.

Verra looked up sharply. "Through... an electromagnetic vibration I've made them into statues."

Deles fell silent. It was impossible to hold a conversation with her. Just when he thought he was getting somewhere she retreated from logic, rendering the dialogue useless.

"They're not inside the statues anymore," Verra said. "They're either here or on the Other side... they visit me sometimes... and then they go away... They can go over to the Other side whenever they please." She giggled.

"Tell me about the Other side," Deles said.

"There are really many sides, an infinity of sides. In fact, this is just one of them."

"Tartarus, you mean?"

"Not only Tartarus," she said disdainfully. "Our whole universe... the universe. Oh, how I'll miss it when it's gone."

"We'll all miss it," Deles said. "But tell me about these sides."

"The sides are not really sides, they're more like lines. But not really lines, either. They go curving across each continuum infinitely, but they converge at a point in several different universes. This is that point in ours."

"This chamber? The lines converge here?"

"Yes." She was quite lucid now, almost like the Verra he remembered. "Lines from the other sides—other dimensions, you might say."

"All the dimensions meet here?" This was sheer madness, and yet...

"No, no, not all of them. You have to go through some to get to others... and besides, these are only lines of time and force extending from other dimensions."

"I still don't understand."

Bursting into hideous laughter, Verra rose and danced on the sparking web, whirling with a grace belying her wasted body.

She pirouettes along the dimensional lines, Deles thought, and it has driven her mad. He too was falling prey to illogic, he feared; he must guard against it. It was as if this place were a drug, the most powerfully addictive narcotic in all creation. It had been too much for Verra, who had once possessed one of the finest minds in the solar system. Would it destroy him, too, if he stepped inside the web?

"The lines drew me here," Verra said, cackling.

"How?" Deles asked.

"And you claim to be Deles," she said contemptuously. "Deles would know about such things."

"Why do you say that? What do I have to do with all this?"

"Deles was born to come here, but he died before he could fulfill his destiny."

Taken aback, he crouched between two of the standing corpses. What did she mean? Was she only trying to frighten him, or did she really know something about him, about his birth?

"If you know that I was born to come here then you must know who my father was," he said, determined to find out if this was more babbling or the truth. "Tell me who he was . . . or is."

The response was a bleak, immense howling, as if the elements themselves had deserted the natural places where they raged, seeking to secrete themselves here. But there was more: he thought he detected a savage intelligence in the straining energy captured in this cavern. Blending with the terrible cacophony was Verra's laughter.

"The End!" she shrieked. "The beginning! The truth!"

"What is the truth?" Deles asked sarcastically.

"Look around you. The truth is here." Verra gestured at the brilliant points of light surrounding her. "Perhaps the only truth."

"The *only* truth?"

"There is only one essential truth," she said, "and it's strongest right here."

"How do you know?"

"I can feel it. Here it's a concrete thing—its strength is overpowering." She became pensive. "Before I came to Tartarus, I thought I grasped a little of it, but after I was brought here . . ."

"*Brought* here? Who brought you?"

She opened her mouth to speak, but her voice was lost in the frightful winds. Bits of her discorporated, reappearing while other segments temporarily vanished. "I move through dimensional lines as if I were an Other," she said sadly as the winds calmed and she became whole once again, "but I can't stay in any dimension but ours for very long. It's like breathing on Tartarus with an oxygen recycler, or looking at the sun with unprotected eyes."

"Perhaps the truth is too much for us, then?"

"Perhaps," she said, and then suddenly became as still as one of the corpses. Her face seemed lit from within, and Deles assumed that the effect was a result of the multidimensional forces energizing the web. "But if I am defeated by the truth, the rest of our people won't even face it. Otherwise the human race would be long since gone."

"What are you talking about?"

"I'm talking about the truth," Verra said with a tone of exasperation. "If humans had faced it, they'd have gone away. Other races reach a point where they grasp Otherhood too. Few remain who have not. But even among these, Man's folly is preeminent. Only Man, in his arrogance, presumes to determine what will follow the End of All Things—using an artifact of his technology—so that he might somehow endure. Machine or no Machine, though, the End comes soon."

"We all know that, Verra."

"Do we? Then why do we, as a race, refuse to give up this paltry existence?"

"Man has never given up easily, has he?"

"All intelligent races possess tenacity, but they come to realize that they can only go on for so long. Look at what the Rocinthans left behind. Don't you think they could have gone on clinging to the delusion of eternal life, too?"

Confused by this moribund lecture, Deles decided to consult the orb. He held the ragged sphere up before his eyes and effortlessly began to sift through its images, seeking information about the events leading up to the Rocinthan departure.

Something pulled him back.

The disc seemed joined to his flesh now, embedded in his palm, as if it were becoming part of him. It began to vibrate rapidly and powerfully until Deles was almost sickened by the sensation. Suddenly it was still again, and he suspected that the vibration it had somehow retarded and absorbed was electromagnetic. It had left him dazed and nauseated, unable to think clearly.

Verra raised her head, the tubes coiling around her face like angry serpents. She channeled the energies of the converging dimensional lines through the strange headpiece. Had it not been for the disc, Deles's cells would have constricted, turning him to stone. Turning him to ice. She had led him on, patiently waiting for him to lower his guard, and then she had tried to murder him.

"You . . . ." Deles advanced on her, his horror transmogrifying into anger.

"No!" Verra cried. "You can't be alive! You can never make it through if you're alive!"

Through his searing rage, Deles saw her twisted sense of

mission. She would save him by making him an Other—by killing him. But there was far too much left for him to do before he accepted Otherness. He must live. He approached the web, unmindful of the danger it posed to him if his oxygen were to ignite. The time for caution was past.

As he neared the cowering Verra, he was enclosed by the web.

"No!" she shrieked, her voice piercing him like a hail of neutrinos. But she would not escape his wrath.

His hand was on her throat when he was ripped from his body in blinding blue light. Blue light so cold and pure he did not think he could tolerate it. The intricate pattern of the web had become prismatic, an agonizingly beautiful rainbow-faceted infinity on which he moved gracefully with Verra in a *pas de deux* of death.

"You're not human!" she screamed. "You're not human!"

But her cries no longer possessed elemental power, and Deles's hand was strong. Her flesh was warm, the cords of her throat supple. He wrenched her head around. As the bones snapped he was again torn from his body. In a formless, alternative existence, a detached Deles watched himself kill Verra. He broke her neck with his left hand, the orb quivering in his right. He took pleasure in the killing—a low animal glee coupled with a kind of sick spiritual joy. And there was an inevitable horror in it—horror not only that he could commit such a monstrous act but that he could enjoy it so much.

And while he killed her, he knew Verra's last words had been true—he wasn't completely human.

But he would never tell him so again. Her limp jaw languished against the back of his hand. Her tongue lolled ludicrously. She was dead.

An infinite number of universes sighed appreciatively. The truth nexus had not been served properly by Verra. Would he be forced to take her place?

He saw a billion worlds, a billion billion worlds, all dead and deserted. He saw the interstices between the worlds, alive as they had never been before . . . waiting.

But waiting for what.

Waiting for the End . . . and for you.

For me? he thought.

For you, if you will serve.

"No," he said, "I have too many things left undone."

Upon his refusal to serve, all the worlds and stars and gaseous clouds became as one, and they whirled in a mighty vortex through his hand as he touched the coiling tubes on Verra's cold head.

There was darkness, and there was light.

And then . . . Lehana was speaking to him: *You have done well, Deles.*

"Lehana," he said, "how did you . . . ?" He was about to ask her how she had come to be on the web, when he realized that he was passing back out through the oval, leaving the place of the web. He had been walking as if he were a somnambulist. He remembered a fleeting image of grinning corpses, and now he was walking away from that terrible place where . . . he had murdered Verra.

Look at your hand, Deles.

Slowly, he opened the fingers of his left hand. The disc was still embedded in the flesh of his palm, and linked to it was an amorphous, flickering shape.

Yes, he remembered now. He had torn away the living tubes to find this marvel underneath them. This thing had been drawn to the disc, and he had cast the biological construct aside, the tubes hissing as they flew into infinity.

I will take you to what is left of their provisions now. Verra has eaten little of the food, preoccupied as she has been in recent days. With the food that is left you can survive the journey to their ship, and then back to your own ship.

"We need the mnemonic cylinder," Deles said. "Take me to it. I must get away from this place."

Do not torment yourself because you have killed Verra.

"But I took pleasure in it," Deles whispered.

Come.

A serpentine shape rose from the shadows and embraced him. And, in spite of the terrible weight of his guilt, exhaustion overcame him almost immediately. The construct shot him away into the darkness, and, sheathed securely in its binding softness, he soon slept.

Chapter Eighteen

Up from the Underworld

A mighty fire raged in the distance, casting a hazy red glow through the methane-ammonia clouds breaking against Deles's graviton shield. He carried the mnemonic cylinder from Verra's wrecked ship in a sling he had fashioned from fibrous plants. Little of the ship's guts had been intact and he felt fortunate that the cylinder was in one piece. He was very tired, but in spite of his fatigue Lehana urged him on, assuring him that he was almost back to the pit.

Just up this hill and you will be there.

As he began to trudge up the slope, he noticed that she wasn't coming with him. Would she reappear later? He didn't think so; there was a sense of finality about the way she hung back.

"Are you coming?" he asked.

I can do no more to help you, Deles. My part in this is finished, and I must say goodbye to you here.

"Grandmother, I need you." But even as he spoke, the flaming blue woman faded. He doubted that he would ever see her again while he lived. But one day he would be like her. Perhaps then . . . but that day would come all too soon.

You no longer need me, Lehana said. *You are on your own.*

He somehow knew that she would not bend, and so he didn't try to dissuade her. "Goodbye, Lehana," he said as she vanished. He started to climb the slope once again. At the top he passed between the jutting rocks and stood looking down at the people of the pit.

He had expected to see their dead tendrils strewn about the bowl-shaped depression. Instead the creatures crawled complacently about their business. How could they have managed so well without the sensorium? It didn't matter; he had promised Bilyf that he would return it to them, and he intended to keep that promise. If things hadn't gone as badly for the people of the pit as he had expected, that was all to the good.

He climbed down into the pit, not stumbling as he had done

the first time. One of the pit's denizens, a large one, groped
about with an ad hoc limb, and Deles approached it. He held
the orb in the path of its sweeping feeler, which, as luck would
have it, passed over the sensorium by only a few inches. Deles
went to the creature's other side, and this time the connection
was made. Before he removed his hand from the orb, he linked
with the creature.

Confusion, first, and then elation, blooming like a Sriphan
wildflower. Another creature touched the first, immediately
sharing in the joy of the sensorium's return. A third joined
them, and then a fourth. Soon the entire village was linked,
reveling in regaining their sight, their memory. Even the infant
shared their elation, though it did not understand why. It had
grown since Deles had last seen it.

Surprisingly, they were not angry at Deles for stealing the
orb. Rather, they loved him for returning it to them. He was
moved by their magnanimity. In spite of their gratitude, however, he wasn't really a part of their celebration. He released
the orb and made his way up the side of the pit as the creatures
bore the orb to the pool. He dug his toes into the steep side of
the pit and struggled toward the top. As he glanced up to check
on his progress, he saw a pair of stumpy, pearl-white legs.

"Bilyf!"

"One sees—that the young master—has returned."

"What are you doing here?" Deles bounded the last few
steps. "I thought you'd be back at the ship."

"One sees—that there is—a need here."

"Not anymore," Deles said happily. "I've returned the orb to
them—and look at this," he said as he swung the mnemonic
cylinder over his shoulder. "I found it in Verra's ship."

"And what has—become of—the Prime Mystagogue?"

Deles's enthusiasm was instantly dampened. He looked
down as he said darkly, "I killed her."

Silence reigned for a little while, until Bilyf began to explain
why he had come back to the pit.

"One has provided food—for the poor creatures—below."
Bilyf indicated a contraption on crude wheels behind him. The
base of a water-catching plant had been truncated and set over
knobby axles, which were cut from immature stalks. A rough
harness had been attached, made from woven plant fibers like
Deles's sling. The wheels appeared to be round slabs of igneous
rock. This makeshift cart was piled high with the viscid foods
that sustained the people of the pit. On Sripha a child could
have pulled it, but here on Tartarus it must have been agonizing
just to budge it.

"Have you any nutritional beads left?" Deles asked.

"One has—no more food."

"I have plenty here." Deles patted a sack dangling from his waist. He had taken as much as he could from Verra's hoard. "I'm sure you can find something here that you can eat."

"Perhaps," Bilyf said. "One must not—after all—permit oneself—to starve."

"Try a little bit," Deles said, "and if it doesn't make you sick you can eat more."

"One sees that Deles—cares for Bilyf—and allows the people of the pit—to care for themselves."

"I promised that I would, didn't I? I felt something when I gave it back, a joy that radiated from them. It was the first time I've felt so good in a long time."

"One believes that—such emotion is indeed—universal."

"Bilyf, I need rest . . . I've been through so much since I last saw you."

"One sees that Deles—has been changed."

"Yes, something in me has been triggered, something that's been lying dormant all my life. I don't know what it is, but it has affected every cell in me." It disturbed Deles that he could speak of it only in these vague terms. Perhaps it was just that he was so tired. "I can't think clearly now."

"The young master—must sleep."

Bilyf unfurled a suspensor bed from the provisions box. Deles lay down on it, every muscle of his body aching. He had wanted to tell Bilyf what had happened to him, but he couldn't. No one would ever really know but him . . . It would be his secret until . . . until. . . .

They made their way toward the open place where the ship had landed. Great, churning clouds rose over the chasm walls above, tinted orange by the encroaching sea of flame. At last the narrow corridor of stone widened, and there was the ship exactly as they had left it, except for a giant millipede draped over the port cone of its hourglass fuselage. The creature crawled rapidly away with a clanking, staccato sound, vanishing in the mist.

The raging fire threatened to intrude into the chasm at any moment, and Deles feared that they would be engulfed in flames before they could reach the ship. To their left rose a thunderous, blazing tsunami that was coming dangerously close to their oxygen bubbles. It shriveled a fungous growth in front of them. From the right, a fiery column of burning gases shot across their path. Now Deles couldn't see the ship at all.

"This way, Bilyf," he said, moving toward one of the few spots not bathed in fire. He hoped that there would be an ave-

nue leading through the inferno to the ship, but their sanctuary
quickly shrank to within two meters on all sides. Cowering from
the blistering heat, he held out his hand in a futile gesture.

The flame became cool and blue. This was not the same fire
that threatened them, but fire from within, somehow rechannel-
ing the blaze. No longer was he within his own body. His power
was as great as his detachment. He would deal with this threat,
and he would do it with unerring calm.

A corridor stretched before them, through the fire. At its
end was the ship, waiting. As they approached it, the ship's
sensors observed them and its memory recognized them. They
could enter it, though it would not respond to their commands if
they tried to lift off. The hatch opened.

Deles observed himself entering the airlock with Bilyf. A
moment later he was inside his own body once again. He sagged
to his knees as the hiss of oxygen filled the cramped space.
Removing the recycling unit from behind his ear, he tucked it
into his ragged tunic. A flood of odors assailed his nostrils, for
he had smelled nothing but himself since leaving the ship. The
inner hatch swung open, and they helped one another inside.

"We must get away from here," Deles said, feeling entirely
drained of strength, "or the fire will . . ."

"First the cylinder—must be placed."

Bilyf removed the sling from Deles's shoulder and set to
work immediately, his digits running through the intricacies of
the memory node like white liquid. In spite of Bilyf's compo-
sure, Deles noted the muscles pulled taut and thin over the ba-
roque Mennon rib cage. Nevertheless, Bilyf had soon removed
the original mnemonic cylinder and was connecting Verra's cylinder to the ship's nervous system.

In the interim, Deles had sat down in the webbing. If anything went wrong now, when they were so close to leaving
Tartarus . . . Everything depended on the new cylinder.

Looking down at his hand, he saw the tiny disc, and next to it
the thing his eyes could not focus on. These were parts of him
now, and would surely draw their power from whatever sources
were available, just as they had done with the fire. He possessed
a terrible weapon, and a shield to protect him from that very
weapon. But how could a mere human be trusted with something like this? Verra's last words came back to him with chilling
clarity: "You're not human!"

"One has replaced—the mnemonic cylinder—" Bilyf said,
"—and now we will see—if it responds to the commands—of
Verra alone."

It was an intolerable thought, but it had to be faced. To come this far only to find that the cylinder's memory had been keyed to only one voice—Verra's.

Verra. He could still see her face, lit from within, horribly bony and pitted with scabs... and the coiling serpentine crown, a monstrous nest for....

"There is only one way to find out," Deles said, and yet he hesitated. In a way he didn't want to go back home. He envisioned a trail of carnage following him from Tartarus to Sripha and beyond. Where would his bloody destiny lead him? Ultimately, he imagined, to his own death, for surely he—of all men—was not to enjoy immortality. Still, he could not remain here.

"Take us to Sripha," he commanded the ship.

Neither he nor Bilyf spoke in the ensuing silence. Deles tasted sweat trickling into a corner of his mouth. Nothing happened. It was over then, he thought. They were going to die on Tartarus after all.

Then he thought he detected a faint vibration, almost indiscernible... or was it merely his imagination? No, the sensation grew stronger, building. The visual scan suddenly enveloped them, showing the drab surrounding landscape as if through a distorting lens. Topographical features slowly began to shrink and disappear into fiery mist. Then the flaming sea diminished until it was nothing but a glowing spot on an immense gray-brown hemisphere.

"It's working, Bilyf!" Deles shouted. "We're going home!"

One saw that the young master was mistaken, that he was on a most circuitous route to his true home. But one also saw prudence in not telling him this. Deles would learn the truth in his own way. Besides, Bilyf could not see *where* Deles was bound.

Tartarus's immense gravity worked in reverse, sending the ship hurtling faster and faster. But while Bilyf rode in the ship with Deles, he travelled in another ship, as a tiny eggsharer, with Acrios. Through the darkness of space they sped...

... farther

and

farther...

... from the Mennon homeworld.

"I'll name you Bilyf," Acrios was saying. "After all, I can't very well call you eggsharer, can I?"

Bilyf, unable to speak like a human, didn't answer. Still, he saw that he was capable of making the strange, barking noises that seemed to communicate so much to Acrios and his kind. It was not unlike the Mennon mode of communication, in a way.

"With you to help me, Bilyf," Acrios said, "things will be

much easier. The Gift has made me great, but add to that the aid of a Mennon chronopath, and you really have something."

Did this being not realize that an eggsharer could not willingly participate in its quest for power? That would be unethical in the extreme, though Bilyf's immature mind could not yet fully comprehend the details of such a moral position. The issue was further complicated by the fact that this creature was clearly the master...the one whom the eggsharer must serve...at least until...until what?...Bilyf did not not know, but he did know that one day he would serve another, and that there would be no question in his mind who that other was, once the time came.

But at this moment, the Now That Seems to Be, Bilyf saw great difficulty arising from this moral dilemma, even to the point of physical pain being inflicted upon him when he would not, or could not, cooperate with Acrios. Still, there was genuine affection for him in the master's heart. Bilyf saw that this dichotomy between selfishness and love was Acrios's undoing— a much greater burden than Bilyf himself bore. A complex being, Man—so often torn between the expedient and the ideal...

...and now here was Deles, as torn as Acrios...

Did the young master live only to destroy? Bilyf could hardly believe so, but neither could he tell for certain. He could not see the forces that moved Deles, that commanded him as surely as Deles himself had commanded the ship to rise from Tartarus's surface.

What did they possess, these humans, that made them of such grave significance in the vast scheme of things? Or was their part really any greater than his own? His conception of humankind was doubtless colored by spending his life among humans. They were, after all, exceedingly vain creatures.

It was difficult to grasp the essence of things when one was so far from the eggsac and the wisdom of the knowledge sharers, and from the love of the mother. In his ambivalence, he had doubtless committed many immoral acts...but these could not concern him in the Now That Seems to Be...

...for he must bridge the gap between worlds, and thus...
    the
       events
            that
                  transpire
                        between
                            Tartarus
                            and
                            Rocinth

pass

through

an

effort

of the will. . . .

Sripha was green and blue, swathed in clouds. Deles thought it looked tiny and make-believe, like a jewel compared to Tartarus. As its three-dimensional image hung before him inside the ship, he imagined that he could hold Sripha in the palm of his hand. He could crush it if he wanted to, and it pleased him in a perverse way to think so. He knew that Bilyf would never approve of such malevolent whimsy—he barely did himself—but as much as he loved Bilyf, he was on his own now, just as Lehana had told him.

The star fields were hidden behind Sripha's bright curve too abruptly. Something was wrong.

"Bilyf, we're coming in too fast."

"One sees that—the ship's memory—makes no allowance —for difference in mass—between this ship—and the Prime Mystagogue's ship."

Checking its reentry speed, the ship corrected its angle and slowed. Relieved, Deles said, "Take us to Ploydektum."

"One sees—that it does not—know the way."

"But how can that be possible?" Deles asked, seeing that they were flying over regions he'd never visited. He nervously directed his next question to the ship: "Aren't you equipped with charts of Sripha?" He had forgotten for the moment that it wasn't a speaking craft. With the evidence at hand, he had to assume its reply would have been in the negative.

"Bring us down," he commanded.

Obediently, the ship settled onto a lush field near a lake, the golden frame of a dark mirror. Forests lined other lakes, for there were thousands of deep holes filled with water, the result of ancient meteor storms.

"Well," Deles said, "this certainly isn't Ploydektum."

"Ploydektum—is far from here."

"At least we're down safely. Do you see in which direction our destination lies?"

"One—does not."

"Let's go outside and see if we can find someone who can tell us where we are." Deles stepped into the airlock as the inner hatch opened. Sensing free-floating oxygen, the ship immediately lowered the outside hatch, and he walked straight through. It was a warm, sunny day. Exhilarated, he breathed deeply of the fresh air. But even as he moved effortlessly in the

low gravity, he felt trepidation. The terrible thing was the sense
of inevitability. He did not know what was to come, only *that* it
was to come.

"One sees that—Deles is pleased—to once again be on Sripha."

"Yes." Deles turned to look at his friend, a pale ghost against
the metallic hue of the sky. Could Bilyf no longer detect the
underlying currents of fear and doubt in him? It had always
seemed that the Mennon could read his mind, but now . .
Perhaps Bilyf still perceived Deles's problems, but did not care
to comment on them for some reason? Either way, it was an
indication of the profound changes that had been wrought in
Deles on Tartarus. "It's so calm here."

"The calm—may be deceptive."

"No doubt," Deles said.

Together they set out along the lakefront, hoping to find
someone to tell them how to get to Ploydektum. Deles pondered how long it would be before the deceptive calm was shattered. He closed his fingers over the alien device in his palm as
he walked.

Chapter Nineteen

Deles's Rage

After walking a good distance around the black lake, Deles and Bilyf began to doubt that they would find any human habitation on it. They decided to try higher ground. Moving away from the lake, they topped a rise. Another lake, a little larger, was on the other side. There were forested mountains in the distance, and a bit past the lake, another hill, which they walked to and climbed. They stood looking down on a mosaic of ebony ponds and lakes stretching into the haze on the horizon.

"Our luck is not good," Deles said. There were many such lake regions on Sripha, and this one struck no note of familiarity.

"There is—a settlement," Bilyf said.

Indeed, as he looked in the indicated direction, Deles made out huts and stone piers lining some of the larger lakefronts. But his first sight of human life did not fill him with joy, for the lake dwellers were known to be a hostile breed of men. Still, they *were* human beings—extremely independent human beings, at that—and Deles could not resist going down to see them. He had hoped to find a lone passerby, but he consoled himself with the thought that tales of the Sriphan wilderness were as often as not exaggerated.

They made their way toward the nearest village. These people were descendants of dissidents, Deles knew; they had rejected the power of the provincial estates and their tyrannical masters.

The walk was all downhill, and they were soon close enough to make out boats skimming the dark water. Soon they could see the men and women piloting them. A few minutes later they heard muffled voices coming from behind the wooden buildings set in a rough semicircle along the lakefront.

"Let's not rush in," Deles whispered. "We'll find out what they're doing first." He didn't want to intrude on some ritual or religious observance if he could avoid such a gaffe. Creeping up to the nearest hut, they peered into the village.

The first person Deles saw was a woman with dark, leathery skin. She was speaking to a group of five children seated cross-legged on the ground. It was difficult to tell what she was saying, the dialect was so unfamiliar. The gist of it was the need to give things up for the greater good of the village. The children were solemn as she spoke of the necessity for sacrifice, staring at her as if in rapt attention. But as soon as she turned around to pick up a slate, the children began to punch and slap each other. Depending on which end of a blow they were on, they giggled or sobbed. Deles had to stifle his laughter at this display of childish human nature, the first such he had witnessed in a very long time.

"That's all for today," the woman said. She herded the children away, leaving Deles and Bilyf hiding behind a hut with nobody to watch. They cautiously threaded their way between huts until the lakefront came into sight.

Those on the fishing boats were busy hauling in their nets. On each vessel was a man or woman armed with a pike. Deles suspected that these were guards, watching for trun.

"Do you think we should make ourselves known?" he asked, noting that there were a few people, mainly children, watching the boats from the ramshackle piers.

"We cannot—obtain the information—we require—without doing so."

Several of the boats were steering towards shore. Deles and Bilyf waited until the catch was brought in. Soon the boats were docked and people were straining at the nets, pulling them up to the shore.

"Now," Deles said, walking boldly out into the open. He shouted at the villagers, "Hello!"

Everyone turned toward him, several villagers having stopped dead in their tracks at the sound of his voice. It was only then that Deles thought how odd it was that there had been so little noise rising from their labors. Ominous, he thought, almost as if they had been expecting him. The silence was complete now, except for the wet flopping of the dying fish. Their smell, and the heat of the day, suddenly seemed oppressive.

"Look!" a woman cried, pointing past Deles at Bilyf. They had never seen a Mennon. Rare as he was here, however, the villagers showed no signs of appreciating him. Several of them hefted spears.

"It's all right," Deles said to them, "he won't harm you." Saying this about Bilyf, the most civilized being he had ever known, struck Deles as absurd, and yet necessary.

"What do you want?" a surly, bearded man demanded.

"Uh, we're lost," Deles said. "We want to go to Ploydektum."

The man frowned. "Ploydektum?" He turned to the others.

"I've heard of Ploydektum," a woman said. "It's over the mountains—on the other side of the world."

"We were afraid of that," Deles said. He recognized the woman as the same one who had been giving the children their lesson. "Our ship didn't know the way."

"You can't depend on machines," the man said.

"This is—often so," said Bilyf.

The villagers stared at him in disbelief. Aliens were rare enough on provincial Sripha, but a talking one had their mouths agape. They exchanged glances, perhaps hoping that someone among them had heard of such a thing.

"My friend is a Mennon," Deles explained. "He has vocal chords like us."

"Such things are not unheard of," said the woman with the leathery face, "but we rarely see them here."

"We're seeing it now," the bearded man said, "and I don't think I like it."

Murmurs of approval came from the crowd.

"No, no," Deles said. "In all my life I've never known a finer person than Bilyf."

"Just what do you and this . . . fine person want with us?" said the bearded man.

"I've already told you once," Deles replied, trying not to show his annoyance. "We're lost. We set down near here after coming from Tartarus."

An incredulous gasp rose from the crowd.

"Tartarus!" the bearded man bellowed. "Nobody comes back from Tartarus."

"We did," Deles stated flatly.

The bearded man seemed to be about to challenge this claim, but he didn't open his mouth. The crowd waited to see what would happen next. Now the waning sun and the fish odor were overpowering, but Deles stood his ground, staring directly at the hostile man.

"Are you and your friend hungry?" The woman broke the silence.

"Very," Deles said, not taking his eyes from the man.

"Then come to my home and I'll feed you."

Some of the villagers grumbled, but one of them said, "What's the harm in it?" Apparently no one had an answer to that, for they dispersed. Deles and Bilyf followed the woman along the lakefront to her hut, which seemed unremarkable among the crude dwellings lined up along the shore.

After they passed into the cool darkness of the woman's home, Deles realized that his fist was clenched so tightly that his nails had torn the skin of his palm almost to the point of bleeding. When he thought of the destructive potential in his hand, he was a little afraid of what might have happened had there not been an amicable ending to the brief confrontation outside.

As evening settled in, the woman got a blaze started in her fireplace. The firelight showed simple furnishings that were sturdy and well-crafted, and that the floor was swept. In one corner was a spring flowing into an opening in the stone floor, a common feature in Sriphan homes. There was an orderly air about the place that Deles found agreeable. But didn't he detect sadness, even despair, in the woman's manner . . . and in the manner of all the villagers? Bilyf sat quietly on a bench as the woman busied herself stoking the fire and preparing fish for cooking.

"Do you live alone?" Deles asked her.

"No." In the firelight, her face blanched. "My daughter lives with me."

Deles wondered why she reacted so strangely. Perhaps her daughter was ill. "I hope she's well," he said.

"Edorna's healthy enough," she said, smiling wryly, as if she had heard an ironic remark.

"Oh . . . I'm very glad to hear that."

The woman indicated that Deles should take his place at table. He sat down and she poured water from a ladle into a cup set in front of him. Then she handed a cup to Bilyf and held the ladle over it. "Do you want this?" she asked.

"One cannot—consume water—in this fashion."

"How does . . . one . . . do it?"

"One—demonstrates." Bilyf waddled to the spring, across the room from the fireplace. Bending down, he immersed his entire head underwater. Deles knew that Bilyf could have merely dipped his oral folds to slake his thirst, but this was far more amusing. Bilyf was trying to cheer up the woman.

Her expression showed nothing, however. She returned to her chores while Deles listened to the soft bubbling sound Bilyf made in the springwater.

"What is your name?" he asked the woman.

"Matta."

"Matta . . . a pleasant name . . . and your daughter is Edorna?" He was curious about the girl, or young woman; why did Matta react so oddly to his questions about her?

"Yes, Edorna is her name."

Clearly, she didn't want to talk about her daughter. He would respect her wishes. In any case, he was beginning to real-

ize just how exhausted he was. The soft flickering of the fire
compensated for the increasing evening cold, which was beginning to seep through the hut's crudely mortised joints. The tem-
perature dropped rapidly here in the lake country. The cool air
and the weight of his impossibly tired limbs dragged him into a
deep slumber. In his dream, the weathered faces of the villagers
turned away from the sun, toward the Stygian depths of the
lake.

Oddly, he knew that it was silence, and not noise, that had
awakened him—even the birdsong had abruptly ceased. As he
opened his eyes he saw that the fire was reduced to its last
graying embers, and that he and Bilyf were alone. His neck was
stiff from falling asleep in the chair, and he rubbed it to get the
kinks out. Bilyf was lying on the stone floor in the peculiar
resting position of Mennons, looking for all the world as if he
were tied in knots.

"Bilyf," Deles said softly.

"One sees—that the young master—is disturbed."

"You too, or you wouldn't be awake."

"Death—is nearby."

Matta came out of the adjoining room, staring at Bilyf. "You
know then?"

"One does not—see clearly—but one does see—that it is
your daughter—who faces death."

Tears came to Matta's eyes and ran down her lined face. It
was the first sign of emotion that she had displayed and the
meaning of her lesson on the necessity of sacrifice became
poignantly clear. Deles wanted to help her, but he was confused.

"You said she was in good health," he said.

Matta turned mutely and pointed toward the lake. As if following a command, Deles rose and went outside. He squinted
into the bright morning sun as people walked by him, making
their way to the lakefront. Gathering by the largest pier, they
watched a boat, its oars plied by two men, which carried a girl
out onto the smooth black water. Edorna?

Now a second boat started out from the pier, this one piloted
by a single muscular man, though it was the same size as the
other boat. The two vessels glided silently for about two
hundred meters, and the men in the first boat raised their oars.
Seconds later the lone rower caught up with them. The man at
the stern of the first boat extended an oar, and the newcomer
grasped it to pull his boat toward the two men, who boarded his
boat. The three of them started back toward shore, leaving the
girl alone.

"Trun," Deles said aloud. Edorna was being sacrificed, the mirror reversal of the atavistic spectacle he had witnessed on the night he had been exiled from Sripha. But this time he would not stand idly by. He sprinted toward the shore, changing direction when he saw that there were no more boats moored at the pier. He ran to the next pier, shoving onlookers out of the way. He awkwardly boarded a skiff, and a murmuring rose from the crowd. But as he hurriedly unwound the line from a bollard, nobody tried to stop him. They quietened as he wrested the oar from the gunwales and slapped them into the water. Pulling at them as hard as he could, he soon gained on the sacrificial boat. Toward him drifted the boat containing the three men.

The people on the shore began to chant.

Now the girl, a tiny figure clothes in white, looked up from the water and saw him. Deles could not judge her expression from this distance, but he was sure she was surprised.

"What do you think you're doing?" one of the men called from the bow of the oncoming boat.

"Out of the way!" Deles shouted, brandishing a dripping oar.

They let him skim past, undoubtedly believing that he too would be taken by the trun. Unimpeded, he strained to reach Edorna. For a few seconds he thought he might get there before it was too late. But now the water on the starboard side of the sacrificial boat boiled white, and black claws shot over a gunwale, glistening in the bright morning sun. Edorna crouched against the futtocks, but the dripping trun reached inside the boat and lifted her high over its plated head. She didn't cry out; it was as if she had prepared for this moment all her life.

Dozens of frenzied trun now swarmed just under and on the surface. Edorna was plunged into the black water, and the flashing of scaled backs abruptly ceased.

"No!" Deles shouted, for he was at the sacrificial boat before the water stopped churning. The villagers stopped chanting, the echo of their voices still carrying across the lake.

Deles filled his lungs with the crisp morning air. Without hesitation, he went over the side, the cold water shocking him.

Sunlight didn't penetrate very far below the surface, but Edorna's white robe still showed through the aqueous gloom. The trun who had abducted her swam straight toward the bottom, a vague shadow soon to be gone forever.

Lungs aching, Deles remembered the oxygen recycler. He had put the device in a fold of his tattered garment before leaving Tartarus, but was it still there? His fingers, like the rest of his body, were so numbed by the cold water that he could barely feel anything. He fumbled, the exertion straining his lungs horribly. Where was it? He doubted that he could make it back to the surface, and the speck of white was now barely visible in the murk.

The tip of his index finger touched something small and hard. It had to be the recycler. Yes, he had it now, between his thumb and index finger. But before he could put it in place behind his ear, it slipped from his numbed fingers. Crying out involuntarily, a torrent of bubbles escaped his mouth and he inhaled water. He tried to keep from gagging as he searched for the recycler. His only chance was to dive below it. He thrust with his legs and dived down, circling back to where he estimated the recycler might plummet. In the murk, it seemed hopeless. He looked up and the sunlight rippled brilliantly through the water above. The recycler was a slowly falling black dot in the light. Deles reached out and caught it, carefully pressed it into the flesh behind his right ear, feeling the water pressure pushing away from him in a relief-giving rush. Without hesitation, he dove deeper.

For a little while he found it difficult to maneuver, turning end over end. Then he got the knack—he had only to point himself down and kick both legs together. Now the trun were swimming capriciously in circles. Below them were dark mounds, heaps of some organic material. It was the surface of their underwater village. If the trun took her in there, she wouldn't have a chance. It was riddled with tunnel mouths, from which other trun now emerged. But the group who had taken Edorna did not join them. Instead they swam back and forth, her abductor holding her just out of reach of their claws. If they kept playing this sadistic game, he might overtake them —but could Edorna last? The big, streamlined bodies of the trun were gliding easily now, still teasing those below them as they turned gracefully. Like a school of fish, they changed direction en masse, and Deles saw that he could cut them off if he angled his descent precisely. Bucking furiously to propel himself, he set out to make the attempt.

Now he was just above them. Edorna's abductors didn't see him, not suspecting that anyone could have followed them. With one last, prodigious kick Deles was upon them, snatching Edorna out of her captor's claws. Before he could swim away, something pulled at his clothing. He glanced over his shoulder to see the trun's claw clutching his ragged tunic. Pulling his knee up toward his chin, Deles kicked the creature in the head with all his strength. The exertion propelled him and Edorna upward as the creature clutched at its injured face. Dark fluid billowed between its claws as it curled up in pain.

Hugging Edorna close, Deles pressed her face to his chest, forcing her mouth and nose inside the oxygen bubble. Fearing that she was already dead, he swam toward the surface, the trun right behind him. The buoyancy of the oxygen bubble shot them upward very rapidly. Light played tantalizingly through the ripples, seemingly just out of reach. With each thrust, Deles expected his head to clear the water, but each time he was disappointed. He glanced down quickly and saw that the trun had made rapid gains. Hundreds of them cut through the water after him. The shimmering light seemed as far away as ever, but he redoubled his effort. Suddenly his head broke the surface.

There was the boat, only a few meters away. He swam for it. With a wrenching effort, he reached it and rolled Edorna over the gunwale. She collapsed in the bottom of the boat. As he started to haul himself over the side, something pulled him back. He felt a sharp pain in his calf. Kicking with all his remaining strength, he struck armor plating with his heel. His captured leg was released, and momentum heaved him up. He fell gasping into the boat next to Edorna.

She was alive, eyes wide with terror as the first trun reared over the open boat, its jaws distended, its claws outstretched.

Deles could not pick up an oar in time. He covered Edorna with his body and threw up his hand. His fingers opened, palm pointed directly at the attacking trun. There was a tearing sensation throughout his body, and then he was altogether outside his skin, coolly looking on. It seemed that all the energy of the distant sun, all the binding, strong, weak, electromagnetic forces of nature, were working for him, passing through his hand like the water cascading over the trun's scales.

The trun's assault was arrested. It froze, its claws poised ominously over Edorna, and then sank into the black water. None of the other trun showed themselves, and within seconds there was barely a ripple on the lake.

Deles crouched in the boat, breathing raggedly and grimacing from the pain in his leg. Blood seeped from it in ragged rivulets, pooling with the bilge water he lay in. Now that it wasn't being washed away, it flowed in a scarlet flood. He was so weak, he could hardly keep hs eyes open, in spite of his agony. The pain...oh, the *pain*. It spread over his body like flames on dry straw. It was intolerable. He clutched at the center of the pain, his torn calf, and his fingers were submerged in blood. He threw back his head and screamed, and the last thing he saw was Edorna's frightened face.

"Well," Matta was saying, "so you're finally coming around."

As her face grew clearer, Deles snatched at a fading dream. All he remembered about it was that Matta's face had not belonged in the watery dreamworld. Other than that it eluded him, the underwater world now replaced by the hut, in which stood Bilyf and Edorna, as well as Matta.

"Edorna saved your life," Matta said, "just after you saved hers."

The girl blushed as Deles's eyes found hers. She was lovely, he thought, with her dark hair and eyes.

"She tore the clothes off her own body to stanch your wound," Matta continued. "Otherwise you'd have bled to death."

'Yes," Deles said, his trembling voice revealing just how frail the ordeal had left him.

"Do you think you can swallow some of this broth?" Matta asked.

Bilyf helped him to lift his head, the tentacular digits firm yet gentle. "Deles has acted—with great courage—and compassion."

"I couldn't let her die like that," Deles said. "I saw . . . someone die like that once."

"Your people sacrifice to the *trun*, too?" Matta asked.

"Deles knew better than to explain to her that it was a trun he had seen butchered by humans, at Ploydektum's solstitial feast. She would never understand that there was something wrong with that. So, instead of talking, he stared at Edorna as her mother ladled out the broth. She was not pretty, he thought, she was beautiful. Her skin was unblemished, translucent, her lips delicate yet full. He was glad he had not let her be taken by the trun.

After he had eaten he felt much better, though his leg was sore. He coaxed Edorna into talking a little, and found that she was not as shy as he thought.

"What would the trun have done to you?" he asked.

"They would have taken me into their underwater city and eaten me," she said.

If she hadn't been so serious, Deles might have laughed. It seemed ludicrous that the lake people could believe such a thing. No doubt the trun took the victims because they were offered. Each human they drowned, after all, was one less enemy. Women must have been considered preferable because of their maternal potential, particularly young women. And yet folklore had generated its own explanation for the ritual.

"There's going to be trouble over this," Matta said.

"Really?"

"Yes," said Edorna. "I've disgraced Mother."

"Edorna," Matta said, setting down the utensils and embracing her, "you could never disgrace me—I love you."

Both of them started weeping. This affected Deles, who

asked Edorna, "Why do you believe you've disgraced your mother?"

"Because I'm still alive, and there may be reprisals."

"If that happens, your people will simply have to stand up to the trun."

"The trun live in the lakes," Matta said, "and we survive by fishing."

"There is technology that can subdue them."

"We don't have it here," Matta said, "and I doubt that the master of any estate would share his machines with us. Deles, I don't know how you saved my Edorna—though I'm very happy that you did—and I don't know how you killed that trun, but it is going to make trouble."

"I saw how he did it," Edorna said, wide-eyed. "He stretched out his hand, and the monster turned to stone."

"Edorna, you were underwater too long. It causes delusions, you know."

Deles nearly laughed aloud, but somehow managed to keep a straight face. Edorna had suffered no delusion, and she knew it. She shifted her gaze knowingly from Matta to Deles.

"Edorna," he said, "you must be mistaken about being disgraced. Surely your people will be pleased to see you still alive."

"You were unconscious, and so didn't see their reaction," Matta said. "Not one man, woman, or child in Lukerna raised a hand to help you when you were in danger of bleeding to death. Edorna and your friend helped me get you in here to bed."

"But now that the shock has passed, they'll be glad she's still alive."

"One sees—" Bilyf said, "that Deles underestimates—the depth of tradition."

Bilyf's admonition silenced him. All he had been through should have taught him that little was accomplished with the ease he had once imagined. Nevertheless, he could not believe that the lake people could want this innocent girl to die.

"Your friend is right," Matta said. "You come from the other side of the world, and don't understand what it's like to live here. Once you're gone you'll forget all about this, but we'll still be here. Our people will not treat us kindly."

"And who can blame them?" Edorna said, her luminous eyes brimming with tears.

"I can," said Deles.

"It's easy for you. Where you come from people are civilized."

"You would not say that if you spent time in—"

"Edorna!" a man shouted from outside the hut.

The girl looked up, startled. After a moment she called, "What do you want, Phranes?"

The hut door was flung open, and a young man stood within its frame. He was sturdily built, and wore a determined expression on his clean-shaven face. "I want *you,*" he said.

"It's too late for that, isn't it?" Edorna looked away from him, plainly disturbed by his presence.

"I love you," Phranes said.

"Then why didn't *you* come forth when she was being sacrificed?" Matta demanded.

He looked at the floor. "The ritual . . ."

"The ritual remains, I am sure," Matta snapped, "but this man saved Edorna's life."

"That may be," Phranes said, scowling, "but he's not one of us. And besides, Edorna is betrothed to me."

"*Was* betrothed to you, you mean—before she was selected by the widows to be sacrificed."

"You are a widow, Matta," Phranes said, "and so you bear as much responsibility as me. Perhaps more."

"I abstained from the vote," Matta said, reddening.

"It doesn't matter. Edorna is mine by law."

Edorna burst into tears, and the older woman took her into the other room. Left alone, Bilyf separating them, the two young men glared at one another.

"You're not one of us," Phranes said.

"Neither is Edorna now."

"She'll always be one of us."

"Didn't your people set her adrift to be taken by the trun?"

"It proves nothing."

"It proves that she *owes* nothing, to the people of Lukerna —or to you."

"One sees that—both positions may be—logically argued," Bilyf said, in a vain attempt at peacemaking.

"Edorna is mine," Phranes said, paying no attention to Bilyf, "and I'll fight for her."

"Very courageous of you," Deles said coldly. "You'll fight a man who lies in bed after nearly bleeding to death."

"I'll wait until you're well."

"You won't have to." Deles threw back the covers. He winced as his bad leg absorbed the pressure of his weight, and hobbled to the doorway to face Phranes.

"This is not—a wise course," Bilyf said, reaching out to restrain Deles.

Deles pushed him away, a sharp pain piercing his calf. He limped out the door after Phranes the sun nearly blinding him as a crowd quickly gathered. He confronted his enemy.

"I won't fight you until you're well," said Phranes.

"You won't fight me now *or* then," Deles replied, "because you're a coward."

Phranes stiffened, glancing at the people around him. "What did you say?" he demanded.

"I called you a coward," Deles said, enjoying himself immensely. Adrenaline coursed through his weakened body, giving him the illusion of renewed vitality. He folded his arms over his chest, smirking at the livid Phranes in spite of the pain.

"Take it back," Phranes said.

Deles stood his ground.

"Take it back, I say!"

"Coward," Deles repeated.

Phranes lunged, and Deles stretched out his hand to ward him off. Again, Deles was wrenched from his body, transformed into a being of blue fire. Detached, the very elements passing through him as if he were a human lightning rod, he watched Phranes's arrested charge. And then he was back inside his body as Phranes teetered and slowly fell forward. The corpse struck the ground with a thud.

A cry rose from the crowd as Phranes's body bounced and rolled to a stop at Deles's feet. The feral snarl of rage was still on Phranes's face, so swiftly had the cells stiffened. His arms were outstretched, much as the trun's had been, and his feet were poised for running. He looked most ungainly lying on the ground in his action pose.

Deles laughed.

"Other," someone said, and the crowd shrank from Deles.

"No," he said doubting that they would believe his denial, but not really caring if they did or not.

"He's an Other." It was the bearded man, his eyes fearful.

Why should he deny it? At least he would be certain that they wouldn't bother him now. He backed into Matta's hut and closed the door behind himself.

"Deles—has killed again," Bilyf said, from the shadows.

"I had to." Now that the heat of anger was gone, Deles felt sick and weak and tired. He crossed the room and collapsed in a chair. In spite of his condition he was flushed with an exhilarating sense of power. He frightened himself. "I had to," he repeated.

"One sees—that the young master—believes this to be true."

"Are you telling me it isn't true, Bilyf?"

"One—cannot see."

"You have no vision," Deles said, "because this is all too great to be understood just now."

"The Now That—Seems to Be."

"Yes." Deles grasped the concept of the continuum as fluid, a plastic medium to be used for one's own purposes . . . if only one knew how to use it. "Yes, the Now That Seems to Be."

Chapter Twenty

Vengeance

It had been a long, grueling journey, and Deles had been forced to do regrettable things along the way. The worst had been the murder of two sentry-clones to get the graviton platform he and his companions rode to complete the last leg of the journey to Ploydektum.

Now the platform, bearing Bilyf and Edorna as well as Deles himself, settled on a hillcrest overlooking Ploydektum.

"Tomorrow," Deles said to Edorna, "Bilyf will take you to Naktra, a village not far from here. The technicians live there who care for Ploydekt's machines." He pondered his enemy's power while he gazed at the mazelike, half-submerged estate.

Edorna nodded. New as the world was to her, she always looked to Deles for guidance. She was in love with him, he knew, and he had grown very fond of her. Bilyf would take care of her until Deles had done what he must; probably better care than she would receive at his own hands, at that.

"I wish you wouldn't go," Edorna said.

"But I must." Deles twisted a sliver of bright metal, which projected a curved field around them, two meters on all sides. It responded to the distinctive vibrations of their bodies so that they could pass in and out of its radius, while nothing else could, not even a raindrop. Bilyf unfurled suspensor beds as Edorna ignited a heat triangle to keep them warm through the coming night. Deles stood staring at the estate laid in the darkening valley floor.

When Bilyf had finished his chore, he said, "One sees—the young master—in turmoil."

"Not so much now," Deles replied. "I am prepared for what is to come."

"One cannot approve—of what Deles does."

"I know that, Bilyf—and I understand the principle underlying your objections. But morality cannot apply here. It's quite beyond that." He placed his hand on the striated muscles of Bilyf's shoulder, pleased that they had filled out again since the return to Sripha. "I fear that this is quite beyond our grasp."

"One sees—that this is so—and yet one cannot help grop-ing—in the darkness." He turned away and passed out of the protective field, seeking solitude.

Deles knelt on one knee, looking down at his anthroform shell. He noted that his scar was healed, and that the cicatrix would soon vanish without a trace. Such were the results of countless ages of perfecting the human body. But there was to be no immortality for Man, no matter how physically perfect he made himself. Nature had struck no bargain with humankind, though humans had foolishly tried to conquer her. Even if im-mortality were possible, what good would it be to him person-ally if he didn't avenge his mother and himself? Death was no stranger to him anymore—he had dealt it from his own hand. He turned his palm upward and gazed at the embedded disc . . . and the shapeless thing dancing around it.

Edorna's fingertips touched his elbow lightly. He looked into her dark eyes and saw love there, love that he could not respond to as he felt he should.

"Don't go," she said.

"I have no choice."

"You have a whole universe of choices."

Deles smiled. "You are so optimistic, just like your people. The lake people are the only humans in the solar system who continue to have a lot of children. Don't you know that the End gathers momentum even now to erase all that has ever been?"

"It doesn't matter," Edorna said. "We are alive now, and we must go on until the End."

"Is that all there is to it?"

"Why must there be more?"

"Perhaps there isn't," Deles said. "But I cannot settle for that."

Edorna wept.

He embraced her, and she held him more tightly than he would have believed possible, her warm tears washing his neck and soaking into the shoulder of his tunic. He was moved but unswayed. Even if he had been capable of love, and Edorna had been the woman he loved, he would still have gone to face Ploydekt.

The sun sank toward the gently rounded horizon as Deles made his way down the hillside. He had sent Edorna to Naktra with Bilyf in the morning. He had watched them riding the gra-viton platform until they diminished into a tiny speck in the clouds. Then he had eaten lightly and meditated until afternoon. After the sun had passed overhead, he had begun the walk to Ploydektum.

The dark walls of the estate reared slowly upward as he approached them. In the distance he could see riders on shaggy mounts, and the breeze carried the muffled sounds of merriment. He had chosen the day of his return carefully. Tonight was the night of the solstitial feast.

Only the orange tip of the sun glowed in the heavens as the revelers straggled into the estate. They were on their way to the banquet. They would choke on the meal, for Deles intended to join them. Surmounting the last gentle hill, where he had so often practiced his dikoit throw, Deles saw the banquet hall slide open to admit the guests. He stood for a few moments under the starry canopy of night, waiting until all were inside.

It was completely dark when he began to walk the last few hundred paces. He came to the gaping south entrance, a glowing mouth in the face of darkness. He went inside, to the banquet hall.

At first nobody noticed him. Amid the hubbub of drunken conversation and laughter, he strode toward the head table. There were a few grunts of recognition. The voices softened and faded. Before him was Ploydekt, flanked by a pretty young boy and Dictys.

The stillness had made Ploydekt raise his jowly head. For a moment he registered irritation, then puzzlement, and at last incredulous recognition. Deles walked to the head table, gazing across it into Ploydekt's rheumic eyes.

No one spoke, not even Dictys, as Ploydekt was held spellbound by this apparition from the past.

"I told you I'd be back," Deles said.

For a moment Ploydekt was speechless. Then his mouth opened, and he croaked, "So you did, Deles."

"You seem surprised to see me."

"I am, a bit." Ploydekt glanced at Deles's apparently empty hands. An unarmed enemy, he must have been thinking, posed no threat. He had only to call his guards and . . . He sank back into his chair, secure with the certainty that he could not be harmed.

"I found Verra," Deles said, savoring the murmur that arose from the guests.

"You did?" Ploydekt leaned forward again in spite of himself. "Have you brought her back with you?"

"No."

"Then how can we know that you're telling the truth?" A hint of malicious pleasure crossed Ploydekt's bloated face.

"You can't."

"So you admit that we have no reason to believe that you ever searched for her at all."

"But I did search for her," Deles said, "and I found her."

In a theatrically strident voice, Ploydekt demanded: "Then why didn't you bring her to Sripha?"

"Because she's dead."

The crowd, which had become noisier as Ploydekt gained confidence, was once again subdued. The master's depraved face now showed fear, doubtless unwittingly, and his diffidence frightened them.

"You . . . found her body?" Ploydekt asked.

"No."

"Then . . . ?"

"I killed her."

As a commotion erupted in the banquet hall, Ploydekt's face twisted into a smirk. Clearly, he believed that Deles's statement was tantamount to suicide. No one would sympathize with Verra's murderer. "You were sent to save her life," he said, "not to take it."

"Was that why I was sent to Tartarus?" said Deles. "I thought it was because you wanted me to see a most interesting world firsthand. A holiday."

"You try my patience," said a scowling Ploydekt, his voice barely audible over the angry shouting of the crowd. "But that may be excused. Murder, however, may not." He raised his hand to signal his sentries.

Deles matched Ploydekt's gesture, lifting his hand, palm outward. Fear found Ploydekt once again as he saw the amorphous shape capering about the disc embedded in Deles's palm. He knew at that moment that he was going to die. The horror on his fat face would be preserved until it rotted away, Deles thought with grim satisfaction.

The power exploded in Deles, wrenching him out of his body in an agonizing blue-white shock. Fueled by his hatred, it ripped at his spirit, his very soul. There was no calm center this time, no detachment. The flames of murder consumed him. He tried to cry out, fearing his own destruction if he did not fight against this horror from within, but he was overwhelmed. No sound came, nor was there sight, smell, hearing, or touch. There was only the immolation of his own spirit.

And still the flames did not abate, even as his essence shriveled and blackened. Soon there would be nothing but ashes where there had once been the being Deles; there would be only hate where there had been a man. He could not bear to lose so much.

Then, like the abrupt awakening from a bad dream, he was

back in the banquet hall. Back in his own body once again, dizzy, head aching. Gradually he became aware of the stillness, the quiet of death. The silence unnerved him as he stared at the frozen face of Ploydekt.

"You should be cheering the death of this monster!" he shouted, turning to the revelers.

But no one answered him. No one even moved. And, as he looked at them, he began to understand why.

He had destroyed them all.

"Dictys," he whispered, turning back to see his cousin, mouth open as if to speak, hand outstretched toward him.

"No!" he cried. But then he remembered that Dictys had betrayed him. If he did not keep that in mind, he knew, he would have to face the fact that he had killed someone whose only sin was weakness; that he had killed someone who, in spite of all, had loved him. "What have I done?"

All the guests stared at him, for he had not moved from the spot where he had done the terrible thing. The accusing faces did not appear to be dead. As he swayed, nearly fainting, the light reflected in their eyes sparkled, creating the illusion of life.

Get out, he told himself, get out of here now. Get away from this place before you go mad. He would go to his mother. At least *she* had not been here. He stumbled toward the entrance to underground Ploydektum.

But before he could escape the frozen nightmare tableau, he was compelled to look once again at Dictys's remains. He could not avert his eyes, though he wanted to turn away more than he had ever wanted anything before.

Dictys had been in the act of rising from the table, a strangely imploring expression on his face. Had he been trying to intercede for Deles when his life had ended, when he had been turned to stone?

Deles tried to cry out but could not; only a strangled gasp struggled from his throat. Nor could he weep, somehow. He could not even walk away. He was made of stone, like his victims.

At last he forced himself to move. He staggered toward the exit that would lead him down to his mother's quarters. As soon as the darkness of the corridor engulfed him, he was able to convince himself that things were not as they seemed. After all, everything had been arranged by the Others. He was their tool, and nothing was so simple that it could be understood on a human level anymore.

Ploydekt was dead, and he must console himself with that fact. The rest was out of his hands. He tried to convince himself of his innocence as he followed a winding tunnel deeper and deeper under the surface. Only Phranes had died in that confrontation in Lukerna. Why had this been different? Why was Dictys dead?

Bitter tears flowed from his eyes. His hatred had destroyed one who loved him, and now his remorse threatened to destroy him. How could he go on? This was no dream, no illusion, and he could not blame the Others for what he had done. Some monstrous thing had risen up from inside him like a malignant cancer and, lusting for vengeance, had overpowered all that was decent.

He wanted to die. Instead, he vomited.

When his heaving was finished, he wiped his chin with the back of his hand. His mother was still alive, at least, and so was Bilyf . . . and Edorna. There was still much for him to live for. It was over now; he had taken his revenge. The price had been terrible, awesome, but it was done. Ploydekt was dead.

"Deles?" a voice reverberated through the corridor.

He looked up and saw a woman in blue facing him. Lehana? No, this woman did not speak directly to his mind. "Mother?"

"You're back," she said, stepping out of the shadows. "I knew you'd come back." She hurried to him and embraced him. "Does anybody know you're here?"

He could barely suppress a bitter laugh. He shook his head.

"They're all at the feast," she said. "You're safe for now."

"And for a good, long while to come. Ploydekt will never harm us—or anyone else—again."

"Then . . ."

"He's dead."

"Dead." Danna shut her eyes, as if in silent prayer.

"I killed him."

Danna fell silent. Perhaps, Deles speculated, she did not believe him. She knew nothing of the weapon he had brought with him from Tartarus, and without it how could he have killed a man who was surrounded by his own guards? She might have thought he had gone mad.

"Your journey must have been very difficult," she said.

"A nightmare," said Deles, certain that the nightmare was by no means at an end.

"And Bilyf? Is he all right?"

"Fine. I sent him to Naktra."

"Of course," Danna said conspiratorially, "he would have been too conspicuous. But surely someone will recognize you anyway, and report your presence to Ploydekt."

"Mother . . ."

"I must hide you, Deles. If Ploydekt finds out that you are here . . ."

"Mother, I've already told you—Ploydekt is dead."

"Perhaps there are other estates on Sripha who will take us in. If not, we must go back to Rocinth. After we deal with my—with Acrios, we can return to settle with Ploydekt."

"Come with me." Deles took her by the hand and led her up to the surface, where the stars shone down onto the motionless revelers at Ploydekt's festival of death. The only sound was the rustling of Danna's skirts as she walked across the tiled floor.

"You say they are dead," Danna said, "and yet they don't look dead." But when she had wandered through the banquet hall, like a spectator at some ghoulish sculpture exhibition, she took her son down to her rooms. Deles was emotionally numb by the time she drew back her curtain to admit them to her salon. It was not that he had killed Dictys. No, he had come to accept that all too quickly.

Danna sat him in webbing and poured a goblet of wine for him out of a crystal carafe. He downed it in one long draught, and she refilled it for him.

"How did you do it?" she asked him.

"With this." He showed her the disc and the shapeless, moving thing encircling it.

Danna stared at them in fascination. "You found these on Tartarus?"

"Yes."

"The Others," Danna said triumphantly. "They planned the whole thing, Deles. You lead a charmed life—and your charms are the Others."

"But what of poor Dictys?" he said forlornly.

"Dictys betrayed us."

Deles was suddenly reminded of his mother's indifference upon hearing of Verra's forced landing on Tartarus. She so easily dismissed the deaths of these innocent people, people to whom she had been close. How could she be so callous? Had the horrors of her life permanently unsettled her mind?

"Mother," he said, "they're all dead."

"There's nothing we can do about that, is there?"

"You don't seem to understand. I killed them."

"We must look ahead to Rocinth now," she went on as if she hadn't heard him. "We must prepare to deal with Acrios."

"Mother, I have killed innocent people. I can't go on as though it never happened."

"You're distraught, my son, but you must remember that there is only one task remaining—and with the weapon you've brought back from Tartarus it will not be a difficult one."

She was mad. There could be no doubt of it. And so was he. But he had to stay with her and help her. Bilyf would know what to do. But Deles's optimism was overshadowed by the gnawing realization that Danna had been like this since before he was born.

"Tomorrow I'll go to Naktra and fetch Bilyf," he said, having decided not to mention Edorna just yet. "When I come back, we'll talk about what must be done next."

"We know what must be done."

"Tomorrow," he repeated, trying to sound self-assured, but he feared that she was right, that there actually was no doubt about what he must do. The only remaining question was whether it was what Danna expected, or something that only the Others knew. He was more fearful now than he had been in Verra's presence. Then he had trusted the Others out of necessity; now he was able to assess what they had done to him through their manipulation. He didn't like it. They had made him into a murderer.

Or had they merely stripped away a veneer of humanism to reveal the essential killer underneath it?

"Tomorrow you'll go after Bilyf then, Deles?" Danna asked.

"Yes, tomorrow."

"And after that?"

"After that . . . we'll see."

Part Three

Chapter Twenty-one

Return to Rocinth

"Touch me, Deles," Edorna said, "please."

He did as she asked, turning over in the webbing and caressing her bare flesh as tenderly as he could. But he knew that it was not enough. Edorna trembled pleasurably, to show him how much she loved having his hands on her. He obliged her, but his heart was not in it. Impulsively, he held his open hand before her eyes in the half-light.

"Why do you show me that now?" she asked, pain and confusion evident through her lake country accent. Her face was eerily lit by the dancing amorphous shape.

"I think of it now as the Destroyer," Deles said, unmindful of her question, "but perhaps I am attributing to it my own nature."

Edorna turned his hand and kissed the back of it. Even while covered, the Destroyer illuminated her face with a faint blue glow, making her look lovelier than ever. "Are old memories troubling you?"

"Old memories . . . and new commitments."

Edorna drew away from him. She had grown fond of Danna since she'd come to Ploydektum, but she had always been horrified by Danna's insistence that Deles kill his grandfather. She had never really believed that he would do it, but now she wasn't so sure.

"You are going to Rocinth, aren't you, Deles?" she asked.

"Yes. It's not what you think, though. Everything will be all right."

"If you go to Rocinth, how is that possible? Do you think Bilyf's vision can be so easily dismissed?"

"His vision was not clear in its details," Deles replied, surprised at how logically forceful the usually submissive Edorna had suddenly become.

"Clear enough that your grandfather will die by your hand."

He sighed. "If it is to be, it will happen whether I go to Rocinth or not."

"You must do everything in your power to prevent it, Deles."

"That is what I intend to do!" he said, raising his voice.

Defiantly, she stared straight into his eyes, saying nothing.

"You don't undersand," he said, getting out of the webbing to pace the floor. "This is all quite beyond my grasp, so how can I expect you to understand?"

"Do you think I'm a fool, Deles, to tell me that you are being forced to go to Rocinth? This is *your* decision."

"I can't begin to explain it to you. You must trust me."

"Trust you! You've had every woman in Ploydektum!"

"It's hardly the same thing, Edorna," Deles sighed, discouraged that she could equate one with the other. "I don't owe you fidelity, in the first place. Furthermore, you are free to enjoy other men if you so desire . . . or women, for that matter."

"What a decadent place this is," she said. "Why must we accede to this immoral climate?"

"Accede? I see nothing wrong with it."

She moaned in exasperation, falling back on the webbing.

"You must abandon the notion that your provincial tribe's morality is superior to the freedom of the estates," he said.

"Even in Ploydektum, murder is not sanctioned."

"I have told you once," he said with annoyance, "I do not intend to kill my grandfather."

Edorna rose from the webbing and thrust herself at him, burying her face in his chest. He felt the moist warmth of her tears on his skin and could not be angry with her. If anything, he should have wept himself.

"Please, Deles," she cried, "don't go."

"I must. It is not my choice, or even my mother's—though she imagines that she is the force behind all this. It is the Others who pull the thread through the tapestry."

"The Others?" She raised her teary face and stared at him in disbelief. *"The Others?"*

A thunderhead reared darkly ahead, and for a moment Acrios fancied that he could make the storm do his bidding, as in the past. But as the immense gray sheet of falling water drew nearer, he remembered how far he had fallen since those halcyon days. Why hadn't he thought to bring a protective bubble to shield himself from the elements?

"Addlepated old fool," he said. He would freeze to death if he tried to ride the graviton platform over the clouds. There was nothing for it now but to suffer the discomfort of getting wet. How ignominious.

But when he was within a few hundred yards of the rain, the cloud began to separate as if it had been cleaved by a sword, and he sailed through a narrow passageway that remained dry, though on either side the roiling clouds gushed rain. Lucky; the mundomentus had assessed the environmental difficulty such a course would entail, and found that keeping Acrios dry was no threat to Rocinth's ecology. It would have done the same for any anthroform on the planet, and yet this act of kindness lent Acrios new hope. Things might be accomplished without the nearly divine powers of the Receptor. Perhaps he would die, as Bilyf's vision suggested, but as he sailed between the restless gray cloud banks, he knew he would not die willingly . . . at least not yet.

He had emerged from the storm into the golden twilight, daring to feel triumphant, when a severe pain coursed through him, ravaging his body. He dropped to his knees on the platform and cried out in anguish, "The searcher!"

For a few moments, the clouds, the sun, the endless verdant lands below vanished, and he lived in a world of pain as the searcher made its way through the pulsing gyri of his brain. And then it was over and he knelt gasping, the wind flapping his white robe. He shook and the sweat drenched his face, but he soon felt better. If only he could remember where he had been going when the seizure had begun. . . .

One sees the madness in little Danna and Edorna. There can be no doubt that their emotional states are genuine. To them, Deles's decision to leave means that *he will no longer be with them.*

But of course he will always be with them.

In the Now That Seems to Be . . .

. . . in the Past That is . . .

. . . and in the Now That Will Be . . .

But Bilyf is confused. It seems that the principles instilled in him in the eggsac are, for the first time, inadequate. He cannot see clearly. He suspects that his involvement with humans has corrupted his understanding of the values taught him by the mother and the knowledge sharers. And yet . . .

. . . he is certain that . . .

. . . there is . . .

. . . more . . .

Deles walked down the corridor. The clones didn't speak as he passed them, more from respect than fear. They had grown to love their new master—overcoming their initial terror, generated by the spectacle of the frozen dead at the solstitial feast

—but today they dared not speak to him. Something momentous was afoot. The atmosphere was so charged that even the most oblivious drone sensed the heavy touch of destiny's hand.

Deles had called for a ship.

He emerged from Ploydektum's bowels onto the bright surface of the world. Wispy clouds drifted through the metallic sky as he made his way up the hill. Why did Bilyf treat him in this manner? Surely he understood that all the prophecies of a dying universe couldn't make Deles kill again. Bilyf had once admitted that his sight was obscured regarding Deles's future. Surely his strange behavior arose from his confusion over his myopic prescience.

It didn't matter. The Others might be driving Deles to Rocinth in some mysterious way, but they couldn't force him to kill. Or could they?

He stopped short and gazed at the Destroyer embedded in his hand. The finest robots on Sripha—Ploydekt's personal physicians among them—had tried without success to remove it. The Destroyer, as Deles had come to call it, was inextricably linked to his nervous system. Nothing short of chopping off his own hand would ever rid him of the monstrous thing.

He resumed walking. Now he was well away from the estate, out in the hills. His hills. The ship would come to him here, from Naktra. This ship, Ploydekt's finest, would not only provide him with the precise information he needed for his journey, but with good company as well.

Currently, Rocinth's ellipse was only slightly closer to the sun than Sripha's, very convenient for trade between the two planets. He would be there in a matter of days. Strangely, even that thought made him uncomfortable.

The wind picked up, gently stirring his hair as he waited on the hillcrest. He was lost in thought when a shadow blanketed him. It was the ship.

It settled onto the grass in front of him, a great silver egg. He had never been inside a ship this large, or this elaborate. Indeed, only a select few had ever traveled with Ploydekt to Rocinth. But now the ship, like all the master's possessions, belonged to Deles. That was the law on Sripha. If you killed a powerful man, all that he had was yours.

Perhaps his mother was right. Perhaps Sripha was less civilized than Rocinth. He would soon find out. Turning around, he took one last look at the earthen walls of Ploydektum and backed into the airlock. He knew that his mother was watching.

The hatch rang shut, blocking out Ploydektum, and the innerdoor opened. A slight vibration started as the ship asked in mellifluous, androgynous tones, "Do you require exterior visuals?"

"No," he replied, making his way to the webbing. "I have to think. No distractions." He sat down and buried his face in his hands. The Destroyer was hard and gemlike against his cheek. Why couldn't he get rid of it? Hadn't it served its purpose?

Perhaps Edorna was right; perhaps his journey to Rocinth could result only in death. Perhaps he could still turn back. But he knew that the glowing Destroyer, the shapeless dancer of death, would permit nothing of the kind.

As the ovoid ship lifted from the hillcrest and shot into the clouds, Danna stood at the window of what was once Ploydekt's bedroom. The air was rent by a powerful cracking sensation as the ship sped away. She allowed herself to enjoy a thrill at the prospect of her imminent vengeance.

"Very soon now, Father," she said. Deles could not fail, armed with a weapon that turned men into stone. It was all working out for the best; even Deles's banishment had led ultimately to Acrios's destruction. There could be no doubt of it— this was destiny. While Deles had languished about the estate, grieving over Dictys, she had known that he would go to Rocinth eventually, in spite of Edorna's wishes to the contrary. And now he was on his way.

"One sees—that death—is near."

She turned to see Bilyf shambling into the spacious chamber. "*Justice* is near, you mean," she said.

"There is no justice—if there is—no crime."

"Bilyf, are you saying that we can't be held accountable for our deeds? Surely the knowledge sharers would disagree."

"Little Danna—twists Bilyf's meaning."

"What do you ask of me?" she demanded, uncomfortable in Bilyf's presence on this of all days.

"One has not come—to impugn—but to ask—a favor."

This was certainly an unexpected turn. "Name it."

"A ship—with which one—might return to—Mennon."

Danna could not speak for a moment. At last she found her voice. "Are you leaving me?" she managed to say.

"One must return—to Mennon."

It was probably just as well. At least now Bilyf would not be gurgling his disapproval whenever she happened upon him.

"Very well, I'll get you a ship, Bilyf."

"One is grateful—to little Danna."

Bilyf drifted in space. The small private ship he had taken

from Sripha was insufficient for the long journey to Mennon.
He had left it docked at Prosep, a world of the neighboring solar
system, a barren and ugly planet that served as a port.

He traveled from there on a tradesman's ship with fifty
others. Though there were thirty-seven humans aboard, the remaining thirteen numbered no Mennon among them. Vanor-
gan, ri'ith, Vulg, Forn, but not a single eggsharer. Still, they got
along well enough, one of the ri'ith possessing a mild chronopathic ability, and the others being affable enough traveling
companions.

Even so, Bilyf often went alone to stare at the stars through
the visual scan. One such occasion transported him, as if his
ability had never waned, to . . .

    . . . the ship that bore Deles . . .

        . . . the young master, to . . . .

           . . . Rocinth . . .

Deles dreamed of reconciliation, of love, as he passed
through images of the starfields. he doubted that he could succeed in his mercy mission, but he knew that he must try.

    . . . all this . . .

        . . . he thought as he looked at the stars, and so
little happiness. He was nearly defeated by the hopelessness of
reuniting his mother and Acrios, and yet he pressed on. Bilyf
loved him the more for that . . .

    . . . as the one starfield metamorphosed into another, one
that had no place on the short journey from Sripha to Rocinth.

He viewed the starfield through his own eyes and Deles's
eyes simultaneously. Dread bloomed in him like a dark flower,
and he shivered in the cold of the Now That Seems to Be. There
was no comfort, and there would be no relief. The love that he
and Deles felt for one another was drowned in the enormity of
their fear.

One star among the millions stood out, slowly growing as
they neared it. The purity of its light was somehow tainted as
they came ever closer. They were bathed in the icy fires of the
Blue Star.

There was no escape.

Chapter Twenty-two

The Pursuit of Acrios

As his ship followed the coastline, Deles watched the visuals in dread anticipation. The course veered away from the sea and a ragged hole appeared on the manicured land nearby, a well. And there was the villa itself, elegant and imposing even from a bird's-eye view. The lawn rushed up to meet him, and the ship was down.

"Your destination," it said grandly. "The estate of Acrios."

"Thank you." Deles rose slowly from the webbing, reluctant to leave the safety and comfort of the ship. Nevertheless, he must not dally, for this was a crucial moment. His mother had worked on him from the time he was a baby, but he had no intention of harming Acrios. He had no intention of harming anyone.

The outer hatch dropped as he passed through the airlock, admitting him to the warm twilight of Rocinth. As he set foot on the grass, a small animal leaped and landed at his feet, staring at him through huge eyes. Its mouth opened, tongue vibrating like gut on a stringed instrument. Soon an insect was lured by the hum, and once it was inside the predator's jaws, teeth snapped shut around it. All the while, the tiny hunter continued to stare at Deles, its many legs unmoving. The fearless creature was a naf.

"I remember you," Deles said. "Or at least others like you. I chased them outside the house we lived in when I was a boy."

The naf scratched itself with a spindly leg and hopped away at its leisure. Deles smiled, seeing this as a good omen. At least the first being he met on Rocinth was not hostile.

He started toward the villa. In the tenebrous light of dusk he stumbled onto a pathway which led to a crystal garden. He stopped to admire the garden's prismatic complexity, for his mother had described it to him more than once. The rambling villa sat on the hill above, the most beautiful structure Deles had ever seen. How peaceful it was this evening, in comparison to the first time he had been here.

He paused in front of the massive stone slabs that served as steps. A colonnade supported a roof that looked as vast as the sky from where he stood. Ploydektum was larger, but mostly underground, not boldly proclaiming its glory under the dying sun like this. For a moment, he studied the frieze running the breadth of the house, and then mounted the steps to go inside.

Here was the spacious dining hall, its braziers cold, but the room was imposing even in the gloom of the setting sun. Deles walked past the long table at its center.

"Is there anyone here?" he called out.

An echo was the only answer.

"Robots?" Something had to be caring for the villa and its grounds. A telltale buzzing emanated from the nearest wall as soon as the word was spoken. A panel slid open, revealing the shiny metal casing of a robot. Its appearence was appropriate for this room, its design as important as its function. Aesthetically pleasing, it resembled a stylized sculpture of an armored warrior. Extricating itself from its hiding place, it walked toward him with precise steps. A meter in front of him, it stopped and said, "At your service, sir."

"Where is your master?"

"This he has not told me. Of late, the master's mind tends to wander," the robot confided. "It is the searcher that causes this —the delusions, as well as the sharp physical pains he suffers on occasion. These ill effects, it seems, cannot be avoided."

"Then he might not remember to come home for some time."

"Eventually the mundomentus will send him home on a graviton platform, or even a ship, if necessary."

"Has he forgotten who he is?"

"This possibility is likely, though how long Acrios might go without someone reminding him of his identity is difficult to determine. He has often stated that he would like to forget who he is, but even if he were successful in such an endeavor, it would not be for long."

"Then you think he's deliberately staying away?"

"If so, it would not be in my master's best interests to announce it to you, a stranger."

"I suppose not." Through its logic, however, the robot had revealed the truth. Acrios had fled the estate, somehow knowing that Deles was coming. But how had he known?

"The Gift," he said, answering his own question aloud. In spite of the searcher, Acrios still possesssed his unique power.

Deles dismissed the robot, and as it returned to its niche, he mounted the stairs that wound around the villa's interior above the dining hall, leading to sumptuous rooms and the highest chamber of all, which housed the reception pool. Deles observed the dry tiles at the bottom of the pool, imagining what it had been like for Acrios to absorb the signals sent by the Machine. Shaking his head, he walked out a door on the far side of the room. Slanting rays of pale sunlight striped the pastel corridor, as he emerged onto a balcony.

From here he could see all of the spacious grounds. A garden lay before him, its thousand bright colors bisected by a path. Like a jewel, an ornate peak of crystal jutted out of the flowered shrubs. Beyond this were copses, more shrubs and a topiary of strange creatures. A stable of garoms was nearly hidden behind some hedges. It was a lovely scene, and yet he was not at ease as he savored its pastoral details.

In the hazy distance the trees were not so sculptured, and there was a dark spot among their motley limbs that commanded his attention. He couldn't make it out very well, but he knew that it was the well he had seen from the sky. He felt drawn to it.

He would go down and take a look. In minutes he was on the path. Along the way he lingered to examine the intricate, icy patterns of the crystal garden. Before he was born, Danna had nurtured it, and now it threatened to overrun the path. Strange that the robots had permitted such untidiness. Had Acrios commanded them to leave it alone?

A little further on, he heard a whuffing sound, and just past the last clump of crystals, he found its source. Here were the garoms, a dozen of the finest he had ever seen, their fur sleek, their powerful haunches and legs suitable for racing. They snorted as he passed them, doubtless hoping that he would feed them.

Now the path became rougher, weeds intruding onto it. The last rays of the sun were fading as he reached the overgrown rim of the well. He felt an urge to climb down into its dark depths. His foot dislodged some loose earth, and it hissed as it slid into the blackness. Some of it thumped solidly, and, as his eyes became accustomed to the dark, he saw a ledge spiraling down into the well. The impulse to go down grew stronger.

It was foolish. This would not help him to find Acrios. . . . But how could he be so sure of that? His grandfather might be down there even now. Unlikely, but . . . his feet seemed to find their own way onto the ledge. He would go down and see what had so magnetized him, if anything. Fortunately, he carried a glowpin in his tunic. Walking briskly, except where the ledge had crumbled here and there, he soon found himself in total darkness. The sky was a rough circle only marginally lighter than the towering walls of the well. He had descended to a great

depth in a very short time, but was in such a dreamlike state
that he hardly noticed the passage of time. . . .

Deeper and deeper he went, in a seemingly endless spiral
. . . a gyre, diminishing into . . .

Tunnels yawned like the mouths of giant beasts, revealed by
the glowpin's light. But he would have none of them . . . until he
came at last to the right one. But how would he know the *right*
one? Once more he looked up, and in the tiny speck of sky he
thought he saw, nestled in the Nidus Constellation, the moons
of Rocinth forming a familiar configuration. Though why it
seemed familiar, he could not say. A delusion, most likely. In
this mysterious place, he might see anything.

The tunnel mouth waited. He knew it when he came to it,
and holding up the glowpin, he went inside. He walked a very
long distance, though it seemed to take hardly any time at all.
At first a faint glow illuminated the tunnel ahead, and, as Deles
pushed languidly on, he came eventually to its source. It was a
large chamber, its vaulted ceiling encrusted with luminescent,
microscopic lifeforms.

"This way?" Deles mused aloud. How many thousands, or
even millions of such passageways existed beneath Rocinth's
surface? It would be so easy to get lost . . . and yet the prospect
did not frighten him, not after Tartarus.

He wandered into a branching tunnel, as if pulled there by
an unseen hand. The urge to go on had become an obsession.
He walked faster, though still in a trancelike state. Soon he was
almost running, no light to guide him other than the feeble rays
of his glowpin. He loped along in the dark, and then sprinted.

His right foot caught on something, and he tumbled painfully
down an incline. When he came to rest, he found himself on a
smooth, flat surface. A few sore spots and a scraped knee were
the extent of his injuries. He stood gingerly, making sure that he
could walk. He saw the glowpin lying on the floor, picked it up
and took a look around him.

He had landed in a cubicle or small room. It was boxlike, the
walls, floor, and ceiling featureless and made of slate. It was a
dreadfully gray and lifeless place. Behind him was the open
panel through which he had fallen. He saw that the panel was
set on a runner so that it could be shut quickly. Even if it didn't
lock from the outside, one couldn't possibly find the proper
footing on the incline to move such a heavy door. This was
obviously the work of a human hand. He had seen enough Rocinthan ruins to know that. But why this one cubicle, so far
removed from all human habitation? And why had he been
drawn so ineluctably to this chamber?

Something protruded from the back wall, catching the glow-

pin's light. It wasn't very large, but it was clearly there by design, no mere flaw on the otherwise blank wall. He saw as he
moved toward it that it was a handle of some kind, set on a wire
or thin rod a centimeter from the wall.

His hand trembled as he reached toward it. He hesitated for
as long as he could, fearing the consequences of touching it.
Impulsively, as if it had a mind of its own—the Destroyer's?—
his hand leaped onto the protrusion. It moved under his fingertips. For a moment he was poised on a great, silent brink, and
then . . .

A rainbow loped through his head, an exaggerated human
figure limned in a dazzling array of colors. It leapt and cavorted,
capering, twisting, dancing. An enormous hand reached out of
it and twisted a brilliantly hued rod.

It was instructive. The running figure was him, a distorted
self image running down a corridor. It had been gleaned from
his own mind, and now a method was being extrapolated by
which he might turn the rod . . . but to what purpose?

He twisted the handle.

The wall bulged, distending, forming a snakelike appendage.
It moved swiftly, coiling about his waist and pulling him into an
oval opening that widened just enough to admit him. Amazed
that he had not dropped the glowpin, he tucked it into his tunic.
With both hands free, he tugged at the coil, but couldn't budge
it. He was rushed through the darkness, the forward movement
blowing back his hair. Abruptly, the coil changed direction, not
once but several times. It bore him at a uniform speed until it
came to a sudden stop, dumping him into a heap of soft, warm
stuff.

A dim light issued from somewhere, illuminating a bubble
that was in the process of forming around him. He was afraid of
smothering until he felt cool oxygen filling his lungs.

Floating in a trough of sweet smelling, viscous fluid, he was
warm and serene. He knew his placidity was artificially induced,
and something in his core told him to fight against it. The power
was his in his hand . . . the Destroyer. . . . But he was lulled by
the easy movement of the bubble, now one in a veritable sea of
bubbles. Why should he want to harm them?

Ahead was a clump of whipping dark strands, oddly juxta-
posed so that they resembled a hand, but with tentacles instead
of fingers . . . tentacles that plucked the bubbles from the stream
one at a time, examining them and depositing them in a huge
vat. Opposite them was a wall with hundreds of holes in it.
Whenever the handlike thing found a bubble with something in
it, it tore apart the bubble and bridged the stream to place the

contents in one of the niches, dropping the bubble's remains in the vat.

Now Deles was directly underneath it, the tentacles looming over him, reaching down. Though he knew he could strike at them with the Destroyer, he couldn't raise his hand to do so. Somewhere in the back of his mind, he knew he should have been afraid, but he was far too relaxed to feel anything but pleasure.

The tentacles wrapped themselves around his bubble, and he was lifted giddily over the trench. Even the tactile sensation of having the bubble peeled from his body was enjoyable. Firmly gripped by two tentacles, he was carefully carried to the wall and placed in a niche, where he lay in perfect comfort, surveying the nightmarish scene below through uncaring, heavy-lidded eyes.

Suddenly his view was obstructed by a sticky, pink gob, splashed over him. It ran inside the niche, which quickly filled up to his chin. But he didn't mind, for it was warm and pleasant, molding itself to his body. He rather liked it, in fact.

"Shouldn't I . . . ?" Shouldn't he what? He couldn't remember.

The tentacles snaked toward him, and he felt their tips caress his shoulder. Then they were under his armpits, and he was borne aloft over the trough once again. The pink stuff had dried, molding itself to his form, a lumpy pink leotard.

The tentacles tossed him through the air and he tumbled in a long arc, too delirious to even be surprised. A screen of thin filaments formed in front of him in silence. The screen tilted and caught him, and he felt as comfortable as he would in his own webbing back in Ploydektum. More comfortable.

Strands periscoped out of the screen as new filaments knitted themselves into a fabric to replace the displaced mass. The loose ends touched him gently, beginning to work over his body—massaging, rubbing. As the filaments stroked his temples and forehead, he saw that they had bifurcated tips. Twice as many to please him, he thought happily. Every nerve in his body responded as if these filaments were the soft hands of a woman. They caressed him expertly, delicate and teasing, over every bit of his flesh. His head lolled as he was blanketed in warm snow, the tendrils clearing the pink sheath away from his genitalia, working on his testicles, his penis . . . working . . . working . . . working . . . until his loins exploded in a rain of blinding gold.

He rested in a dark, humming place, a living place that responded to the beat of his heart, the heaving of his lungs, the rhythms of his life force.

He opened his eyes. A man stood over him, bearded and stooped. They were inside a cave, its arch textured like delicate crosshatching in a pen-and-ink drawing.

"Are you all right?" the man asked in a rasping voice. Words seemed to come to him only with great difficulty.

"Yes," Deles replied, "I think so."

"When you were carted in here, they brought me out of stasis," the old man said. "I've been down here ever since I tried to kill myself. I'm kept in stasis except when there is something a human hand can do better than these damned things." He gestured behind him. "That's a rare enough occurrence."

"The ... constructs, you mean?" Deles asked.

"Is that what you call them?"

"Yes, biological constructs—living things, but designed for specific functions ... like machines."

"I call them roborgs, short for robot organisms," the man muttered, stalking out of the cave as if he had forgotten Deles.

Deles sat up. He was naked, except for a few dried pink crusts still clinging to his skin. Feeling fine, he stood and followed the strange man outside.

The cave, he found, was actually a violet dome at the summit of a series of piled tiers. These spread out before him like hemispherical stairs, leading to the strange tableau wherein he had been lulled and seduced, a kilometer or more below. He could see the clump of tentacles, busily plucking and peeling bubbles —all empty now—from the oily stream.

"What is this place?" he asked the bearded man, who squatted on the edge of this topmost tier.

He turned and squinted at Deles. "It's a factory," he said, "a genetic factory. It examines organisms, and then it ... takes care of them—gives them what they need, genetically speaking."

Deles leaned against the violet dome, frightened and confused. What had been done to him? Was this what had happened to his mother? Was this how he was conceived? And he had always wanted to know his father's identity, never understanding why Danna would not reveal it....

He became angry, frustration boiling up inside him. A twinge in his palm, as it rubbed against the soft, convex dome, reminded him that the Destroyer responded to anger. He stifled his resentment. He could easily demolish the genetic factory. But he might kill this man in the process.

"How did you come to find yourself down here?" the bearded man asked.

"I don't know. I just couldn't help myself. It was like a dream."

"Um, so it was for me, too." The bearded man stretched out

his hand to indicate the factory. "Something called us here, something that has been here since before Man's First Coming."

"Man's First Coming? What are you talking about?"

"Has even that been forgotten now? Once Man left Rocinth —and the rest of the solar system, too. Left it all behind. For some reason he can't remember where he went, or even when he came back, and now he's forgotten the whole thing, if I'm to believe you."

"I've never heard of such a thing," Deles said, "I assure you."

"Strange," said the bearded man, "but it only proves that Stallea was right."

"Stallea!" Deles cried. "Are you Leptos?"

"The very same." Leptos rubbed his beard.

"Acrios is your son."

"Yes." Leptos seemed embarrassed by this admission. "I'm afraid I haven't done very well by him, but I am his father."

Deles lunged at the startled Leptos and smothered him in an embrace. Leptos sputtered in confusion.

"I am Deles, your great-grandson!"

Chapter Twenty-three

The Worldmind's Reply

As Leptos rambled on about the past, Deles could not resist grinning at this unlikely meeting.

"You think I'm funny, do you?" Leptos demanded.

"No," Deles lied. "Please go on."

"Well, it was a terrible thing I did to my boy," he said, "a terrible thing . . . and then the Seers coming to take him. . . ."

Deles began to pay more attention.

"It seems Acrios has the Gift . . ."

"Like no one before him or since, I've heard."

"You know Acrios?"

"Mostly by reputation," Deles said. "I've lived most of my life on Sripha."

"Beautiful world, Sripha, but primitive."

"Yes . . . but please go on."

"Well," Leptos said, "it was only when I locked him in the antechamber that he found his Gift. I didn't know why I was doing it, but the compulsion was so strong that I couldn't resist."

"Compulsion?"

"To bring him down here and lock him up." Leptos peered into the distance. "His mother heard his mind crying. She was nearly as frightened as he. After that, she . . . she never spoke to me again. I couldn't make her see that I had no choice in the matter, that I wasn't to blame."

"Who *was* to blame?"

"Why, the Others. I was little more than their tool. And they've held me down here who knows how long."

"Do you know the way out of here?" Deles asked.

"Yes, but they won't let us go."

"We have to make the attempt."

"It can't be done. As soon as we try, they'll snatch us up and put us in stasis."

"What if I were to tell you that I have a way to stop the— what did you call them? Roborgs?"

Leptos nodded, frowning.

"Do you see this?" Deles held his palm out toward Leptos, exposing the Destroyer. Its glow lent a ghastly pallor to Leptos's already white face. "What is it?" Leptos asked, eyes ablaze with wonder.

"Our passage out of here."

"I don't understand," Leptos protested.

"It's time for you to go home," Deles said. "You have been down here too long."

"How long?" Leptos gazed intently at him.

"I'm not sure . . ."

"Deles, I'm afraid to face what has happened up there. Do you know what's become of Stallea?"

"You'll learn all about that later," Deles temporized. "Just now we must get up to the surface." But Deles began to have his doubts. After all, this man had been down here for thousands of years.

"At least tell me about Acrios," Leptos insisted.

"He became Receptor of Rocinth."

"Receptor!" Leptos's eyes widened. "I knew he would be great. You should have been there when the lightship came. It was awesome, monumental. . . . If only Stallea had understood that it wasn't my doing . . . I never wanted to lock my boy in that room." Tears came to his eyes, and his scrawny body quaked with emotion.

"You want to see Acrios, don't you?" Deles asked. "I've come from Sripha to find him, so the two of us have a common interest."

Leptos wiped his eyes. "He won't hate me?"

"I think he'll understand."

"All right then, if you can get us out of here, let's go."

Deles grinned at him and leapt down to the next tier. He fell to his knees, and his forearms and hands took the shock easily. He stood and held out his arms.

"Jump, Leptos," he said. "I won't let you fall."

Looking down from a three-meter height, Leptos nodded. The tendons in his skinny legs strained as he readied himself. But his body suddenly stiffened, and he pointed past Deles.

Several tiers below, a seam, where one level emerged from another, bulged. The protrusion erupted into a long, waving strand, reaching toward Deles.

Don't lose control, Deles told himself. Don't get angry. He raised his hand while the strand twisted ever nearer. It formed a noose over his head . . . as the blue fire transported him.

Detached, he watched the vibration freeze the noose and work its way down the strand. Each gyrating curve was stilled, all the way to the seam, eight tiers below. Then he was back in his body, suffering little ill-effect. He had not unleashed the Destroyer through blind emotion, but in self-defense; apparently that made a great deal of difference.

"I'm not sure I believe it," Leptos said, "but I saw it." He jumped, and Deles caught him under the arms, staggering.

"You see," Deles puffed, "nothing to it."

"That was only one—there are dozens of levels to go."

"Then we'd better not waste any more time talking."

They had only made it as far as the next tier when they were attacked once again, this time from above. Roborgs resembling immense dragonflies were maneuvering overhead. Blurred wings sprouted from stiff, tubular bodies, mounted on thoraces behind heads completely covered with photoreceptors. Wiry limbs dangled from underneath the banks of eyes, culminating in powerful hands, a most noninsectile feature.

Leptos moaned in fear as the nearest of the swarm swooped toward them. Its fingers, each the length of a human arm, nearly touched his shoulder before Deles struck. Leptos might have been crushed under the falling roborg, but Deles had no choice.

Blue fire consumed Deles, taking him from his body once again.

The dragonfly turned to stone, Leptos darting out of its way as it dropped. It tumbled over the edge and struck the next tier, a wing smashing into a hundred fragments. A deafening clatter followed as it was reduced to a powder, colliding with one tier after another. Its remains rained into the oily stream; moments later the tentacles were peeling clear bubbles from the pieces.

Deles helped Leptos to his feet, nearly stumbling himself. The second assault had left him considerably weaker than the first.

"Look at you—you can barely stand," cried Leptos. "Don't you realize there are hundreds of roborgs?"

"I can stop them."

"The factory is already in the process of making more."

Deles suspected that Leptos was correct, and he wasn't sure how much longer he could rebuff these assaults. They leapt down to the next level. This time a white, gelatinous mass advanced like a vast, one-celled animal, closing in on them from all sides.

"It's hopeless," Leptos said.

But before the shapeless stuff touched them, Deles raised the Destroyer a third time. The menace was quickly halted, but he sensed that he was farther from his physical self than he had ever been. Could he get back to his body?

He swam in waters more formidable than any Sriphan lake, fearing to drown in this nether world between life and Otherness. Somehow he did return to his body, nearly fainting, and somehow he survived the attack of massed threads that undulated from below and threatened to carry them back to the stasis dome. After that, he was barely conscious. Still, he kept moving.

"Deles!" Leptos cried, shaking him by the shoulder. "You're doing it!"

But Leptos's elation was short lived. The glowing factory ceiling, a vast arch festooned with luminous bacteria, was obscured by a monstrous tube, wide as a man was tall, a grainy green mouth at its end that puckered and sucked with tremendous force. It would pull them in unless Deles destroyed it. But he didn't know if he could survive such an effort.

As the gaping maw's hoselike body curved over the dome, Deles saw that they had descended no more than ten meters. And life was draining out of him each time he fought the roborgs. Leptos had been right. It was hopeless. He sank to his knees.

"Deles!" cried Leptos. "Hang on!"

Why? Was it worth it to go on? Should he try to fight this thing and risk death? After all, the roborgs weren't going to kill them. They would just put them in stasis . . . forever.

"No!" Deles screamed as the maw was about to engulf him in darkness. He could feel himself being lifted, and he saw Leptos's body flip around, limbs flailing as he flew toward the ravenous behemoth. As if to ward off the roborg, Deles raised his hand.

Blue flame carried him through stars that were not stars, worlds that were not worlds. Apocalyptic visions of destruction passed before him, as did glorious hints of creation. Were they not one and the same? But he had no chance to ponder this grand mystery, before . . .

. . . he was back in his body, falling on his hands and knees. Leptos thudded onto the tier beside him. And the liquid sounds of the roborgs were silent at last.

Dazed and shaken, Deles looked at the still tableau—still as the banquet hall in Ploydektum—with its motionless monsters poised for action. The great mouth yawned above him. Below, the dark stream had ceased to flow, and the tentacles clutched a bubble that would never be peeled. And Leptos . . . Leptos too was still.

Unable to walk, Deles called his name. There was no answer. Deles crawled to him, every inch an agony. Had he killed another innocent soul? Reaching Leptos's supine figure, Deles touched him on the shoulder.

Leptos jerked his head around and stared at Deles. "You did it," he said with reverence.

"Yes," Deles replied weakly, leaning against the base of a tier.

"You don't look well, Deles," Leptos said. "You're very pale."

"Just let me rest awhile." The strange odors wafting up from the factory were making Deles sick. He was thankful that he hadn't eaten in some time. "I'll be all right."

"All we have to do now," said Leptos, "is find our way back to the well."

"That might not be easy," Deles said, still breathing heavily from his exertions. He suffered occasional spasms, but they went away, and he began to feel a little better. "The way I came in is probably sealed off."

"There is more than one way in and out—several, in fact."

"Good." And it was good. The Destroyer had not been out of control this time. Deles had not wanted Leptos to die, and his great-grandfather still lived, though every other living thing in sight had been killed.

"There is greatness in you," Leptos said, "like Acrios."

"There is nothing in me that is great." Acrios's greatness was questionable, too, Deles thought, but if the notion helped to sustain Leptos, he would say nothing to contradict it. "The Destroyer, not I, has saved us."

"Oh, but you saved us, all right. The Destroyer is part of you."

"I'll show you to your room, sir," the attending robot said.

Acrios followed, marveling that he could have forgotten the beauty of the sea where it met the scarp at the foot of Tornaj Mountain. And how could he have forgotten this hotel, its face bearing this peculiar, rippling design? At first glance the design appeared to be natural, but it was altogether *too* natural. It had actually been carved into the cliffside by the ancient Rocinthans, who had also hollowed out the passageways and chambers that humans had later outfitted for their own use. Though the rooms were oddly shaped, one soon became accustomed to them. How long ago had he been here? Five hundred years? A thousand?

They climbed up several levels, Acrios becoming a trifle winded by the exertion. But at last the robot indicated a low entrance at the end of a gloomy corridor, and Acrios went inside. In spite of its considerable spaciousness, he found a Spar-

tan room, with a mattress on the floor and an empty stasis field
for food. One corner held a sprayer for cleaning his body, and
another sheltered an imagemaker, a dream-disc, and a visual
scan for watching the upcoming games from inside. In the past,
that is precisely what he would have done—in much more
sumptuous surroundings—with half a dozen lovers of both
sexes. Those days were gone forever, though, and, surprisingly,
he missed them very little. He took a comfort in his solitude that
he never would have dreamt of when he was Receptor. His
power had not saved him from his downfall. Rather, it could be
argued, power had pushed him toward it.

And yet, he thought as he sat on the mattress, if he could do
it all again he would not do it differently. Now and again he
tried to convince himself that it could be otherwise, imagining
that he could reshape himself into a man of cool reason, selfless-
ness, compassion . . . but then he wouldn't be Acrios, would he?

He thought about watching through the scan, but decided to
go out and see the real thing instead, for the games were beginning today. Millions of people had come over the mountains and
across the sea to watch them, and that would make this provincial town the best hiding place on Rocinth for weeks to come.

He rose and walked back out to the corridor. In the dim light
he couldn't tell where the corridor branched, and soon found
himself on a ledge nestled in one of the cliffside's carved ripples,
high above the town of Trapathe. From here he could see the
milling crowds below, though the major events would not begin
until tomorrow.

The wind was strong, reminding Acrios of the days when he
had been capable of riding the storm, when the mundomentus
had provided such a dramatic mode of travel for him, all the
while maintaining a flawless meteorological balance. The
worldmind was unlikely to permit the murder of Rocinth's
former Receptor.

A vast sward stretched beyond the marketplace. Most of the
crowd was headed there. Perhaps they wanted to be able to say
that they had walked on the gaming field, for none of them
would be permitted on its blue-green surface after today. From
the scarp to the sea—now hazily visible in the distance—every
habitation would be filled by morning. The overflow would spill
out, and those without housing would resort to bubble fields
and tents. Acrios had an urge to go down and join them, these
teeming millions, to become one of them . . . one with them . . .
before Deles found him.

Deles. The very name terrified him. He often brooded on
the possibility that his actions had fulfilled the prophecy; that if
he had not acted against Deles, it might never have come to

this. Of course, Bilyf had predicted his end, so his best guess was that it would have happened one way or another, no matter what he did. In his arrogance, he had hoped to change his own destiny, but that wasn't to be.

He traced his footsteps back to his room and found the corridor that would take him back down to the scarp. If he must die by Deles's hand, why didn't he just face the boy and be done with it? But that wouldn't be Acrios.

No, it was his responsibility to live as long as he could. *That* he had decided long ago. He had committed many crimes in his headlong pursuit of immortality, and he regretted these, but he did not for one moment regret his decision to live.

"Ah." He had come to the bottom at last. As he came out into the light, he blinked at the passing throngs before going on. He looked for a young man who had come from another world to take his life, a life so long he had ceased counting first the years, then the decades, and finally the centuries. He remembered the events of his childhood more clearly than he remembered yesterday. Perhaps he had lived long enough. Before he died, however, he would lead that boy on a merry chase.

"Fresh fish!" an offworlder shouted. The vendor was an Eiy, and his clamplike fists turned sizzling fillets expertly on his portable grill. They smelled delicious, and Acrios was tempted to try one. As a blue-eyed woman passed him in the crowd, he stopped. Did he know her? Was it Verra? There, among the babbling thousands, she walked, his former lover, the Prime Mystagogue herself! But no, Verra was dead . . . or was she? Where had she gone? Tartarus, or was she lost somewhere in that milling mass of humanity somewhere, now lost from sight . . . if she had ever really been there at all? It made little difference, he supposed, if she *were* an hallucination. He was no longer the Receptor, and Verra was gone, but they had both been mighty once. Fortune had not been kind to him in the past few years, but what a life he had lived before that! No one in the history of the human race had ever exercised the Gift with *his* power and conviction. He had been the greatest Receptor in all Rocinth's history—in all the histories of all the worlds in all the galaxy. He had the answer to the greatest riddle of all, the riddle of the End of All Things, locked up in his brain . . . locked up somewhere even the searcher could not go. And it was destroying him.

"No, no," he muttered. He was going to live forever. This was merely a temporary setback. He still had his Gift, and it would someday restore him to his former glory.

He had forgotten his meal, he suddenly realized, in his preoccupation with the blue-eyed phantom. He passed the pa-

tient Eiy a few coins. Accepting the fish in a thin wrapper, he
realized that he wasn't hungry anymore. But he had to eat; even
an anthroform could conceivably starve to death. He removed
the wrapper and tore away a bit of the hot, white flesh. It burnt
his fingers and tongue, but he managed to swallow it. Even so,
he was having trouble grasping his food in his hands. It wasn't
that it was too hot, just that he couldn't seem to . . .

Ah, the pain! It bent him so cruelly that his skin nearly
struck the vendor's table. His fingers wriggled like dying worms.
He groaned at the passersby through a rictus of pain—and, oh,
what exquisite pain it was, almost pleasurable in a terribly perverse way—a relief from the burden of his madness.

A second spasm straightened his spine like a trun pike, and
his neck twisted to one side. Falling, he thought how interesting
the texture of the ground looked as it rose to meet him. Strange
that he hadn't noticed it before.

And then there was a vague something—the Gift?—before
the merciful darkness engulfed all.

How long did the mystagogues expect him to wait? Deles
chafed at the time lost sitting in this featureless antechamber to
the mundomentus, waiting to be granted admittance.

He grasped his ankles to stretch his muscles. He felt cramped
and hungry. Had he been in this room all night? It hadn't taken
this long for him and Leptos to fight their way out of the well
and climb to the surface. At least Leptos was comfortably en-
sconced in Acrios's villa now. Under the circumstances, Deles
hadn't felt as if he were letting his grandfather down by traveling to Nathe so soon after Leptos's return to the world.

Deles had felt such exhilaration while coming in over the
great city, images flashing in the night sky around his ship. As
he had landed in an empty plaza, he had believed his search to
be nearly over. And now . . . But what a magnificent city it was!
He had assumed beforehand that his recollections of its gran-
deur were the exaggerated impressions of childhood magnified
and distorted over the years. But it was just as he remembered
it, as if time had stood still: the clonarium rising like an immense plug among the brilliantly lit buildings; the gigantic
docking bays with their thousands of graviton platforms; the
bustling marketplace with goods from hundreds of worlds; the
colorful projections. And most imposing of all, the great dome
of the mundomentus.

He had wasted no time in coming to the mystagogues for
help. That was his purpose in returning to Nathe, after all, not
mere nostalgia. But he wished that he had taken time to explore
the city, now that he was subjected to this interminable wait.

Were the mystagogues watching him? Was this some kind of test to determine if he was worthy of the mundomentus's time? Or did they know about the alien artifacts implanted in his hand? That might explain why no living soul had come near him since he'd been ushered into this antechamber. If so, the mystagogues were keeping him prisoner . . . a sobering thought.

He cleared his throat, the sound echoing through the bleak cubicle. Was it possible that they had forgotten him? Perhaps if he called out? . . .

No, the mystagogues knew he was here. No matter how inscrutable their reasoning, it was important to remember that there *was* reasoning behind his detention. They were aware of his identity, and so was the mundomentus. But did the world-mind know his purpose?

A panel in the smooth wall slid to one side, and a cowled figure entered. "Deles," the mystagogue said.

"Yes."

"Why have you come here?"

"I stated my purpose before I was locked in here. I want the mundomentus to help me find someone."

"To what end?"

"Certainly to no evil end," Deles replied. "A family matter."

"Are your intentions such that you must conceal them?"

Deles nearly snapped at his inquisitor, but he managed restraint. He couldn't be sure what the mystagogue was getting at. "My intentions are for the mundomentus alone to know," he said.

"Such arrogance will not help you."

"Perhaps it will help if I tell you this: I have been to Tartarus, and I have spoken to the Prime Mystagogue."

Strangely, the cowled figure showed no reaction, unless silence could be interpreted as such. Perhaps what Deles had said was too incredible, but he had been willing to take that chance. Another day in this antechamber would be intolerable, and so he had boldly spoken of his encounter with Verra.

Behind the mystagogue, a clone carrying a food tray entered. He set it on the floor next to Deles and backed out of the room. The mystagogue was silent, lost in thought. Deles tried to read something in the deep-set eyes, or in the set of the mouth in that white face. But there was nothing.

"Your message will be conveyed to the mundomentus," the mystagogue said, abruptly turning and leaving the room. The panel slid shut behind her.

"Well . . ." It seemed that Deles was at last getting somewhere. Or was he? For all he knew the mundomentus would discount his message as a fabrication. The mystagogue's visit might have been intended only as a feeding, for that matter.

Which reminded him that he was famished. He selected one of three utensils from a tray and cut off a bite of steaming fish. It was nearly raw in the middle, the way he liked it. He ate it greedily. There were some vegetables too, which he also made short work of, washing down his meal with a goblet of wine. If it had been offered, he could have eaten more. But the silence of the chamber remained undisturbed until after he had fallen asleep on the floor.

A foot nudged him awake, and he thought that here was something to add to his agitation. Wasn't it enough that his shoulder was sore from sleeping on this hard surface without . . .

Then he remembered where he was and what he had been waiting for.

Through sleep-swollen eyelids he looked up at a mystagogue. Was it the same one? The mystagogue's hood and the dim light made it impossible to tell. "What is it?" he asked.

"Deles," the mystagogue said.

"Yes." He sat up, leaning his back against the wall.

"You have been granted an audience with the mundomentus." This was stated as blandly as if the mystagogue were asking if he had enjoyed his meal.

Deles stood, stretching his limbs as he did so. Now he would have the opportunity to present his case to the Rocinthan people's surrogate, and to ask for its help.

"When may I go in?" he asked the mystagogue.

"Now." The mystagogue turned and walked through the open panel, Deles following. They passed through a dark, yet gleaming corridor, and then onto a ramp that took them to a considerable height. This turned into a path that lay like a suspended ribbon passing through the winking synapses of the worldmind. Above was the diaphanous sphere at its core. The mystagogue led him to a diverging path. Higher and higher they rose, Deles looking down at a seemingly bottomless expanse of scintillant light.

Three receptacles appeared in the sparking brilliance, coffin-like boxes set in a cul-de-sac at the path's end. The sphere loomed like a moon next to them as the mystagogue pointed to the center sarcophagus.

"Lie down inside it," the mystagogue said.

Deles obeyed, confident that the mundomentus meant him no harm. His head rested in a cavity that molded itself to the curve of his skull.

The image of a network, complex almost beyond imagining, leapt into his mind. It was not a representational image, but it conveyed the idea of the mundomentus' function conceptually,

particularly its power. And at the same time it took from him
what it needed.

There was no pain, nor even discomfort. There was merely
the temporary darkening of portions of his mind. The light returned before its absence could frighten him. Information had
been removed, encoded, and replaced in the twinkling of an
eye.

It knew that he had killed Verra.

But there was no hint of reprisal, no indication that the mundomentus even found this bit of information unusual. Its communications were the roar of the ocean heard through a
seashell, the faint echo of creation. But no, Deles thought, this
is a man-made entity, finite in its knowledge and power. The
brain of a world, true, but nothing more. He understood now
that the conglomerate mind of the people of Rocinth was, by
and large, just and compassionate. Understanding was all. Just
as Deles understood the nature of the mundomentus, the mundomentus understood why he had killed the Prime Mystagogue.
He was not to be held accountable.

Strangely, he was not relieved, as he would have expected.
"Why am I not accountable?" he asked, his voice distant and
unfamiliar.

No answer was forthcoming. Instead, the mundomentus
asked him: Why have you come?

"Don't you know?" Was it testing him?

You have come to find Acrios.

"Yes, to find my grandfather."

You have forgiven him.

"I desire no more misery or hatred . . . for anyone." Deles's
eyes misted unexpectedly. "I don't want any more suffering."

Your guilt is a terrible thing.

The tears flowed now, and Deles did not try to stop them.

"I am a murderer," he cried. "I enjoyed killing."

You enjoy it no longer.

"I now see what a monster I have become."

His lament was barely a disturbance in the mundomentus's
all-encompassing wisdom.

Acrios fears you.

"He has no reason to fear me, in spite of his crimes."

You do not understand him.

"No . . . but I want to."

Very well.

And the transcendent pain and glory of Acrios's passion
flooded him, transfixing and transforming. Never had he conceived of the cosmos's wonder as he did through the mind of
Acrios. The mystery, the terror, the beauty—the passion! No

human being could absorb it for long without going mad.

There was more. Acrios had been the unfortunate pawn of beings beyond his understanding. Manipulated, haunted by the most terrible knowledge in the universe, twisted this way and that by the Others, his sanity had given out. He had never been a temperate man, but now he submerged himself in excess to escape the anguish of his burden. His vices had made him madder yet.

The answer to the riddle of the End was in him, and he could not bring it out. Neither could the mundomentus, even through a searcher. Here Deles witnessed the implantation of the searcher into Acrios's brain. A simple operation, the scalp cut away, then the skull. The left hemisphere was exposed. The tiny wormlike searcher was placed in a ventricle in the occipital region. The sealing of the skull, replacement of the scalp, accelerated healing, and cosmetics were quickly attended to, and Acrios was able to walk away within the hour. But he would never be the same, even if he lived for the eternity he desired.

Now his pain was localized, and he suffered frequent hallucinations as a searcher crawled slowly from one hemisphere to the other, touching sensitive spots in different gyri on its microcosmic odyssey. And still he would not let go of life.

"He needs rest . . . and love," Deles said. "I must find him and take him home."

Your compassion is great.

"Compassion?" Deles shrugged. "I don't think my sympathy was entirely genuine before. I feared my own destruction more than anything else. But now . . . now I think I'm beginning to understand. The past can never be changed, perhaps not even the future . . . but Acrios's greatness will live on."

Man may never come so close to the answer as did Acrios, before the End. He was the Seers' greatest hope, and his accomplishments cannot be denied. But it is unlikely that his knowledge will ever be freed from the prison of his mind.

Deles wept.

Acrios is in Trapathe, the mundomentus told him. Go to him and give him your love.

Chapter Twenty-four

An Old Friend

Lying in his dark room, Acrios reflected on just how decrepit his mind had become. An intimation of Deles's whereabouts had been aborted by the wracking pain only last night. He was losing the Gift . . . it was being driven from his brain by the searcher as his sanity ebbed like the tide of an evaporating sea. At first he had been certain of Deles's proximity, but then . . . then the image had been distanced by pain. Or had the entire vision been nothing more than a delusion brought on by the searcher? It was possible.

Sitting up, he cast his rheumed eyes on the bottle of wine he had purchased after the last seizure. Did he dare to take a drink? He raised his aching bones from the mattress and squatted next to the bottle. Look how it shines, Acrios thought. It is like the life you once lived, a beautiful thing, symmetrical and polished, but inside it, ah—there is a substance that induces an irrational mental state.

His trembling fingers touched the smooth glass and trembled no more. With difficulty he raised it to his lips, for it seemed very heavy. But now the pungent liquid washed over his tongue. He swallowed in great gulps, gasping between them. The cold glass bottle was soon empty, and he wiped his lips with the back of his hand. Deles was farther from Acrios's mind than he had been for quite some time.

He must have another bottle, that much was clear. He stood on wobbling legs, bound for the street. But this time he had no trouble finding his way down through the dark corridors; he had done it often enough. And each time he'd been out, he had passed vendors hawking wine and liquors. On a number of occasions he had been sorely tempted to purchase a bottle. After that last terrible spasm he had decided that he must have a drink, especially if Deles's proximity was, as he suspected, no delusion.

Staggering through the crowds—already substantial at dawn —he approached the first wine merchant he saw and bought three bottles, as much as he could carry. He downed the contents of the first bottle in a few long swallows and immediately started on the second. By the time the third cool glass rim touched his lips he didn't care if he lived or died.

Then he thought he saw the blue-eyed woman (Verra?) again.

"You!" he called to her. But, as before, she disappeared into the crowd without answering. Thinking that he heard someone laughing, he shrank into the cliff's shadow.

"What is happening to me?" he said aloud. What if it was Verra? Was she an Other? Or was it merely another symptom of brain damage?

What did it matter? He had come to Trapathe to enjoy himself, and he resolved to do just that. He would spend the day drinking, wandering from one game to the other. And tomorrow he would attend the eliminations and ultimately witness the decision on the first major event, the dikoit throw.

"Deles!"

He froze. Who could be calling to him from this enormous crowd? Acrios? He turned and saw a hulking figure emerge from a sea of merrymakers.

"Don't you remember me?" asked the muscular young man.

"Of course." Deles grinned to see such a friendly face. "How could I ever forget the man who beat me at the dikoit throw. Zetik, from Baregtum."

"The last time I saw you," said Zetik, "you had more on your mind than the dikoit throw." He shook his head. "I never thought I'd see you again."

"Nor I you."

"What brings you to Trapathe, Deles? As if I didn't know."

"The dikoit throw." It was best not to explain his real reason for being here. He would enter the dikoit throw tomorrow. It might take weeks to find Acrios in this crowd, and he had to do something in the meantime. If he became acquainted with some of the athletes, he might learn something from them. He had already asked a few questions of vendors, but they regarded him with suspicion. Who wouldn't be suspicious of questions on a planet where all the citizens were linked by the mundomentus? The athletes wouldn't mind, though, once they knew him. It was a good idea to compete. He looked forward to throwing the dikoit again.

"Have you entered your name as a competitor yet?" Zetik asked.

"Not yet. I just arrived a few hours ago."

"I'll show you what to do." Putting his arm around Deles's

shoulder, Zetik led him across the sward. He had been on Rocinth for some time now, he explained along the way. In fact, the horrible spectacle of Ploydekt's solstitial feast had convinced him to leave his homeworld.

"They say that you killed Ploydekt," said Zetik. "Is it true?"

"He's dead."

Zetik looked curiously at him. "They say he died strangely."

"What else do they say, Zetik?"

Zetik's discomfort was evident from the way he averted his eyes. "They said everyone at the feast died . . . not just Ploydekt."

"It's true," Deles replied.

"I understand how you must have felt, having been there the night he banished you from Ploydektum," Zetik said, his square-jawed face sincere. "Still, the lives of all those people."

"You could have been there, too," Deles said.

"Easily."

They had come to a spire set in the sward, a three-meter-tall needle. Its long shadow fell between them.

"Here is where offworlders register," said Zetik.

Deles laughed. "I wondered what this thing was doing here in the gaming area."

"Tell it who you are," Zetik said, "so it can let the mundomentus know."

"But the mundomentus already knows I'm on Rocinth," Deles protested. "Isn't that enough?"

"You have to do it if you're going to participate."

"All right." Deles knew that the worldmind could be trusted, but he still didn't like to be watched. Nevertheless, he stepped up to the spire.

"Your name, please," it said in an officious, but not unpleasant voice.

"Deles."

"There is no record of your neural imprint."

"The mundomentus knows me," Deles said. "It even knows that I am in Trapathe."

"So the mundomentus has just informed me," the spire said. "You were born on Rocinth."

"Yes."

"And yet there is no neural imprint."

"My mother withheld it." Deles was beginning to wish that he had never agreed to compete.

"What event do you wish to enter?"

"The dikoit."

"The mundomentus approves," said the spire. "You will compete today, number six in the thirteenth group."

"How many are registered?" Zetik asked.

"Eighty-two so far, Zetik," the spire replied. "It is one of the most popular events, since anthroform humans are particularly skilled at it."

"May I be rescheduled to the thirteenth group," Zetik asked, "so that my friend and I will be together?"

There was a slight pause, and then the spire said, "You will be number five, since the original number five has dropped out of competition. You may take his place."

"What good fortune!" Zetik said, beaming. "I was going to have to wait until the last group. Not only that, but I'll be throwing just before you."

Deles smiled, but he felt the ghostly hand of Otherness intervening here. It was all just a bit too fortuitous to be mere coincidence. Even encountering Zetik made him suspicious, though he was certain that the big athlete was quite innocent of all but the most common myths about the Others.

"We'd better get something to eat," Zetik said, slapping Deles on the shoulder. "We'll need our strength."

Deles looked up at the strange rippling scarp with its stone balconies, wondering if he was doing the wisest thing.

"Do you have a place to stay?" Zetik asked.

"Not yet," Deles said, trying to forget his gloomy thoughts in the face of Zetik's cheerful camaraderie.

"You'd have done better to come a few days in advance. But don't worry, there's plenty of room in my quarters. All we have to do is find another mattress for you."

The two companions walked across the sward, laughing and chatting.

"Good luck," the spire called after them.

"A different shore," Acrios croaked. For a while he had thought that he was somewhere near his villa, until he remembered that he was thousands of kilometers from home. Then he had laughed until his coughing forced him to be silent. He was walking adequately now, barely staggering at all . . . even if he did find himself grasping people's arms and propping himself against buildings even more than usual. Once he had leaned against a tent so heavily that it collapsed, its occupants cursing him until he reeled out of earshot.

"At least you're still alive, old thing," he reminded himself aloud. That damned boy was still after him, and Bilyf's prophecy rang as freshly in his memory as if he were a chronopath himself. And Danna . . . where was his baby now?

"You old monster," he muttered. There was no worse anthroform in the galaxy than old Acrios. But he had paid the

price for his hideous acts. Oh, how he had suffered . . . he who
possessed the ultimate answer . . . Or did it possess him?

It was getting dark. He preferred the night these days, now
that he didn't have to spend it in the reception pool. But it
couldn't be night time. It was still morning, wasn't it?

"Ah." He saw what it was. Clouds. Nothing but clouds. The
mundomentus was providing a little rain to freshen the sward.
He'd have to go back to his room. It was just as well, since he'd
been drinking since dawn. He was simply too tired to go on
much longer without a nap. Best to go back to that wormhole
where he slept. He no longer cared that people shunned him; it
wasn't because he was Acrios anymore, but because he was a
drunk. At least that made him human. He sighed. Here was the
main entrance of the hostel right in front of him. Amazing how
these things worked out. He should get drunk more often.

"In we go," he said, staggering through the dark archway.
For a little way he moved with assurance, and then wondered if
he was going in the right direction. There was always someone
coming in or going out; he would ask the first person he saw.
But there was no one in sight.

"The place is empty," he said. Everyone was outside waiting
for the games to begin or, like him, getting drunk. Well, he
would just have to find the way by himself, wouldn't he?

"Here we are." This seemed like the best way to go, he
thought, staring up at a sloping corridor. He found it to be hard
going, though, since he was on the downhill end. When he came
to a junction, he took the opportunity to sag to the floor for a
rest. His breathing was wet and ragged, his limbs sore, trembling. But he would be all right in a moment.

"I wish . . ." What did he wish? So many things—none of
them within the realm of possibility, unfortunately. "I wish I had
a drink."

He rose slowly to his feet. Propping one arm against the
wall, he set off once again, more unsteadily than before.

"Now which way?" He couldn't remember the direction he'd
been going in when he stopped to rest, much less the way to his
room. He sank into a corner, immediately regretting it. He
couldn't get up.

"You just don't want to badly enough," he muttered. That
was the truth. He would lie here until someone tripped over
him, and then he would get up and start drinking again. His
body would repair itself faster than he could destroy it, a result
of Man's perennial biological tinkering. In the past, people had
live and died in a natural cycle, like a naf or a flower. A beginning, a middle, an end . . . but now there was no end. One was

born, grew to maturity, even middle age, and stayed that way forever.

But had Man ever truly lost the need for death?

"The need for death . . . ?" He had never before thought of death as something one needed. As a desire, as an obsession, but never as a need. Surely there was truth in it, though.

Life could only have meaning for so long. But while that essential knowledge was trapped inside his brain, didn't his life continue to have meaning? Why had he buried it so deeply that not even the searcher could ferret it out? To prolong life past this excruciating point? To live forever?

"Nobody will live forever," he rasped into the darkness. A part of him had known that since he was a little boy, thousands of years ago. He had become aware of that immutable fact the day his father had locked him in that dark room.

"Father!" he cried, just he had cried then. And, then as now, there was no answer.

He whimpered, wondering if anyone would ever come to get him. He had followed his father here out of curiosity. Leptos had gone down into the well every day, but nobody had known what he did there. Acrios had been afraid to ask, because his father had been acting very strange of late. Consequently, Acrios had been careful to keep to the shadows, never losing sight of Leptos's glowpin.

Suddenly the light had been extinguished.

Panicking, Acrios had run ahead, toward where he imagined his father to be. A hand had seized his wrist like a vise, and he had been dragged to this dark room. The door had slammed shut, and he had been here ever since.

"Father!" he screamed. "Let me out!"

His voice echoed in the darkness, a pitiful attenuating wail. But crying would do him no good . . . he might never be freed . . . he was going to die here of hunger or thirst . . . of neglect . . . No one loved him.

"Father! Please!"

The echoes died away, reminding him that he was in another place now, another time. Was he a Mennon, that he had trouble making such a distinction? He was here in Trapathe, in his fading years, and Deles was closing in on him.

Deles . . . The boy was the spawn of whatever hellish thing had driven Leptos mad. He could not be human. No human could have done what Deles had done.

"You fool, Acrios," he said. "You drunken, arrogant fool." His father had made him into a monster by locking him into that room, and he had done worse to Danna. Deles had defied the very universe to come back and avenge her.

"Not that you don't deserve it, you old monster." He buried his face in his hands and wept. There was no reason to go on with his life. He was unloved, unwanted; the lives of all those he had touched were in ruins, or they were dead because of him; worst of all, he who had promised to be the greatest of all Receptors had failed miserably, after coming so close to revealing the answer to the riddle, to the End of All Things, to humankind. He derived no pleasure from life anymore.

And if he died he would pass into myth. In a sense, he would once again become great . . . in a very real sense. But if he went on, he would become a lesser being, until he was lowlier than the most miserable clone. No matter how he looked at the future, it remained bleak. His life was over.

He coughed, a liquid sound echoing in the dark. Had he really just entertained the thought that his life was, for all intents and purposes, as good as over? He had, and he did not regret it. It was the truth, nothing more or less. He had no reason to live. He wanted to shout recriminations at himself. Madness! the survivor in him would cry, and he would pick himself up and go on living. But *that* would be madness, because nobody lives forever.

He had only one nagging doubt. Though it was unlikely that the searcher would ever be able to unearth the secret buried in his brain, one thing was still possible. And as long as it was possible, he had to go on.

"Ah." A light. Someone was coming at last. But it didn't seem to be the glow of a lantern, glowstick, or glowpin. This was a flickering, icy blue fire.

Others!

Spiral swirls of blue flame capered through the corridors, illuminating the concave walls. Like the elements themselves, the Others seemed to affect the atmosphere in profound ways; Acrios felt a breeze stir his hair. But how could there be wind half a kilometer inside a cliff?

He tried to remain calm as they came closer to him, but he found himself cowering like a frightened animal. They were godlike, awesome. Did he dare become one of them?

"Of course you do," he said. "You can do anything. You are *Acrios.*" He stood and faced them, blinking in the face of their brilliance. They whorled about him, closer and closer, obscuring the corridor, engulfing him in burning cobalt. "You have been the greatest man in the galaxy, and now you can become even greater. Only fear holds you back."

Acrios, the Others called to him, *join us.*

"Yes! Yes, I'll join you! But not yet . . . not until the searcher has found the answer."

Join us. The answer will be given.

"Given? By someone else?" Some of his pride returned. "Whose Gift is greater than mine, that he might give the answer?"

Your Gift is the greatest. So great that you have found the answer before its time.

"Before its time? I don't understand."

You snatched it from the galactic subconscious prematurely.

"But Man has to know the answer!"

The answer will be known in time. But you will not be the instrument of revelation. It will be Deles.

"Deles . . . ?" Of course. It was all so obvious. Deles, the Gift in his blood, created to provide the answer . . . which meant that Acrios was no longer needed . . . that he did not have to go on . . . that he could die. . . . But did he dare?

There is time.

"Time? For what?"

For you to join us in Otherhood.

"Yes, I need a little more time," Acrios said. "I'm not quite ready for Otherness yet. There's something I must see to first, but . . . but I'm not sure what it is. Do you know?"

Yes.

"Tell me, then—tell me so I can get it over with and rest."

You must meet Deles.

"Yes, yes, of course," Acrios laughed. "And to think that I was afraid. To think that I . . ."

The blue flames vanished. Acrios's clothing no longer billowed, and his hair settled onto his scalp as the strange wind died. He was alone, but no longer afraid. He understood now, for the first time, where his greatness lay. He was Deles's grandfather. In his arrogance, he had never dreamt that the boy was the key to the answer, but there it was . . .

It was out of his hands now, he thought as he calmly made his way down the corridor. Resignation followed by acceptance . . . as natural as death following life.

But now he needed rest. Where was his bed?

"I'll find it if it takes me all night," he said, without a trace of drunkenness in his voice.

Chapter Twenty-five

The Games

The sun was bright now, but not terribly hot. It was a good day for the games. In the morning, after registration, Deles had taken some light exercise before eating. He and Zetik had then gone to Zetik's humble room in the labyrinthine cliffside hostel. After resting an hour, they had gone out, struggling through the growing crowd and onto the sward.

Now a troupe of Ygon acrobats were performing, their spindly yellow limbs a blur of rapid, complex movements. They competed against Charn ambisexuals possessing equally supple limbs, though that was where the resemblance ended, for the Charn were much smaller, and—to human eyes at least—much more attractive, possessing four limbs and vaguely anthropomorphic features. No humans competed in this contest; they simply weren't equipped for it.

Humans did, however, compete in the Shroov flip. The Shroov were deceptively plump-looking people with hollow bones, able to toss one another about like so many sacks of flour. Human acrobats were capable of mastering the Shroov flip, though nearly always losing to its originators. Such was the case today.

Still, the spectators applauded the human athletes warmly. And they were appreciative as the Ygon and Shroov teams received their medallions.

"The first and second groups of the day," Zetik said. "We have a long wait ahead of us."

Deles smiled. "If they're all as entertaining as these first two, I won't mind."

And many of them were just as interesting, some downright fascinating. The strain of muscle and tendon, the streaming sweat, the grimace of effort, lent weight to the deceptive lightness of the human athletes' movements. The alien athletes, too, showed strain in their various exotic ways. The blazing sun rose high over one contest after another, until at last the spire announced the first dikoit group.

213

Deles had feared that it would be too hot, but the sea breeze was picking up. Granted that they still had some time to go before they threw, it appeared that the weather would be ideal.

It didn't take long for twelve groups of six to throw, and soon Deles and Zetik were threading their way through the ranks of spectators. The spire announced that two competitors had registered to complete the fourteenth and final group as they struggled through the pressing bodies. Since their arrival early in the morning, the crowd had swollen into millions. Deles had never seen so many people in one place at the same time. He found it somewhat intimidating, even frightening. But at last they were free of the ocean of sweaty bodies, crossing the sward to the area reserved for athletic competition.

"Good luck," Zetik said as they approached the spire, which had extended itself to over five meters in height. They stopped in front of it, where the other four dikoit throwers already stood, and the spire announced their names and told the first four to take their places for the event.

"Zetik, from the province of Baregtum, Sripha, take your place with the others."

Zetik did so, walking over to join the assembled athletes. The crowd was omnipresent, a ceaseless background rumbling.

"Deles of Ploydektum, Sripha, formerly of Rocinth, take your place."

The rumbling took an ambivalent turn, Deles thought. All these Rocinthans knew who he was, but apparently the mundo-mentus had not revealed his presence to them . . . until now. This disturbed him, but there was nothing he could do but join the other athletes.

"Forty-eight dikoit throwers have been eliminated. More will be winnowed out from the final twelve," the spire intoned. "Each player will throw once, beginning now."

The spire's tip threw out an image of a great cube, hundreds of meters square. Within the cube were millions of tiny hairline calibrations by which the athletes' efforts would be judged. The spire demonstrated how the cube could be turned in any direction or extended to any necessary dimensions.

"Number one: Pruive of Luthas."

Pruive, a tall woman, graceful and sturdily built, stepped to the edge of the cube image, took a breath, crouched, spun, and let fly her dikoit. It soared into the immense image, performing little acrobatic stunts as it went, describing figure after figure while remaining inside the cube. A good throw, thought Deles, but nothing extraordinary.

The next contestant, one Niros of Popothe, made a poor showing, but he was followed by a fellow from Nathe whose effort required an extension of the cube's southern parameter. The crowd began to show some signs of life.

The next throw was adequate but unexciting. Then it was Zetik's turn.

"Good luck," Deles said, slapping him on the shoulder.

Zetik stepped up to the cube, paused, and then, spinning like a dancer, let fly.

Acrios slipped through the crowd, trying to get as close to the cube as possible. He hadn't been able to sleep, so joyful—so *enraptured*—was he. Coming out into the sunlight, he had seen that the dikoit throw was in progress. This was an event he had always enjoyed, though racing had been his own sport.

Now he was at the fringes of the crowd, nearly on the playing field itself. Yes, he could see the players clearly, the transparent cube rising above them like a ghostly palace, crowd and ocean alike visible through it. And there was the dikoit itself, spinning, climbing, pirouetting—what a magnificent throw! The cube shifted, extending in a dozen different directions, all unexpected. It was a challenge for the eye to follow. But at last the dikoit eased back toward the sward, taking little dips and rolls as it came, settling into the athlete's hand like a bird.

The audience was wildly appreciative, applauding and cheering for several minutes. Acrios clapped and shouted, too, pleased to be a part of things. That young man had certainly made a fine showing. And to think he had almost missed this!

Now the next thrower was taking his place, a tall, strong young man with curly blond hair. But Acrios wasn't really looking at him. The woman with blue eyes stood next to him. Was it Verra? He couldn't focus on her. She turned toward him, smiling beatifically, her lips forming a word.

His name? He couldn't hear over the crowd, loud as the roaring of the ocean—but somehow he knew that she spoke his name.

"It's good to see you again," he said politely.

She was close enough to touch now, a radiant vision among the millions. Acrios lost himself in the breathtaking cerulean of her eyes. "If you are not Verra, then you are someone else I have known, aren't you? Someone I've always known."

She nodded, and then turned toward the dikoit thrower. Acrios followed her gaze. If she was a delusion, he thought, did that really make her any less real than a flesh and blood woman?

She came closer, her face nearly touching his. He felt her warm breath on his neck. Was she going to kiss him? No, she whispered to him, a single word. "Deles."

"Deles . . . ?" He looked back at the dikoit thrower.

And saw the boy spinning, powerful legs flexing. The dikoit was released to dance within the cube and beyond. Well out over the sea it soared, almost skimming the waves here, flying high above them there. Then a long, gliding motion brought it back over the sward unexpectedly, and the crowd gasped. It was overhead now, and they craned their necks to watch its balletic movements. Extending the cube farther and farther, forcing it to shift position again and again, the dikoit continued its unpredictable, dazzling flight.

Now it dipped so low it sank out of sight behind the cliff, and the woman stared at Acrios solemnly, her eyes as timeless and blue as the sea. The cube foreshortened, coming toward him like the jaws of some immense, transparent beast.

He might have been alone in the crowd, the way the dikoit so relentlessly sought him out. At that moment he knew that, though he had not found the answer, he was not a failure. His life had been worth a great deal. If no one wept for him, it did not matter.

All the world was blue at that moment: blue sky, blue sea, blue eyes sparkling in the sun as the woman watched.

Incredibly, he was at peace as the dikoit spat out of the beast's jaws. He had lived for this moment, and now that it had come he was not afraid.

His death flew toward him on the wind of destiny.

Deles heard thousands moan like a single wounded animal. The dikoit had flown too low and entered the crowd, out of control.

"Get a physician for this man!" somebody shouted. Deles ran to the crowd as several people bent over a crumpled figure.

"No!" the fallen man commanded them. There was something in his tone that made them obey him. The few who had started to fetch a physician stopped in their tracks while others backed away as if they somehow feared the stricken man. Deles saw only a thin figure lying on the grass, gray hair slick with blood. The dikoit lay on the grass next to him.

Something sour rose in Deles's gorge.

The man's gray eyes caught him and held him fast.

"Deles," the injured man said.

Chilled, Deles knelt and lifted the bloody head onto his lap. "Forgive me, Grandfather . . . I didn't mean to . . ."

"There is nothing to forgive . . . as time and space must end, so must my life."

"No, no," Deles protested, "you can still be repaired."

Acrios's bloody hand clutched his wrist. "I want to die," he said. "I *will* myself to die . . . to Otherhood."

"You wish to be an Other? Then why did you run away?"

The cold hand pulled Deles close, and Acrios whispered, "A revelation . . . the Others. . . ."

"A revelation," Deles said, stroking the old man's bloodied head. The gaunt face was illuminated by the Destroyer, and Acrios stared at him through heavy lids.

"I am not the one," he said. "It is you, Deles. You."

"I . . . I don't understand."

"You will give humankind the answer."

Deles wanted to believe that Acrios was delirious, but the dying man's conviction was palpable. Perhaps it was not what Deles thought, nevertheless. "What answer, Grandfather?"

"The answer that I, and the other Receptors, and the Machine, and the mundomentus have searched for in vain all these millennia. How humankind—how we—can survive the End of All Things."

Deles shook his head in disbelief. "I possess the Gift only in small measure, if at all. How can I provide the great answer?"

"I cannot tell you how," Acrios rasped, "only that you will."

Something distracted Acrios, his rheumic eyes slowly focusing on a robot physician as it climbed down from a graviton platform.

"Stay away from me," he ordered the machine, his voice surprisingly strong.

The physician froze, sunlight glinting off its oblong head.

"You'll die," Zetik said. Deles had forgotten about his friend, but Zetik stood beside him. "Let the physician treat you."

"No, I will be an Other soon. Then I will be far greater than any Receptor . . . greater than any living human being."

"Grandfather," Deles said, "I wish that we could have known one another."

"Then you have forgiven me, Deles . . . in spite of all . . ."

"Yes." Deles spoke the single syllable with perfect conviction.

"And your mother?" The tired eyes searched his face, preventing Deles from lying.

"She is still bitter."

"I can't blame her, after the terrible things I did to her . . . and to you."

"There is no blame to be assigned to anyone," Deles said, "but Mother is blind to that fact."

"We are all blind to something," Acrios wheezed. "I was blind to many things. . . . the mighty Receptor . . . such power

was in my hands that I thought nothing could affect me. I rode
the clouds, my will the center of the storm . . ."

"I remember, Grandfather."

"Yes, of course you do . . . I took you once . . . not under the
best of circumstances, I'm afraid . . . I'm sorry."

"It's all right, Grandfather."

"I feared death so much, Deles . . . if I had only known the
truth . . ."

And, staring directly into Deles's eyes, he ceased breathing.
His hand on Acrios's brow, Deles felt the pulsing terminate, and
knew that it was over. The prophecy was fulfilled.

Gently, he lifted the scrawny figure and carried him through
the parting crowd. Not a word was spoken, for by now all knew
who this dead man had been.

The tart smell of the sea stung Deles's eyes as he approached
the spire.

"Call the storm to take him," he demanded.

"That is impossible," the spire replied.

"Nothing is impossible," Deles said. "Have the mundomentus call the storm."

"I repeat that it cannot be done."

Deles carried the body toward the beach. Down from the
sward he walked, the crowd following. His feet sank into the
soft sand as he made his way to the lapping shore. He laid the
body of Acrios down by the tide. Standing over it, he looked to
the sky.

The people waited silently, Deles having forgotten them in
their millions.

He raised his hand.

Far out over the swells loomed a gray sheet of rain. Nearer,
white fleecy clouds stirred and quickened. Like the high priest
of an ancient cult, Deles commanded the elements, defying the
might of the worldmind.

The dark clouds swirled as Deles's will emerged, a being of
blue flame. It spiraled into the storm, entering its core, its essence. Funneling, the clouds curved toward the beach, a sinuous
tentacle. Deles was barely aware that his body stood on the
beach. He did not care that the screaming crowd broke ranks
and scattered in terror. Godlike, he directed an elemental sarcophagus, lifting the body of Acrios gently skyward in a blaze of
blue glory.

Chapter Twenty-six

The Eggsharer's Return

Bilyf is disturbed. Because of his long stay in the society of Man, it is difficult for him to perceive in the pure Mennon manner. Nevertheless, it *can* be done, for many of the knowledge sharers have served different species . . . not the least of whom is Man.

It is just such a knowledge sharer Bilyf seeks now, one who has spent more than half a lifetime on Utrops, a world across the galactic rim where humankind flourishes. Into the mist goes Bilyf, wading through the swamp water. He comes to a hut made of dried splintertree branches; he enters. In the darkness within, he sees a shadowy figure, the knowledge sharer, huddled beneath a blanket of woven plant fibers.

"One sees that the eggsharer is restless," says the knowledge sharer.

"One sees that the knowledge sharer is correct," Bilyf replies, enjoying the use of his native tongue as it flows fluently from his oral folds.

"Have you not shaken away the odor of Man?"

"No."

"And yet you would be a knowledge sharer?"

"One must pursue a worthy goal."

Bilyf's host falls silent. As he waits, Bilyf sees the death of Acrios with startling clarity. Otherness surely follows, the master's life vindicated by his good end. . . . But will Acrios suffer another End . . . ? The gesture of the young master certainly suggests that nothing is resolved . . . but then, is there truly a resolution for anything?

"One sees," the knowledge sharer begins.

"Yes."

"One sees that you are not to be a knowledge sharer, that you are to return to Rocinth."

At once Bilyf sees the inevitability of this prophecy. He has always known that his own end would not be on Mennon . . . and has he not foreseen the Blue Star in his own future? He has

misinterpreted his own visions, allowed himself to assist in the
immoral acts of the driven Acrios, and turned his back on
Deles. This the knowledge sharer has shown him obliquely.
Like the opening of a flower, the one simple truth—that Bilyf is
not to be a knowledge sharer, but is instead destined to return
to Rocinth—reveals to him the intricate, beautiful structure beneath.

But now...

he visits...

the oviparious...

Mother...

...huge and warm she is, the Mother of them all. She
spreads her bulk over this huge chamber in the nest, where she
is fertilized twice a year, high above the swamp. The nest has
grown from the scum that floats on the swamp. Dried and piled
high, it is easily shaped into habitations, some even larger than
those harboring the eggsac. The Mother exhales a fond greet-
ing.

"One returns, Mother," Bilyf says.

"Much grown, your Mother sees." Her heavy limbs reach
out to him, the embrace of her tentacular digits sheathing his
body. "Your Mother loves you."

"One sees that you are fat with new eggs," Bilyf says, stroking her distended belly.

"Always, my eggsharer, always."

"Here with you, Mother, one is still small," Bilyf says politely, "and I do not speak only of your bulk."

"You will always be small, my eggsharer, as you were when
the human came and tore my heart even as he tore the eggsac."

"It was not a wound beyond repair, even so," Bilyf reminds
her.

"So many wounds have been inflicted upon your Mother's
heart, but the wound of the eggsac remains the sorest."

"And yet my Mother loves selflessly, as ever."

"Does your Mother not feed the tiny eggsharers with the
fluids from her own body? Is my life not the life of many? Is
there not joy to overwhelm the sadness that must come as surely
as comes the dreaded fogbeast?"

"One sees that one's thinking becomes twisted by one's proximity to humans," Bilyf says. "The humans would not tolerate
the fear of the fogbeast. They would seek it out and kill it with
their weapons, thus becoming even more terrible than it."

"There is more folly in this than wisdom," the Mother says,
"for surely the killer gives away more of himself than could be
taken by death."

"The humans do not believe so."

"And do they believe that the fogbeast has no right to its life?"

"If it threatens them, they suffer little remorse in destroying it," Bilyf replies. "World after world has suffered the loss of species upon species after the coming of Man."

"Was this true after the First Coming of Man, as well?"

"One does not see the Mother's meaning."

"Man has colonized the galaxy twice."

"One defers to the Mother's superior knowledge."

"The disappearance of Man," the Mother says, "is a mystery to the Mennon race. But disappear the anthroforms did, and there was peace . . . until they returned to plague us again."

Remembering that he had been born to serve Man, Bilyf said, "In spite of his violence, Man is not without compassion."

"One sees that he possesses greatness," the Mother agrees. "He persists while other species die."

"But his self-loathing is strong, is it not?"

"One sees that he fails to reproduce in sufficient numbers, even while he struggles to survive on the worlds he has made fit for his kind."

"One sees Man's ambivalance toward the End."

"And yet," the Mother says, "you have grown to love them."

"One believes that this is so."

"Then you have served your master well."

"Yes." But now . . .

. . . the master is . . .

. . . no more . . .

. . . and still Bilyf must serve. This time Deles, the young master, has need of him. The vision of death has blinded him to this, but the wisdom and love of the Mother now makes it plain . . . and yet this journey to Mennon has been necessary, a confirmation of those values imprinted upon his consciousness in the eggsac . . . a return to the beginning. He has been as needful of this as Deles has been of his journey to Rocinth. There has been no choice but to go.

"Your Mother sees that you must return to your new master. You have been created to serve him. The genes long ago were implanted for this purpose."

"You have had a vision, Mother."

"Yes." Like him, she sees death with sobering clarity—as big and beautiful as a fogbeast, and with claws just as terrifying. "Yes, the wrong must be righted. It was seen long ago, in the Now That Seems to Be, and you will help to put things aright."

"Yes."

"But there are no ships," says the Mother. "It will not be a simple matter for you to return."

"One sees that this is so," Bilyf replies, the image of the fogbeast fading into the mist, "and yet sees that it will be done."

"In the Now That Seems to Be . . ."

". . . And the Now That Is Always."

Bilyf

      meditates

              by the eggsac

                        just after the Mother

has delivered it, and sees . . .

                              the birth . . .

      of Deles's children . . .

                twins . . .

                      Deles loves them dearly . . .

                            and yet . . .

                                he is as . . .

                                  preoccupied . . .

                      with what is to come . . .

as is Bilyf . . .

Siule and Siula, he has named the twins, much to Edorna's annoyance.

"Those are clones' names," she protests, but Deles turns a deaf ear. Daily, he walks to the well—having taken possession of Acrios's estate—and follows its winding ledge to the level where the antechamber is. He does not enter, but stands without, pondering his strange conception.

Although Edorna's announcement of her pregnancy had frightened him, the twins are not teratological genetic mutations. They have grown to be both beautiful and intelligent, and he loves them dearly.

And yet, as he stares into the black pit, he longs for Bilyf's counsel and friendship. He fears that all is not well, despite appearances. In his mind he relives the day he told his mother that Acrios was dead.

"You're sure of it?" she had asked, like a little girl. "And there was nothing from which another might be cloned?"

"Nothing," he said. "Acrios is gone forever."

She turned away from him then, sighing. Perhaps at that moment she did not think of the tortured Acrios, but of the man who had taken her to the theater when she was little. Bilyf cannot be certain. Indeed, Bilyf can be certain of nothing except that he must return to Rocinth. There is still much to be done, and so he must locate a ship. He will be forced to go halfway around Mennon to the mineral deposits of Foras, where an occasional merchant ship loads in the argillaceous quarries.

On the way he will be attacked by a fogbeast, he knows, its

tusks distended through its flaring oral folds, claws poised to rend and tear. But it will not kill him (Does he bear the odor of death, of tainted meat, that this will be so?), it will not even come near. It slinks back into the drifting mists of the swamp as if it has had a vision of its own. Perhaps it has not expected an adult eggsharer—or perhaps it simply is not hungry. Brackish water fills its big, notched tracks in the clay, and Bilyf pushes on through the swamp. He will not die on Mennon.

He will

not die

until . . .

. . . he sees . . .

. . . Parnassus . . .

. . . and the Blue Star . . .

He will never see the Mother, or Mennon, again.

One dark, one light, the twins reminded Danna of Deles as they frolicked here in the nursery. Danna had frequented this brightly decorated room as a child herself. Its comical, capering images were calculated to amuse children for hours. Nevertheless, it didn't seem to be working for the twins today.

She watched them wrestling on the floor. In spite of his black hair, inherited from Edorna, Siule looked more like his father. Still, Siula's golden curls often reminded her of those halcyon days when Deles chased nafs outside their little house in Nathe. Often quiet in the presence of their father, the twins were most lively with Edorna, and yet one sensed that they loved Deles no less than their mother, perhaps even more.

Deles entered the nursery now, and the twins stopped laughing immediately. His effect on them was typically sobering.

"Where is your mother?" he asked, tousling their heads.

"Watching a dreamdisc," Siula said.

"No she isn't," Siule argued. "She's reading."

"Edorna can never learn too much," Danna said.

"Mother," Deles said. "I didn't see you sitting over there in the corner."

"I just wanted to be with the children. If only they liked studying as much as their mother does."

"Well, Edorna feels that she missed a great deal growing up in Lukerna. Though in some ways life is much better there."

"I'm sure," Danna said skeptically.

Deles ignored her comment, squatting to pat the children on their rumps. "Go find your mother," he said.

They went off reluctantly, casting mournful looks behind them. No doubt they wondered why they were being excluded. Indeed, Deles was in a brown study, even more than usual.

"Are you all right, my son?" Danna asked.

"Yes, I'm fine."

"Something is troubling you."

"Yes, you're right, there is something I haven't told you . . . it's about the well."

"The well. Is it about Leptos?"

"Not Leptos. Me."

"You?" Danna said. "Deles, what are you talking about?" He hadn't been the same since he left Sripha, and moving into Acrios's villa had made him worse. She was beginning to doubt his sanity, so peculiar had his actions been of late. She suspected that Acrios's death had been the catalyst. It was like her father to reach out of the grave to contaminate their lives. But she couldn't really blame a dead man, not when she had ruined Deles's life with her single-minded insistence that he punish Acrios. She hated to think what he would have been like if he hadn't had the children.

"Mother," Deles said, "I think I know how I was conceived."

For a moment, Danna didn't breathe. Did he really know? And, if so, had Leptos told him?

"Mother, I know what happened to you in the factory. Something happened to *me* there, too."

"Happened to you . . . ?" What was he saying? Would he ever be his old self again?

"It changed me," Deles said, "genetically."

"But all that was years ago," Danna said. "You have two lovely children now, so it couldn't have made any difference."

"You had a normal child, too, Mother."

"Yes, and you turned out well." She was desperate to convince him that it didn't matter.

"If you think a killer has turned out well, then I have."

"Deles, *I* made you kill Acrios." But she wondered if it were true. It seemed to her now that this could never have been a matter between just a few people. There was a reason why members of her family put their offspring into that tiny room leading to the factory. There they could be analyzed, to see if their genetic material was suitable for the purposes of the Others. But what *were* the Others' purposes?

Deles stared at her, not without compassion.

"My son," she said, "try to understand. I have only had one obsession since I was a young girl. I am not sure that it was not meant to be that way, but whether it was or not, my wish was fulfilled. I found no satisfaction in it."

"*I've* found little satisfaction in anything since I've come back up to the surface," Leptos said, entering. "Where are the children?"

"Gone to find their mother," said Deles, his mood lightening somewhat at the sight of his great-grandfather.

"They brighten this strange house," Leptos said. "The place would be intolerable without them."

"You are bored, Grandfather."

"Sometimes I feel like a ghost wandering through this place," Leptos said. "And it wasn't even built during my lifetime."

"Your lifetime is still going on," Deles said.

"When I go upstairs and look at that reception pool..." He shook his head. "How can I believe that little Acrios lay there, absorbing information from the Machine itself? And how can I believe he's now an Other while I still live?"

Deles's heart went out to the confused Leptos. The patriarch did not fully understand what had happened while he was in stasis, and he believed that Acrios's death was an accident.

"You know," Leptos said, pacing the nursery, "at least I had a purpose down in the factory. Here I serve no function. No function whatsoever."

"You don't have to," Danna said. "You're our grandfather, not a robot. You can do as you please here."

"Nothing gives me any pleasure except the twins." Leptos's blue eyes stared sincerely out of his hirsute face. "I've found the changes in the world not much to my liking."

"Things have not changed so much, Grandfather," Danna said.

"Perhaps not, but at least there was a place for me in the old days. It was only when I hurt my son that things became unbearable. I threw myself into that well out there, intending to never see the light of day again... and I wish I hadn't seen it again, most of the time."

"Why don't you take a trip to Nathe?" asked Danna.

"And get out of your way, hmm?"

"Grandfather," she rebuked him.

"It's the truth, and I don't blame you for it. I make you uncomfortable—why, I make myself uncomfortable, for that matter. Deles should have left me down there in the factory. At least I had a purpose there."

"You said that before," Deles reminded him.

"I'm perfectly aware of that," Leptos said. "You may not realize just how much I *am* aware of."

"Oh?" Deles had long since discovered that such a taunt alleviated Leptos's despondency, replacing it with contentiousness. The patriarch enjoyed a good argument.

"Quite so," Deles," he said. "For example, I know that you

are in a quandary. You feel you must take action, but you don't know what action to take. Is this not so?"

"True enough," Deles replied, "as far as it goes."

"As far as it goes! How can I go any farther than you have? Indecision is your problem, Deles, just as boredom and confusion vex me."

"Well, what decision should I make?"

"I don't know," Leptos admitted, falling back into his depression. "I don't know much of anything anymore."

"Come, come, Grandfather," Danna said, taking his hand. "Let's go for a walk."

"I've been for a walk," he said, but allowed her to lead him out into the corridor.

Standing alone in the nursery, Deles wondered how he could be so transparent that even Leptos could see through him. He *was* indecisive; he could not make up his mind to stay with the family or go into space. But where was he to go if he left Rocinth? And why did he feel such an urge in the first place?

Was he being manipulated by the Others? By the Machine? Or was it only his own sickened spirit, hungry for renewal?

It didn't matter. He wasn't going anywhere. His place was here with his family. After all he had been through, he had a right to enjoy watching his children grow. And Danna needed him to help her through a period of change after Acrios's death. Leptos had needed help in adjusting, too . . . and before him, Edorna . . .

He walked out of the nursery and down the adjoining corridor, deep in thought. He would go outside for some fresh air. As he approached the central arch, he heard the children laughing.

"Siule!" Edorna's voice cut through the twilight as Deles stepped onto the grass. "Don't be so rough with your sister."

The setting sun oversaw the wrestling twins and their mother. Edorna's white gown appeared as pastel violet, and her skin seemed healthy and tanned—dusk's illusion, for in reality she was as pale as garom's milk. The twins continued to grapple on the lawn.

"You heard your mother," Deles said softly.

The giggling twins became silent, and their energetic squirming ceased. They stood on their plump legs obediently as he approached them. Squatting, he took one small head in each hand.

Under the lurid sky, their blue eyes seemed to burn like tiny suns. Another trick of the light, Deles told himself.

"You want to go away, don't you, Father?" Siula asked.

Surprised, Deles could only stare at the twins, certain that they both shared this knowledge. Indeed, Siule eyed Deles as knowingly as his sister. "Yes, I want to get away," Deles said.

He heard a stifled sob. Turning his head toward the house, he saw Edorna running inside, her hand to her face.

"Mother doesn't understand," Siula said, "but we do."

Deles stood and took them by their hands, not knowing what to say, or if he should say anything. He only knew that his children's bizarre ancestry was beginning to show in them at last.

Chapter Twenty-seven

The Little Others

Siula asked to be carried, and Deles obliged her, hefting the little girl onto his shoulder as they made their way down the path. Siule preferred walking next to his father, his short legs having no difficulty in keeping up with Deles's reluctant pace.

"This is where your grandmother used to play," Deles said, pointing at the crystal garden as they neared it.

"Why doesn't she come here anymore?" asked Siule.

The question disturbed Deles. Why didn't she cultivate the crystals? Why wasn't anything *right*? They had a family, a home; what else did they need? "She has other things to keep her busy."

"What does she do?"

"Well . . ."

"Does she talk to the blue people?" Siule asked.

Deles put her down. "Blue people?" he said. "Like fire?"

"Yes," Siule said, "like fire."

They passed the garoms and came to the edge of the well. It was a warm evening, so the three of them sat in the grass, the dark hole yawning a few meters away.

"Do you know what we call those fiery blue people?" he asked the twins.

"Others," said Siula.

"You see them?"

"Yes—and talk to them."

So this was the result of the factory's tampering with his body: his children were able to sense the Others with no artificial aids. "What do you talk about?" he asked.

"Lots of things," Siule said, laconic as usual.

"But mostly . . ." Siula added, looking sidewise at her brother, ". . . mostly about what it's like to be an Other."

"What *is* it like? Have the Others told you?"

"It's better."

"Better than what? The anthroform?"

"Yes."

228

Deles thought that he should point out to the twins the pleasure of the anthroform, the joy of feeling the wind in one's hair and the springy grass underfoot. But for all he knew the Others experienced these sensations more acutely than he. The arguments that he had heard as a boy against choosing Otherness would not work with his own children.

"I know we've never spent as much time together as we would have liked," he said, though it wasn't true. He had been a conscientious parent, showering the twins with attention. "When I have punished you," he said slowly, haltingly, "it wasn't because I wanted to hurt you. It was to teach you to be good people . . . because . . . because I love you."

"We know," Siula said, "the Others told us."

"Told you what?"

"Told us about you. Where you came from. And they told us where they came from, too."

Deles felt a chill, and it wasn't the wind. "Have you told your mother about this?"

"No," Siula replied, "the Others told us not to."

Deles was relieved. "Good. I'll talk to her."

"Why?" Siule asked.

"Why? Because she's your mother."

"She won't understand."

"That may be true, but she has a right to know."

"All right," the twins said in unison.

Deles rose and walked the few paces to the well. It was completely dark now, the stars were out, and the moons were lining up in a familiar pattern. Beneath his feet the pit yawned like death itself. Restlessness was replaced by dread, for Deles knew what was soon to come. If he could have prevented this, he would gladly have suffered all his tribulations up to now a thousandfold. His suffering had only begun.

Acrios, an Other; Stallea, gone; all the world changed, giving the lie to the old saw about nothing ever changing on Rocinth. On one of his endless nocturnal walks, Leptos considered just how much things had changed. It wasn't only his personal life, but the way everyone lived. Their dependence on dreamdiscs, imagemakers, and violent sport was much more pronounced. Even here in this house, pent-up emotions threatened to explode at any moment. Though they called him patriarch, Leptos was a stranger among them.

Still, he considered as he set an art object spinning with the touch of his finger, he could not ignore their antagonisms; these were not petty squabbles. There was a great deal at stake here, but his part in it was long since over—over for thousands of years.

Shouting came from a room at the end of the corridor. Should he listen? Why not? They never paid any attention to him anyway. Besides, he might gain some insight by overhearing this argument—a particularly vehement one, judging from its volume. He drew closer to the curtained chamber.

"You're holding something back from me." It was Edorna, her voice strident. "You know what's wrong with the twins, don't you. *Don't you?*" Her tone was accusing.

"There is nothing *wrong* with them." Deles.

"Oh," she huffed. "Don't you think I can sense a change in my own children?"

"Change is not always for the worst, Edorna."

"Then why are you so evasive? Don't patronize me."

"Calm yourself."

"Is that all you can say?"

"Edorna, when I brought you to Rocinth, I told you it was better not to have children. This is not Lukerna, nor even Sripha."

"How deftly you avoid the point," she said.

"I am not avoiding it. I am merely stating that few people have children on Rocinth."

"What are you getting at?"

"Imposing the values of Lukerna on Rocinth simply won't work."

"Lukernan values are strong."

"Oh, come now," Deles said. "You were willing enough to abandon those values after your people sacrificed you to the trun."

"Deles . . ."

"Don't look at me like that," he said. "You know it's true."

"None of this has anything to do with the twins."

"Edorna," Deles said, his voice lowering, "Siula and Siule must make their own decision."

"How can they?" she demanded, her voice breaking with emotion. "They are only babies!"

"They have reached the age of reason," he said. "It is the way of Rocinth. I explained it all to you when you first came here."

"Deles, what are you saying?"

"I'm trying to prepare you for what's going to happen."

"Deles—"

"They have reached the age of reason," he repeated. "Now they must decide in which form they'll continue, anthroform or Other."

"You mean alive or *dead!*" Edorna screamed.

"Those are antiquated terms," he said in exasperation.

"Deles, how can you stand there lecturing me while our children plan to kill themselves? We must stop them."

"We can't stop them—even if we lock them away in the darkest chamber underground."

"But surely we can dissuade them, use reason, convince them that there is much to live for."

"Edorna, we must accept this," Deles said softly. "It is inevitable."

"Why? I've heard of parents talking their children out of it."

"It wouldn't work in this case."

"Don't you want them to live?" Edorna cried. "Your children?"

"They must make their own way, whether as anthroform . . . or as Other."

The children, Leptos thought with terror, the children. As he slowly backed away from the curtained chamber, a long, anguished scream issued from within, reverberating through the estate like an echo of the End of All Things itself.

Danna barely raised her head as Deles entered, and it occurred to him that he had spent half his life seeking her out in her rooms on two worlds. Never before, though, had she been so despondent. He stood over her as she worked on a tapestry, and was reminded of people in the distant past who had aged, withering and dying like plants. He sat on the webbing to be on her level, but she didn't look him in the eye.

"You know, don't you?" he said at length.

"I know nothing," she replied. "You have told me as much on several occasions."

"That's not what I said—ever."

"Ah, but what difference does it make, Deles? You were right. My life has been one long delusion, a red haze of hatred."

"Terrible things were done to you," Deles said. "You couldn't help the way you felt."

"I lived only for my father's death."

"And now *he* is dead."

"But it does my heart no good. Nothing is as I had hoped. Even though his death was by your hand, it was not your doing . . . and even if it had been, I would have had no satisfaction. There is precious little joy in vengeance, after all . . . but without vengeance I have no purpose."

"You will find another purpose, Mother."

"I think not," she said, ceasing her weaving. "It was Bilyf's vision that evening that shaped my life . . . our lives."

"We all did what we had to," Deles said.

"And now the twins are to become Others?"

"I am afraid so."

"It is difficult to imagine," she said. "They are so full of life. I don't know if I will be able to stand it."

"Might it not be preferable to the anthroform?"

"Those of us who have clung to life cannot bring ourselves to believe so."

"Even Acrios decided ultimately that Otherness was for the best," Deles pointed out, "and no one ever resisted the end more than he."

"The burden of life becomes too ponderous, even in a life as short as mine," Danna said. "Imagine what it was like for him, living for century after century with all that sin on his conscience . . . worse, knowing that his entire life had been spent in a meaningless quest for power."

"Purpose gets us through life, doesn't it, whether or not there is meaning?"

"Oh, how I'll miss those little ones," Danna said. "They are a constant delight and surprise to me. They make me think of you when you were a child . . . how it might have been had you grown up in this house."

"The result would have been the same."

"Yes," Danna sighed. "As if we were nothing more than laboratory specimens, tended by a hand we barely discern."

"Then perhaps it is best that the twins choose Otherness."

"Can it be that they *won't* choose it?" Danna asked.

"I don't know, Mother, but I doubt it."

"We'll find out soon enough, I suppose," Danna said, turning back to her tapestry. She did not turn her head toward him again and did not speak, so at last he rose and left her rooms.

The day arrived sooner than Deles had hoped, and later than he had expected. Danna would not go with them, and Edorna could not. But the twins were cheerful as they walked down the garden path with their father.

Deles was about to watch his children die.

No, he thought, he came to watch them be born . . . born on the other side, as Verra had put it. Things would be better there—not perfect, perhaps, but better. He had to believe that.

The three of them stopped near the edge of the well. Here they had sat and talked many times, at this quiet weed-strewn spot. It occurred to Deles that he had never really known the twins; there was a bond between his children that excluded everyone else. Still, he had been closer to them than anyone, even their mother.

"I'll miss you," he said.

"But you'll be an Other some day, too," Siula said, shaking her blonde curls out of her eyes. "Then we'll be together again."

"Will we?"

"Yes," said Siule, "the Others have told us so."

"Have they told you if Otherness is forever?" Deles asked. "Or must that too come to an end?"

"They never said." Siule frowned.

"What *have* they told you about Otherness?"

"It's hard to explain," said Siule, unusually talkative in his last minutes. And how terribly implausible it was, Deles thought, that these were the last minutes of this little boy, so dear to him and yet so strange. Siule glanced at his sister for aid.

"The Others don't talk out loud," Siula said. "They talk inside your head."

"Yes, that much I know."

"And they say you have to decide for yourself if you're going to be an Other."

"If they haven't tried to influence you, what made you decide to . . . join them?"

Both of them looked at him sharply. Neither spoke, and Deles feared what they thought. And yet he had to know. "Well, what made you decide?"

"No one is happy here," Siula said solemnly. "That is what made up our minds."

Deles wasn't sure if his daughter's answer was innocent or profound. Perhaps it was both.

"You know how badly this will hurt your mother and your grandmother?" he said.

Their blue eyes were sincere. "There is nothing we can do about that," Siule said, his sister nodding in agreement. The remark was not callous, simply the truth. Deles found their answers somehow reassuring, almost convincing him that this was not death they faced, not really. In their guilelessness they might have divined the true nature of Otherness. It had to be. When he was a child, there had been no Others to guide him. . . .

No one is happy here.

A deep longing overcame him, and he could think of nothing more to say. Alien as was Otherness to him, he had little to offer his children now, except . . .

"I love you." He gathered them in his arms as he began to weep.

"We love you too, Father," Siula said.

"Do you?" Deles's voice cracked like an adolescent's. Holding them close, he smelled their scrubbed childish scent through his salt tears. "Do you love me?"

"Yes, Father," Siule said, "we love you, but you'll always be unhappy here. Why don't you come with us?"

"I wish I could, but there is still much for me to do in this life."

"What?"

"I—I don't know yet. I only know that there is more for me to do before I become an Other."

"Haven't you done enough, Father?"

"Whatever I have accomplished is a mere prelude to what is to come, I suspect." Deles studied their rapt faces. "Do you understand what I'm saying?"

The twins nodded simultaneously.

"Just as you are doing what you have to," he went on, "so am I doing what I must . . . though it is not all clear to me yet."

"Why not?"

"I don't know, but it never has been. Bilyf used to say that I was being pulled through life like a thread through a tapestry. He was right, I think." How he missed Bilyf's quiet strength now. "But when I am finished I will join you, I promise you that."

The twins hugged him again and then drew back. They lay in the grass together.

The time had come.

Determined to see it through, Deles stood watch over them. He dared not speak, for concentration was essential.

The sun sank low, and still the twins lay beside the well. An occasional twitch was the only signal that they still lived. The sky was beautiful, a layering of magenta, damask, royal purple, and indigo. Against these bright hues, Deles noticed a flicker of blue.

A trick of the light? No, there was another. And another. Soon there were half a dozen azure flashes; they coalesced, flaming spirals issuing from an amorphous shape suspended over the well.

"You come to take my children," he whispered. "And you take my heart with them."

Like an insect's antennae, the spirals of blue fire reached toward the supine twins. Deles fought the urge to run at them, to try and stop them. But they were no more solid than the air he breathed. How could he affect them?

The flaming mass divided into humanoid figures, two of them hovering just over the twins. These two he had perceived as antennae.

A wind rose, not from the sea, but from inland. It washed

over his face, rippling his clothing. Growing in strength, it became an assault, challenging him to stand against it.

Leaning into the wind, he made his way closer to the twins, more determined than ever to last out the transformation. This was the last time he would see his babies alive. He wouldn't let the Others drive him away.

But the wind was so strong that he could barely advance against it. It threatened to lift him off his feet and hurl him back toward the villa, to crush him against its stones like an insect.

"Damn you!" he shouted. "I won't go!"

But the wind tore at him even more savagely. The dying light was a backdrop for hundreds of flaming blue figures now, thousands. Deles pitched himself into the gale, stumbling toward the Others, cursing and weeping.

Deles.

"You're dead things!" he screamed. "The very essence of corruption!" He raised his hand. The Destroyer would deal with them.

Deles.

They were addressing him, something he thought would never again happen while he lived. Was Lehana among them? And even if she was, how could he see and hear them without the sensorium?

"You know me?" he demanded.

We know you.

"You've persuaded my children to join you!" he accused, not really believing what he was saying. "Why?"

It is for the best that they become Others. In their innocence they have found the freedom that eludes the anthroform.

"Freedom? Then this really is their choice?"

Yes. Did you ever doubt it?

He knew that it was true, that the twins had perceived an intrinsic happiness in Others that did not exist among anthroform humans. He had no right to question their decision.

Do you fear Otherness?

"I fear death," Deles said.

Do you know what it is?

An unexpected question, for which Deles had no answer. He braced himself against the wind as the two Others brushed flaming fingertips over the twins. There was nothing he could do.

The two antennae flared, and there were four Others where there had been two. For a moment they shimmered in the encroaching darkness with the multitude of fiery, blue figures.

Goodbye, Father.

"My children!" he cried, but the figures once again coalesced into one immense glowing sphere and imploded into nothingness.

The wind abated and was gone.

For a very long time, Deles could not bring himself to move. He could make out two tiny white shapes in the darkness, but he could not believe that they were all that remained of his beautiful twins. At last his mind stirred from that illogical place and forced him to see the irrefutable. In a few minutes he had gathered enough strength to approach the bodies.

They might have only been sleeping, he thought. Their plump faces had not yet paled, and their eyes were closed. It was only the unnatural stillness that betrayed the semblance of life, like an unmoving projection, a frozen image designed for aesthetic pleasure. But it was not an image. It was real . . . so very real. And there was nothing he could do.

"But you're their father," he said. "You have to do something."

Yes, there was something he could do, and somehow he knew it was right. One at a time, he picked up the tiny bodies and carried them to the edge of the well, Siule first, and then Siula. They were limp, but they didn't weigh very much, and it was easy to drop them into the well. They disappeared into its black depths without a sound. And then it was over.

As if in a dream, Deles started back up the path. His only thought was that the bodies had still been warm when he lifted them and threw them over the edge. But he was nearly as relieved as he was emotionally numbed. At least it was done . . . and the twins would be happier now. He must remember that when their laughing faces haunted him, awake or dreaming.

Chapter Twenty-eight

Deles's Renewal

The roborgs had stopped Leptos from killing himself once, but they couldn't do it again; Deles had seen to that. The Destroyer had done its work well. Dying now would be finishing a task too long left undone. Leptos ambled down the path toward the well. It was a fine day to join the twins—birds sang, flowers bloomed in a glorious profusion of colors, the sun shone brilliantly—and there was no need to hurry.

They'd never miss him anyway. Being alive like the three of them in that house was worse than being dead or becoming an Other. He wasn't quite sure which he would be, and it didn't much matter to him. As far as he could see, it was all the same.

Life, or whatever passed for it, would go on. It wouldn't have seemed like life to him without Siule and Siula. The adults were all caught up in their own worlds, and he didn't know how to get through to them. Why, they didn't even know that this was the Second Coming of Man! They dismissed it as *his* fantasy. What ignorance. Not that he had ever fathomed the Second Coming's significance himself, but at least he was aware of it. He'd had some interests besides self-pity, unlike these people.

"They don't see anything," he said aloud as he passed the whuffing garoms. And to think that it had all started with him. Of course, he couldn't be held responsible; the entire business was out of his hands. There was no guilt where there was no blame . . . or at least there shouldn't be. Such problems wouldn't vex him for much longer, he thought as he came to the well's edge. Down there he had at least had a purpose. That purpose was gone, but now he could go to sleep.

With the wind of destiny at his back, he leapt to his death.

"Leptos," Deles called, the echo swallowed by the ocean's roar. He had ranged from the forest bordering the estate on the west to the sea, and had seen no sign of his great-grandfather. He stepped carefully along the clifftop, staring down at the whitecaps. Moss made for slippery footing, but he moved swiftly in spite of it as he started back toward the villa.

Where could Leptos have gone? Bethes, to see a play? Popothes, to the races? Nathe? He had been despondent since the twins had become Others, nearly as bad as Edorna. Perhaps he had merely gone off in search of some entertainment. Of course, Deles had already taken him to the city, and truth be told, Leptos hadn't exhibited much interest in the diversions there. It seemed likely that he had gone somewhere much farther away than Nathe.

Deles missed him, though he had to admit to himself that none of them had paid much attention to Leptos since . . . since things had begun to fall apart.

It was up to Deles to buoy Edorna's spirits now, but it was so difficult for him to talk to her, almost impossible. He hardly knew her at all anymore. Indeed, he hardly knew anyone.

The clifftop was above him now, so that the wind at his back was cut off. His footfalls seemed inordinately noisy in the ensuing silence. He could even hear his own slightly labored breathing. If the acrid salt smell hadn't continued to sting his nostrils, he wouldn't have been able to tell that the sea was only a hundred meters behind him.

"Deles!"

He looked up to see a white figure running toward him—Edorna. Had she found Leptos? Something had agitated her; she kept shouting as she ran, her gown trailing awkwardly behind her.

She reached him in a few moments, redfaced, clutching at his arm as if to pull him toward the villa. Her nails dug into his skin, threatening to break through and draw blood. What had brought on this hysteria?

"Edorna . . . ?"

"Deles," she gasped, "it's your mother!"

"Mother!" Deles pushed her away and ran up from the sea and across the sward. As fast as he sprinted, the house didn't seem to draw any closer. But at last he was bounding up the huge slab steps, dashing through the dining halls and up the stairs. Tearing the curtain aside, he entered his mother's quarters. She lay on the floor next to her unfinished tapestry, two crimson streams extending from her wrists, filling the cracks between the tiles.

"Get a physician!" It was Edorna; she had followed him upstairs. "She might be repaired!"

"No." Deles shook his head savagely. "It's better this way."

"Better? How can it be better? She's dead!"

He pushed Edorna back through the swirling curtains. "That is what she wanted."

"Deles..." Edorna said, her eyes wild, "...the children... and now your mother...."

Deles pulled her through the corridor and down the winding stairs. In the banquet hall, he jerked a chair back from the table, the scraping sound echoing through the huge, empty room.

"Please sit down," he said.

She did as he asked, and he poured wine for both of them out of a sparkling carafe. In the dim light he spilled some on the polished wooden tabletop. Angrily, he ordered the robots to clean it up and to fire the braziers so that he could see. Without leaving its wall niche, one of them fired two bursts from its fingertips, igniting the braziers, while the other hurried to the table and wiped up the spilled wine.

Firelight twinkled on the glasses as Deles refilled them. Deles didn't like it; darkness or the harsh glare of artificial lighting would have been more appropriate.

"Edorna..." he stammered, not knowing what to say.

"You're mad," she said. "Your entire family is—was—mad, and you're the craziest of them all."

"Perhaps." He gulped down his glass of wine in one long draught.

"Look at you," Edorna said. "You're a marionette, dancing to the Others' tune."

"How do you know who's playing the tune?" he asked, wiping his mouth with the back of his hand.

"Who else could it be but the Others? They want us all to be dead, like them."

"Perhaps."

"After all the terrible things they've done...If you had any courage you'd defy them."

"Edorna..."

"But you won't, because you're insane...you.... You've ruined your own life, and mine."

Deles didn't argue with her, for what she was saying was undeniable. She had no idea of his strange conception, nor of the genetic tampering that had shaped the twins. Was their birth a mistake, or some part of a great scheme known only to the Others? He had almost told her about the factory once, thinking that it might relieve her worrying, but now he saw that it would have only added to her misery.

"I'm going back to Sripha," Edorna said.

"Very well."

She didn't touch her wine, but sat staring at the crystalline lip of the glass. "My babies," she whispered once, and then became silent.

Deles refilled his glass and downed its contents. Edorna murmured something incomprehensible.

"What did you say?" he asked.

"I asked you what you will do now."

"Wait, I suppose."

"For what?"

"For a sign—to tell me what must come."

"I've never been to Rocinth before," Matta said, her weathered face sincere as she stepped back from Deles after a brief embrace, "or even to the big estates on my own world. That's why I didn't hesitate to step aboard the ship you sent to Lukerna when the robot invited me inside . . . though my neighbors warned me not to go."

"It's a good thing you didn't listen to them," said Deles. "It would be difficult for Edorna to make the trip alone."

"Well, the robot didn't explain what had happened, only that Edorna needed me."

"It was a terrible shock to her," Deles said, "first to lose the children, and then my mother, and Leptos disappearing the way he did." They had never found Leptos's body, and yet Deles was quite certain that his great-grandfather was an Other by this time.

"You are strong, Deles," Matta said, "to accept these things."

"I'm not so strong—I've been drinking a great deal—but this is the way things are, and I cannot change them."

"We have a different attitude toward death in Lukerna," Matta said, "perhaps because we live only a few centuries at most, a result of our separation from the rest of humankind. Well, it's our own choice to live in the lake country, so we have nothing to complain about."

"Perhaps not," Deles said absently. "Would you like something to eat, Matta?" The robots had set out food and potables on a table in the sun.

"Fish, if you have any," she said, sitting down at table and reaching for a piece of broiled seafood. Plopping it onto her plate, she began to devour it. Deles enjoyed her robust manner, a welcome change these days.

"You may live in Ploydektum, if you like," he said. "By Sriphan law it is mine to give, and no provincial tyrant would dare deny it."

"Might makes right on my world, it's true," Matta replied,

"and no one in the solar system is mightier than Deles, I daresay. But I think we'll go home to Lukerna."

"As you wish."

Matta swallowed and looked at him. "Will you be all right here, Deles?" she asked. "This house is full of ghosts."

Deles shrugged, pouring himself a glass of wine.

"The day you and Bilyf wandered into our village, I sensed something noble in you, and the following day you saved my daughter's life. Now look how she repays you."

"Edorna has shown more patience than is good for her," Deles replied, "I assure you of that."

"You *are* noble, Deles, to be so charitable."

Deles laughed.

"I've always known it," Matta persisted.

"So you have the Gift?"

"You're making fun of me now," Matta said, "but you know that we all have the Gift in some measure."

"My mother certainly did."

Matta stopped chewing and looked at him sympathetically. "She must have been a remarkable woman. I wish I'd known her."

"Life was often unkind to Mother. She . . . never fully recovered from a shock she suffered as a young girl."

Shaking her head sadly, Matta said, "At least in Lukerna we know where the danger is, hiding in the lakes. But here it seems to be in the human heart."

Her words remained in Deles's mind throughout the day, until Edorna was prepared to leave at dusk. He had not seen his wife in several days, but it was just as well, for he didn't have anything to say to her.

Now, as she came down the stairs dressed in a severe gray wrap, he wanted to run to her, hold her, comfort her. But her cold stare warned him to keep his distance.

"Edorna." Matta embraced her.

"I am ready to go home, Mother."

A robot stepped lightly behind her, carrying a number of bundles under its armatures. She beckoned for it to follow as she crossed the dining hall and started out through the main archway. But now the sun was low, and the shadows inside the villa deepened.

Without a word, Deles trailed Matta, Edorna, and the robot outside. It was a cool twilight, and the ship was perched on a cliff overlooking the sea, not fifty meters from where Deles had been standing the day his mother died. In the dusk, its silvery bulk resembled a pyramid placed there as a monument to the dead, perhaps intended to last forever. But it would remain only a few more minutes; the last of his mortal ties would vanish in the darkening sky.

"Edorna," he said.

She hesitated, now just a few meters from the ship. Would she stop and speak to him before she left Rocinth? Deles prayed that she would, but for all his power he could not make her do so.

She turned and searched his face with her dark eyes. Deles could discern no emotion in them, not even disgust. "Goodbye, Deles," she said.

He watched her gesture toward the triangular hatch. The robot clambered aboard with her bundles. How absurdly domestic this scene is, he thought, as if Edorna were merely going for a few days holiday to Bethes, instead of leaving him.

"Don't bother to tell me that you love me," she said.

He would not argue. He didn't want her to go; didn't want to be left here, like some ancient prophet waiting for the will of the Others to manifest itself. He didn't want to be alone. Surely she understood that he was fond of her. Wasn't that enough?

"Perhaps I don't love you in the same way that you have loved me," he said, "but you are still the mother of my children."

"*Dead* children!" she screamed. "Dead! And you did nothing to stop it!" Tears streamed down her finely chiseled face. He could not make her see, for she had not been touched by the Others . . .

"I had hoped that you would not hate me, at least," he said.

"I don't hate you, Deles," she said, wiping her face with the back of her hand. "I pity you."

She turned away before he could comment, and rushed to the ship. The hatch clanked shut behind her.

A low thrum, and the pyramid lifted slowly into the setting sun, whitecaps licking under it as it moved horizontally. And then there was a slight trembling in the air and in the earth, an after-image remaining for an instant. The image faded, and Deles stood alone, looking out over the sea.

No doubt the mystagogues wondered at his return, but he noticed a certain deference in their manner, upon his entering the mundomentus, that had not existed the first time he had come here.

As the panel of the waiting cell slid back, he congratulated himself—this time there would be no lengthy wait.

"Deles," said the mystagogue who entered, "the mundomentus will receive you now."

"Thank you." He rose and made his way through the corridor, passed through a portal, and mounted the suspended walk-way. At the path's summit he lay down in the sarcophagus with-out hesitation. There were no preliminary thought shapes, no images. The mundomentus began: Why have you come?

"To ask your advice."

The worldmind waited.

"There is some task in store for me, and I still don't know what it is, much less how to go about it."

Still the mundomentus remained silent.

"Do *you* know?" Deles asked.

No.

"Then what shall I do? I am as restless as a garom in heat, obsessed with . . . with I don't know what. Some force geneti-cally imposed upon me . . . imperfectly, at that."

Acrios believed that you will supply the answer to human-kind's question.

"He was dying when he said that . . . delirious."

Nevertheless, it is true.

"But how? I have no special knowledge. The roborgs failed when they created me."

Did they?

"They must have. It should have been me who was able to communicate with the Others, rather than my children."

Are you certain of that? Do you know the Others well enough to divine their purpose?

Deles fell silent.

You cannot abdicate your responsibility, the worldmind went on. Mankind and all the other remaining intelligent species de-pend on you.

On him? Deles lay like a dead man, the weight of the mun-domentus' pronouncement crushing him like an insect. This could not be.

"Are you not linked to the Machine?" he said at last.

Yes.

"Will you ask it if what you claim is true?"

The machine will not comment on this subject.

"Why not?"

There was no reply.

After watching the riderless graviton platform veer out over the sea on its way back to Nathe, Deles walked reluctantly to-ward the villa. What would he do now, pace aimlessly, read, take a garom for a ride, get drunk? Midway between the sea cliffs and the well he subsisted, day after day, a futile existence. Even if he accepted the role of universal savior, he thought as he mounted the villa's steps, what did it mean?

In the dining hall, he walked to the table and hefted a carafe.

"To frustration," he said after filling a glass. The wine was tart, stinging his tongue. Some of it dribbled down his chin, and he wiped it with the back of his hand. He considered having another, then thought better of it.

Turning from the table, he was startled by a figure outlined in the archway. Short and pale, with long, wriggling fingers and a crested, piscean head; no human, this, Deles realized with mounting joy.

"Bilyf!" he shouted, running to embrace his old friend. His arms sank into Bilyf's striated musculature. "What are *you* doing here?"

"One sees—that the eggsharer—sets out for his home—and ultimately returns to it."

"You've come from Mennon?"

"Yes."

"All that way... Did you see the Mother?"

"One has—seen the Mother."

"I'm glad to hear that." Deles knew how important this had been to Bilyf. "How did you get back?"

"One finds—traders and merchants—on the homeworld."

"Seven, nearly eight years."

"The Now—That Seems—to Be."

Deles relished the cadence of Bilyf's speech. But how much did his old friend know? "Edorna and I have had children, Bilyf, and..."

"And—they are gone—and Deles grieves."

"Do you know about Mother?"

"One does not—easily recover—from the death—of little Danna."

"You foresaw it all," Deles said. "All their deaths."

"One sees—that Deles's heart bears—no hatred."

"That's not enough to console me. I watched Acrios die... and then the children...Leptos...Mother...Edorna leaving...."

"One sees—that Deles's life—is difficult."

"As are all lives, I suppose, but at least they are genuine lives. I am not even human. I'm some sort of biological machine like those things in the well."

"And yet—Deles feels pain." Bilyf drew his eyes back into their sockets thoughtfully, commiserating.

"If they wanted an automaton, why did they permit me to have emotions?" Deles cried.

"Perhaps the Others—need more than—a machine."

"But why? What do they need but a device to carry out their bidding?"

"Perhaps you will be—required to make judgments—based on love."

"Love?" Deles stared at the Mennon. "Bilyf, I've killed people. I've schemed to do terrible things."

"This—is so."

"How can *I* make judgments based on love?"

"Deles is desirous of love—though he has difficulty finding it—in himself."

"How can I ever hope to love while my life is being so horribly manipulated?"

"Deles *must*—do his best."

Surprised by Bilyf's emphatic tone, the like of which he had never heard before, Deles fell silent. At once he saw that Bilyf was correct, that his self-pitying tirade was a waste of breath. After a long pause he said, "You've come a long way, Bilyf. Are you hungry?"

"One is in need—of nourishment."

To the robots, Deles said, "Nutritional beads for my friend."

One of the robots stepped from its niche and strutted out of the dining hall in search of the beads.

"You know, Bilyf," said Deles, "except for that brief time just before Acrios exiled us, we've never been together in this house."

"One sees—that this is so."

"Now we have the place to ourselves—and here is your food."

The robot had already returned from the stasis field with some black beads set in a small tray. These were presented to Bilyf, who set the tray on the table and plucked a morsel from it.

Deles was certain that his friend must have been weak from hunger, or he wouldn't have asked for food. It was so good to have him back. Bilyf couldn't have arrived at a more opportune moment. "I've felt trapped in this house, Bilyf," Deles said. "My life seems to be enclosed by the space between the well and the sea."

"One sees that—Deles must act."

"Clearly . . . but I don't know what to do."

"Deles must—undertake a journey."

"You see that?"

"One sees—that Deles has been created—for this purpose."

"Created for this purpose . . ." Perhaps he would at last know the truth, he dared hope. But elation was dampened by doubt. "But what if my genetic programming is askew, and I cannot accomplish the . . . task I was made for?"

"This is—a possibility."

"More than a possibility," Deles said. "A likelihood. It might even account for the deaths of all these people, Bilyf. What if it's all a mistake? It must have been planned so long ago, and the roborgs are so old . . ."

"One sees—no alternative."

"All those deaths."

"One sees—how heavily the deaths—weigh on Deles."

Deles snorted. "A machine with a conscience?"

"Not—a machine."

"I'm a half-human construct, then, no better than the roborgs. Bilyf, not only have I killed my loved ones, but two people who might have found the answer to Man's question, as well."

"One sees—that Deles and Deles alone—can provide the answer."

An icy needle pierced Deles's heart. "How?" he asked.

"One sees—a journey," Bilyf repeated.

He was frightened, not only of beginning this final phase of his life—which he knew it must be—but of being alone. In fact, he was more frightened of being alone. "Will you go with me, Bilyf?"

Deles bowed in profound sincerity. "One—accompanies—Deles."

Deles was relieved, but still afraid of what was to come. "Where are we going, Bilyf?" he asked softly, as he had asked Bilyf so many times in his childhood.

"To the Blue Star—to Parnassus—in the Now That Seems to Be."

Chapter Twenty-nine

Parnassus

The journey required a timeship, for the Blue Star was far across the galactic rim. Doubtless for the last time, Deles had traveled to Nathe to consult with the mundomentus, to ask it to entrust him with the precious craft. The worldmind had not hesitated to supply it.

"Have we stocked everything we need?" he asked Bilyf as the last of the robots emerged from the round opening of the timeship, which was itself a great sphere.

"One—believes so."

The salt air smelled fine as Deles walked around the timeship, which rested on a cliff. They had brought it back to the estate to outfit it and themselves for the journey. There was a sense of symmetry in starting out at the point of their first journey together.

"It's nothing but a big, stippled ball," Deles said as he circled around to where he could see Bilyf beneath the timeship's curve. "It's the plainest ship I've ever seen. Even a graviton platform has more grace."

"It is—functional."

"I hope so." Deles had never understood how timeships aligned themselves with the forces of nature, slipping entirely out of one space/time continuum without entering another. At the end of its—for want of a more descriptive word—trajectory, it reentered the original continuum in a different time and place. Through experimentation, fairly accurate trajectories had been developed, though Deles had heard of timeships that never returned. It was a risk they had to take; the Blue Star was simply too far away to reach in any conventional manner. And with Bilyf along, he felt that he could accomplish anything. The indecision that had plagued him since Edorna's departure was gone. Here was a new adventure . . . the one that he had been created for. It was for the best; of that much he was certain.

"All that remains—is to board—the timeship."

Deles nodded, and the two of them passed through the

hatch. Once inside the airlock, they entered a brightly lighted interior.

"It looks comfortable enough," he said. "I've never seen a ship with so much room inside it."

"One sees that it is—*more* than adequate."

The hatches shut after them, sealing Deles off forever from the planet of his birth. A vague presentiment of the End tormented him, but he shook it off.

"Visuals," he said, embarrassed by the trembling of his voice.

They were suddenly submerged in the estate's manicured grounds, the ocean below them. The villa itself was oddly warped by the imaging sensors.

They rose slowly, hovering over the estate for a moment. The world shrank suddenly into a blue bhel-melon, a distant pearl, a light mote. It became lost in a myriad of stars. And then the stars themselves blended into a single dazzling jewel, filling the eye and the mind.

"*This is...*" But Deles couldn't find the words.

"One believes—it is extracontinuum travel."

"Yes." Words to describe the indescribable. It seemed that he looked at Bilyf through a dreamdisc. He could see all around the Mennon, from every conceivable vantage, and he could even look at himself in the same way, he realized with a start. From the *outside*. Himself, complete. He didn't like what he saw. He was fragmented: a twisted, tortured thing.

"Bilyf," he cried, "help me."

"One sees—that Deles requires no assistance—that he must bear with—the timeship's effects—in the Mennon way."

Of course, the Mennon conception of time would serve well under these conditions. If only Deles could recall the little he had learned about the Mennon way. He wanted to ask Bilyf to explain it to him again, but Bilyf's voice was now so faint and distant, heard through the hissing of blackbody radiation, it seemed, the sound of the universe itself.

Deles clutched the webbing, trying to retain some sensory ground in reality. But his fingers grasped an airy nothing, and he could not hold on. He drifted aimlessly, a billion shards of self, scattered throughout the void. The shards turned in upon themselves, revealing endless facets. Were these the Deleses that were or those that might have been? Whatever their nature, their endless complexity fascinated him, making his agony a little easier to bear.

But where was Bilyf?

Were these bits of matter—if indeed they *were* matter—all that was left of Bilyf? If so, they had mingled with his own fragments incontrovertibly now, and he and Bilyf were . . . ? Not one, surely. Two entities, yet indistinct.

"Bilyf," he called.

"One—is here," came the reply. And though time and space had lost all meaning, the journey was not empty. Here was love, in spite of all.

Abruptly, all sensations ceased. Deles held a trembling hand before his eyes, and saw it with normal binocular vision. Was it truly as pale as it seemed, or was it merely the light? Beyond the hand was Bilyf.

"Are you all right?" Deles asked him.

"One—perseveres."

Swinging his head around to loosen the cramped muscles of his neck and shoulders, Deles gazed up into the image of a blazing blue sun.

"So soon?" he said, but the journey might have taken a million years.

"One sees—that our destination—is the fourth world—of this solar system."

"Parnassus . . . the Machine . . ." Deles was confused. Could they really have traversed the galaxy? Was this indeed the Blue Star, the end of his quest? Now that it was so near, all was trivialized under its baleful glare.

Icy fire radiated from the sun. In the field of stars suspended in the firmament surrounding it, no planets were discernible.

"In spite of everything, we are here," said Deles.

Bilyf's silence reminded Deles that Bilyf had always known that this moment would come.

One of the stars grew larger, gaining definition as they approached it, until Deles saw that it was not a star at all, but the fourth world. The ship knew the way, and soon they observed a blasted, bare orb, spattered with the refuse of space.

"Can this be Parnassus?" There was no sign of Machine, Seers, or lightships. This planet was dead. Yet there was nothing for it but to watch as it loomed ever larger, seeming—through the visuals—to fill the ship's interior, overpowering in its bleakness.

"Scan for a surface entrance," Deles said. The ship began to orbit tightly as its sensors searched for evidence of a passageway leading beneath the surface.

"There is no apparent entrance," the ship reported after a lengthy interval. They had gone around Parnassus once.

"But that's impossible," said Deles. "There has to be some way for the lightships to get in and out."

"We must—be patient," Bilyf said.

"But we can't orbit this world forever. And we can't go back to where we came from. How can you speak of patience at a time like this?"

"One sees—that Deles speaks of—the Now That Seems to Be—and forgets his purpose—in coming—to Parnassus."

This admonition quieted Deles. But he was still frightened. This place embodied the end of all time and space. Its desolation affected him as deeply as the sight of death itself. There was no need for simile or metaphor; this place *was* the sight of death.

"One sees that—there is a solution."

"Are you having a vision?"

Bilyf didn't answer, and Deles felt a cold knot in his guts as a result. His mother had always claimed that everyone possessed a little of the Gift, and it seemed that the Gift pervaded his soul with a sense of doom now. But there was no certainty that the feeling was a presentiment. It might have been nothing more than his fear bubbling to the surface. He struggled to control it.

"Change course, uh . . . ninety degrees," he commanded the ship.

"One sees the wisdom—in this."

"We have to try something." The scan might have missed an entrance, so they would modify their orbit to compensate. But they circled the planet again, with no result. Deles was tired, querulous. He should have slept by this time, but he couldn't manage it. The ship sent out as powerful a signal as it could muster, but nothing came back from the planet. In spite of his efforts to subdue it, Deles's feeling of desolation increased.

"Bilyf, I may have been born to come here," he said, "but now that I'm here, I don't know what to do."

"One sees that—the solution will come."

"Will it? Or are you just saying that to calm me?"

"One sees—one sees—one sees," Bilyf said, as close to annoyance as Deles could ever recall seeing him.

"I'm sorry, Bilyf," Deles said, mollified, "I know my anxiety isn't doing us much good."

But it became clear that optimism was not enough, as the timeship orbited Parnassus again and again, altering its course slightly each time to accommodate the capacity of its sensors. The landscape curved endlessly beneath them.

"How long can we orbit before we run out of food?"

"There is food enough—to sustain us—for quite some time."

"Good," Deles murmured. He thought of Acrios in his last moments, and was ashamed. If death was to come, then he must not fear it; he must resign himself.

"Bilyf, are you not afraid?"

"One—knows fear."

"Was that why you went away? Because of fear?"

"At least—in part."

Deles was disconcerted to think of the stoic Bilyf being afraid. But even Bilyf had the right to fear his own death. He himself had been whining since their arrival, and he had been indecisive before that. Now his panic began to subside, though a sense of urgency remained. Bilyf's acceptance calmed him.

Again and again the blasted panorama passed under them, inducing a contemplative, dreamlike state.

"I'm beginning to feel that I understand the Mennon concept of time a little," Deles said. "While events transpire once in a direct way, they have always been and will always be in another way. Am I correct?"

"Perhaps."

Deles grimaced. "Why is that whenever I feel I have started to grasp Mennon metaphysics, you show me that I don't understand anything about it?"

"One merely suggests that—the Mennon conception of time —is as imperfect as any other."

"But surely it suggests the truth about time?"

"One is not certain—that there is—a particular truth."

"Then why have we come here?"

"One sees that—we *must* be here."

For the second time, Deles was startled by Bilyf's emphatic tone. If there was no question in Bilyf's mind that they had to be here, how had he come to this conclusion?

After the ship had mapped every square kilometer of Parnassus's surface, finding neither life nor technology, Deles was, surprisingly, not at his wit's end. He knew what had to be done; they must contact the Machine. It already knew that they were here, of course. Perhaps he and Bilyf were deemed insignificant, beneath the Machine's notice. . . .

"Bilyf," he said, "the Machine is ignoring us for some reason, and may continue to do so for as long as we are in orbit. Isn't that likely?"

"One—believes so."

"But if we go down to the surface, walk on the Machine's skin, then it will be forced to acknowledge us."

"One does not—believe so."

"Surely it won't let us die down there."

"One does not—see."

Disturbed by Bilyf's reticence, Deles nevertheless said, "I think it's the only way."

"This—may be so."

Deles commanded the ship to touch down, and the pock-marked plains of Parnassus rose to meet them. Minutes later, they settled onto a relatively flat surface. Beneath them was the Machine. Only their timeship and the radiation-scarred surface stood between them and it. But for all of that, they might as well have been back on Rocinth. Deles burned with resentment at this treatment. If it was intentional, at least that meant the Machine knew they were here. Otherwise...

A clear, gleaming bubble on the console contained units to neutralize dangerous radiation within a close-fitting field around the body. The field also cycled oxygen, of course, but did not resist gravity. There was no need for a gravity shield on such a small, low-gravity planet. Deles opened the bubble and re-moved two of the minute units, placing one underneath Bilyf's oral folds, and the other behind his own ear.

"Open the airlock door," he commanded.

The ship did so, and they stepped outside. When the inner hatch closed, they pressed their units and felt the familiar hair-raising static charge, and then a rush of cool air.

"Open the hatch."

The hatch obediently irised open, a ramp extending into the merciless blue landscape beyond.

They moved out onto the wasted plain. It was a cracked, brittle desert shimmering in the impossible heat. Ridges and ragged crenelations showed the impact of cosmic detritus, and a scarp rose in the distance, a failed mountain range.

"It's not a very large world," Deles said. "We could cover a great deal of it on foot, given time."

Setting out, Deles thought how odd it was that he now felt eager, while Bilyf was hesitant. It was as if they had exchanged personalities. Yes, Bilyf truly *was* a part of him now.

They tramped across a blazing, sapphire plain like figures in a dream.

"This rock must be virtually colorless," Deles said, "to re-flect light as it does."

"One—believes so."

They came upon a pool of liquid rock, thick stuff melting and running from the scarp to fill it.

"One sees—that the stone—solidifies—when the planet faces—away from the sun."

"And melts again each day?" said Deles. "How does it get back up onto the scarp?"

"One sees—that it does not—but that the pool grows larger —as it is filled—with melting stone."

"But how was such a scarp formed in the first place?"

"One supposes that—it was thrown up—by the impact of—large bodies."

Moving on, they passed craters large enough to contain Nathe, and larger. There was nothing to suggest artifice anywhere. All was an irregular blue, curving jaggedly to the horizon.

"Perhaps the Machine doesn't really exist," said a despairing Deles at one point. "Perhaps it's only a myth."

"One sees—that it is—no myth."

"A vision?"

"One—sees."

It was no good trying to coax these things out of Bilyf. And yet Deles could barely contain his desire to know what was going to happen here on this scorched world, for Parnassus was all there was in his life now, except for Bilyf. How many centuries had passed since they left Rocinth? How had the universe further dwindled? It could all be calculated, but it was a meaningless exercise. All that mattered was that he was here, searching for a way inside the Machine.

"Isn't it odd that there are no mountains," he said in an effort to divert himself.

"The surface is roughly uniform—due to the engineering of the Seers—One can hardly expect to see—evidence of recent geological activity."

"Of course." Parnassus was almost entirely hollowed out and refitted with the gigantic intricacies of the Machine for a depth of several kilometers planetwide. Using core taps as an energy source, the Machine was shielded by a thick layer of bedrock on its underside. The excavation had been accomplished incrementally, burned out in stages over several millennia. Mineral was then replaced by a technological behemoth, installed section by cavernous section, until Man's most wondrous creation was complete.

"One sees—that the ship—is out of sight."

Deles glanced over his shoulder and saw that Bilyf was right. Even on this virtually featureless landscape they had lost sight of it. Deep in thought, they had walked quite some distance, several kilometers at least. Deles was getting tired.

"Do you think we should go back?" he asked. "This doesn't seem to be doing us much good."

"It is wise to return—to the ship for rest—and then to set out—in another direction."

They trudged back. An hour passed, and then another hour. There was still no sign of the timeship.

"We must have come back the wrong way," Deles said at last.

"One does not—believe so."

Chilled, Deles stared at Bilyf, whose white body appeared a shimmering blue in the sunlight. "Then we should be able to see it from here, shouldn't we?"

"One—believes so."

"Then . . . ?"

"Then the timeship—has been taken."

The Seers were trying to kill them! But why? He had expected them to welcome him gratefully, proclaiming him as the one they had awaited. Instead, they had tricked him into leaving the timeship so that they could steal, it, leaving him and Bilyf to die.

"But why did they do it?"

"One—does not see."

"Doesn't the Machine realize that we have to get inside?"

Bilyf sat down, saying nothing. He seemed to tie his limbs in knots as he rested on his pelvis in the Mennon fashion.

Deles decided against disturbing Bilyf's meditation. He was frustrated, angry, and fearful, and didn't really feel like talking. It shouldn't have happened like this. Any of it. How could it have turned out to be such a cruel joke? He paced back and forth before Bilyf's still figure. It seemed to him that years passed, that time had lost all meaning in the human sense . . . or perhaps in any sense. Indeed, the only hope now was Bilyf's chronopathic talent.

But he could no longer depend on Bilyf. This was *his* mission. It was up to *him* to find a way into the heart of the Machine. If he didn't, their lives would end here in futility. His shoulders alone bore the responsibility, and yet . . . and yet, Bilyf had helped him so many times in the past that he dared feel a bit of hope even in the face of this drastic situation.

He stopped pacing and looked at his old friend.

The Blue Star sears Bilyf's soul, burning fiercely through his eyes, forcing them to retract ever deeper into the darkness inside his skull. Even there, however, there is no respite from the heat.

For this heat

       is

          more

             than

                heat

This is   the Blue Star . . .

. . . and if the end must come, it comes here for Bilyf, but his suffering will not be meaningless. He has seen—has he not?— the way it will be. But oh, let the lessons of the knowledge sharers, of the mother, not be forgotten now. To serve ... to love ...

These are reality ... and the rest ...

   ... ah, the rest ...
    —is—

        —nothing—

... and now the Blue Star's burning acquires a quality that breathes life into Deles's soul ...

 ... but death to the body of Bilyf ...

  ... life ...

   ... death ...

       ... death ...

  ... life ...

    —joy—
    —joy—
   —and pain—

... if he were human, it would be only a fleeting thing, this pain. But he is Mennon, and so he endures it forever. He has languished since the beginning, all the while knowing the end ... but he is slipping into human temporal conceits, the purity of his thinking sullied by Man's restrictive ratiocination.

He has been dying always, and will always die ...

 ... he must transcend ...

  ... the pain ...

     ... the pain ...
   —! the pain! —!

A shortness of breath assailed Deles, and he withered under a tide of heat that should have been blocked by the shield. But these sensations were so fleeting that he considered them mere psychological manifestations of stress. If they were more, it meant that the apparatus keeping him alive was failing, in danger of winking out like a candle's flame in a draft.

But no, these were no more than symptoms of anxiety so intense, frustration so great that ...

Here it was again, threatening to blister his flesh and crisp the hair on the backs of his hands. He couldn't catch his breath. Again, it lasted just long enough to frighten him, but this time there could be no doubt of its physical reality. His protective unit was not functioning properly. He was going to die.

"Bilyf!" he cried, a strangled, gasping sound. He needed his friend, now that the end was so abruptly upon him. He needed the sustenance of Bilyf's love. But Bilyf seemed to be in a trance, unable to see or hear him.

    *   *   *

—joy!—
—the meaning of his existence is clear—
—he has been—
—he is—
—for this moment—

—to serve—
—but not to serve Deles alone, or Acrios, or even humankind. To serve all the sapient races of the galaxy, of the universe, for this (joy!) was the truth that eluded Verra, that Acrios
was unable to face until the very end of his life. But the master
had seen the truth, as Bilyf sees it now. Here, on the Machineworld, Deles reveals the truth. He must live—must live—
—Deles must live!—

Each time, the dimming of the field lasted a little longer.
Deles wished that it would simply wink out, killing him instantly. That was what usually happened. Why must he suffer
this agony?

The heat engulfed him again, and this time he thought he
would die. The blue landscape turned crimson, and then darkened.

Now the world was cool, such a relief after the burning... he
drifted on a calm Rocinthan sea, at peace with himself and with
the universe... But wasn't there some reason, he wondered,
why he must return to shore, however temporarily?

First he had to turn his eyes to the sun; he was certain of that
much. But why should he, when he could float so pleasurably
for as long as he wished? He was finally alone, completely
alone. He had always feared utter solitude, but he now found
that it agreed with him. *Was* he entirely alone, though? It
seemed that someone was here with him. Whoever it was, Deles
felt no desire to turn into the sun to face... to face... whom?

Very well, he would see who it was, but only for the briefest
moment... just long enough to be polite.

But he found that he could not turn his head.

A shadow passed before his eyes, deepening the shadows of
the vague blue world. Perhaps he didn't have to move at all;
perhaps he had only to open his eyes to see who it was. Even if
he *were* to do that, to leave the shadowy ocean, it would be
possible to return and resume floating later, wouldn't it?

"Deles—one sees—that the time—has come."

"Time?" said the incredulous Deles. Was this Bilyf speaking
of time like a human being? Bilyf, here on the ocean with him?
Of course, Bilyf would *never* desert him. Bilyf loved him.

"Bilyf, my friend." He opened his eyes.

Heat blasted his lungs as Bilyf's tentacular digits reached toward his face. And he knew that there was no sea, for the blue was the aqueous color of Hades, a glare under which no living organism could survive.

He felt Bilyf's gentle touch just behind his ear. The multi-jointed fingers pressed firmly, and then snaked away.

Bilyf had given Deles his oxygen-recycling unit.

"No!" Deles cried. "You'll die!" He slapped his hand to his neck, thinking what the lack of a radiation shield meant on this infernal blue surface.

But it was too late. Bilyf took a step backwards on his stumpy legs, stumbled and fell. Quaking, he emitted a terrible wail as his limbs thrashed wildly. His nacreous flesh shriveled. His digits writhed like dying worms. His oral folds fluttered. His skin became parchment, blackening under the rays of the Blue Star.

His remains burst into flames. But the fire flared for only an instant without oxygen. Ashes fell like black snow, blanketing Deles's vision of the Blue Star.

Trying to stand, Deles found that he could not.

"No!" he screamed, but his cry was sealed inside the protective shell Bilyf had given him. He would never see Bilyf again, he thought as he slumped to his knees, never again in his life.

Chapter Thirty

The Machine's Soul

Deles watched Bilyf's ashes settle upon the blue stones, and upon the charred remains of the rococo skeleton that had supported flesh and blood, organs and nerves, heart and brain. The skeleton resembled the decayed hulk of some mysterious machine, left on the surface of Parnassus thousands of years ago. Could this be Bilyf?

Beyond tears, Deles rose and insensately continued the march back toward the spot where they had left the timeship. He located the melting scarp, though he was now on the other side of it. A portion of the huge meteor whose impact had created it was visible.

Soon he found the imprint of the timeship, thousands of tiny points on a rounded impression in the dust. Sitting down, he felt the air bubble cushion his rump. He had not believed that the Seers would let him die, but Bilyf was gone, a martyr to their mission. The cool flow of oxygen over his body might have been blood, he thought bitterly. But his anger alternated with the deepest sadness he had ever known.

He held up his hand, the in-turned palm casting a preternatural glow undiminished by the Blue Star's glare.

But before he could strike, a sparkling white light on the horizon caught his eye. The sun was behind him; could this have been its reflection on some glassy protuberance of fused sand? If so, why had he not noticed similar coruscations before?

The sparkling coalesced into an incandescent, fluttering triangle, and bloomed into a graceful birdlike shape that filled the empty sky with rectilinear flow, leaving behind it strange parabolic glints that faded into the blue of the sun.

"A lightship!" Deles cried. He craned his neck as the glorious vision, dimming the Blue Star with its nimbus, passed overhead in a stately arc. Soon it had traversed the sky, vanishing into the too-near horizon on the face of the sun.

The Seers had passed him by. Not content to let him perish as his shield failed or he died of thirst, they had felt that it was necessary to taunt him, to show him that they knew where he was and that they did not care. But perhaps that was too superficial a reading of their mocking flight; perhaps they cared a great deal, else why should they go to such trouble to make him believe otherwise?

He turned his gaze to the ground, feeling very old and fragile. Was it possible that his body was aging, that the alien part of him was genetically inferior in that regard? So much had happened. When he left Rocinth he was still in his twenties, but that meant nothing anymore. If time as he understood it existed at all, a great deal of it had passed since then. He must act now.

He stared into the ship's imprint, at the dust beneath his feet. He held his hand out toward it, as if to grasp something indefinable from the airless space there. Outstretching his fingers, he focused consciousness on what he must do. He thought of Bilyf's death and the rage boiled inside him, releasing the Destroyer's power.

The wrenching sensation was more familiar now, but no less terrible than it had been in the past. This time it was blue on blue, as the light of the sun paled under the icy conflagration erupting from his hand.

Crackling and leaping, the blue flame opened the ground at his feet. A crevice several meters wide split the plain for half a kilometer. Teetering at its edge, Deles nearly fell in. As he backed away from the abyss, his feet started little drifts of sand that sifted into unfathomable darkness.

As if in reply, a deep rumbling issued from below, a chugging, mechanical sound, elemental in its profundity. The ground shook, and Deles hurled himself onto his belly. Before him, the walls of the crevice began to crumble, pouring down furiously as great dust clouds rose, obscuring everything in sight.

Deles would have been ill had there been anything in his stomach. As it was, he gagged and trembled as the quake abruptly subsided. It ceased altogether as he lay still on his comforting cushion of air. Then he slowly stood on wobbly legs. The dust was clearing, but there was now no sign of the crevice. The Machine had quickly healed the wound Deles had inflicted upon its skin.

Apparently the possibility of forcible entry had been taken into account when the Seers designed the Machine.

"This won't stop me!" Deles shouted. He would rend the mantel of this planet again and again, until he met with success. Even so, fear nagged at him; he was weakened by his first assault on the Machineworld. How many times would he have to strike?

But he recovered with surprising speed. There was much

strength in reserve, and he would use it all if necessary. Ripped from his body a second time, he cracked the Machineworld's hide with more determination. The fissure was longer and deeper, but the Machine closed the wound quickly.

His body was holding up well. Perhaps it was because he had not used Verra's hideous legacy against a living thing. In any case, he felt capable of making a third attempt. It seemed that the sealing process took a bit longer, but he couldn't be sure. Steeling himself against nausea and fatigue, he resolved to find out.

Like an angry god, he fired awesome blue bolts from his fingertips. This time he was certain that the closure had slowed. If he kept at it, he would win . . . but he was growing weaker each time he cast the energy of his passion through the transforming Destroyer.

When he was nearly at the end of his tether, the ground still buckled at a snail's pace until the rift was filled, leaving a shallow depression of sand and stone snaking away from him. The dust cleared slowly, leaving him standing shakily over this Procrustean valley.

He didn't know if he could do it again. Fighting a desire to lie down forever on his cushion of oxygen, he extended his hand, spreading his trembling, pale fingers. Somehow he found the strength.

Wrenched from his body in a blue nightmare that instantly turned the deepest shade of black, he felt himself fall. But through his unconsciousness, the fall produced only a vague sense of disequilibrium, and the crashing pain of his descent's end was barely noticeable in his dream, wherein all his loved ones still lived and forgave him.

He awoke slowly, wondering why the ground had ceased vibrating, why there was no longer the terrible noise of rocks being grated and crushed, why there were no longer great clouds of dust drifting like Rocinthan sea mist.

For quite some time he lay quietly, contemplating his failure, anticipating his ultimate demise here on the barren face of Parnassus. He had no strength left; as coldly as he had used it, his passion still had limits. There was nothing to do now but wait for the end . . . just as the rest of the universe must wait, for the End.

He averted his eyes from the ceaseless blue glare, and as he turned his head he saw that he lay beside an open rift so deep that its sifting sides were lost in shadow.

He had defeated the Machine! At least in this first test of strength, he was victorious. But now he had to descend into its depths somehow, and, if he survived that, it seemed likely that the Seers and the Machine would take up the challenge.

He crawled to the very edge of the abyss he had created. If he threw himself inside, would there be antigraviton fields to buoy him up before he was dashed on the cold Machine surfaces? He would die if he remained here, so it was a risk well worth taking. And yet his mouth was dry, and his throat twitched nervously. Even given such a choice, he did not find it easy to dive into a bottomless pit. If he failed, then at least his end would be mercifully brief.

Taking a deep breath, Deles tensed his hams and sprang. His leap took him farther than he had anticipated, due to the low gravity. It was a soaring, breathless arc, carrying him into a sky so blue that it bordered on purple, and then into pitch blackness.

The fall seemed to last for hours, a drift through blank time-lessness that somehow put Deles at peace with himself. But it must have been only a few moments in actuality. Deles saw a faint luminescence, and then splashed into a foul-smelling liquid. He sank rapidly, fearful of drowning, able to move his limbs only with difficulty in the thick stuff. But his sluggish flailings were unnecessary, for he was buoyed up by the fluid itself, and soon floated on its surface as easily as a twig on the ocean.

"Well, well," he said, laughing. But his mirth was checked when he got a look at his surroundings. He had fallen into another crevice, albeit a much more tidily constructed one. It was no more than ten meters wide, a tributary of lubricant cutting between two enormous banks of machinery ... at least he assumed that it was machinery, though it might have been a darkened city, so monolithic were its structures. He floated by them until he came to a notch in the otherwise perfectly straight edge of the bank. Catching the corner with his fingertips, he pulled himself inside the notch, which was barely a meter wide. Dripping, he soon found a landing with steps leading down into the darkness. Did the Seers sail down the lubricant rivers in order to effect repairs? Clearly, this was a mode of egress designed for humanoid form.

As he walked down the steps, he heard the rhythmic rumbling as the crevice closed up on the surface. Sand and boulder began to fall in a hissing, banging echo. As he found shelter under an overhang on the steps, it occurred to him that the monoliths were protective casing for the delicate machinery. And the faint light revealed the crusted layer of bedrock, hanging between the bracing buttresses that towered over the monoliths.

"Miraculous that you still live," he said. The Others? He had seen no signs of them since they had taken Siule and Siula, but that wasn't evidence that they weren't with him now. How else could he have miraculously plunged into this greasy sea to survive? Be that as it may, he was now inside the Machineworld. He would be forced to deal with the Seers sooner or later, if he didn't lose himself forever in this technological maze. Surely his entry into the Machine showed them that he was no ordinary man; they could no longer afford to ignore him. Were they watching him now?

"I haven't come to damage anything," he shouted when the clangorous rocks ceased falling at last. "I've come to help you."

As he moved deeper into the labyrinthine depths of the Machine, his body heat triggered illumination, so that there was a perpetual aura about him, though the rest of the world remained in darkness. The effect was somewhat enervating, as if the Machine followed his every step, his every breath. He was reminded of the blue glow of the Others, who he hoped were with him.

But what could the Others do to help him if the Seers took it upon themselves to rid the Machine of this unwanted intrusion? It was up to him to fight his way through to the End, with or without help.

Music sounded faintly . . . the suggestion of singing voices . . . was it orchestration? Or something quite apart from his conception of music, though equally pleasing to the ear? Pleasing, and yet subtly disturbing at the same time. If only he could hear it more clearly. It wasn't muffled by distance; he sensed that it was all around him. Why was it so hard to hear?

The narrow crack broadened, the steps ending as it became a small plaza. Here were several peaked doorways, charming in their incongruity. One of them was ajar, emitting a slice of green light. Deles entered cautiously, finding a long, low room or passageway dimly lit with constantly changing characters on the walls. These figures, resembling ideograms, glowed so faintly that it would have been impossible to get a good look at them even if they had remained stationary. As it was, Deles could make no sense of them. At the end of the room, so shrouded in gloom that he had not at first noticed, was a figure.

A Seer? Deles didn't know, for no one had ever described one to him. He couldn't see very well, but from where he stood the figure looked humanoid.

"Hello," he said, drawing closer.

The creature lifted a wispy hand into the cyan glow of the flickering characters, revealing fingers half a meter long but no broader than straws. It was couched in a transparent mem-

brane, its spindly legs mere vestigial members. There were no
genitalia that Deles could see; the torso was so long and fragile
that it reminded him of a flower's stem. The head was equally
thin, the planes of the face in high relief; a pointed chin below
pursed, razor-thin lips; two tiny slits for nostrils; ears mere
bumps set low on the extremities of the jawline. Fully half the
head was covered by the eyes, two hemispheres of luminous
blue. Characters flashed behind it as well as in front, and these
were observed simultaneously, or so it appeared to Deles.

"You disturb my labors," it said in a thin, reedy voice.

"Forgive me," Deles said, "but I am on an urgent mission."

The rumbling cadences of the Machineworld sealing its broken skin filtered into the room, and the Seer gestured.

"You are most determined," it said, "Deles."

"Then you know who I am. Why did you try to keep me
out?"

"Are you *in* now?"

Deles was having none of it. "It would seem so," he said.

Like gossamer in the wind, the edges of the membrane advanced slightly, bringing the Seer forward. Deles did not fear
the puny creature, nor was he repulsed by it. Indeed, there was
a strange beauty about it.

"You will not succeed," the Seer hissed.

"Won't I?"

"What compels you to even try?" the Seer demanded, so
close now that Deles could see into its toothless mouth.

"The Others," he answered truthfully.

Tiny nostrils flaring, monstrous eyes twitching, the Seer
whispered, "The Others? You lie."

The narrow room was abruptly plunged into darkness.

Deles spun around and dashed for the door. But the door
had vanished. A queasy, spinning sensation overtook him, and
he braced himself with a hand against the wall. As his dizziness
left him, the sensation of motion remained. The entire room
was turning!

A pattern appeared before him, of endless angles and
curves, flickering with the eerie green glow the characters had
formerly exhibited. Through it a rectangle slowly spun, rhomboids and parallelograms moving aside to fit neatly, jigsawlike,
into one position after another. Behind him, the facing wall
showed the room's descent into the Machine's depths, in the
same fashion.

It began to sink more swiftly. He was hurled to the floor, no
longer able to maintain his balance. Above him, the Seer jiggled
in its gossamer web. Was that a smile on its thin lips?

At last the room ceased its descent, and Deles saw that it

adjoined a large oval. The Seer retreated through an opening in the darkness, suspended on its ghostly threads. Deles tried the door behind him, but it would not budge. Reluctantly, he followed the Seer, emerging into an oval room filled with hundreds of other Seers, who hung like spiders from the curved ceiling. Everywhere the green characters flickered, spectral communications from the Machine.

"At our request, our sibling has brought you to us," one of them said.

"Good," said Deles, "though I'm not quite sure how you managed it."

There was a great communal sigh, a bellows sound that temporarily obscured the omnipresent musical tinkling. It answered his question more efficiently than words. Theirs was a community mind, at least in part. They were used to knowing what one another thought . . . but not what *he* thought. Like a blind man, he might possess other, sharper senses than they.

"You resent my intrusion," he said, "but surely you know that it was necessary—no mere adventuring, I assure you."

The Seers said nothing.

"Has the machine not revealed to you my purpose?"

"The Machine has told us that you have come out of a misguided sense of duty," the spokesman said. "Because you possess great power, your sensibility has become imbued with evangelical fervor. Go back to where you came from, Deles, and leave the riddle of the End to the Machine."

How could this be? The Machine must have at least an inkling of the truth, and yet it had presented this gross distortion to the Seers. Why? He tried to hold his temper as he spoke.

"The Receptor of Rocinth told me at his death that I was to divine the riddle," he said. "Since he was my grandfather, I did not take his dying message lightly. Furthermore, a Mennon chronopath—my dearest friend, whom you allowed to die on the surface of this planet—has foreseen the same purpose for me, and Mennon chronopaths are reputed to never err in their visionary traumas."

Still they remained silent, apparently unmoved. They had no reason to disbelieve the Machine, and still less reason to believe him, a mad stranger. It angered him to think that humanity had placed its trust in a technological monster and its foolish servants.

At length the Seers stirred on their cobwebs, and their spokesman resumed the discussion. "If you do not leave us, there will be dire consequences."

"How could I leave without my timeship?" Deles asked. "Even if I wanted to?"

"Your ship will be returned to you," the Seer replied, "once we have exacted your promise to go and never return."

"I'll do as you ask . . . if you'll just put me in communication with the Machine for a few minutes."

This elicited a response that might have been either amusement or exasperation, but certainly not agreement.

"Do you not see," the spokesman asked, "that the Machine hears all, sees all?"

Deles disliked the sneering, imperious tone, but he remained cool. "I believe that mine is a special relationship to the Machine. Perhaps it does not even realize this itself."

"Such impudence cannot be ignored," the spokesman said, "not even the impudence of one so ludicrous as yourself. Do you actually think that your knowledge is superior to that of the Machine?"

"No, no, that isn't what I'm saying. It's the Others—"

"The Others! You would have us believe that you are favored above all men to talk to the Others?"

"I am different. . . . My grandfather . . . my children . . ." How could he explain?

"And why has the Machine not informed us of your unique status?" the spokesman demanded. "Why have we been led to believe that you have forced your way in here, brandishing a destructive device like a child with a toy?"

"I don't know," Deles pleaded, "but if you'd only let me . . ."

The tenebrous light vanished entirely, as if a pall had been drawn over him. He was engulfed in an impenetrable gloom, his feet no longer touching a solid surface. He floated like a fetus in the dark. The Seers had imprisoned him as a dangerous criminal, a usurper to the machine.

Or was this the work of the Machine itself?

An eerie glow cut through the darkness like a sword. Colorless, neither good nor evil, the Destroyer responded to what was in Deles's heart. And what was in his heart was murder.

Like paper cut by a razor, the dark was torn by blue light. Deles watched his black prison dissolve.

"No!" he cried, and closed his fingers over the Destroyer.

He did not look up for some time, certain of what he would see, but at last he forced himself. Frozen on their gossamer webs, thin lips drawn back in from white toothless gums, the Seers gaped at him. He stood there, wondering what to do without their help. He had barely scratched the Machine's surface. This first clot of Seers might represent only a few hundred out of millions, even billions. An entire world, like an insect hive, infested with enemies—enemies who communicated mind to mind.

"It seems that you are powerless to strike us down," a Seer said. Perhaps he could have. He didn't know. Perhaps his invasion of the Machine was madness. The words of a dying man could have been meaningless, the vision of a Mennon misinterpreted, rendering his quest a bloody folly. But where did that leave him?

"You will have to deal with me!" he bellowed at the Seers. "I will crawl through the Machine's guts until you do! Do you hear me?"

The chamber darkened again, and a figure materialized before him. An Other, he wondered as it took shape, or...

It was an exact replica of Deles, a mockery.

"You will have to deal with me!" it shouted at him. "Do you hear me?"

Deles had seen realistic projections before, but none so startling as this. If he reached out and touched it, he would almost expect to encounter warm flesh. And yet there was the hint of exaggeration in the curl of its sneering lip, the wildness of its eyes, the hulking triangle of its neck and shoulders. It looked insane.

"Very amusing," he said, "but hardly productive."

"Very amusing," the doppelganger said, "but hardly productive."

Deles turned away from the image, annoyed by such cheap japery. It ran in a circle around him, laughing out loud.

"Why do you do this to me?" he cried. "I have come here in good faith, to do what is required of me."

He tried not to listen as his double repeated his every word. Better to remain silent, gesture minimally; give the Machine less to draw on for its maddening charade. Passing through the endless hanging bodies, he permitted the image to follow him without comment.

"Murderer," it said, as if it had read his mind.

"*You* forced me to kill!" he shouted, losing his temper.

"Your grandfather?" his own voice demanded. "Your cousin?"

"You know the circumstances. These were accidents."

"Ploydekt? Verra?"

"Honor. Duty."

"Your children? Your mother?"

"No!" he lunged at the apparition, and his fingers clasped muscle and skin. Another trick, he told himself, though the tactile realism of it shocked him. Supple and warm, the throat resisted his grip. But not enough. His thumbs were buried in soft flesh up to the knuckles. He watched his own eyes roll upwards, until only the whites showed, his tongue blackening and protruding from his twisted mouth. Then the satisfying wheezing and gasping. And, as his fingers grew numb from the effort, a popping that signaled the end. The lifeless jaw languished against the backs of his hands, the swollen tongue lolled from flaccid lips.

For just a moment, Deles imagined that he knew the sweet peace of death, that this delusion so flawlessly impersonated. It was as if he had killed himself without experiencing death's pain. A transitory delight, unexcelled by anything he had ever known.

He released the still warm throat, and the corpse sank into a morass of shadows, vanishing without a trace. Backing away from the scene of his own death, he thought he heard voices behind him. Festive, laughing voices. The Seers?

Slowly he turned, not to see the Seers hanging from their gossamer webs as he expected, but instead a crowd of *Homo sapiens* gathered about tables under the stars.

"Ploydektum . . ." It was the solstitial feast as surely as . . . as surely as he had just killed himself.

"Don't be afraid," he said, advancing toward the chatting revelers, who turned their faces to him en masse, as if his softly spoken words had been directed at them. "It's only a delusion."

All of them had his face.

"What are you doing to me?" he screamed, his hand raising involuntarily at the sight of his own leering face multiplied by hundreds. The faces blanched under the blue heat of his fear, and when he had returned to himself, they no longer moved. They sat staring at him, an army of silent monuments to the horror he had created.

"No!" he screamed. "No!"

He fled the banquet hall, clutching his temples as he ran, sobbing, through the dim corridors and chambers of the Machine. Wherever he looked, the green characters now spelled out the accusation, "Deles, you destroy." He stumbled and fell, battering his knees and elbows. As he rolled on his back in pain, his eyes met the same words emblazoned overhead: "Deles, you destroy."

Chapter Thirty-one

The Rebellious One

Deles had come to think of himself as a kind of searcher, like the microscopic bio-construct that had crawled through Acrios's brain. His search differed in that hallucinations were inflicted upon him instead of his host, the Machine. And yet, like the searcher, his quest was to find the answer to the riddle of the End.

Now, as he made his way along a ledge over a symmetrical canyon, he noted that this was a likely spot for the Machine to vex him, here where he might easily fall to his death. He wouldn't permit himself to be killed, for he had a mission. The Destroyer would assure him of ultimate success, if he lived long enough.

His eyes, grown accustomed to the dim light, shifted constantly in search of anomalies. Sometimes he thought that they must have grown large and would soon cover his head like the eyes of a Seer. Idle fancy, of course; the Seer's optical appendages were the result of precise engineering, not magical transformation.

The ledge slanted down under the canyon's rim, and he noticed the flickering green of a Seer Cubicle. He would attempt to pass it by quickly, before the attendant Seer could come out of its trance long enough to detect his presence. By the time it absorbed the information tracing his path, he would be gone. It really didn't matter very much, since the Seers denied his very existence anyway. And yet, as he passed by the peaked entrance, he could not resist glancing inside.

What he saw surprised him. There was indeed a Seer in there, but a Seer wearing a dark cover over its eyes, pipestem arms crossed over its scrawny breast as it lay in repose. Was it asleep?

Information was materializing at the usual rapid rate, but the Seer obviously wasn't reading it. This was something Deles had never seen before. Ordinarily the cubicle walls darkened for the duration of the Seer's rest period. Was this Seer violating the rules, and thus defying the Machine?

Deles couldn't decide whether to move on, or to stay and try to figure out what the Seer was doing. Up to now, Deles had thought of his enemies as little more than intelligent insects, but here was evidence that the Seers might possess some individuality. This might somehow work to his advantage . . . though if it didn't communicate with him, he didn't see how.

He crept into the cubicle. The Seer did not move, even when Deles was close enough to hear its shallow breathing. Even when he was close enough to smell its peculiar, musty odor. He barely resisted the urge to tear the cover from its head.

But what if he was wrong? What if this was some form of meditation practiced by the Seers? Why then, he reasoned, were there still symbols appearing on the walls? Wouldn't the Machine stop generating information during meditation?

There was only one way to find out. Deles snatched the cover, a silky cowl, and exposed the startled optic hemispheres of the sleeping Seer.

It shrieked in fear and confusion.

"It's all right," Deles said. "I won't hurt you."

The Seer shrank into its gossamer web as if it had been struck. "What do you want?" it hissed.

"I only want to talk to you," said Deles, surprised that it had spoken.

A shrill, mocking sound issued from the Seer's mouth. "You want to kill me, you mean."

"No."

His denial seemed to calm the Seer. It waited for him to say more.

"Why are you talking to me?"

"Why not? You are talking to me, aren't you?"

"What were you doing when I came in here?" Deles asked.

The Seer said nothing.

"Were you defying the Machine?"

"Defying it? There is no way to defy it. I was merely hiding from it."

"Did I spoil your retreat?"

"No."

"Well, then?"

"I am able to resist the intrusions of my siblings, as well as those of the Machine."

"Then the Machine's power is limited."

"Like everything else."

Deles suddenly saw a Seer as a human being for the first

time. This strange being stood alone against its own fellows and against the Machine, just like Deles.

"Do your siblings know I'm here now?" he asked.

"Why should I tell you that?"

"Why? Because we might be able to work together."

"To what end?"

"You obviously have no love for the Machine, or you wouldn't try to . . . hide from it."

"So that means I will collaborate with you, does it?" Was that a sneer on its tiny slit of a mouth?

"I have not come here to harm anyone, and yet the Machine has punished me."

"I too have been punished." The Seer's voice was barely audible.

"Why?"

With its spidery hand, the Seer reached back and pulled the cowl over its orbs. "I learned something about the Machine."

"And what was that?"

"It fears the End as much as humankind itself does."

"The Machine fears the End? Why did it punish you for finding that out?"

"It cannot face its own deficiencies," the Seer said. "For example, this conversation would ordinarily be monitored by my siblings, and through them, the Machine would record it."

Deles was somehow gratified to know that the Seers took note of his activities in spite of their pretense of ignoring him. "And that isn't happening?"

"Do you think I would tell you these things if it were?"

Could this be a trap? It seemed incredible that this Seer was talking to him in this way. And yet the walls continued to flash the green ideograms. Beyond that, there was no movement, no sign that anyone heard or saw.

"Does the Machine fear *me,* as well as the End?" Deles asked.

"Perhaps."

Did the Machine fear him because of the Destroyer? Surely it knew that he only used it when he was driven to do so. Perhaps the Machine had some inkling of his purpose here. Perhaps he would be horrified himself, if he only knew what that purpose was.

"I must get through to the Machine," he said, "even if it does fear me."

"Its fear is logical, a protective mechanism."

"Somehow I doubt that," Deles said. "It seems to me that it should be detached, empirical, not experiencing an emotion such as fear."

"Indeed." The Seer looked almost human with the cowl pulled over its eyes.

"Do you disagree?" Deles asked.

"I don't know. You might say that I have very little knowledge of the Machine's thought processes."

"But didn't you—the Seers—design and build the Machine?"

"Yes, and together we have a certain overview that is impossible for me alone to comprehend."

Clearly, Deles thought, there were limitations to a hivemind. Still, the Seer knew infinitely more than he about the workings of the Machine. And it didn't seem so hostile now. If he could win its confidence, it might yet be persuaded to help him.

"What do you do when you're . . . hiding?" Deles asked.

"I dream."

"Dream?"

"Without sleeping, I dream. I live, at these moments, in a world of my own creation."

"All humankind does this."

"But Seers are not permitted to do it. Our dreams are shared by all, and even these are programmed by the Machine."

Deles was moved. The Seer was declaring its humanity to him, though it was of a breed that had developed into something barely recognizable as human. In spite of the bioengineering, certain human traits had not been extinguished. There was hope, then, that the Seer might become his ally.

"I have dreams, too," he said. "My dreams concern Man's place at the End of All Things. I have some special knowledge to impart."

"And what is your special knowledge?"

"I don't know," Deles admitted.

"You don't know what knowledge you have?" The Seer burst into a high, shrill laugh. Grotesque as the sound was, it made the Seer seem more human than ever to Deles. He found himself laughing along with it.

"It's a compulsion," Deles said. "My life is only a vehicle for the Others."

"*The Others?*"

"Yes, they created me."

"The Others . . . The Machine has kept all this from us, if what you say is true."

"Why else would I have come to Parnassus? Do you think I could be so megalomaniacal, to come here challenging the Machine, unless I had no alternative? This"—he held up the Destroyer—"was given to me by the Others. It lay in an airless cavern for millions of years, waiting for me to come and claim it."

The Destroyer cast an eerie glow on the Seer's thin face. The constantly shifting characters all around him might have represented his thoughts. But at last he lifted his hood, once again revealing the enormous eyes. "How can I help?" he asked.

"I must find a way to make the Machine see that it is wrong," Deles said. "I don't know how to go about this, but perhaps the two of us can manage it."

"We are not just two," the Seer said. "I share the common mind of all Seers, with the special insights inherent in all natives of Parnassus. I know as much about the Machine as any living being. If you are to succeed, you must have my cooperation."

Deles knew that this was true, but the Seer's comments smacked of arrogance. "You think I can't get along without you."

"That is correct."

"I've managed alone thus far."

"Managed? You have blundered into our world, tormented by the Machine, stealing food from our stores, ineffectually fighting the simulacra and delusions the Machine visits upon you.'"

"Nevertheless, I have survived. I will either find my way or face the End, like every other being in this universe."

"If you die, won't you have failed in your mission?"

"I can only try."

"That is not enough, Deles," the Seer said. "To try is not enough. You must succeed, even if the Machine fights you every step of the way."

"Why does it fight me?" Deles asked. "Why doesn't it see that my coming is inevitable?"

"Because it is mad."

As Deles searched for a place to rest, he pondered his dialogue with the Seer. There was no doubt that their collaboration was a major breakthrough for him, but it seemed trivial beside the revelation that the Machine was mad. It would have been so much easier to go on hoping that it could be reasoned with.

He crawled under an overhanging curve of burnished steel. Used to sleeping on hard surfaces now, he was comfortable enough as he stretched out in the overhang's shadow. He closed his eyes, wishing that he could forget where he was, that he could be a boy on Sripha once again, the only happy time of his life.

"Deles," a voice whispered, whether in his ear or in his dream he couldn't say. If it was in his ear, it was only one of the

Machine's illusions and could be ignored, no matter how convincing and substantial it seemed.

"Deles," the voice repeated. "Deles, do you know who is mad? Is it the Machine or the one who speaks of the Machine's madness?"

"Does it matter?" Deles said. "I must do what I have come here to do, and I will take any help offered me."

"Is that wise?"

"How can you talk to me about wisdom? If I am wise, I'll ignore you."

"You cannot."

"Can't I?" Deles rolled over onto his side, cushioning his head on his bent elbow.

"No."

The world fell away under him, and he flailed his arms as he flew through the dark. Sickened by the falling sensation, he yet resigned himself to the end. Why hadn't the Machine done this long ago? Perhaps it hadn't considered him a threat until he attempted to form an alliance with a Seer. But what difference could it possibly make now? He was finished.

His descent seemed to last forever. He was a stone plummeting to earth, a raindrop, a falling tear. A flower about to bloom in red, liquid beauty. No, there would be no color here in the darkness, just an end. The End, for Deles. The End. . . .

His body struck a surface so rigid that every bone in his body shattered, a good many of them piercing the skin, pointed shards cutting through like daggers. Like pins from a pincushion.

The mass of torn, bleeding flesh and splintered bone bounced, colliding with the hard surface again and sliding on its own wet effluvium.

There was no pain. The collision was too sudden, the destruction too complete. There was nothing anymore. No love, no hate. Nothing.

So this is how the universe Ends. . . .

Deles opened his eyes. It was dark, but there was a faint green light flickering someplace far away. No, not so far away. Just beyond the overhang. His hip was sore from lying on the metal. He was sweating, and he felt terrible, but he was alive and in one piece. Sweat poured down his twitching face.

"Amusing," he croaked. "Very amusing. Do you have any other tricks?"

"You cannot ignore me," the disembodied voice repeated.

"Can't I?" Deles said, wiping his face with the back of his hand. He closed his eyes and went back to sleep.

Chapter Thirty-two

Confrontation

So long had Deles wandered through the Machine's bowels, that it seemed to him all that had gone before his journey to Parnassus was a mere prelude, a prologue, the briefest of prefaces.

He had died a thousand times or more, sometimes in ingenious manner, often by his own hand. He had to remind himself that these suicides were also the work of the Machine, but it was hard to believe, so real were they . . . so personal.

He supposed, in his life of endless descent into the Machine, that it really didn't much matter. He had become inured to his own death . . . and yet the Machine still didn't kill him. Finality was now Deles's definition of real death, and that, he suspected, wouldn't come until his mission was completed. At least that suspicion left room for hope.

But what did he hope for? A continuation of his suffering until . . . until what? Until he found a way to reach the Machine? It seemed determined to keep him at bay, and his alliance with the Seer had come to little. The Machine was perhaps right about the Seer being mad, but mad or not, the Seer was the only friend Deles had now.

Through the blinking green maze he walked, threading his way around corners and through meter-wide cracks between the towering sheaths of the Machine's myriad components. Occasionally he came upon Seers, who invariably shrank against the casings until he passed. How many levels had he climbed through? It seemed that he had continued going down, down, ever down, for a hundred years . . . or even a thousand. Did time exist here? For that matter, did it exist anywhere?

"Deles." A strained whisper.

"What do you want?" he sighed. Would the Machine never tire of its cruel games?

"Don't you recognize me?" Something loomed off to his right. It was a Seer, web pulled along by wispy threads that found holds here and there in the sharp metal corners. It must be his friend, though Deles couldn't tell it from any other Seer at a glance.

"I'm glad to see you," he said, "but I'm afraid the Machine knows what we've been up to."

"Yes, I have been punished for my crime of conspiracy," the Seer said, razor-thin lips pursed in memory of its punishment. "But the Machine will not kill me."

"Why not?"

"It hopes to rehabilitate me."

"Can't it just create another to take your place? It might be better for you if you forgot about trying to help me?"

"No, I have already suffered for the crime of conspiracy. The Machine will not punish me for the same crime twice."

"But you haven't really done anything," Deles said. "Have you been punished for your *intentions?*"

"Yes, intentions are most important."

"Then if you still intend to defy the Machine, won't you be punished a second time?"

"No, because my intentions remain the same. I have already been punished for helping you in your effort to talk to the Machine."

"The Machine *has* talked to me. It was a rather one-sided conversation."

"There are methods of overriding the Machine's intransigence," the Seer said, "known to my siblings. Unfortunately, I am no longer privy to this knowledge."

Deles felt a faint hope stirring. "Do you remember anything about these methods?"

"My memory, in that regard, has been wiped clean."

Deles threw up his hands in despair. Turning his back on the Seer, he began to walk through the narrow passageway. He arched his back as something brushed lightly against it. Looking over his shoulder he saw the Seer following him in its cocoon.

"Where are you going?" the Seer asked.

Deles laughed bitterly. "Where is there to go?"

"To the core of the Machine's mind," the Seer said, "to the very soul, if necessary."

"Rhetoric," Deles snorted. "Useless words. I have come no closer to my goal than if I had stayed on Rocinth."

"That is not true," the Seer said. "I've learned that much from my siblings, in spite of my ostracism."

"You have been ostracized for trying to help me?" Deles asked, stopping to look at the Seer more closely.

"Yes, they try to block me out of the group mind, but I'm too much a part of them for that to succeed completely. I can sense that you have them very worried. They are frightened by your persistence, and they cannot understand why the Machine has not disposed of you once and for all."

"Neither can I."

"Don't you see? The Machine knows that you bear a message far too important to be casually destroyed. Eventually it will have to receive you."

"Seer, I wish I were as certain of that as you are."

"You will either find a way to appeal to it or it will capitulate," the Seer said. "That is the prognostication of my siblings, and I concur with them."

"But you say the Machine is mad," Deles said. "What is to stop it from changing its deranged mind?"

"I suspect that it *cannot* kill you, Deles, and that this same restriction on its impulses will lead ultimately to your triumph."

Deles thought about this as the Seer's words rang through the crooked passageways. He continued walking, soon coming to a stairway that wound around a gigantic, cylindrical shaft that disappeared into the green shadows above and below.

"Why are there steps everywhere?" he asked. "You and your siblings certainly don't need them."

"Our bodies were altered after the Machine was completed. Our cocoons respond to mental commands, feeling their way as they carry us about, but once we walked on two legs like you."

"When Acrios was here?"

"Oh no, that wasn't so long ago. We were the same then as we are now."

"You knew him?"

"No, that was long before my time, but I know him through the siblings' memories. He was the most talented Receptor we have ever trained."

"Does the Machine believe that, too? That Acrios was the most talented of all those with the Gift?"

"Certainly." The Seer's hemispherical eyes pulsed slightly.

"Then perhaps it should consider what the Others have revealed: It is my destiny to achieve what Acrios set out to do."

The Seer gaped.

"Did you think it could be anything less?" said Deles.

Leaving the Seer with its mouth open, Deles started down the curving stairway. On the way down, he occasionally felt the light touch of the Seer's tendrils at his back. They continued on in silence, until they came to an opening in the cylindrical shaft, two meters high and very dark on the inside.

"What's in here?" Deles asked.

"A synaptical auxiliary shaft doesn't have anything in it, actually. A charge passes through it, capable of carrying an information load if there is a breakdown elsewhere."

"I see." Deles went inside. There was no light at all, for all the information currently being transferred was either above or below. Even the usual faint green light was absent.

"You'd better not stay in there," the Seer warned.

"Why not? Nothing is happening."

"But the charge is . . ."

Deles was blinded by an explosion of brilliant white light. For a moment he thought he had somehow excited the Destroyer accidentally. But no, this was different. He was caught in the flow of the synaptical charge, which was set off by his intrusion into the chamber.

The current passed through his body, holding him in a rigid standing position. He clenched his teeth, trembling as he was possessed by the surging power.

Through the blinding light, he thought he saw the Seer's horrified face. Strangely, he wondered at that moment if the Seer had a name. If so, he had never learned what it was.

He relaxed his muscles, finding that the current was not at all unpleasant. How refined his energy must be, he thought. Perhaps it is actually intended for this purpose—using living beings as receptacles for its enormous communication energies.

A hissing filled his ears. Could he reach the Machine this way? Slowly, he moved his head. He saw that he stood on a grill of some kind, a finely worked grating through which lines of force leapt, dazzlingly pure, white threads that traversed his body without harming him.

It seemed that something probed his brain, much the same way that he probed the Machine's corners and curves. Much the same way that the searcher had probed Acrios's brain.

And yet the Machine was gentle. It was an assault on the soul, rather than the mind. And the soul's secrets could not be pried loose carelessly, for through their stirrings they ultimately cut deep and lasting scars in the psyche that might never be healed. The Machine knew this and probed accordingly.

"Don't you already know about me?" Deles asked. "Is there no communication with the Others?"

There was no answer.

The threads of light spun around him, forming an egg shape that enveloped him, with almost imperceptible slowness. Descending, Deles curled up, knees tucked under his chin. Suspended in the blazing egg, his mind opened to the Machine.

"Where are you taking me?" But he did not expect an answer. He was not afraid, because he was certain—or nearly so—that the Machine did not intend to kill him.

The egg came to the shaft's bottom, floating out into a vast open area. It was a dark place, suffused with an ever-changing, tenebrous light that lent it a mysterious, shadowy quality. Deles thought he could make out the outline of mazelike passageways below, for now the threads of light had dimmed so that they were nearly invisible. But they weren't passageways; they glowed ever more brightly, spelling out "Deles, you destroy."

"No," he protested, "I haven't come here to destroy."

The enormous characters burned brilliantly, pulsing with emerald fire.

"Why do you fear me?" he said.

But there was no reply, only a darkening of the green letters. The absence of light became so pervasive, Deles felt trapped by it. Unease plagued him as he floated in the transparent egg.

"Imprisoning me won't help matters," he said. "The Others have sent me here, and they are more powerful than you." He wasn't sure that this was true, but perhaps the Machine believed it.

The green glow blossomed once again. "You have corrupted one of the Seers."

Deles snorted. "He is more aware than the other siblings, able to think for himself. It is not my doing."

"You have disrupted the Seers with the seduction of this innocent," the Machine spelled out in flaming green.

"It is good for them," Deles said. "They were not intended to be your slaves."

"What do you know of their purpose?"

"They are human. They built you to serve humankind. You have no right to punish them."

The green characters dimmed, shifting as a reply appeared. At least this debate was a kind of communication. Deles would keep it going for as long as he could.

"My rights were defined by the Seers themselves," the Machine wrote.

"So you have used your rights, so generously provided by the Seers, to enslave them."

"Their function," the Machine replied, "was determined by a consensus of humankind."

"That matters little, considering the steps you have taken."

"I perform the task I was designed and built for."

"That is a lie!" Deles shouted, no longer arguing merely for the sake of argument. With conviction, he catalogued the abuses of the Machine as he saw them: "You have tormented me, played with me as if I were less than human; you have punished the one Seer who has tried to help me; you have failed to take into account the possibility that my mission is one that cannot be ignored; in fact—and this is doubtless the worst of all—you have done everything in your power to make me fail, short of murder."

"My actions have been weighed," the machine wrote, "and there can be no doubt that they have been for the best."

"No doubt?" Deles laughed bitterly. "Are you perfection itself, to say such a thing? There is little in this universe *but* doubt, so far as I can determine. You were created because of doubt, but I see that you somehow discovered arrogance, and have cultivated it instead of reason."

"You speak of arrogance," the Machine wrote in scathing letters. "You who have come as the savior of humankind."

"You at once misinterpret my intentions and my self-perception. I have not come to—as you say—save humankind. I don't know why I have come. All I know is that I was created to come here. That I *have* come seems to be essential to the answer."

"The answer?"

"To the riddle of the End of All Things? Perhaps you have heard of this while you are disciplining the Seers like so many delinquent children?"

The green letters darkened, and no others appeared to replace them. It seemed that Deles had ended the argument in spite of himself. And yet, he just might have reached the Machine this time.

He remained in the egg until he began to fear death by thirst or starvation. He began to suspect that the Seer he had befriended had lured him to the shaft. That the Seer was working against him.

But no, he wasn't thinking clearly. The Seer had warned him not to venture inside the shaft. He had only himself to blame. Besides, the Machine could have imprisoned him like this at any time. It must have had a reason for doing so now . . . just when he was getting through to it. He had been communicating with it synaptically, if the Seer was to be believed, and then it had taken him away to its impersonal fiery letters where he could not affect it. . . . Or was he dreaming? Could he ever really have any influence on this titan? It seemed that he was merely an annoyance the Machine tolerated for the Others' sake. Defeatist, he thought, this is not the kind of thinking that will see you through to the End.

Chapter Thirty-three

Resurrection

"Are you testing me to see if I am really the one?" Deles asked. He had been dreaming, and this answer had suddenly occurred to him—the Machine was neither mad nor vicious, but simply had to be certain Deles was the one who would somehow provide, or at least lead to, the answer. But how long might that take? Until it was too late? "Are you testing me?"

There was no reply, of course. If the Machine was testing him, it didn't want him to know it. In case he was a megalomaniac, the Machine would make it impossible for anyone but a genetically designed, hapless mutant to succeed. Therefore, Deles reasoned, the timing of his mission was crucial. The Machine did not intend to waste a moment with him if he wasn't the genuine article. And yet, it had to spend a great deal of time trying to determine if he was indeed this reluctant messiah. It was a paradox.

"You've been waiting for me all this time," he said. "I never wanted to come here. All I ever wanted was happiness."

Threads of light curved silently around, and the Machine did not answer.

"I am just an ordinary anthroform human being. There is only one thing unusual about me."

Silence.

"Don't you even want to know what it is?"

Silence.

Deles felt the long beard trailing over his chest. His ribs protruded underneath it. He still had been provided no food, though a fat globule of water floated before him. When he had awakened to find it there, he had drunk so much it had almost made him sick, but now he sipped only a few drops at a time.

He found that he did not miss food very much. In fact, his mind seemed clearer without it. He had experienced privation before, on Tartarus. It had only served to enrage him then, to make him plan his revenge all the more carefully. Now he wanted to preserve, not destroy. Ultimately the Machine must see that.

But what was it that he had been trying to explain to the Machine? Oh yes, about how ordinary he was; how there was only one unusual thing about him.

"This," he said, holding up his hand. "This is the only thing unusual about me."

The Destroyer glimmered.

"Without this I would be long since dead . . . several times over."

Silence.

"It is not such an amazing device, except that it is so old. Its magic is that it provides just the right thing when I am in need."

Silence.

"Don't you see the significance of that?" he asked. "It means that the Others were able to see precisely what I would need in each case. Of all the artifacts on Tartarus, they knew that this was the one—and they knew where to find it. What vision."

Silence.

"The length and breadth and depth of time—if time possesses such dimensions—are as nothing to them. They see all, like gods. They touched my children, and my children became Others. Do you know what that was like?"

Silence.

"No, of course you don't. You're only a Machine, after all. You can't know what it's like to lose a child. It's intolerable." Tears welled up, and he leaned back his head as he sat cross-legged in the egg of light, letting them run down his bony cheeks. "It's intolerable. My little girl and boy, gone forever . . . forever."

Silence.

"If I succeed I might see them again . . . after the End . . . and all the rest of my loved ones. Isn't that enough reason to come here?"

Silence.

"Bilyf must be an Other . . . if Mennons can become Others." Deles stared down at the hard edges of his knees. "Surely he . . ."

Silence.

"Nobody had greater love than Bilyf—love for all living things. It would be such an injustice if he . . ." Deles considered just how much injustice he had seen in his lifetime, and realized that his emotional argument might well be pointless. Unjust or not, things were as they were. He had to hope that Bilyf was an Other, that he would see his dear friend again. Perhaps Mennons had an Otherness of their own. . . . But why should they? It might have been a solely human trait, accounting for the differences between the two species' outlooks.

The thought was monstrous, but it had to be taken into consideration. If it was true, then at least Bilyf would have no more worries. But it seemed impossible that Bilyf might be deprived of a noncorporeal existence; he had virtually led such a life while he breathed. Bilyf had been unafraid to give up his life to save Deles. Surely he was entitled to Otherness, if anyone Deles ever knew was.

"What do you know about Otherness?" he asked the Machine.

Silence.

"What good are you?" Deles shouted. "You know nothing and you fight my efforts to help you. The Seer was right—you're mad."

Somewhere far away, there was a rumbling. Deles couldn't be sure if it was in his mind, or if it came from the unplumbed abyss of the Machine.

The egg spun, darkening as a vortex pulled Deles down faster and faster. He spun dizzily through layer after layer of machinery. All the while the rumbling grew louder, even more profound. Like the voice of a world it roared in his ears, through every molecule in his body, to his very soul.

"What are you doing to me?" he screamed.

He spun faster, the roaring grew even louder, the darkness deepened. But in spite of the nauseous motion sickness, he was unafraid. The Machine would not kill him. He had the dismal feeling that he was no closer to his goal than he had been on the surface of Parnassus, or even back on Rocinth. He felt very tired.

He went to sleep, and when he awoke, he was lying on cold, hard metal. It took some time for him to get to his feet, and his joints creaked, but at least he was free of the light egg now. Walking was difficult at first, but soon his legs regained some of their former assurance. He hadn't been imprisoned in the egg for so long then, if his muscles hadn't atrophied. He gained confidence as he walked. Sooner or later he would win, he knew with ever increasing conviction; he *had* to win this contest of wills with the Machine, for the survival of trillions was at stake. It was more than vindication that he hoped for, it was salvation —the salvation of all humankind.

Surely that was reason enough for him to continue, reason enough for him to refuse to quit. He pushed on past the place where the images from the past had appeared, into the dark, without fear.

Soon the ubiquitous green characters began to form, dimly lighting the way.

"You'll have to kill me," he said. "I won't stop trying as long as I live."

The echo of this vow trailed down the endless, mazelike passageways, and Deles fancied that it reverberated through every nook and cranny of the Machine.

Just now, though, it was time to look for food stores; the Machine had imposed this fast on him for far too long.

Deles sat cross-legged in a Seer's cubicle, recalling the first time he had ever seen one of these peculiar little rooms. He had thought it was a corridor or passageway, and perhaps it was, in a sense. If he could learn to read the glowing green symbols, then he might be linked with the Machine in some heretofore unseen fashion.

He needed the Seer who had tried to help—the rebellious one. But could the Seer be trusted? Come to think of it, it probably didn't matter; the Machine was watching him all the time now, whether the Seer was with him or not. The worst that could happen was that he would learn nothing from the Seer, and in that case he would be no worse off than he was now.

But where was the rebellious Seer? Deles hadn't seen the creature in quite some time. He would search for it now; better still, he would call for it. Surely it would hear the echoes in the minds of its siblings. He rose, inhaling a deep draught of the Machine's stale air.

"Seer," he called, "I have need of you."

"Seer... Seer... Seer..." His voice echoed through the twisted passageways.

"Seer, I have need of you."

"Need... need... need..."

"Seer!"

"Seer... Seer... Seer..."

But the Seer didn't come. Eventually, Deles stopped calling, trudging ever deeper into the Machine's intricate pathways. A zigzag crack in a slab revealed a food store. He grasped its edge and pulled it open. Inside, protein bubbled up through tubes running from the processing vats, oozing into clear tubs that sealed themselves once full.

Deles smashed the top of a tub with his clenched fist, scooping up the runny protein and slurping it down. Nearly tasteless, the stuff slid down his throat like bland honey.

Carotene tubs lined one wall, and Deles helped himself to some of that syrupy substance next. It helped his disposition somewhat, for he had been depressed thinking of the odds against his success. If only he knew what he was supposed to do.

When he had finished his meal, he started out again on his seemingly eternal quest. Soon he came to an open place with a shaft of black metal extending up into the shadows. His footfalls echoed through the dark as he approached the shaft.

"And what have we here?" he said.

The shaft split open, top to bottom, revealing a crimson glow. Fascinated by its scintillant brilliance, Deles slowly neared it. He felt no radiant heat, surprisingly. But as he walked, elation grew in him, almost geometrically enlarging in proximity to the open shaft. Could it be that the Machine was finally opening up to him?

"Are you going to help me?" he asked, dreamily recalling the conversations he had recently had with the Machine.

The two halves of the shaft seemed to reach toward him, blazing now, scarlet stroboscopic light playing on his mind like a fever. This was it; this was the Machine's response to all his suffering, to the love and hate and pain and death he had known. He stepped gladly within the fiery confines of the shaft, believing that his quest had come to an end.

"Deles!"

Who was this now, calling to him, interrupting him at such a crucial moment? Deles turned his head in annoyance to see the rebellious Seer, tendrils groping as it hurried toward him.

"Deles, get out of there!" it shouted.

"Why? This is what I've been searching for," Deles called back. "Do you think I can stop now?"

"Deles, what do you think this is?"

"Isn't it obvious? The Machine is opening itself to me at last."

"No, no, this is a *euthanasia chamber.*"

A euthanasia chamber? How could that be?

"Don't go any farther!"

Preposterous . . . and yet the Seer's advice had been sound in the past. If he had listened, he would have been spared the ordeal in the light egg. Still, even knowing this, he could barely resist walking inside the shaft's tantalizing opening.

"Deles, get out of there!" the Seer shouted.

Deles took a step backwards.

"Keep going! Come back toward me!"

Reluctantly, Deles retreated two more steps. He felt the Seer's wispy hand on his wrist, tugging, trying to pull him free from the crimson coruscations' lure. The Seer hadn't the strength to pull him back if Deles didn't cooperate. He couldn't make up his mind. What the Seer said seemed reasonable enough, but his feeling was that the shaft's secrets were those for which he had been searching. As he allowed the Seer to pull him farther and farther from it, however, this reasoning seemed less sound. In seconds he was convinced of the madness of it. But, as the huge shaft closed seamlessly, Deles experienced a moment of longing...as if he had lost something precious.

The moment passed quickly.

"It would have broken you down and stored your essential chemicals," the Seer said.

"It lulled me into a sense of security," Deles said, beginning to realize how close he had come to suicide.

"Yes, many who have lost the will to live are still afraid to die," the Seer explained. "So the Machine makes it impossible for them to renege past this point." He gestured at the shaft.

Deles shuddered.

"If I hadn't distracted you...."

"I would have walked right into it," Deles said, "happily."

"You can see how efficient it is."

"Frighteningly so. But why is this shaft here? Surely not just for me?"

"The Machine can't have a lot of despondent Seers around. It's best that they pass on their genes and die. A new life is usually an optimistic one."

Deles was moved by the crushing hollowness of the Seer's words. It must have considered this course more than once in its unhappy life, particularly after the Machine's punishments.

"You came to help me," Deles said. "I called and you came."

"Yes, but it wasn't easy to find you. My siblings did their best to prevent me from knowing where you were."

"How *did* you find me?"

"I looked for you in all the most dangerous places." The Seer smiled. "You seem to have a predilection for them."

Deles laughed. It was the first happy moment he had known in a very long time, and it felt good. He had a friend now, and that helped him a great deal, though he was saddened to think of Bilyf.

"I'm glad to see you again," Deles said, "especially under the circumstances. But won't the Machine be angry with you?"

"I suppose so, but I think it is more important now to consider its attitude toward you."

"How so?"

"Isn't it obvious? It was going to let you die...and if it can rationalize letting you walk into your own destruction, it will soon be able to rationalize killing you outright."

Chilled, Deles asked, "Is that possible?"

"It will do anything to preserve itself. It fears that you will destroy it; therefore it must ultimately try to destroy you."

"How can I stop it?"

"You cannot. Only its value system can do that."

"But you say it is mad."

"True, but it still cannot go against what it believes to be best for humankind."

"I am here to help it find the answer. It knows this. How can it justify such behavior?"

"The Machine is megalomaniacal," the Seer replied. "It is a reasoning entity possessing the sum total of all human wisdom. How could it avoid megalomania?"

Behind the immense shaft was a tunnel boring through a solid, burnished black surface. They entered it, the Seer gliding down the sloping floor while Deles walked ahead of it.

"I hope I haven't put any thoughts of killing you into its mind," the Seer said.

Deles stopped walking, turning to look at the Seer. "Perhaps you should have considered that before you spoke."

"I don't think it really matters." The paper-thin lips curved into a smile. "I was only trying to amuse you."

"I see." Deles noted the familiar green flickering of ideographical characters lighting the way ahead. "Do you think you could teach me how to . . . see, like a Seer?"

"Not like a Seer," it replied. "You haven't the eyes for it. But perhaps you could see a little."

"Teach me, then."

"I'll try."

They made their way to the nearest panel of flashing characters, the Seer briefly examining the pattern before passing on to another. Deles felt the filaments extending from the cocoon brush his arm, like cobwebs on his bare skin. At last the Seer reached a satisfactory panel.

"Here," it said. "Here is an easy one."

To Deles, it appeared the same as all the others, but he accepted the Seer's verdict. "What do I do?"

"Just gaze at it for a while," the Seer said, "without trying to see anything in particular. Let be whatever comes to mind."

Deles stared at the constantly shifting figures, seeing nothing.

"Relax," the Seer said.

Deles sat cross-legged on the floor, gazing at the panel, still seeing nothing.

"Concentrate on all the characters at once. An overview."

Deles did as he was instructed, with the same result. After what seemed a very long time, the green figures became blurred. He shook his head and continued to watch them, but they soon went out of focus again. He was falling asleep.

"Don't awaken yourself," the Seer said. "It is best to remain in a trancelike state when you're Seeing."

"You forget that my eyelids close when I fall asleep," Deles said. "I won't be able to see anything at all."

The Seer *tsk*ed. "I hadn't thought of that. You'll have to learn to keep them open."

"Is there no other way?"

"Not that I know of." The Seer's enormous hemispherical eyes twitched. "But if you can accustom yourself to doing it, perhaps you'll learn to keep your eyes open."

"Perhaps," Deles said doubtfully. "Do you think you might give me some idea of what my overview should be like? If I know what to look for, it might help."

"Preconceptions are damaging to a Seer's ability. You must learn to recognize the pattern yourself, or you'll never master Seeing. Try again, Deles. Open your eyes, and let your mind go."

Deles did as he was told. He had no trouble letting his mind drift, but keeping his eyes open was another matter. Still, he did his best, and if his eyes closed at all, they did so only briefly. After a while he began to detect patterns—at least he thought so. Whether these were the designs of the Machine or of his own imagination, he couldn't be sure.

"I'm beginning to see patterns," he whispered, forcing his eyelids to stay open.

"Excellent," said the Seer. "Excellent."

Characters were like rippling waves, slowly forming designs that transformed the shapes on the panel. Lost in this visual poetry, Deles began to notice subtle differences in the ideographical characters themselves. These too were subject to tiny changes in their components, scratchy marks forever dancing, turning, revolving, jumping. No two were alike, nor was there any repetition, even in the most minute detail. Now he couldn't have fallen asleep even if he had wanted to. He was captivated.

"I think I'm getting the knack," he said. "It's a visual representation of thought itself. Fluid, incredibly complex."

"Yes. This one, of course, is only general information, designed to be observed in passing. Once you have mastered these, we can move on to more intricate panels."

"This seems intricate enough to me," Deles said.

"Soon you'll laugh at your present lack of confidence. Fluency will come with experience."

"I hope so." Deles returned to his labors, gazing in mystification at the increasingly legible patterns of green fire. As the designs became clearer, their meanings remained obscure—a seeming paradox.

At last Deles could no longer keep his eyes open. He slept while the Seer watched over him, and upon his awakening, the two of them set out to find food. As soon as they had eaten, they went to a new panel, which Deles dutifully studied for as long as he could keep his eyes open. The routine continued until Deles made a conceptual breakthrough.

"I can see it!" he shouted.

"Yes," the Seer said, "I knew you would. You learn quickly."

"This is a report—or a treatise—on continuum flux."

"What is its thesis?" the Seer asked.

"That the nature of matter should have changed more radically than it has, considering all the empirical evidence."

"This sort of thing has preoccupied the Machine lately," the Seer confided. "It seems far afield of its search for the answer, but there is probably a connection somewhere."

"It would seem obvious, wouldn't it?" Deles said. "If there is an inconsistency in the stuff the universe is made of, then surely the resulting changes would have a direct bearing on the End of All Things. . . ."

"Many Seers fear its direction is too oblique, too tangential to the heart of the matter. Though none would voice that fear."

"None but you," said Deles, smiling. "You know, you never told me your name, Seer. Do you have one?"

"There are no names among the Seers," it replied. "I am merely one among them."

"Or apart from them."

"As the case may be."

"The Machine has tried to take from you the very quality that makes you human," Deles said.

"Perhaps."

"If individuality does not make us human," Deles asked, "then what does?"

"Many things," the Seer replied, "but most of all, I think, it is compassion."

"The most compassionate being I have ever known was not human," Deles said. "The coldest being I have ever known was."

"We have strayed from the business at hand," said the Seer.

Deles nodded. "I grasped the concept that the panel represented, the first one I have had any inkling of . . . rather vaguely, though."

"It will become increasingly clear, and ultimately you will become fascinated by details. Then you will either resign yourself to a life of Seeing or become that rarest of siblings, a rebel."

"I don't think I'll have time for such esoterica," said Deles. "Not if I am to succeed."

To this the Seer said nothing, a slight quivering of one visual hemisphere betraying the fear it felt at the notion of Deles's success.

"Do you believe that what I bring can be worse than the End?" Deles asked.

"I *know* that it cannot be, and yet there is something in me that fears you greatly."

"Why?"

"We have been engineered to fear you, no doubt to protect the Machine."

"So the Machine knew long ago that I was coming."

"Apparently, and it must have known that your arrival would presage the end of its functioning. By allowing you to find your way, to understand your purpose and complete your mission, it would be effectively committing suicide."

"But it's only a Machine, designed and built to serve Man."

"Designed and built by Man, *In his image,* an extension of the human mind. And what greater imperative does the human mind know than survival?"

"Are you saying that the Machine is willing to sacrifice the entire human race, perhaps all sapient races, to preserve itself, in spite of the purpose for which it was created?"

"Yes," the Seer said, "but of course it doesn't see it that way at all. It has convinced itself that you are dangerous to it, and therefore dangerous to the human race."

"It *is* mad." Though the Seer had been telling him this all along, it now struck Deles as a revelation. "Do the Seers all know it?"

"They are beginning to suspect a flaw. For example, it claims that you are insignificant, while tacitly admitting your significance by its hostility."

"I see. And yet the siblings continue to follow the Machine."

"Because they were designed to follow the Machine. They have little choice."

"*You* defy the Machine."

"Yes, I am deficient in that regard."

"Don't you find it odd that you are the only one who does so?"

The Seer smiled. "Extremely."

Chapter Thirty-four

The Final Journey

As time passed, Deles's reading of the panels did indeed grow more proficient, though much of what he read continued to confuse him. At last the Seer deemed him sufficiently advanced to enter one of the cubicles.

"The information here is theoretical," it said. "This will allow your imagination free rein."

"There is more than one interpretation possible?" Deles pointed at the flickering green wall.

"As many interpretations as there are Seers."

"Then how can the Machine justify the rigidity of its pronouncements?"

"The laws of probability are on its side," the Seer explained. "All the Seers working together form a whole that is far greater than the sum of their parts. Our consensus on a theory is thus considered fact by the Machine."

Incredulous, Deles said, "Madness! Vagaries made into laws."

"Suppositions must be made. How else can the machine progress from one point to the next?"

Deles laughed. "I'm beginning to think that this entire, mammoth construction is useless, just something to pass the time until the Others make me do whatever needs to be done."

"What?" The tendrils involuntarily pulled the Seer back a few inches.

"It might all be a facade," Deles said. "There must be something *hidden* in this great mass machinery that is the key."

"Why do you say that?"

"Fear of its destruction, perhaps," Deles said, not hearing the Seer's question. "Or a matter of timing."

"Timing?"

"Yes, perhaps it cannot be unleashed yet . . . whatever *it* is."

"I thought of something just now that is even more heretical."

Deles looked at the bulbous eyes of the Seer, which reflected the green light surrounding them.

"What if the Machine—and the Seers—have been created to *stop* you from fulfilling your mission?"

"Is that possible?" Deles whispered.

"It explains why the Machine is mad, and why my siblings oppose you without question."

"Except for you."

"It's true," the Seer said. "At the moment of awakening, I felt that not all of the information in my brain was accurate. I don't know how this happened, but it made me more skeptical than my siblings."

"Your awakening? Do you mean that Seers are born with knowledge?"

"Yes. The Machine composes us more or less as you see me now. Why bother with children?"

"How long have you been alive?" Deles asked.

"I was created just before you entered the Machine."

Part of the Machine had been inactive for thousands of years, Deles discovered in his travels with his rebel friend. None of the hive could account for the function of an immense section hidden behind cyclopean, black walls.

"Perhaps this is the key to my mission," Deles said as they stood before the walls, "and knowing this in advance, the Machine simply shut it down."

"That is logical," the Seer replied, "but I don't think so. It has not been deactivated, but is merely dormant."

"Waiting for a new life to come . . ." At least Deles hoped so. If this closed-off, silent piece of the Machine was his destination, then he had to find a way to reopen it.

"Perhaps, perhaps," the Seer said, "but we cannot know for certain."

"Not until we reactivate it," Deles said. "How do we do that?"

"Seers are not programmed with that knowledge."

"No, of course not." Deles had to think this through; if only Bilyf were here to help him now. No, it was his problem . . . his and this one Seer's, for some reason. But why *this* sibling and none of the rest?

"Perhaps the Others sent you to help me, Seer," he said.

"I don't believe in miracles. I help you because I want to."

"Do you? Would you know if it were otherwise?"

"You have a point," the Seer admitted.

"Somehow you came out differently than the other Seers,

just when I needed somebody to help me. Could that be a coincidence?"

"I don't know." The Seer's eyes twitched nervously. "Perhaps the Machine has created me to entrap you—is that what you think?"

"No." But now that the possibility had been mentioned, Deles thought about just how likely it was.

"If it *is* true, I am not aware of it," the Seer said. "And it seems hard to believe that the Machine would suppress the very thought from my mind if it wanted me to betray you."

"Agreed, unless you *are* fully aware of your spoiler destiny, and you are simply lying to me."

"But why would I even bring up the possibility? Why not remain covert?"

"To obviate any suspicion I might voice."

"Logical enough, Deles . . . but now you have *no one* you can trust."

"Oh, but I trust you."

"You do? After all that?"

"You warned me not to enter that synaptical shaft."

"True, but that might have been part of my sinister plan."

Deles chuckled. "I'll take my chances. Why should I fear you while I am surrounded by the Machine?"

"The Machine has much to occupy it. I, not so much. I could serve as the Machine's eyes and ears."

"Especially the eyes," Deles said drily.

The Seer didn't seem to mind this little joke, but rather seemed relieved that Deles had decided that it was not his enemy.

"You said before that you remember Acrios," Deles said, "and yet you were only created when I came to Parnassus."

"While you were still on the surface, actually."

"Then how could you have known Acrios?"

"I have a memory of him, instilled by the Machine."

"Oh yes, so each Seer is provided a selective history at birth. That is convenient for your programming, no doubt."

"No doubt."

"It still doesn't make sense. You shouldn't be any different from the other siblings."

"Nevertheless, I am . . . and I have suffered because of it."

"And yet you came into the world with precisely the same knowledge as the other siblings. You must be a product of the Others' interventions."

"If so, I know no more about it than you do."

"Less, I should think. But what I know took me years to

discover. It is the accumulated knowledge of a lifetime, and little of it was easily learned."

"You come into the world knowing nothing, a *tabula rasa*, while Seers are born mature. I can understand why you are so mystified by my individuality, Deles. But it is a *human* trait, as you have said. And I am human, though I barely seem so to you."

"That's not true," Deles protested. "I am your friend."

This silenced the contentious Seer, who pursed its lips in emotion. Friendship was new to it.

"We must not become preoccupied with these discussions," Deles said. "Our purpose is clear. We must enter the forbidden part of the Machine."

In a fretful tone, the Seer said, "I fear the consequences."

"No more than I, but we have no choice in the matter. Stop and think of the consequences if we do not act. We must prepare ourselves for this final reckoning, Seer. Will you go with me?"

The Seer sighed. "Yes, I will."

"Then it's settled. We'll rest, and then we'll launch an assault on the condemned sector, as you call it. We won't rest again until we have succeeded . . . or succumbed."

"Agreed," the Seer said, nodding so that green glinted on its eyes, dark globes hiding the mystery of its thoughts.

Deles lay down in the cubicle, perhaps for the last time. The Seer retreated to a corner, where its tendrils enclosed it as it rested.

The knowledge that he had a companion, a friend, to help him aided Deles's sleep a little, but he was uncertain if he should risk all on this one venture. If it failed, might the Machine not still become angry that he stormed the condemned sector? It could serve as the excuse it needed to dispose of him once and for all. His troubled dreams relived all the deaths the Machine had visited upon him. Again and again, he awoke in a cold sweat.

"No!" he cried, as he was crushed between two walls, or burned alive, or eaten away by a corrosive acid. Each time he awoke to see the patterns of green figures converging on his consciousness. But he drifted off again before he could study them.

But once—and only once—the panel showed something different. Deles forced himself to stay awake, to keep his eyes open. Was he really seeing this, or was it just another nightmare? Whatever it was, it was different from any pattern he had yet seen. There was something . . . *incongruous* about it.

He raised himself on one elbow, feeling the stiffness in his neck, the lack of feeling in one arm where he had lain on it. This was no dream.

Barely noticing the sleeping Seer, he sat up and stared at the panels. There could be no doubt that each showed an anomaly, a distortion or flaw in the pattern.

Soon he perceived the designs of each panel as composed of rectangles, spheres, rhomboids, parallelograms, tesseracts... like the one he had seen in the moving cubicle. What he was seeing now, as he had then, was a diagram of the Machine itself. Each panel showed a cross section at a slightly different angle than the contiguous panel. But at the center of one sector was an anomaly. It pulsed and rippled as if the solid metal of the machine was melting, turning to liquid.

"The power source," Deles said.

It was a large area, surrounded by long tunnels. There was no movement or activity of any kind near it. Could it be the condemned sector?

"Seer!" Deles shouted. "Wake up and look at this!"

The Seer stirred, and Deles lunged to the corner where it slept to remove its cowl. Its visual hemispheres flexed in surprise.

"What are you doing?" it asked sleepily.

"Look at the panels," Deles said.

He need not have told the Seer what to do. Once exposed to the flickering green patterns, the Seer studied them involuntarily.

"Is it the condemned sector?" Deles asked as the image faded into obscurity, to be momentarily replaced by another.

"Yes," the Seer said, "yes it is, Deles. But how could...?"

"There's something in there, something the Machine itself is confused by. I wasn't sure when I dozed off, but there is no doubt in my mind now. The condemned sector is my goal."

"*Our* goal," the Seer said, correcting him.

Deles decided to try climbing the outside face of the condemned sector. They found no entrance on this level, however, and they couldn't find a way to get to a lower level anywhere in the vicinity of the condemned sector, so the only solution was to go up. This proved easier than they had anticipated, for there was a covered walkway zigzagging up the side of the burnished metal wall. The Seer was able to climb this quite competently, its tendrils finding graspable surfaces above, below, and on either side.

"Look at this," Deles said at the first landing. He referred to a seam in the center of the landing, running to the height of the overhead covering.

"For repairs, doubtless," the Seer said. "The Machine couldn't always fix itself."

"I suspect that it still cannot fix itself," Deles said, "at least while it believes itself to be infallible."

"You may be right," the Seer said, strawlike fingers probing the seam. "It is unaware of the possibility of its own illness, and therefore cannot conceive of being wrong."

"That does seem to be the case," Deles agreed. "So, if we succeed, it might actually help the Machine . . . for all the good it will do at the End."

The Seer said nothing, preoccupied with examining the seam.

"I don't suppose we can hope to get through here." Deles, too, touched the seam. "It's quite well sealed."

"It can't be pried open," the Seer said.

Deles lifted his hand and stared at the Destroyer.

"I don't think we should use that too hastily," the Seer said, "judging from what I have seen of its power. Why don't we go farther up and look at the other seams? Perhaps we'll find one that's partially opened, and you can save the Destroyer for when—and if—it's needed."

Deles nodded. He didn't think that there was any question that the Destroyer ultimately would be used. The Machine was far too obstinate a foe for them to expect to make progress otherwise. But had the Machine prepared contingency plans in case he used the Destroyer? It seemed likely; inevitable, in fact. Unless, of course, they had misunderstood the Machine's madness. It might have been self-destructive, not self-preserving.

They made their way to the next landing, Deles staring down at the flickering green among the twisting shadows, the Seer again probing the seam with its spidery fingers.

"It's as tight as the first seam," the Seer said after a few moments.

"Well, we didn't expect this to be easy." The Destroyer itched in Deles's palm.

"Few things are, where the Machine is concerned."

"Do you think it means to make me *use* the Destroyer?" Deles asked.

"*Make* you use it?"

"Yes . . . give me no choice . . . force me to use it."

"You think that it wants you to destroy it? That it is trying to commit suicide?"

"I don't know." By now they were well on their way up to the next landing, and Deles thought that he heard the same soft music he had heard upon entering the Machine.

"Listen," he said.

"To what?"

"Music. All around us . . . but somehow distant. I've heard it before."

"I hear nothing."

At the next landing, they were no luckier than they had been at the previous two. They had achieved a truly awesome height, and still the walkway disappeared into the shadows above.

"How many more levels can there be?" Deles asked as they climbed steadily upward.

"This sector extends all the way to the mantel."

"Then there will be no entrance at the summit?"

"I think not, but we'll see."

A dozen more locked portals had been bypassed before they came to the top. Immense struts were propped against the solid rock above, leaving avenues by which they might travel. But there were no glowing panels here to light the way.

"It will be hard going," Deles said.

"But we must risk it," the Seer said. "We've come this far. Besides, it's the only way."

They started across the top of the condemned sector, the struts jutting at angles, as big as Rocinthan public buildings, penetrating the solid stone just a few meters overhead.

Soon they were lost in the darkness, only the light of the Destroyer to guide them, as Deles held his hand out in front of himself like a torch.

"I wonder if we can find our way back," the Seer said.

Occasionally, as they wound their way around the immense struts, they heard the thump of falling rocks striking metal, muffled under the layers of dust and sand and stone already lying on the ancient steel.

"Someday this will collapse," Deles said.

"If that day comes before the End, it will be repaired post-haste. If not, it will make no difference."

Deles couldn't argue with that. He forged through the forest of metal and stone in silence, wondering how he could possibly hope to penetrate this adamantine monolith . . . unless he used the Destroyer.

Was that what the Machine really wanted? What of it? It was not his destiny to analyze the Machine, to help or hinder it, to destroy or preserve it. It fell on him to find the answer . . . whether he had to use the Destroyer or not.

Chapter Thirty-five

The End

"Deles!"

He spun, holding his hand up to light the deep gloom. He heard a swishing sound, as of rustling gravel, and saw the fine white threads of the Seer receding into the darkness. There was a shallow depression in the dirt to mark its passing. Deles backed away quickly, lest he too be swallowed up.

"So you're afraid we'll get in, are you?" he taunted the Machine. "You're going to kill us before we can get at you, is that it?" He turned and fled, fearing entrapment. Stumbling, he fell and immediately picked himself up and rushed headlong into the dark, the Destroyer barely lighting the way a pace ahead of him. He had scraped his knees several times before he came to the wall.

It rose straight up, a slightly concave eminence embedded in the solid rock above. It did not shine like the lower wall, covered as it was in dust. There was no doubt that it was impassable.

The metal groaned.

Deles stood his ground as the wall slowly curved around him, the rock above grumbling, chunks of it falling with booming, irregular percussion on the transforming surface. There must be terrific quakes on the surface, Deles thought, a cataclysm tearing at a dead world just to capture one lonely man.

He was enclosed in a gigantic cylinder now, and a sheet of metal skimmed over his head, sealing him in like a bug in a bottle. The floor began to sink. He was frightened, but he still had the Destroyer. If the Machine didn't kill him now . . .

"You have come a long way to die like this," a voice said from the darkness.

"You'd better kill me now," said Deles. "You can't hold me."

"I won't try." The voice was silky smooth and accommodating.

A circular opening appeared at Deles's feet, emitting a ray of light so brilliant that he winced. Stairs curved below, and he

wasted no time stepping down onto them. They were brightly
lit, but all else was shrouded in darkness.

"Why did you kill my friend?" he demanded, stopping to
peer out into the fathomless gloom.

"How do you know that the Seer is dead?" the Machine
asked.

"I don't . . . at least I can't be sure of it."

"Can one be sure of anything?"

"I'm sure you killed my friend Bilyf," Deles said bitterly. "If
you murdered once, you are capable of murdering again."

"Doubtless, but couldn't the same be said about you?"

Angered, Deles shouted, "Was I so cold-blooded? So
damned arbitrary about it?"

"At times. Don't you remember Phranes?"

"Do you know *everything?* My god, there wasn't a single
witness to that who is linked to the mundomentus. How *could*
you know about it?"

"I learned it from you, Deles."

"From me? I've never told you."

"But your dreams have."

"My dreams?"

"How do you think the Seers' interpretations are transmitted
to me? There are thousands of areas in me that are sensitive to
the emanations of dreams, and you have lingered in many of
them."

Deles was about to lash out, when it occurred to him that he
might have benefited from the Machine's spying. His dreams,
his longing, must have somehow drawn what he needed from
the Machine's subconscious.

"You have nothing to say, Deles?"

"You know my dreams. What more could you want?"

"Tell me why you believe yourself to be a god."

"I don't believe any such thing. But even if I did, it wouldn't
matter. I have no choice in any of this. Compare what I am
doing to your task of sifting information from the stars, if you
must have an analogy."

"I will concede that your claim is not impossible, Deles, but
your compulsion is not evidence that you are the creature of the
Others, as you believe."

"I *know* what I am."

"But I do not."

"If you have examined my dreams, you *must* know it."

"I only know what you believe—an extraordinary life, filled
with great events, violence and tragedy. But all explainable as
coincidence, passion, hallucination, and the regrettably mystical
influence of the Mennon Bilyf."

"Ludicrous," Deles snorted. "How could I possibly have found Verra, alone on that vast planet, without the help of the Others?"

"The sensorium, which you stole from a degenerate tribe of Tartarans, could have led you to the disc, as well as to Verra."

"The sensorium did nothing but permit me to *see* Lehana," Deles said. "And besides, she led us to the pit in the first place."

"You believe that the Others guide you, Deles," the Machine said. "I have never doubted that."

"That's very kind of you. But whether or not you believe me is irrelevant. Things are as they are."

"They need not be so immutable as you would have them."

"Is that a threat?" Deles said, taking a step down toward the darkness.

"My comment could mean any number of things."

"I tire of being toyed with," Deles said, descending the stairs. "If you cannot speak to me straightforwardly, then I see no reason to continue the discussion." At this point, Deles felt that he had nothing to lose by a show of defiance.

"I caution you," the Machine said, a hint of menace creeping into the silky voice.

"I am not afraid of you," Deles said.

"You should be."

"Should I?" Deles held up the Destroyer. "Your repertoire of cheap tricks has nothing to compare with this in terms of power."

"Are you so certain of that?"

The stairs were gone, leaving only a perfect, impenetrable darkness through which Deles floated, a bubble in a wine-dark sea.

"Is this the worst you can do?" he asked.

"Since you require a demonstration." A white speck appeared in the distance, slowly enlarging as it approached. It became the scrawny figure of a Seer, bereft of its cocoon and tendrils. It was not just any Seer; it was Deles's friend, the rebellious sibling.

"Deles!" it called. "Help me!"

For a moment, Deles was too astonished to move. In spite of the Machine's hint to the contrary, he had believed the Seer to be dead. He reached out to the slowly spinning body, drifting toward it. Swimming motions didn't help; he made no progress. End over end the crying Seer went, spidery, white hands outstretched in stark relief against the pitch black.

"My disobedient child," the disembodied voice of the Machine said, "you have committed another infraction of my law.

You tried to enter the condemned sector. For this you must be punished most severely, since you did not learn your lesson the first time."

"Please," the Seer wailed. "No. Deles, help me."

But Deles could only watch as the Seer spun faster and faster and faster. Its splayed feet and thin hands became blurred. It was a white pinwheel, its screaming mouth a streak of red spinning on the outside.

The Seer careened suddenly toward Deles like a buzz saw, so close now that he could almost touch it. Something warm sprayed over Deles.

Blood.

A strangled cry became a rattle, oscillating as the Seer's body spun still faster.

"Stop it!" Deles screamed. "Please stop it!"

The Machine stopped it. The Seer's spinning ceased so abruptly that Deles could hear the bones snap in its neck and spine. Blood poured from the gaping mouth, coating the emaciated torso. For a few more seconds the death rattle lingered.

The Seer's body trembled.

Deles tried to speak and found that no words came.

The Seer's limbs kicked spasmodically, and then were still.

Deles covered his eyes with his balled fists, screaming, "You monster!"

"Would you like me to bring the Seer back?" the Machine asked in its calm voice, "or should the Seer remain dead? The choice is yours."

"My choice!" Deles shrieked. "I'll show you my choice!"

He thrust out his hand.

But something emerged from the Seer's drifting, broken body, and Deles stayed his hand. It was a brilliant blue force, a presence beyond the living, that shimmered outward toward him.

It touched him, entered him.

Deles recognized this, this essence. It was not just the Seer.

It was Bilyf.

One's death—occurred too soon.

"Bilyf! It really is you!" Deles cried. "How is it possible?"

One's essence—was transmigrated—to the Seer—at the moment of—its creation.

"But the Seer didn't know..."

One was not—recognized.

Now the two spirits had merged, not only human and Mennon, but human and *Other.* Indeed, this was an Otherness beyond what Deles had seen on Tartarus. At last he comprehended the profundity of the Mennon way: the self-denial, the patience, the commitment to servitude. Most of all, the love for all living things. And to think that he had always believed that it was his destiny alone that had led him to Parnassus. His own spirit was dwarfed by Bilyf's greatness.

Deles must be—patient a little longer.

"Yes, Bilyf, I'll do whatever you ask."

His awe was tempered by Bilyf's affection for him. Otherness was as natural to Bilyf as emotion was to anthroforms. Deles felt himself to be a tributary, a paltry trickle, compared to the great sea of the Mennon's soul. All these years, Bilyf had watched over him—over a seemingly normal boy with a strange compulsion leading ultimately to the Machine. To this moment.

"Extraordinary," the Machine said.

"Now do you see?" Deles asked softly. "Do you understand that a new thing is happening?"

"I have seen an Other," the Machine replied.

One sees—that the Machine—is blind.

"How can we make it see?"

One must learn—to see oneself—before helping another to see.

Deles grinned broadly. It was so good to have his friend back.

"I could strike you dead," the Machine said.

"Then do so!" Deles and Bilyf cried simultaneously.

The Machine was silent.

"Kill me before I kill you!" Deles and Bilyf demanded.

No message came forth from the darkness, but a light glimmered. At first it was the barest spark, but then it erupted into flame.

Deles thrust out his hand and the crackling bolt parted, surrounding his body without harming it.

This attack must be followed to the source.

They were drawn through the bolt like a kite through the wind, music from a horn, a thread through a tapestry. It was like the storm they had ridden so long ago with Acrios, but this time the dark clouds were solid walls of lightning that played threateningly around Deles's body (and Bilyf's now!), but could not enter the field the Destroyer made.

The being that was both Bilyf and Deles sailed through the current for what might have been seconds, minutes, hours, years, centuries, millennia. It might even have been no time at all.

Arrival was imminent, they knew, because the jagged splinters of the bolt began to form a pattern, crisscrossing, an intricate snowflake of refined energy seeming to stretch through infinity. Through all infinities.

They were almost there now, at the anomaly lying at the heart of the Machine. They felt it more than they saw it as they approached, a warp in the fabric of space/time.

Something descended like a giant spider, a dark, hovering shape against the brilliance of the anomaly's web. A second shadowy figure scuttered down from above, and then dozens more. They were Seers, come to try and stop him before it was too late.

They were everywhere now, carried along in the same powerful flux as Deles/Bilyf, intent on stopping the usurper, even though they knew it was suicide for all of them.

"I don't want to harm them," Deles said, his voice hollow and unfamiliar, "but if I must..."

They can do nothing—to stop us.

As if to bear out Bilyf's prediction, the Seers were swept into the torrential flux, an energy gyre funneling into the anomalous web.

Deles had seen such a web before, on Tartarus, but it had been as nothing in comparison to this. A truth nexus.

The Machine had been built to hide it. But why?

One sees that—the answer lies—within Deles's grasp.

"Within *our* grasp, Bilyf. We could not have come here if you hadn't told me to ride the bolt."

At the sparkling points wherein lines of energy converged, ethereal blue figures emerged, dancing within the eternal web. There was ritual in their movements, these Others.

One witnesses—a game.

"A game?"

Deles/Bilyf lighted on the web, which Deles now perceived as the playing field. He belonged here now, he knew. Not forever, perhaps, but at least for now. He and Bilyf.

The strands of the web encircled all universes simultaneously, piercing each one in a sequence that was reality to the inhabitants of each. Few in any cosmos guessed that their universe could be reshaped by the players if the game grew stale, but there were always those who guessed at the truth—sometimes by the design of the players, sometimes in spite of them. Acrios had been one of the latter.

One perceives—the true measure—of the master's greatness—at last, thought Bilyf.

Many, especially the anthroforms, had lost sight of their true nature. They played at corporeal existence in a cosmos modeled on the universe of the dim past. Stars had been created, planets orbiting them suitable for habitation. Those who chose this game anticipated idyllic millennia on pastoral worlds, but they had forgotten the dark side of the human psyche—the myths of old Earth—murder and incest, gods and demons, beggars and prophets. Yearning for sensuous life, the anthroforms had immersed themselves in pain as well as pleasure.

"We are not what we seem?" Deles/Bilyf asked.

You are Others, the truth resonated, *and you must escape those bodies to which you cling.*

"But why?" Deles recalled the transformation of his children into Others. In their innocence, they had known something that he had been unable to see. "Why must we escape our bodies?"

But he knew why, even as the answer touched him.

In the implosion of matter that will soon complete the continuum you now inhabit, all life-forms will be destroyed. Many will be trapped within the field of imploding energy.

"Verra tried to tell me this," Deles said.

She tried to return you to Otherness too soon.

Deles heard music. It was somehow familiar—he had heard its distant echoes from time to time since entering the Machine. Magical, haunting, he knew now what it was: the symphony of the universe as the final movement began, its natural death. All the collapsing matter converging at one point; all the primordial black holes whirling toward their ultimate union. The End of All Things.

"But why secrecy?" Deles/Bilyf demanded. "Why didn't you simply show us the truth?"

The game must be played out.

"But you helped humankind by creating me. Was that part of the game?"

Others helped you only when you could not help yourself.

"What if I had failed?"

Then the beings of your universe would have lost the game.

"How can you dismiss all those trillions upon trillions of lives so easily?" Deles/Bilyf demanded. "How can you make it into a mere game?"

Do not those who choose anthroform play their own game, even when confronted with the truth?

"Perhaps, but if you tasted life, you'd understand why."

Deles/Bilyf sensed amusement at this riposte. All was understood; all was benign here. Humankind and the other intelligent races would win their game. Their goal would be reached through Deles/Bilyf.

"But how will they know?"

You alone will show them.

"Alone?"

Deles/Bilyf separated, Deles remaining in his own body while Bilyf flowed from him like a flaming blue river, pouring joyously into the endless, timeless, limitless web.

"Bilyf!" Deles called.

One returns now—to the eggsac—to the knowledge sharers—and to the mother.

They would soon be together again, Deles knew, Bilyf and all the Others. Sadly, there were those who were forever lost, and Deles bore the responsibility for some of them. But for them it was all over, at least. They had played the game and lost.

"What must I do?" Deles asked.

The threads of the infinite web curved and twisted over him, enclosing him in a structure of pure energy. Motile, the radiant structure returned to the universe of Deles's anthroform life, passing through the the monolithic casings of the Machine as if they were nothing but ghost images. As the radiant wedge (for that was how Deles now perceived the structure) moved, Seers were collected—hundreds, thousands, millions, billions, their enormous hemispherical eyes glistening with emotion. They knew now that they had been wrong about this man who had come to Parnassus to fight a contest of wills with the Machine.

Purposefully, the wedge—a lightship!—rose from the blasted surface of the Machineworld toward the Blue Star. Against the blackness of space, Deles and the entire population of Parnassus rode toward the End of All Things.

But it was not the End after all.

Streaming, whirling, playing against the night, the Others traveled with them. The lightship was as big as a planet, as minute as the tiniest subatomic particle. It was a bridge to the cobalt sun, a geometrically perfect flow.

Deles's breath was taken away. There had never been such splendor in this or any universe, he thought. He had been created for this moment.

Now the gigantic blue orb filled his vision with its cold fire. A creation of the Others, like all the stars and quasars, galaxies and dust clouds, the Blue Star consumed the lightship. Its heat did not burn, but nourished. In its fiery bosom, Deles saw the true universe of his birth. It bore no resemblance to that in which he had agonized for so long. Expanded far beyond the cosmos of humankind's creation, the universe demanded a new evolutionary phase to survive. And yet, such was the ingenuity of the Others that they had still been capable of playing at being human once again, a second childhood. The Second Coming of Man.

But now the time for playing was past, and the Others must venture through the final collapse . . . perhaps to evolve into an even higher form . . . ?

It fell upon Deles to show the malingerers what they must do.

"But how will they know?" he cried. "How can they even guess at what is happening here in the heart of this star?"

And the Others answered him: *The Blue Star is an inchoate spark linked to the mind of every Other trapped inside a body. Your action here will ignite a corresponding, cognitive spark in the mind of each and every one of them.*

"Then it is truly all up to me now?"

It is all up to you, and you will not fail.

"No," he said, "I won't fail." The intricate, patterned glow of the lightship merged with the impossibly brilliant glare of the Blue Star. Deles perceived that the great Machine reflected the anthroform's intuitive effort to duplicate the function of the Blue Star—perhaps a stirring of racial memory, ill-fated but groping in the right direction.

Unharmed, though surrounded by heat intense enough to instantly crisp a world, Deles drifted alone. I must choose, he thought. His body would not be consumed until the choice was made, a choice that must trigger a cosmic spark of recognition ... a choice that could wait no longer.

Eyes wide open, Deles commanded his living heart to cease beating.

And Others saw. In all the worlds circling the myriad suns in every galaxy of the universe of Deles's birth, incarnate Others recognized the forms they inhabited as empty vessels bound for destruction. Joyously, they cast their worlds aside to grasp the freedom of eternal light.

Epilogue

I wait no longer. Chastened, healed by what has happened, I attend the cold, quickening demise of the stars. How could I have known what was hidden in my core? Did the anthroform recognize the Other in his soul?

Perhaps I was not meant to guess the truth before the hour at hand. My antagonism to Deles might even have been part of the plan. Adversity made the prize that much sweeter in the End, did it not? I suspect that I was humankind's self-destructive urge personified, their ultimate death wish, purged once and for all, so that nothing could interfere with the final transformation.

Still, I am mollified, lonely as the End approaches. I turn to the dwindling balls of fire in those darkening heavens and ask myself if there might not be a kind of Machine Otherness. I am an intelligence, after all. Not such a formidable intelligence as I once believed, perhaps, but an intelligence nevertheless. Is there no chance that I might be reborn in the cosmic egg, that I might live and grow in the new hyperuniverse?

I will soon know. One by one I shut down my synaptical shafts, each sector growing cold as space, and *will* myself into Otherness. . . .

Afterword

A Note on the Rocinthan Moons

by Dictys of Ploydektum, Sripha

The first human inhabitants of Rocinth were forced to redistribute the mass of one moon after another, in order to simulate the gravitational pull of the earth and to approximate the movements of the tides on the homeworld. Nevertheless, all twelve moons remained in the Rocinthan sky, brighter than any heavenly body other than the sun, which was called Mnemosyne.

This mammoth engineering feat caused the moons to rotate nearer together and exert a force on the tides that aided terraforming greatly, but was never perfected. Still, the huge tsunamis of antiquity were no more. Smaller, more frequent disturbances had taken their place. These spouts and eddies often created a colorful spectacle, but made navigation quite dangerous. Consequently, little sailing was done on Rocinth, unlike her sister planet Sripha.

Three of the moons are closely connected—two small satellites orbiting the largest of them all, Clotho. Like Clotho, these tiny moons are named for the Fates, Lachesis and Atropos. The other nine moons are named for the Muses. These are Urania, Thalia, Melpomene, Terpsichore, Clio, Calliope, Erato, Euterpe, and Polyhymnia.

Because of their unique gravitational movements, the three Fates are always isolated from the nine Muses, sometimes encircled by them, at times beneath them or above them, depending where the observer stands on the surface of Rocinth.

At times, the configuration of the twelve moons corresponds precisely to the constellation Perseus, as seen from Earth in ancient times.

TIM SULLIVAN has published more than twenty short stories and dozens of articles. DESTINY'S END is his fourth novel, and his fifth, as yet untitled, will be published in the future by Avon Books. He is also at work editing an anthology, *Tropical Chill*, for Avon Books.

Mr. Sullivan is the winner of the 1986 Daedalus Award for short science fiction and was a finalist for the Nebula Award in 1982 for his short story "Zeke." In 1983, Donald A. Wollheim selected Mr. Sullivan's story "The Comedian" for inclusion in that year's *Annual Best Science Fiction* anthology. Mr. Sullivan is the author of three original novels based on the former NBC television series *V—V: The Florida Project, V: The New England Resistance*, and *V: To Conquer the Throne*.

In addition to his writing, Mr. Sullivan has served as Membership Chairman of the Science Fiction Writers of America and has taught classes in science fiction and creative writing at Florida Atlantic University and at the Woodlawn School.